TEX

A YOUNG BROTHERS NOVEL, CORAL CANYON COWBOYS BOOK 1

LIZ ISAACSON

TEX

CHAPTER
ONE

Tex Young drove past the sign welcoming him to Coral Canyon about the same time he realized another song hadn't come up on the radio. He glanced over to his son, who reminded him more of a man than a teenager.

Bryce was seventeen now, with only one more year of high school before he'd be unleashed on the world as an adult. His son met his eye and hastily reached for his phone. "Sorry. I was thinking about something."

Tex thought it was probably some*one*, but he didn't say anything. He didn't quite know how, and living in a permanent place wasn't going to be the only brand new thing Tex would have to learn how to do this summer.

He'd always had Bryce with him in the summers, and he'd loved taking his son around to various cities in the US as he traveled with Country Quad, the family band he'd founded and led for the past fifteen years.

He smiled at his son and said, "Maybe something that isn't country."

"Are you insane?" Bryce asked with a chuckle. "There is no music other than country that's worth listening to." The twangs of guitar came through the speakers, and Tex did love a good guitar. He'd been playing since he was four years old, and he never felt quite as at-home as he did on a front porch with an instrument in his hands.

Even better was when Bryce sat next to him and sang the songs Tex had written over the years. Otis, one of his brothers in the band, wrote a lot of music and lyrics for the family band, and Tex admired his brother's gift.

Tex shifted in his seat, a question on his mind. He reached to turn down the radio, which also drew Bryce's attention. "You sure you want to stay here for senior year?" he asked.

Bryce looked away, out his passenger window. The boy had been growing facial hair for over a year, and he hadn't shaved since the last day of school, over a week now. Tex and Bryce had been living in Boise, and they'd spent the past few weeks packing everything after Tex sold his house. Now, all they owned rode in the truck or the trailer currently attached to the hitch behind them.

"Yeah, Dad," he said.

"You never have told me why," Tex said as gently as he could. "Your mother's had you for years."

"Only because you traveled so much," Bryce said. "I came over to your place on every break when you were home."

"Yeah." Tex had traveled three hundred days a year,

and while he maintained a residence in Boise, he'd sold that house and rented one in Coral Canyon, Wyoming. He glanced around at the town, noting all the changes. "Wow, look at this medical center."

He'd brought Bryce to his hometown before, most recently when one of his brothers, Mav, had gotten married a few months ago. They'd also come when his father had announced he was going to sell the family ranch. Tex had eight brothers, but none of them had felt a deep love for Wyoming land, and no one had wanted the ranch a decade ago, Tex included.

They'd all converged to help Daddy pack, clean, and move out of the farmhouse and into a more sensible place in the middle of town. He and Mama lived with men and women their own age now, without any yardwork, animals to be fed three times a day, or howling winds and snowstorms to navigate to the barn.

Tex actually missed the cowboy life, and he wanted to get back to it. The house he'd rented sat on the other side of town from the ranch where he'd grown up, and he suddenly decided to drive by the farmhouse he'd known so well.

"How are you feeling? Need to use the bathroom? Can we drive by the farmhouse?"

"Sure," Bryce said. "I'm good."

Tex watched the new developments pass by the window, and he saw several unfamiliar restaurants along this extension of Main Street. "Looks like some great new places to eat," he said. "Even since April."

"Let's try 'em all," Bryce said, referring to a summer he

and Tex had spent together a few years ago, where they'd tried as many new restaurants as they could, in as many towns and cities as possible.

"Deal," Tex said with a smile. He passed the road that led back to the high school, then City Hall, then the library. Tex couldn't remember the last book he'd read, and he wondered if he should make a list of things he wanted to try this summer.

Reading would go on it. *Getting back to his cowboy roots* would too. *Writing a new song, getting and riding a new horse*, and *hiking* would definitely be on it.

"Maybe we should make a summer list," he said, glancing over to his son. "Things we haven't done in a while we want to do, or things around Coral Canyon we can't do anywhere else."

"Like the balloon festival,"

"Yeah," Tex said, grinning. "Like that."

"Grandpa said there's a police dog academy here," Bryce said. "And they do tours."

"We'll look it up when we get to the house." Tex made another turn, and the road led past a couple of office buildings and then the residential part of Coral Canyon opened up. The houses along these streets sat fairly close together, and the farther they got from the historic Main Street, the more land surrounded the houses.

"Did you like growing up out here?" Bryce asked.

"Yeah," Tex said, sighing. "We had a pond right on the property. We could ride our bikes anywhere. Dad let us go fishing every Sunday after church." He grinned at his son. "It was an easy, slow life."

He had liked it, and the tender part of his heart longed for that life again. He'd stepped back from Country Quad to do exactly that, hadn't he? Relax more. Travel less. Find a community to belong to.

He had, and his chest swelled with another breath, which he blew out slowly. "It was a good life." He looked at his son again. "What happened in Boise to make you want to leave everything you've known and come do your senior year here?"

His dad had always shot straight with him, and Tex wasn't doing his son any favors by not making him talk. He'd stayed in touch with his son over the years, but Tex wouldn't label himself a good father.

He could talk to his son, and he'd given his advice, but he hadn't been involved in the day-to-day parenting the way his ex-wife had. He knew that had been a major source of annoyance to Corrie, the woman he'd been married to for only two years before that marriage had dissolved.

He was actually looking forward to this summer and this year and all of this time off. While he still had an album to make for his record label, he would finally be able to dedicate time and energy to Bryce, and they'd talked about this year a lot already on the drive here from Boise.

"Mom's...she's been saying some things."

Tex kept his gaze out the windshield. "What kind of things?"

"Lots of stuff," he said. "When she said she had put her whole life on hold to have me and she couldn't wait to do what she wanted, I got pretty mad at her. There was…sort of a…blow up."

Tex didn't know what to say. He was always the brother who observed and listened before he spoke. His chest stormed and his stomach turned inside out. "She loves you," he said.

"She told me she hated being a mom," Bryce said. "That's when I called you."

Tex whipped his attention to Bryce, suddenly all of his listening skills gone. "She did not say that."

"She said she wished she'd never had kids." Bryce kept his gaze out the window. "It's fine. I don't believe her, and I know she's been stressed."

"About what?" Tex demanded, trying to keep his grip on the steering wheel loose and his temper in check. He wasn't the Young brother who went from zero to annoyed in one second. "All the money I send her for the two of you? Her summers off from teaching? That perfect, two-story house that looks like it came out of a storybook?"

Bryce said nothing, and Tex stewed in his anger. Corrie had no right to make Bryce feel like he was unwanted.

"Bud," he said, exhaling all of his irritation from his body. "I'm sorry. I know she didn't mean any of those things."

"Yeah, I know too," he said. "But since I moved in with you, and we always have the summers, I just figured, why not senior year too?"

"Jenny's why not senior year too," Tex said, sliding his man-son a look out of the corner of his eye. "You're still talking to her, right?"

"Yeah," Bryce said with a sigh. "We talk."

"You goin' with her?"

"I don't know what that means, Dad," he teased.

"It means she's your girlfriend." Tex gave him a full look. "Your mother told me about the Sweethearts dance and the prom, and then the other prom…."

"Yeah, well, she lives in Boise, and I live here now."

Tex made another turn, this time not looking at his son. "Once we have a real chance, we'll look around and buy something. I'm going to stay here for a while." The right side of the road didn't have any houses, and the places out here were spaced far apart.

"Whenever," Bryce said. "We can put it on our summer list."

"I used to go with the girl who lived next door to me," Tex said, infusing a smile into his voice.

"You've told me, Dad," Bryce said dryly.

"See? You know what goin' with someone means."

Bryce scoffed—or maybe laughed—and shook his head. "All right, Pops."

Tex laughed too, saying, "It's right up here."

"You sure?" Bryce asked. "I've been here before, and it didn't look like this."

Tex frowned out the window too, because his son was right. The land sat in shades of yellow and brown. The fence that ran around the pasture that bordered the road looked like it could collapse if a two-ounce bird swooped down and landed on it.

"Maybe no one lives here," he mused. He didn't know who his father had sold the ranch to, and it had been ten years anyway. The property could've changed hands more than once by now.

The pasture gave way to the house and lawn, but it too looked abandoned. No one lived here, that was for sure.

"Look," Bryce said. "There's a sign. Is the house for sale?"

Tex's heart jumped right up into his throat. If this house and ranch was up for sale, he wanted to buy it. "Is it?" He slowed the truck he'd owned for years and turned into the gravel driveway. Weeds and grass grew through the rocks, along with some pretty pink wildflowers Tex had long forgotten the name of.

He brought the vehicle to a stop long before the end of the driveway, which would take him all the way to the back steps. His mother would throw a fit if she saw the state of the front porch she'd once loved and tended to.

Tex could remember trimming this lawn behind a push mower, and he knew how to fix fences, tend to horses and cattle, and paint houses. His father had made his boys do scads of chores as they grew up, and he'd pitched in plenty.

He must be so disappointed in us, Tex thought as he looked at the house. Half of the brothers had passed on inheriting the ranch because of the band. Blaze and Jem were still heavily entrenched in the rodeo, and the twins had barely been out of the house when Daddy had decided he was too old and too weak to keep up the two-hundred-acre ranch.

"Dad," Bryce said, and Tex blinked his eyes to get himself to stop looking at the peeling paint and the faded front door. He hadn't even noticed his son getting out of the truck. Bryce stood on the lawn—the crispy, brown grass—and waved at Tex to come over.

He heaved a sigh and got out of the truck, the heat of the day punching him in the lungs. It wasn't usually hot in the mountains, but the whole country was experiencing a heat wave this week.

"What is it?" he asked.

"There's an auction on this property," Bryce said. "Tomorrow."

"Tomorrow?" Tex arrived and looked at the sign, but the type was way too small to hold his attention for long. He'd always had such a short attention span, and he forced himself to read the big, blocky, black letters.

The property would be sold as-is to the highest bidder. The auction would be at the library at ten a.m. in the morning, and Tex's only thought was that he'd better be there.

"We should go," Bryce said. "You have money, right, Dad?"

"Yeah," Tex said. Country Quad had done well on tour last year, but they'd postponed their next album, and he had to split everything with the other band members and the staff. Touring wasn't cheap, and the record label only paid for so much.

This was a cash auction, and Tex wondered how much it would go for. In Coral Canyon, Wyoming? A town of maybe ten thousand? After a rush of growth? With other houses sitting empty?

"Let's look at the market," Tex said.

"I want to sit on the porch where you kissed Nina," Bryce said, chuckling as he jogged across the grass.

"That was eons ago," Tex called after his son. He returned his attention to his phone, and he started looking up the real estate market in Coral Canyon. The town had enjoyed a boom a few years ago, but the growth had stalled, and Tex didn't see anything out of his price range.

A broken-down, abandoned ranch further from town? No one would want this place, and Tex suddenly did. He could call Otis, Luke, and Trace and find out if they'd like to go in on the ranch with him. Well, maybe Luke and Trace.

The band was taking a break this summer, as his brothers were trying to figure out if they wanted to rebrand Country Quad into Country Trio—or some other name—and continue making music, or if anyone else was ready to do something different with his life.

Tex knew Otis didn't want to keep traveling. He'd been talking to a woman pretty seriously over a dating app, and he'd gone to Florida to meet her. Tex was expecting a text announcing his brother's engagement any moment now.

Luke and Trace had stayed in Nashville for now, but they were taking time off. Tex could text them both about chipping in for the ranch and get them out here to Wyoming by next weekend.

Cash only, streamed through his head. Tex had always had enough for his needs, to send to Corrie and Bryce, and to enjoy himself without thinking too hard about how he'd pay for his next meal.

"You can't be on this property," a woman said, and Tex

looked up from his phone. The sunlight glinted off his front windshield, momentarily blinding him. The woman's voice tickled something familiar inside him, but he couldn't quite place it.

"This is private property," she said. "We don't need any land sharks coming into our town." She marched on toward him, her long legs clad in jeans despite the heat. She wore a blue and white striped tank top and cowgirl boots on her feet. Her limbs were long, and she ate up the distance between them in a few last strides.

Tex knew then exactly who she was. Fireworks popped inside him, burning his lungs and rendering his voice mute.

Abigail Ingalls put one hand on her hip and gestured toward the porch. "Do you mind getting him off the porch?"

"Sure," Tex said, the word catching in his throat. He whistled through his teeth, something he'd always done to call his son and get him to come back to him. He'd been doing it since the boy could crawl, and it worked now too. Tex could barely look away from Abby, but in the brief moment he did, he saw Bryce coming down the steps and toward him.

"Sorry, Abby," he said, reaching up to tip his cowboy hat at her. He was suddenly so glad he always wore it, because it hid his graying hair, something he'd become more and more self-conscious about in the past couple of years.

The woman folded her arms now. "Do I know you?"

Bryce jogged up, and Tex indicated the truck. "We should go."

"Yeah, sure," he said, but he simply looked at Tex and then Abby. Abby looked back and forth between the two of them, her gaze finally landing on Tex, her eyebrows cocked high as she obviously waited for him to explain.

"You should know me," he said. "I took you to plenty of drive-in movies. A dance or two. I think I even told my son here about how I used to sneak into your barn so we could sneak a kiss." He grinned at Abby, but a horrified expression filled her face instead of the fun, flirty vibe Tex had been trying for.

CHAPTER
TWO

Abigail Ingalls could not believe the man standing in front of her was Tex Young. He was the only one she'd ever shimmied into the barn to meet for a kiss, so it had to be. The young man with him looked like a mini-him—except he had the height. The head full of dark hair. The deep, penetrating eyes that seemed to see more than she wanted him to.

Tex still had that grin on his face, and Abby told herself to wait until it slipped. The man exuded confidence; he always had. But he wasn't infallible, and Abby knew if she waited long enough, he'd slip.

He blinked, and she saw it. The corners of his mouth drooped, and satisfaction dove through her. "Hello, Tex," she said coolly, arranging her face into something she hoped was passive and placid.

This man and his good looks did not influence her. Never mind that he hadn't lost an ounce of his charm or his good looks. He'd aged well, from what she could see, and she sure did like a man in a big, white cowboy hat, as much as she hated to admit that.

She would never tell him, that was for sure. Not again.

"This is my son, Bryce," he said, slinging his arm around his son's shoulders. "We're moving to Coral Canyon today."

Abby flicked her gaze toward the truck and trailer in the driveway. They weren't brand new, but she'd still expected to find a land shark scoping out the house and land, planning a way to raze everything and bring in steel, cement, and glass.

She still lived right next door, and she would not let that happen. She would *not*. She had no less than four alarms set for tomorrow morning just to make sure she showed up at the library on time. Lucky for her, she had a key, and the auction couldn't start without her to open the library. So she wouldn't miss the auction no matter what.

Her stomach still quaked with nerves, and she just wanted it over with already. Once she owned this property, she could hydrate it properly. She could move her horses onto it. She could think about renting out the farmhouse after she'd given it a thorough cleaning.

"Nice to meet you," she said to Bryce, because she did have some manners. "Where are you two staying?"

"We've got a rental over on the other side of town," Tex said. He pointed back to the house. "How long has it been like this?"

"A year maybe," Abby said. "The last couple who owned it left suddenly, and they couldn't sell it. He had a job that came up in intelligence, and they were here one day and gone the next. Neither of them came back, and a for-sale sign appeared a couple of months later. The bank eventually repossessed it, and they're doing an auction tomorrow."

"Yeah, that's what I was looking at," he said, his smile as brilliant as the summer sun shining down today. Abby tried not to find him attractive, but any woman would fail in that quest. Tex had the kind of face a woman longed to touch, if just to feel if that jaw was as strong as it looked.

He had large hands that knew how to coax the most beautiful melodies from a guitar, and Abby would only admit to herself in her quietest moments that she'd watched some of his videos online. He had a series of how-to's for kids to learn to play the guitar, and there were plenty of music videos to choose from.

His son stood as tall as Tex, and while he wasn't quite as filled out in the shoulders, they could both break a woman's heart.

Abby vowed it wasn't going to be hers. Not this time.

"Anyway," Tex said, a high note entering his voice. "We'll get out of your hair. It's too hot to stand out in the sun." He lifted his hat and moved his hand through his hair in such a familiar gesture that Abby blinked, and the world went black.

Black and white. Salt and pepper. Tex had plenty of gray in his hair, and wow, that only made him sexier than he already was.

He and Bryce walked back to their truck, both of them talking in such similar voices, and she still stood on the fried grass. She shook her head and told herself to pull everything together. She'd been around plenty of good-looking cowboys over the years. Tex Young wasn't going to bring her to her knees.

"Oh, no, he is not," she vowed as she crossed the patch of land that used to grow vegetables that separated this ranch from the farm she helped her brother run. Back in the house, she poured herself a big glass of lemonade as Wade wheeled himself into the kitchen.

"Who was it?" he asked. "I'll take some of that." He swiped off his hat and wiped the sweat from his forehead. "I got the pipes moved. We'll get the sprinklers on tonight."

"Okay," Abby said, handing the glass of lemonade to him. "I bet we can get the tomatoes and peas in this week-end. I don't think it'll freeze again."

"The weather is so weird right now," he said, shaking his head. He took a drink and set the glass on the counter. "But I bet you're right."

"So I'll go to the nursery after the auction tomorrow," she said. "We can do them tomorrow night." She'd already spent half a day putting in tomatoes that had then died in a late frost. Abby hated having to do work twice, and she had not been happy with Mother Nature that morning a few weeks ago.

"You're still sure about the auction?" Wade wore doubt in his eyes and wouldn't meet her gaze.

"Yes," Abby said. "We can take care of that land, and if we own it, then we control who lives right next door to us."

"Mm." Wade pushed himself over to the cupboard. "Don't spend more than eighty on it, or we'll be in trouble."

"I know." They'd discussed the budget for her auction habits, though she hadn't really bid on any of the other properties around Coral Canyon.

"Do we have any of that chicken noodle soup?" Wade asked.

"We're in the middle of a heat wave." Abby leaned against the counter and watched him pull out the packet anyway. How he ate that stuff, she'd never know. "I have homemade mac and cheese in the fridge."

"We've eaten that for three days." Her brother filled the electric kettle and set it on the element. After switching it on, he added, "We need to learn how to make smaller meals."

By "we," he meant her, as Wade hadn't actually cooked for years. Since returning from his military service, in fact.

"You're right," she said instead of arguing with him or suggesting he make something for dinner. Secretly, she liked making big pans of food, because then she didn't have to cook every evening. She always had something hot for lunch at the library, and she simply didn't have to use so much mental energy to keep herself and Wade fed.

Lord knew Abby had enough other things taking up the available space in her mind. An image of Tex's handsome, more mature face flashed across her brainwaves, and she pushed him right back out.

She definitely didn't have time for him. "I'll get the

barn door done today," she said. "And I'll bring in the horses tonight. I want to work with Knitted Cotton."

"All right," Wade said, and Abby hadn't expected him to argue with her. Very few people did. She ran the library with firm fairness to the employees and the patrons, and she loved her job there. She loved gardening and prodding the land to produce a lot of what she and Wade needed to live. They had honeybees for honey, and a huge garden that produced plenty of vegetables. Abby had learned how to preserve them from her mother and grandmother, and they lived on spaghetti sauce, stewed tomatoes, bottled peaches, frozen corn and green beans, and more all winter long.

They grew all the hay their horses needed, and their two dozen chickens provided eggs. Abby loved her country life, even if the work was long and hard some days. The ranch next door had been neglected and overgrown since the Youngs had sold it a decade ago. She'd been worried about that, and she'd been right.

This was one time she hadn't wanted to be right, but that didn't change the fact that the two hundred acres next door was a severe eyesore for Mountain View Road, and Abby had always taken pride in where she lived.

She'd told Wade time and again that they didn't have to farm all of the acreage. She'd take care of the gardens and lawns. She'd work on the house over time, and they'd possibly rent it. Or, to prevent her from becoming a complete spinster who lived with her older brother forever, perhaps she'd move into the house next door and they'd each live alone.

After Wade's discharge from the service, he'd spent several months in a hospital in North Carolina, recovering from the loss of both of his legs. They'd been amputated from the knees down, and he had two prosthetics he could use. He said the wheelchair was simply easier in some instances, and Abby couldn't remember the last time he'd put on his prosthetics.

She'd been coming out of a failed engagement at the time and had been more than happy to help her brother transition back to regular life on the farm in Coral Canyon. Her parents had bought a smaller condo in town, and the four of them got along well.

Abby didn't need anything or anyone else.

Certainly not a former boyfriend to sail into town and buy his childhood ranch right out from under her nose. With horror, she realized that if Tex did manage to do that, he'd live right next door to her again. A hundred yards from the side door on her house to the back door on his.

That so wasn't happening.

Abby pulled out her phone and set a fifth alarm just to make sure she got up in time to put on just the right amount of makeup for the auction. After all, if Tex really was going to be there, she'd want to look as powerful as possible, and she knew just how to put bronzer on to shape her face into its power pose.

———

THE FOLLOWING MORNING, ONLY A FEW PEOPLE LINGERED IN the multi-purpose room at the library. Abby wore a denim skirt and a blouse with running stallions on it, her cowgirl boots, and that powerful makeup. She couldn't help glancing around for Tex or Bryce, but she hadn't seen them yet.

Dale Flood had come, and she should've known he'd show his face here. The man came to every auction in Coral Canyon, and he'd bid if only to keep the outsiders out of town. Abby had to say she respected him for that. She didn't want more big corporations in Coral Canyon either.

Justin Wells sat in the front row, but Abby had seen him come to two or three auctions now and never raise his paddle. She wasn't sure what, if any, interest he held in the land out by her.

Zach Zuckerman had just walked in, and the man had a ton of money. He could easily outbid Abby for the ranch, though he lived further north on a pristine piece of property already. She narrowed her eyes at him and wished she could read minds. He simply gave her a friendly smile and asked, "My wife just checked out thirteen books. Isn't there some kind of limit?"

Abby gave him a tight smile. "Not for adults."

He chuckled and shook his head. "She'll probably get through 'em all this week anyway."

His wife worked as the private chef up at Whiskey Mountain Lodge, but apparently she had plenty of time for reading. Abby wouldn't be able to name the last time she had leisure time. She did read a lot, but that was for her job. She had to know the latest bestsellers and be able to answer questions about a variety of books. People came into the library with the oddest questions sometimes, and they often mixed up author names and book titles, then relied on her to unjumble everything.

A couple walked in, and Abby smiled politely at them as they signed up and took their paddle. She knew Gill and Tricia Yardley, and again, she wondered why they were there. They already owned a big corner lot on the last true block before the farms and ranches took over the more rural parts of Coral Canyon. Not only that, but their property sat on the lake side, which was easily twenty minutes from Abby's east side of town.

The clock clicked closer to ten, and Abby glanced toward the stairs, imagining where the elevator would go if she could just get the funding for it. She'd been working on a grant for what felt like forever but had actually only been about a year. She'd made it quite far before realizing she had to bid out everything, and she'd had to start over.

She stepped over to the table and signed herself in, then moved halfway down a row about halfway back from the podium. The big screen had been pulled down for the auctioneer to show the property and go over the rules, but Abby knew both like the back of her hand.

Perhaps that was why she zoned out. She only looked over her shoulder once, and she didn't see Tex. She listened with half an ear as the man up front went over the acreage, the outbuildings, and that the property would be sold as-is.

"It's been appraised for two hundred and fifty thousand dollars, but you can see the land and home and buildings need a lot of work. We'll open the bidding at fifty thousand."

Abby waited, because she wanted to feel out who would really be bidding this morning. Dale lifted his paddle after glancing around at everyone.

"Fifty thousand," the auctioneer said, but he didn't increase in pitch or speed. He simply said it, and she'd learned that these land auctions weren't anything like cattle auctions. She'd worked in that industry for a few years right out of high school before deciding to go to school and get her degree in library science.

"Each bid has to be one thousand dollars more than the one lower," the man said, and Abby lifted her paddle.

"I have fifty-one," the auctioneer said. He wore an expensive suit, because he'd likely come from a bigger city like Cheyenne or even Denver to run this auction. He represented the bank, and they'd take whatever they could get for the property that had been in default for over a year.

"Fifty-two," he said.

Abby lifted her paddle, and he called out her bid.

When they reached sixty-one, Dale put his paddle down on the chair next to him. Abby's heart pounded. Getting that ranch for one-fourth of what it was worth would be a huge steal. A major win.

Excitement beat beneath her breastbone like hummingbird wings, and she swallowed to keep them down where they belonged.

"Sixty-two," the man said, and Abby surveyed the crowd to find who'd bid against her.

Tex Young. The traitor.

Her hummingbird pulse turned into crow's wings. Big, huge flapping things that drove fury through her with every—single—beat.

Tex had some nerve, especially when he got up and moved closer, sitting right on the end of her aisle.

She threw her paddle into the air. So did he.

Back and forth they went until Abby was nearing her ceiling. In fact, if she bid again, she'd be at eighty-one thousand for the ranch.

Tex looked at her, a glint in his eyes that issued a challenge in such a sexy way that she wanted to toss her paddle at his slightly crooked nose and make it even less straight. She gripped the handle of it as if seriously contemplating it.

"Eighty thousand," the auctioneer said again. "Do I have eighty-one?"

Slowly, she put her paddle in the air.

Tex frowned and turned back toward the front, his paddle up already.

Off they went again, and Abby's mind raced. She had no idea what she'd tell Wade. It was almost like she was operating outside of her body, and when she put her paddle up at ninety-three thousand, she called out, "One hundred thousand dollars."

Tex looked at her with wide eyes that didn't blink.

She stared straight back at him, trying to control how quickly her breath went in and out of her lungs. He would break; she'd seen him slip yesterday, and she could force him to do it again.

His shoulders slumped, and Abby could almost taste the victory.

"One hundred thousand," the auctioneer said. "Do I have one-oh-five?"

Tex didn't move for a moment, and she swore the auctioneer waited longer than the rules called for. He bid, and she scowled at him, her paddle already in the air. A few more waves and silent battles later, the bid sat at one-fifty, and Abby was in serious, serious trouble.

Tex put his paddle down and wouldn't look at her, and the auctioneer called, "Sold, to seventeen, for one-hundred-fifty thousand dollars."

The air rushed out of Abby's lungs, and she sagged back into her chair too. A smile touched her face, but it was just a façade. One she needed to keep in place as long as Tex's eyes weighed heavily on the side of her face, as they did now. And one she'd have to wear when she faced her brother and told him how much she'd overspent.

CHAPTER
THREE

Tex got up and left the row where he'd moved to hopefully convey to Abby that his family's farm meant a great deal to him. She obviously hadn't gotten the message. That, or she hadn't cared.

He sat in the back while the room emptied and Abby went to talk to the auctioneer. She spoke in a quiet voice, but he didn't, so Tex clearly heard him say, "Yes, we can handle the transaction in the conference room."

So she'd be paying for the ranch right now. "Cash auction," he murmured to himself. He texted Bryce quickly, telling him he hadn't gotten the ranch and they'd start looking for another house the moment he got back to the house they were renting.

A dose of sadness hit him after he sent the text, and he looked up to see Abby checking around her as if she expected someone to be there listening—and she didn't want them to overhear her.

Something wasn't right. Tex had seen that look on her face before, and it wasn't a good look. He stood and walked up to the podium too. The auctioneer closed his folder and said, "Come with me."

"Is everything okay?" Tex asked, startling Abby. The auctioneer turned and left without answering Tex, but Abby looked at him with wide, nervous eyes. "What's goin' on?"

"Nothing," she said, sliding a mask over her true feelings. Sort of. She'd never been great at hiding how she felt, and that hadn't changed much over the last couple of decades.

He started to smile and stopped himself just in time. That would only fuel the angry fire he found brewing in her eyes, and he didn't need that. He didn't know what to say, and he simply remained quiet while he studied her and tried to figure out what the problem was.

She rolled her neck, her eyes falling closed. "My brother is going to kill me."

"Is he?" Tex asked. Wade was a couple of years older than her, and she was a year behind Tex. "Why?"

She wiped her hand through her auburn hair and glared at him. "You're really nosy, you know that?"

"It's small-town Coral Canyon," he said, rocking back on his heels and tucking his hands in his pockets. "Everyone's nosy."

She cocked her hip and folded her arms. "You've lived here for less than twenty-four hours. You don't get to claim the town."

"I'm not claiming the town," he argued. "Though I did grow up here."

"You left."

"Everyone leaves," he said, spreading his arms wide. He wasn't going to be blamed for leaving Coral Canyon. "You left. For years and years. Last I heard, you were working the library system in Chicago, for crying out loud." His chest heaved, and he wasn't even sure why. Maybe because her hair held strands of gold in it. Her hazel eyes cut through him, and Tex actually liked it.

He was sick, that was for sure. He hadn't expected his life to be so crazy here in Coral Canyon, and here he was, trying to buy his dad's previous ranch and battling his attraction to his old girlfriend from high school.

"Miss Ingalls," the auctioneer said. "My manager says we can't do a loan. It's cash or nothing."

Abby waved both hands at him, her gaze going from arrogantly angry to panicked in less than three seconds. Tex started to chuckle, realizing what the problem was.

"You don't have enough cash for the ranch," he said. "Do you?"

Abby glared at him, but he wasn't going to be the one who backed down this time. He'd let her stare him out of a smile yesterday, but today's wasn't going anywhere.

He maintained his eye contact and raised his eyebrows. Finally, Abby said, "Fine. I don't exactly have all of the cash."

"How much do you have?"

She coughed as she said it, and Tex tipped his head

back and laughed. "I'm not sure what you said, but it wasn't even six digits."

Abby swatted at his chest and said, "Stop it. Don't you have some boxes to unpack or something?"

He danced away from her, laughing. "No," he said. "I've got all day. No job. No obligations. Nothing." He grinned at her, trying not to be so pleased.

She did the folding-arms thing again. "And I suppose you've got plenty of money. Big-city cowboy music star sails into his hometown and buys up all the land."

"Not all the land," Tex said. "Just my *family's land*." He leaned closer to her, hoping to drive home his point. "One of us should've bought it ten years ago when Daddy was selling."

Abby blinked, clearly getting the point.

"Miss Ingalls," the auctioneer barked.

She flinched as she lurched toward him, then looked back to Tex. "Come in with me," she said in a rush. "Maybe we can buy it together."

"Together?" he asked, but she was already striding away with those long legs of hers.

Tex really had no choice but to follow her, and he did with a prayer of, "Lord, some help here would be fantastic," falling from his lips.

The conference room couldn't hold him and Abby, not without some sort of nuclear explosion in the next ten minutes. Tex prayed this transaction would be finished long before then as he sat at the tiny table with her. She looked at him, but he chose to focus on the paperwork in front of him.

He hadn't bought a house for a while, but the amount of paperwork in front of the auctioneer was enough to tell Tex this wouldn't be done in ten minutes.

"You're co-buying?" he asked.

"I can do it if it's not cash only," Abby said. "But, well...I don't have one-hundred-fifty thousand in cash." She twisted her hands together once and then sat on them. Tex swallowed his chuckle, because he'd seen her do that during difficult history tests too, and once while trying to explain to her daddy why she and Tex were in the barn so early in the morning.

He grinned at that memory, and Abby kicked him under the table. "Ow," he said, the word flying from his mouth. "What'd you do that for?"

"He just asked you how much you'd be paying."

He searched her face, telling himself not to zone out inside memories from the past. It was extremely obvious that the two of them wouldn't be recreating any of them, and he'd do best to not even conjure them up.

"I think half," he said, turning back to the auctioneer. "That way, it's fifty-fifty."

"I can pay eighty," she blurted out. "He should only have to pay seventy."

"I can put all of it down now," Tex said, throwing the words at Abby. "Cash. Right now." He reached into his back pocket as if he'd have that much money in his wallet. He wouldn't, but he could get it. He hadn't even called Otis or Trace to talk about them going in on the ranch with him. He'd spent the evening researching the housing market in Coral Canyon, ordering pizza for him and his son, talking to Bryce about possibly living on the farm where he'd grown up, and obsessing over how high to bid.

Abby glared his face down to wax, and Tex sighed. "If you pay up everything you have, how are you going to invest in fixing up the house and land?"

"I—" She cut off when she realized he'd made a good point.

He didn't give her a *so-there* look. He simply switched his attention back to the auctioneer, whose name he'd missed while he'd reminisced privately inside his own mind. "She can do half. I'll do the other half. Seventy-five each."

"That only leaves me with five grand to pay for renovations," she said.

"I get to live on the ranch with my son," he said, turning back to her. Every piece of this complicated puzzle fell into place in Tex's mind. "Rent-free. We'll fix things up in exchange for that. You can file for the water rights. Put your horses on the land. Whatever you wanted it for."

"I wanted it so I could control who I live next door to." She raised one perfectly plucked eyebrow at him, and Tex wouldn't be male if he didn't notice and appreciate her beauty. Oh, yes, Abigail Ingalls was downright gorgeous, and she'd worn the perfect makeup today to prove it.

"Perfect," he said, though she didn't want to live next door to him. "You got yourself some great neighbors." He did smile then, which only made her scoff, roll her eyes, and look up to the corner of the room.

Tex focused on the auctioneer. "If she can't pay, shouldn't it go to me?:

"Wait a second," she said, her hand landing on his arm. "I won."

"But you can't pay." He looked back at the auctioneer. "Shouldn't I get it for one-forty-five? Or even eighty-one thousand? She can't pay more than eighty, and she bid over that." A lot over that, and Tex got reminded of Abby's pride and stubbornness.

"Half each," she blurted out before the auctioneer could say anything. "He gets to live there rent-free, and we'll discuss fixing it up together."

"Sir," he said, his voice calm and controlled. "Ma'am. I don't care what you two do with the land. I just need the one-fifty in cash so we can start signing these papers."

Tex appraised him. He wasn't going to give Tex the property for eighty-one thousand, or even five grand less. Bankers.

"Right," Tex said, shaking his head and deciding not to fight this battle. "Let me call my son."

"I'll be right back," Abby said, and she got up and left the room before Tex could pull his phone from his pocket.

Half an hour later, the auctioneer had his money, and all the documents had been signed. He tucked them away into his briefcase, pushed their copy toward them, and surveyed the two of them. "Good luck," he said before he left, and Tex thought that was a fair assessment of the situation.

He looked at Abby. She gazed back at him, that familiar fire licking through her expression. Tex wanted to get burned by it so badly, but he didn't lean forward. Giving someone with a flame thrower more fuel was never wise.

"I get to live in the house and on the land, with Bryce, for free," Tex said. "We'll get all the utilities back on and in our name. I'll pay all the bills. We'll get the house and yard back in amazing shape."

"What do I get out of it?" she asked. "I paid seventy-five thousand dollars for it, and not so you could live there rent-free."

"You get sweat equity without having to lift a finger," he said. "I paid half too, sweetheart. I'll be doing all the work, paying all the bills, and funding it all. You don't have to do a single thing." He got to his feet to leave. He wasn't going to debate this with her, not right now. He had his family ranch to get to and assess more fully than he had yesterday before she'd run him off the land.

"Equity is only good if we sell it later," she said, scrambling after him. "How long are you going to live there?"

"I don't know," he said. "At least a year until Bryce graduates." He didn't have to tell her he still owed his record label an album. She didn't get to know what his life on tour looked like. She *wasn't* his friend, and he hadn't been her boyfriend for twenty years now.

She caught up to him, and they walked side-by-side toward the steps that led down to the first level of the library. "You have to run everything by me," she said, panting.

"No, I don't," he said, pausing on the landing. "Abigail, think of yourself as a silent investor." *Emphasis on silent,* he added in his head. "Bryce and I will do everything. You don't even have to fund us. You paid an initial investment—which you didn't have to do, by the way. You went nuts in that auction and way overbid yourself, as well as the property."

She glared, her chest rising and falling in quick breaths. Tex felt the same way inside, but he could hide it better. "Investors supply money to the people making things happen. I don't have to run anything by you, because I'm going to be funding the improvements, repairs, and renovations. You get to sleep easy at night knowing I'm not going to tear the house down and build a community of high-rise condominiums."

He started down the steps again, done with this conversation. He tried to channel Mav and Blaze simultaneously, because Mav wouldn't give in on crucial points but he'd be kind about it, and Blaze was the happy-go-lucky type that would agree to things just to end the conversation. Right now, Tex needed both of those qualities, because Abby hadn't changed since high school.

She still wanted supreme control of everything around her. She probably got up in the morning and did the same things in the same order, just like she had back then. Getting her to sneak out into the barn before school so he could kiss her had nearly put her in the hospital, for crying out loud.

His memory tickled again, more news of hospitals and injuries, and the irritation with Abby faded even further. At the bottom of the steps, he paused again and adjusted his cowboy hat as she came down the last couple of stairs. "I'm real sorry about Wade," he said. "I didn't know he'd been injured overseas."

Abby's chin came up, and those eyes…. Those eyes

said so much Tex suspected she would never say out loud. She adored her brother, but she didn't need Tex's pity. She found him attractive, but she'd never admit it. She didn't want to agree to his terms about the ranch, but she would, because she had no real legs to stand on.

"Good to see you, Abby," Tex said, tipping his hat. Then he strode out of the library and over to his truck, where Bryce waited on his phone.

"I have to go, Jen. My dad's back." Bryce ended the call, hope etched in every line on his face. "So? Did you really get it? We can live there?"

Tex put the truck in reverse and ignored Abby as she stood on the front steps of the library. "I got half of it," he said. "But yes, we can live there."

"Good," Bryce said with a sigh.

"It's not nice," Tex said, the outline of the keys he'd gotten from the auctioneer suddenly burning a hole in his jeans. "You saw it yesterday, right? We'll be lucky if it's not full of raccoons."

Bryce laughed and said, "Anything's better than that rental, Dad. I think I swallowed four spiders last night while I was sleeping." He shuddered, and Tex did the same.

"I can't guarantee that won't be the case again tonight," he said. "But bright side—we hardly unpacked any of our boxes, so moving again won't be too bad." He turned to go out to the east side of town. "Let's swing by and see what we're really dealing with, so we can buy groceries and furniture today if we need to."

"This is exciting," Bryce said, shifting in his seat. "A real summer adventure."

"Yeah," Tex said, thinking of Abby and the adventures he'd like to have with her this summer. One look at his son reminded him of what this summer was going to be. Time spent together. Rest and relaxation. Writing songs together.

He couldn't wait to tell his brothers what he'd done, and a quiet vein of excitement and adventure stole through Tex too. This was going to be a great bonding experience for him and Bryce—and hey, maybe he'd get to have a second chance with the girl he'd once gone with in high school too.

The possibilities suddenly seemed endless, and Tex grinned into the summer sunshine as he drove toward the two-hundred acre ranch he now owned half of.

CHAPTER
FOUR

Abby stewed as she watched Tex and his mini-me drive out of the library parking lot. He didn't come to a stop before he pulled onto Main Street, and she scoffed, folded her arms, and marched back inside the building.

It was too hot to be standing outside, obsessing over an ex-boyfriend. "Your new business partner," she muttered to herself. She had to view Tex like that, or her heart would start to whisper scandalous ideas to her mind.

She wasn't working today, but she went back to her office and closed the door. She leaned against it in the cool dimness and pressed her eyes closed. In truth, her heart wasn't beating like a big bass drum because she and Tex had just bought the property next door in a joint venture.

He'd made it very clear he could afford the full one-fifty, and in fact, he'd tried to take the property from her completely. Thankfully, the banker was greedy, and he wanted his one-fifty. Abby had stored the money in her office, and she looked over to the cabinet that still stood open.

She moved to close it, finally admitting the real reason everything hurt when she looked at Tex. He'd broken up with her almost twenty years ago, before he'd left for college. He'd come back the next summer, and then he was off on his next endeavor—starting his country music band.

It hadn't happened right away, but within a few years, she'd heard Country Quad on the radio when their first album came out.

What hurt the most was seeing his son with him. The teen would be a senior in the fall, and that meant he had to be seventeen years old. Or close to it. So within two years of Tex leaving Coral Canyon, he'd met someone else, fallen in love with them, gotten married, and had a son.

Like she'd never existed. Like Tex had never considered being with her for longer than it took him to pass his exams and claim his diploma.

Her heart trembled, and Abby curled her fingers into fists to contain her emotions. She wasn't going to make decisions based on what Tex had or hadn't done two decades ago. Lots of people left their hometowns and went to college, fell in love with classmates or the man down the hall, and moved on.

Heck, even she'd once been in love with someone else. She absolutely refused to think about Jonas for longer than five seconds. He didn't deserve more time than that, and she pushed him and his cheating heart right out of her mind and life. She usually didn't have to work that hard to do it today, but with Tex's reappearance in Coral Canyon—with Bryce—she couldn't help thinking that she had some fundamental flaw that no man would ever be able to see past.

She'd be single forever, and while she'd thought she'd be okay with that, she knew now how lonely and empty she was. Even with Wade at the farmhouse, Abby still felt alone.

He was dating Cheryl Watts, and Abby wouldn't be surprised if her brother asked Cheryl to marry him this summer. They'd been seeing each other for six or seven months, and Cheryl didn't seem to care about Wade's injuries at all. He'd been really concerned about that after his service and surgeries, and he hadn't dated anyone until her.

Abby liked Cheryl a lot, as she was sweet and kind. "You could probably learn something from her," Abby said as she slumped into her desk chair. Her phone rang, and she pulled it from her pocket to answer Wade. "Hey."

"So," he said. "How did it go?"

She reached up to rub her eyes, sighing as she did.

"Not well, I see," he said. "So who bought it?"

"We did," she said. "Kind of."

"Abigail," he said in his military voice. "What does that mean?"

She didn't want to tell him she'd gone crazy and overbid herself by almost double. She also didn't see a way around it. She spilled the whole story in less than a minute, barely taking a moment to breathe.

Wade sat on the other end of the line, silent.

"Say something," she said. "I know I'm an idiot. Proud. Selfish. Impulsive. All of that." She knew, because she wasn't blind. She could see herself clearly, and she had been trying to change. There was just something about Tex Young that irked her.

More like lights you up, she thought. The past twenty-four hours with him back in her life had been more eventful and colorful than the previous twenty-four *months* without him. She couldn't believe she still had this insane crush on the boy next door—and he was once again the boy next door, literally.

He's definitely not a boy, she told herself while Wade made her revel in his judgmental silence.

"I guess that's why Tex and his son just pulled into the driveway," Wade said.

"Yeah," she said, relieved he hadn't launched into a lecture. Wade wouldn't anyway. He usually let what he didn't say weigh more heavily on her mind than what he did.

"I suppose I should go say hello," he said.

"If you want," she said. "I'm still going to get chicken parm from Capolti's, and then I'll be home." Hopefully, Tex and his twin would be gone by then.

"Do you want me to text you when he leaves?" Wade asked.

"No," Abby said. "I'm not that pathetic."

"I didn't say you were pathetic," he said. "You just… went off about him last night, and I thought maybe it would be easier if he's gone before you get home."

"He's going to live there," she said. "I can't avoid him forever." She didn't even want to do that.

"All right," Wade said easily. "Then I want double chicken and an extra breadstick."

"Okay," Abby said. "See you soon." The call ended, and she phoned in her order to Capolti's, which was a newer Italian restaurant that had come to Coral Canyon in the past few years. She didn't hate all the growth and newer restaurants. She just didn't want to look out her back windows and see two hundred new homes instead of the farmland and fields and pastures she'd known for so long.

Now she wouldn't have to, and Tex was right about that. He wouldn't build condos or section off the land and sell it to a builder. He'd revive the ranch where he'd grown up, and Abby couldn't help wondering if he'd mind fixing her up too. He'd already brought back to life part of her that had been dark and dreary for a long time.

Maybe living next door to him now would be as exciting as it was all those years ago. With that hope in her heart, Abby left the library and went to pick up her lunch. The moment she turned onto Mountain View Road, her hope turned into a prayer.

"I will do what You want me to do, Lord," she said. "Help me to be kind to my new neighbors, and help me not to be too sensitive about…well, anything."

She saw Tex's truck parked in the driveway long before she drove past the ranch next door. She turned into her own driveway, her eyes stuck to that midnight black truck.

Tex had always owned a truck, and she shouldn't have expected anything different.

She didn't, other than someone else entirely showing up to bid on the ranch. The fact that he was back, here, now, she didn't understand. When Jerry Young had first listed the property ten years ago, both she and her parents had been surprised one of the nine Young sons hadn't wanted it. None of them had lived in town at the time, and Susan and Jerry Young had moved into a fifty-five-plus community after the sale.

Her parents had done something similar a few years later, leaving the farmhouse to her and Wade when he'd come from North Carolina. They lived in the one and only condo building that had been built in town, and Abby had refused to visit them there for the first year in her own form of protest.

She'd gotten past her irritation with the bigger buildings in downtown Coral Canyon, because she just needed more time with some things. Looking next door as she got out of her own truck, Tex Young would just be one more of those things.

She took the food inside the house and closed off the sight of his truck and that dilapidated farmhouse with a slam. "Oops," she said when Wade looked at her with a frown between his eyes. "The door got away from me."

"Your temper gets away from you," he said, lifting his eyebrows in a challenge. He stood from the table, and Abby's surprise stole through her.

"You put on your prosthetics?" She put the bag of food on the table and started unpacking it. "Why?"

Wade moved over to the fridge to refill his water bottle. His cowboy hat hung beside the back door, and Abby didn't see his wheelchair anywhere. "No reason."

"Liar," she said, staring a hole in the back of his head. "You didn't want Tex to see you in that chair." She wadded up the plastic restaurant bag and lobbed it toward the trash can. "Newsflash, brother. He already knows you were hurt overseas. He said he was real sorry about it at the library."

Wade turned to face her, something challenging in his expression. "It wasn't for Tex," he said. "*I'm* not the one with a schoolgirl crush on the man."

Abby scoffed, her default emotion streaming forward. "I don't have a crush on him."

"Abby," Wade said. "You've been in love with him for twenty-five years." He returned to the table with real silverware, because he hated using the plastic stuff from the restaurant. "You don't have to hide it from me."

"I'm not hiding anything," she said, taking a fork from him. "You can't hide something that doesn't exist."

"Okay," Wade said, sitting down and opening his Styrofoam container of double-chicken parm with extra breadsticks. He grinned at it and then at her. "I put the prosthetics on, because Cheryl wants me to meet her folks today, and they make me more normal."

Abby collapsed into the only other chair at the dining room table in the old-fashioned kitchen. "Wow," she said, her body turning numb. "You're meeting her parents today?"

"Tonight," he said. "For dinner. We're going apple-picking this afternoon, and that's another reason I thought the prosthetics would be better." He put his head down and twirled spaghetti around his fork.

Abby let the subject drop. He didn't like talking about his wheelchair or making Cheryl push him in it over rough terrain. Abby did it without complaint, and Cheryl would too. Until now, they'd stuck to normal dates, like movies and restaurants and walks around town. He could do all of that from his wheelchair.

The apple orchards northwest of town would definitely be much harder in a wheelchair. Harder, not impossible. Abby felt like that summed up Wade's whole life—harder, but not impossible—and she couldn't help applying that same idea to her and Tex's relationship.

It would be harder this time, sure. But not impossible.

"You're going to clean out the stables this afternoon, yes?" Wade's question that wasn't really a question brought Abby back to her real life.

"Yes," she said. "I've got Kent bringing his trailer too. So we'll get all the sawdust down, and he's taking a load of hay for his farm."

Wade nodded, his mouth full of food. He and Abby ran the farm, with a lot of the work landing on Wade's shoulders. Abby worked at the library, and she drove the Bookmobile two nights a week and on Saturdays.

"Then I'll be in Dog Valley tonight," she said.

"Five to seven," he said. "I won't be home until late. Her parents got a reservation at The Branding Iron." He cocked one eyebrow, which said more than his words had.

"Wow," Abby said. "Are you nervous?"

"Yes," he said simply before stuffing his mouth full of food again.

Abby picked at her Caesar salad, not sure how to say what she wanted to. Her family wasn't great at expressing their feelings and emotions. She and Wade were better at it than her parents, so she cleared her throat and said, "You're the most amazing guy in town, Wade. It's going to be fine."

He nodded, his eyes wide. He clearly needed more reassurance.

"It's clear Cheryl *really* likes you," Abby said. "Her parents don't even matter."

He swallowed and said, "She's real close with them, being an only child and all."

"Then they already know how much she *loves you* and they'll be on their best behavior for her." Abby grinned at him as he smiled and shook his head.

Her phone vibrated at the same time Wade's did, and as they both looked at them, the doorbell rang.

Wade's smile really widened then, and he looked up from his phone, glee in his face. "Ohhh, guess who's standing on the porch?"

Abby's stomach dropped to the floor as she saw the image of the sexiest cowboy alive on her video doorbell app too.

Wade chuckled and twirled up more spaghetti. "He's not here to see me, Abs. Wipe your face and go say hello to your boyfriend."

Abby got to her feet, her hands straightening her hair though she didn't consciously tell them to. She glared at her brother and said, "He's *not* my boyfriend."

"Yet," he teased as she swiped her phone and left the kitchen to go see why the devil Tex Young stood on her doorstep.

CHAPTER
FIVE

Tex stood back from the door, because it used to open out. Today, it swung in, and the gorgeous, tall, lanky Abigail Ingalls stood there. He grinned at her, because a woman like her required such a response. "Hey," he said. "Do you happen to have an adjustable wrench we could borrow?"

"Yeah," she said, stepping back. "I think it's in the lean-to." She seemed…calm. Nice. Reserved. Tex knew she could be perfectly pleasant. She could joke and laugh. He'd once swung her around while they both laughed, the snow falling around them and the sun shining in the west. They'd then fallen to the ground and made snow angels, and he'd kissed her completely while the snow melted beneath the heat of their combined breath.

"Do you want to meet me around back?" she asked. "I'm gonna go through the house, because it's too hot."

"Some air conditioning would be nice," he said with a

chuckle. "The house next door has no air conditioning." He entered the house, his smile slipping. "I'd forgotten about that. We used those window coolers."

"There's a couple of those," she said. "In the bedrooms, I think."

"Yeah," he said. "Bryce has been workin' on one of 'em for a minute. We're trying to get the water on too, but the main line has rusted closed." He followed her into the kitchen, and in these older farmhouses, it was its own room.

Next door, the kitchen in the house where he'd grown up sat at the back of the house, with a double-wide doorway leading into it from the front living room. It wasn't quite one room, but he didn't mind so much. He could probably call in a contractor and see if he could knock down that wall to make it more open.

The house was probably over a hundred years old, and Tex once again experienced a horrible flash of regret that he hadn't stepped up as the oldest Young son and bought the farm from his father. Daddy had offered it to him at less than market value, but he'd been so focused on the band.

The band, the band, the band.

Tex's whole life for the past two decades had been the band. His marriage had failed because of the band. He'd missed a lot of years of his son's life because of the band. Some of his brothers didn't return his calls or texts because of the band.

The ranch was just so big, and so physical, and now that Tex was here, he couldn't face the choices he'd made in the past. He'd laid awake for at least two hours last night, filled with regret over focusing solely on his career for so long.

He hadn't known any better, and he'd prayed long and hard for forgiveness—and for guidance now that he wasn't in the band. The album he hadn't finished yet, the one still on his contract, hung over his head, but as he glanced over to Wade sitting at the kitchen table, he pushed it to the back of his mind.

"Howdy, Wade," he said as if he was a real cowboy. He was about to be, if the look of the fences, the pastures, the land, and the farmhouse were any indication. Tex had already called Mav and offered him a job, to which his younger brother had laughed and laughed.

But he was on his way over, because he'd grown up in that house and on that land too, and he wasn't currently employed. He volunteered a little bit, and he took care of his wife and kids. He loved having time to make a hot breakfast in the morning for everyone, take the kids to the swimming pool or the pond in the hills. They went hiking, boating, and more, and Tex could admit the main reason he and Bryce had come here instead of staying in Boise was because Tex wanted to do and experience all of those things with his son too.

"Tex," Wade said with the nod of his head. He didn't move to get up.

"Smells good," Tex said, catching a whiff of Abby's perfume. She didn't know that, of course, and she paused near the back door as he took another couple of steps and reached her.

"It's from a new place in town," she said, downright cordial now. "Capolti's. Have you been yet?"

"No," he said. "We did see it on the way through, though. Good to know it's good."

"We love it," Abby said, and then she went outside. Tex once again followed her, this time taking a moment to appreciate the curves she had as she practically skipped down the steps. He went before she could realize he was ogling her, and they arrived at the lean-to against the back of the house almost at the same time.

She opened the single door, and the hot scent of dust and metal met his nose. Sweat had already started to bead beneath his cowboy hat again, and he told himself to get used to it. The forecast didn't call for rain for another week, and the heat wave that had been drying out the West and Midwest planned to stick around for several more days.

"I was thinkin' of flooding the yard tonight," he said. "The irrigation water is still running. Seems like I remember my daddy tellin' yours when he was gonna do it, because you guys then wouldn't have irrigation water for a bit."

She glanced at him and then stepped into the slim lean-to. "That's fine." Her voice echoed though the space wasn't very big. She backed out with a huge red toolbox in her hands. He grabbed it from her the moment he noticed how badly her arms trembled.

"Thanks," he said. "We might as well try to revive the grass and fields." He looked south, toward his place. "We can't plant much this year, but we could put a cow and horses out there." To his left, on her property, the squabbling of chickens met his ears, and he swung his attention that way.

"Your place is real pretty," he said, meaning it. The two houses sat right next to one another, driveways and a slim piece of lawn separating them. His ranch then went straight back and to the south, while the Ingalls' went back and north. He wasn't exactly sure on their acreage, and he wasn't going to ask.

But all of their fences stood tall and proud and strong. Their chicken coop was new and properly wired so they didn't lose birds to foxes or hounds or wolves. The pastures held grazing animals and greenery, and their grass had been recently clipped, with huge trees clustered in the back corner as well as in the front yard.

"Thank you," Abby said quietly. "You can keep the tools for now. You might need them."

He looked back at her, and the moment froze. She closed her eyes, but everything moved in slow motion so he could see each individual eyelash as it went down and then started back up. Those lovely eyes looked straight at him, and since she really couldn't hide her feelings, he saw her own regret in her expression.

In the past, she never would've apologized. Well, that wasn't true. She'd let the storms blow out of her, and then she'd come over, her hands pressed together and her skinny legs barely able to hold her up as she said she was sorry.

Now, she said, "Tex, I'm sorry about the auction, okay? I shouldn't have lost my mind and overbid so much."

He nodded, his attraction to this woman making his throat too narrow to speak. That, or working in the heat for the past hour, without food, had really addled his brain. That one. He was going to go with that one.

"Do they deliver food out here these days?" he asked, thinking he and Bryce should've probably grabbed something in town the way Abby had.

"Just pizza," she said. "From The Pipeline." She raised her eyebrows, clearly asking him if he was that desperate.

He just might be. He grinned at her, but she'd already started to turn away. She missed the playful grin, and Tex forced it from his face anyway. He wasn't going to ask her out. She'd say no anyway, and then his pride would be hurt and he'd be embarrassed to see her across the way as they went about doing their chores.

"The Pipeline," he said with a laugh. "I can't believe that place is still in business."

"It's good for kids," she said. "They'll eat anything."

He laughed again and said, "I suppose you're right." He lifted the toolbox a few inches. "Thanks. I'll bring 'em back as soon as we're done."

She looked next door and then nodded. "It's a lot of work over there." Their eyes met again, and something teetered between them. She opened her mouth to say something, but her brother called her from inside.

Abby turned that way and went up the steps two at a time and through the door in one fluid motion, already saying, "Wade?"

Tex's heart beat a little faster too, and not just because Wade Ingalls might be in trouble.

"I'm fine," Wade drawled, and the door closed as he said, "It's hot, Abby. We—"

Tex started back toward his own house, counting his steps. It used to be fifty-five from his back door—which really came out of the side of the house—to hers. He must've gotten longer legs, because it only took him fifty-two steps and a whole lot of introspection about the woman Abby had become.

Yes, there were some things about her that were the same. Some things had changed too, and Tex liked the curves, the makeup, the long, curled eyelashes, and her ability to talk to him like a human being. He appreciated the apology, and the way Abby clearly adored and took care of Wade. She hadn't fallen down in her family duties to take over the family farm, and the weight on Tex's shoulders increased as he went up the tall staircase to the door leading into the kitchen.

A set of stairs went down right in front of him, and he needed to install a door there. If Mav brought Beth and Boston here, one of them could go tumbling down to the basement easily. He mentally added it to his miles-long to-do list and went down the steps, calling, "Got the tools. I'm gonna try the water main."

"Okay," Bryce yelled from somewhere in the house—probably on the other side of it, where two bedrooms sat across the hall from one another. A bathroom sat between them, and one sat between the kitchen and the back bedroom too. It was connected to the small master bedroom as well as the hallway.

His parents had raised nine boys in this house, and that

was solely because of the basement. It also had two bathrooms, one in each of the two back corners. A small living room sat at the bottom of the steps and extended below the living room upstairs too. The rest of the space was filled with bedrooms, four in total.

They weren't big, but they could hold a set of bunk beds, a desk, and a closet. For a boy, they didn't need much else. His father had finished this basement with the help of a friend, and Tex wanted to rip everything out of it and make it a family home.

He wanted real carpet pad and carpet on the cement floor, with bigger bedrooms and more family living space. He wanted a storage room full of Christmas decorations, an exercise bike they never used, and extra toilet paper.

The real family dream.

As it was, he went into the bathroom in the back corner of the house below the master bedroom and set the toolbox on the vanity. His parents had done the best they could with what they had and what they could afford. His mother had taught piano lessons in exchange for the horseback riding lessons Blaze had begged to have. His dad had helped others in the community with their basements and farms so he could get the same help in return.

As Tex found the adjustable wrench and started making it the right size, he murmured, "Thank you for good parents, Lord. Help me to tell them how amazing they are, and bless me to learn the lessons I probably should've when I was a boy."

With the aid of the wrench, he managed to get the water main moving. The lever made a terrible moaning sound as he moved it into the on position, and he grunted once it wouldn't move any further. It sat at a right angle now, and Tex sighed.

"All right," he said to himself. "Moment of truth." He turned and twisted the faucet on the bathroom sink, expecting rusty, spurting water to come out.

It didn't.

He waited, because he had some experience with older houses like this one. The rental they'd stayed in last night clearly hadn't been used in a long time, and it had taken a few seconds for the water to make it to the kitchen sink. He'd messaged the landlord and said he and Bryce would not be staying there due to the dirt, grime, and spiderwebs prevalent in the house, and the owner had responded with an apology and a refund.

Water exploded out of the bathroom fixture, and Tex jumped back with a cry of surprise. The lines had air in them, but they seemed to be working. The water came out in spurts and gushes, and yes, it was the color of mud for at least a minute.

He grinned as it started to run in a clear, steady stream. Pure happiness ran through him over something so simple, and Tex needed that. He needed simplicity and hard work, and he looked up to the too-low ceiling and said, "Thank you, Lord."

For the water, sure. But also for this experience, for this ranch, the house, all of it.

He tossed the wrench back into the toolbox and took it upstairs, yelling, "Water's on!" He wanted to celebrate with his son, of course, but faced with the door that led outside and then the possibility of only fifty-two steps until he could rejoice with Abby, Tex had a decision to make.

He turned left and went around the corner into the kitchen. He flipped on the sink there and got spurting, discolored water. He kept going, intending to make sure all the bathrooms were up and running before he and Bryce did anything else.

The house held no furniture—not even a cardboard box they could sit on—so they needed to make another trip to town that day. Fast. His stomach told him the same thing, and after turning on the faucets in both of the upstairs bathrooms, he entered the bedroom that would be Bryce's.

His son turned toward him, a giant grin on his face. "Look what I got running." The window air conditioner hummed beside him, and Tex took off his cowboy hat and tossed it into the air, emitting some wild whoop he'd heard Blaze and Jem do after they'd ridden bulls.

This wasn't quite the same as staying on a two-ton bucking beast for eight seconds, but it sure felt like it.

He grabbed onto his son, and they laughed together. "I'll fix yours too," Bryce said.

"I've got the water on," Tex said. "We have electricity. Now all we need is food…and about fifteen hundred other things." He turned as Bryce went by him and down the hall a jog and into the master bedroom.

"Hey," he said, following. "Leave it for now. Let's get back to town and go shopping."

"If I fix it first, it'll be running while we're gone," he

said, continuing toward the window unit. "I know how now, Dad. It'll be fast."

The logic was sound, so Tex left him to do that while he went to turn off all the water. It ran clear, and he once again praised God for his goodness and miracles. It seemed odd that a being as powerful and all-knowing as God could care so much about providing water for Tex in this small house in the wilds of Wyoming. But as he stood in that house, in Wyoming, amidst an entire universe of people and things and happenings, Tex felt the sure love of the Lord.

He warmed from head to toe, though he was certainly already warm enough, and closed his eyes in silent thanks.

When he opened them, he started making a list of all the things he and Bryce needed. *Food* went on it, as did things like *vacuum, cleaners, mop, broom, medicines,* and *airbeds.*

He started praying that the furniture store could deliver quickly, and then he called Mav.

"Hey," Mav said. "I'm on my way."

"We're going to be leaving in a minute," Tex said in a rush. "Sorry, but there's nothing here and we're starving."

"Oh, sure," Mav said. "Do you want to meet somewhere? I can head out afterward."

"Bryce and I have a ton of shopping to do too," Tex said, plenty of apology in his voice. "There's nothing here. No furniture. Nothing to clean with. I want central air...."

Mav chuckled and said, "Yeah, that house doesn't have central air conditioning. I forgot about that."

"You and me both," Tex grumbled. A new unit that

would power the furnace and air conditioning wasn't cheap, he knew that. That was why his parents hadn't installed one.

"You also said my wife's favorite word," Mav said.

"Hey," Dani said. "Not true."

"Shopping," Mav said anyway. "She's gesturing at me like mad, and I finally figured out her warped sign language."

Tex grinned as Dani started arguing with Mav. They were on the speakerphone, and Mav just laughed while Dani said, "Tex, I know the best place to get everything you need. Please let me come. They're new, and not many people go there."

"Can they deliver, like, last night?" he asked.

"I will call Hilde right now," she said. "They delivered our dining room table the next day."

"It was in stock," Mav said. "So he'll have to pick out what they have."

Tex thought he could do that, and he quickly agreed to meet Mav and his family at Monarch Wash, a fast-casual restaurant that served popular burgers and sandwiches as bowls. It wasn't really Tex's kind of food, but Mav raved about it and Tex didn't want to argue.

"Got it," Bryce said, entering the kitchen. His hands bore black, and he stepped over to the sink to wash them. "This water is freezing."

"It comes from a well," he said. "And the water heater won't have been on long enough to heat much."

"We don't have any soap either," Bryce said, frowning at his hands.

"I have a big list of things," Tex said. "And we're meetin' Mav and Dani for lunch. So let's get going."

Going anywhere from out this way took longer than Tex remembered, and by the time he arrived at Monarch Wash, Mav, Dani, and their kids had ordered. "Sorry," he said to his brother. He grinned at Beth and Boston, and said, "Look at you two. I swear you've grown a million inches since the wedding."

"A million inches, Uncle Tex?" Beth asked. Her mother was oh-so-proper, and she got some of that from Mav's ex-wife. He grinned at her, as did Mav, and sat down.

"Did you order for me?"

"Just drinks," Mav said, indicating the tall glass of soda in front of Tex. Another blessing, and he thanked his brother verbally and the Lord mentally as he unwrapped his straw and got the first taste of delectable Diet Dr. Pepper.

"Where's Bryce?" Mav asked.

"He went to wash his hands," Tex said. "We don't have soap at the house, and he got grimy fixin' the window coolers." He grinned at Dani and then Mav. "So. I bought Daddy's farm, and it's a huge mess."

"You look so happy about it," Mav said dryly.

"You know what?" Tex asked. Then he took another long, ice-cold drink of his soda, feeling it spread its coolness into the warmer parts of his body. "I am."

"Mav would love to come help you with it," Dani said, giving her husband a pointed look.

"No," Mav said quickly, shooting her a glare. "I wouldn't."

"But you're going to," she said. "You can take the kids and everything. It'll be good for all of you."

"She's just sore because *I* get a nap every day when she has to work." Mav grinned at her. "I've earned my naps."

"I never said you haven't," she said. "But your brother needs help. Isn't that why we moved here? To help your family when they need it?"

"Mama and Daddy," he said, enunciating every sylla-ble. He switched his hard look to Tex, but Tex had seen it plenty of times before. Unbothered, he drained the last of his soda just as Bryce joined the party.

"Hey, Uncle Mav." He grinned at him and then Dani. "Aunt Dani."

"Hello, dear," Dani said, looking from him to Tex and back. "Your daddy says you swallowed spiders last night?"

"What?" Beth asked, looking up from her coloring sheet. "He ate spiders? Bryce, why would you do that?" She looked horrified, as did Boston, and Tex adored his niece. He burst out laughing while Dani tried to explain that no, Bryce hadn't eaten the spiders willingly.

He met Mav's eye, the two of them grinning at one another just like they had in the band. "Family," he said, reaching over and clasping his hand over Mav's. "It's good to be home."

"That it is," Mav said. "That it is."

CHAPTER
SIX

A bby hit a bump and cringed as she heard the crash of books in the back of the Bookmobile. "I hate that pothole," she grumbled. She hated worse that she'd forgotten to avoid it. How many times had she driven this road out to Dog Valley? At least a thousand.

The reason she'd forgotten about the pothole rotated in her mind, the perfect specimen of a cowboy. Of a neighbor. Of a man.

She shook her head, but Tex refused to leave, just like she'd laid in bed last night and relived every memory with his lips on hers from yesteryear. Even the purring of her cats hadn't helped soothe her enough to fall asleep. She'd had to get up and take a Simply Sleep just to drive him into her dreams.

Yes, he starred there too, and with the help of the mild sleeping aid, the dreams had been *vivid*.

She frowned to herself and took the corner slowly. She ambled down the road now, her frown turning upside down when she saw the children come running from the playground beside the church, which was her goal.

She made another painstakingly slow turn over the bumpy entrance to the church parking lot, the kids lined up now and their parents coming out from the shade of the trees to join them. Abby's heart squeezed, because she knew all of these people intimately. Many of them had been bringing their children to the Bookmobile for years, and she waved to one fourteen-year-old that Abby had bought a whole series set for only a couple of months ago.

Sandi had turned fourteen, and that was the perfect age for all of the *Coastal Girls* books. Abby had loved them when they'd first come out several years ago, and Sandi had torn through them.

Abby pulled the Bookmobile up to the curb and set the parking brake. The vehicle hissed, and she unbuckled her seatbelt. She could stand in the front of the truck-like Bookmobile, and she stepped through the skinny doorway leading into the back space. Several books lay scattered on the floor from that pothole, and Abby quickly picked them up and replaced them on the bookshelf.

She loved the smell of books and the way their colorful spines all lined up on both sides of the Bookmobile. She knew the kids outside would be anxious for her to unlock and open the door, so she didn't make them wait any longer. She twisted the big lock and pushed the door open as she went down the three steep steps to the asphalt.

"Hello, everyone," she called, her smile genuine and

big as she took in the crowd. She pushed the heavy door open all the way and secured it with the hook she'd drilled into the side of the Bookmobile herself. "Go on," she said to the boy first in line. "Be careful on the steps, remember. They're really tall."

She grinned as the little boy scrambled forward, two books clutched in his arms already. He'd put those into the slot at the top of the steps, and all of the returned books would drop into a bin that sat where the passenger seat normally did.

Abby smiled at everyone as they filed into the Bookmobile, and once it was full, she opened the passenger door and reached for the scanner in the glove compartment. She started checking in the books people had brought back, and once the initial crowd thinned, she'd reshelve them.

Nothing made her happier than providing books for children, teens, and adults, especially in small communities. She'd even started volunteering twice a month for the Books for Prisoners program in Jackson Hole. She didn't like leaving Wade home alone overnight, but he'd been fine for the past eight or nine months since Abby had started driving to Jackson, opening letters, finding books to match the requests, and then packaging them to be mailed to prisons all over the country.

She'd often lost herself between the pages of a good book, and she wanted to provide that for everyone who wanted it.

Tex had never been much of a reader, and as she went through the motions of scanning, stacking, and selecting another book, she wondered if that had changed. When she caught herself thinking about Tex, she frowned and forced him out of her mind again.

"Miss Abby?" a girl asked, and she turned from the bin.

"Yep." She scanned the book's barcode and then looked up at a girl who'd just started junior high last year. Claire.

"Did The Cozy Cat Mystery come back?"

"Yes," Abby said, having just seen that title. "Let me find it for you." She scanned the stack of books, finding the cozy mystery volume near the bottom quickly. She plucked it from the pile and handed it to Claire. "There you go."

Her face lit up, and that was the moment Abby always knew she'd made the right choice in her career. "Thanks." She hurried back up the steps, saying, "Momma, it came back!"

Abby finished checking in all the books, then gathered a stack of them into her arms. The Bookmobile had one aisle down the middle of it, with room for people to look at the shelves on either side. It didn't offer much more than that, but Abby squeezed around the patrons to put the returned books back on the shelves.

The Bookmobile didn't take names for a waitlist the way the library in Coral Canyon did. It was first-come, first-served out of the Bookmobile, and people came every week to get the books they wanted. In a town as small as Dog Valley, people would loan them around before returning them too. Abby didn't care, as long as the books came back within their allotted two-week timeframe.

Patrons checked out themselves, using a wall-mounted scanner right beside the door, and after about thirty minutes, the crowd had thinned to only a few people and Abby. She answered questions, looked up titles for people if they asked her to, and tidied up after children who couldn't quite get the books back in the right place.

There was little that made Abby happier than perfectly alphabetized books, all done by author, of course. The Bookmobile had a very small non-fiction section, which she was working to increase, but donations were hard to come by in small communities.

She once again thought of Tex and if he might donate to her cause. The man certainly seemed to have money growing in the walls of that farmhouse for how much work he'd done in only a few days.

The lawn had started to green up considerably, and he'd already had the window coolers removed when the brand-spanking-new dual heating and cooling unit had been delivered. He and Bryce had sturdied up the front porch and Abby had seen Bryce sanding it that morning. She fully expected to find it painted or stained by the time she pulled into her driveway next door.

Tex had painted both doors leading into and out of the house, and he'd weeded all of the flowerbeds, as well as the driveway. That he'd gotten re-graveled, and Abby was tired just by the progress she'd seen on the outside of the house.

She had no idea what the interior would look like, as she hadn't been inside that house in years. Something itched beneath her skin to go next door and peer through the windows. She could just see herself with her hands cupped around her eyes so she could see in, her back to the road, and her mind whirring with how she was trespassing to even be on the front porch.

"…is that okay?"

Abby blinked at the woman standing in front of her. Rita Norris stood there, a knowing look on her face. She put one hand on her hip and grinned at Abby. "Who are you thinking about?"

"No one," Abby said defensively. "Who says it's a who?"

"You were smiling," Rita said. "I know you, Abby." She wore her dark hair in a messy bun on the very top of her head, and Abby wished she could do that. Whenever she tried, she didn't feel like herself. She looked like she was trying too hard to be casual and cool, when she was hardly ever either of those.

"I was just thinking how glad I am that I'm not working tomorrow," she fibbed. "That's all."

"Sure," Rita said, clearly not believing her. "Whoever he is, I hope you do more than just think about him."

"What did you ask me?" Abby asked, deciding to ignore Rita's statement.

"I asked if it was okay if I took the keys and drove off with the Bookmobile." Rita giggled. "That's how distracted you were by this mystery man."

Abby rolled her eyes. "There is no mystery man." She checked the clock above the highest row of books and gasped. "It's almost time to go."

"You didn't know?" Rita's surprise made Abby uncomfortable. "Wow, he must be something special."

"He's not," Abby said, moving to pick up a book that hadn't been put away properly.

"But there is a *he*," Rita said triumphantly.

Abby sighed as she straightened. With the book back in the right place, she turned to face Rita. They were the only two in the Bookmobile. "Fine," she said. "There's this man who moved in next door. We dated once, and he's...."

Irritating would've fit in that pause. *Handsome* would've too. *Intriguing, sexy*, and *maddening* all would've worked.

Rita waited, her eyebrows sky high.

"He's fixing up the place next door," she said. "That's all."

"Oh, honey, that's not all."

"It is."

"But you don't want it to be."

"Are you getting any books?" Abby asked. "I have to start closing up."

Rita moved over to the scanner and checked out the three books in her arms. She faced Abby again and said, "Remember when I had that huge crush on Stephen? What did you do?"

"I didn't do anything."

"You nagged me to death," Rita said with an enormous grin. "To *death*, Abby, until I finally talked to him. Look at us now."

Abby had attended their wedding three years ago, so she didn't need to look at Stephen and Rita.

"I'm going to nag you to death over this," Rita promised.

"Please don't," Abby said with a moan.

"Then do something about it before I get the chance," Rita said as she went down the steps to the ground. Abby followed her and made sure the passenger door was locked. Then she unhooked the door and pushed it closed. She'd lock it from inside before she drove back to Coral Canyon.

She waved to Rita, got back into the Bookmobile, locked the door, and then sat behind the wheel. The drive usually took twenty-five minutes, but tonight, it passed in the blink of an eye. She didn't remember turns or tunes on the radio, because Tex once again dominated all of her gray matter.

She'd even turned onto Mountain View Road before she realized she hadn't taken the Bookmobile back to the library. She pressed on the brake, indecision raging inside her now. Her stomach needled her for something to eat, while her ethics told her she should return the Bookmobile and get her car.

It was another twenty minutes to town, and then back....

She continued down the lonely road out on the east side of town, slowing to a crawl to go past the farmhouse where Tex and Bryce lived.

The sexiest cowboy alive sat on the newly stained front porch, a guitar across his lap, his fingers coaxing music from the instrument.

"That is so not fair," she muttered to herself as Tex looked up. He caught sight of the Bookmobile—and Abby behind the wheel—and his grin filled his whole face.

"*So* unfair," she said, glad her windows didn't even roll

down. "Really, Lord? He has to have a smile like that? Why can't it be hideously crooked or something?"

The speedometer read two miles per hour as she made the wide turn into her driveway and parked behind Wade's truck. It was fitted with extensions for the pedals for when he wore his prosthetics, and he could drive with just his hands if he wasn't wearing them.

His meet-the-parents date had gone swimmingly well, of course. It was only Abby who couldn't seem to charm anyone or anything. Even Atticus and Scout, her cats, had been aloof this morning. That wasn't super unusual for her cats, but still. She just wanted someone to look like they were excited to see her. Someone over the age of fifteen, that was.

She sighed as she cut the engine and reached under the front seat for her purse. She'd just dropped to the ground, her own feet making shifting noises in the old gravel, when she heard footsteps walking through rocks.

"Hey," Tex said, still wearing that swoon-worthy smile. "Look at the old Bookmobile." He actually patted the side of it, right over the M. "You drive this?"

"Every Monday, Tuesday, and Saturday," she said, unable to look away from him. He really was symmetrical and gorgeous. Only his nose sat a tiny bit askew, from a horseback riding injury when he was sixteen. Abby hated that she knew that while she also enjoyed knowing things about Tex.

"Where'd you go tonight?" he asked, looking at her.

"Dog Valley," she said. "I go out to Coyote Creek on Mondays, and Rusk on Tuesdays."

"Wow, Rusk." He dropped his hand, the other one holding the neck of the guitar. "That's a drive."

"An hour one-way," she said. She should walk away from him and see what Wade made for dinner. Then she remembered that it was Saturday evening, and Wade didn't sit at home like a pathetic spinster, petting her cats and thinking about the cowboy next door on Saturday nights.

Her stomach growled, loud enough for Tex to hear. He chuckled and asked, "Do you have dinner inside?"

"Oh, we'll have something," she said airily.

"Bryce made banana bread French toast and bacon. Remember my mama used to make that?" He nodded toward the farmhouse with his cowboy hat, those eyes sparkling like so many diamonds. That wasn't fair either, and he had to know it. "We have tons. You're welcome to come have some."

"Oh, I...." Abby looked next door too, her mouth watering. She'd eaten the banana bread French toast several times at Tex's house. Everything at his house had been the opposite of hers. She had one brother. He had *eight*. They enjoyed quiet family meals, with please's and thank you's. She had to ask to be excused.

At the Youngs, they were lucky if a brawl didn't break out during dinnertime. She'd actually seen more than one food fight firsthand, and whenever someone finished eating, they simply left the table.

Their mama had taught them to clean up after themselves, and she distinctly remembered the first time Tex had picked up her plate and then his, rinsed them, and put them in the dishwasher. Then he'd looked at her with a million stars in his eyes, and she'd slipped away from the table.

She'd slipped her hand into his, and they'd slipped into the basement. He'd kissed her there while everyone else in his family finished eating, and to Abby, it had felt dangerous and forbidden, and utterly thrilling and special all at the same time.

"What's goin' on in your head?" Tex asked softly, and Abby turned back to him as she pulled herself out of the memories. He stood very, very close now, and her mind blanked.

His hand whispered against hers, barely touching her skin before it was gone. She shivered though it was still plenty warm in Coral Canyon. "Come eat dinner with us," he said, and he wasn't really asking.

If he had, Abby would've said no, because a direct question she could answer. When her mind went soft like this, however, she let Tex take her hand and lead her across the narrow strip of grass and onto his newly graveled driveway.

She let him take her up the stairs and into the house through the back door, and she let him lean his guitar against the door there before she met his gaze again.

She would've let him kiss her had he tried, but his son said, "There you are. I just checked the front porch to tell you dinner was ready." He looked at Abby too, then dropped his eyes to where Tex still held her hand.

Abby pulled away at the same time Tex did, feeling like she'd been caught with the wrong boy by her father, and he said, "I was just talkin' to Abby. It's okay if she eats with us, right, bud?"

Bryce wore open shock on his face, but he said, "Yeah, sure," to his dad. Tex followed Bryce around the corner and into the kitchen, and Abby took a deep breath. It smelled like fresh paint mixed with bacon, and that wasn't wholly appetizing.

The cowboy sticking his head back around the corner and saying, "You comin'?" was, so Abby nodded and forced her feet to move.

CHAPTER
SEVEN

Tex's nerves had all come alive at the same time, about the moment he'd seen Abby behind the wheel of that Bookmobile. He hadn't even known such a thing still existed, but he should've. A small town like Coral Canyon didn't progress as fast as the rest of the world, and he'd experienced a pang of nostalgia at the sight of that vehicle with those huge, black blocky letters on the side of it.

He had no idea why he'd then pressed in close to Abby, nor why he'd felt it natural and normal to hold the woman's hand. She hadn't protested, but she'd also gone into robot-mode. He'd seen her do that before, and he didn't like it.

Thankfully, when she came around the corner, her eyes flowed with liquid fire, the kind that made Tex want to get closer and get burned.

"You've done so much," she said. "It's only been a

week."

"My brother comes to help," Tex said, not wanting to take credit for everything. "And Bryce and I aren't lightweights." He grinned at his son, who had done everything Tex had thrown at him that week.

"The air conditioning is nice." She ran her hand along the cupboards. "These are new, I think."

"Got those in this morning," Tex said, a touch of pride entering his tone. He forced himself to swallow it as Bryce served him two pieces of French toast, his eyebrows up near his hairline. Tex would have so much explaining to do, and he sort of wished his kid was younger, like Beth, so he wouldn't have to.

"We're doing the countertops and floors next," Bryce said as Tex moved past him to the butter and syrup. "And if we don't get a dishwasher soon, I'm going on strike."

Tex chuckled, though he knew Bryce wasn't kidding. "It's comin', bud," he said. "Should be here Monday."

Abby dropped her eyes to the hole in the cabinetry where the dishwasher should be, and then she picked up a paper plate and let Bryce serve her too. "One piece?" he asked. "Or two?"

"Two, please," she said.

"Bacon is down there," Bryce said, setting down the spatula. He started to dip more slices of banana bread for himself, and Tex once again dealt with pangs of regret and embarrassment. He shouldn't have invited Abby over without talking to Bryce first. Yes, he'd made two loaves of banana bread that afternoon, after his girlfriend had sent him a recipe she'd made earlier this week.

That didn't mean Bryce was ready to make both loaves into French toast. Thankfully, he didn't complain about not being able to eat with Tex and Abby, and he kept himself busy in the kitchen after he'd laid the pieces in the pan.

"How long have you been driving the Bookmobile?" Tex asked, flipping over his French toast. He didn't like it too soggy, and this way, all the syrup was on the bottom, without gravity to pull it through the bread.

"About five years," she said. "Since I moved back to town."

"You've only been back for five years?"

"Yes," she said. "Wade got transferred out of the hospital in North Carolina at that time, and…." She trailed off, sudden anxiety in her expression.

"You came back to help him," Tex supplied. "Right?"

"Yes," she said, shifting in her seat.

Oh, Tex wanted to go further down this road. "Where were you before that?" he asked as casually as he could. He was much better at hiding his true feelings, and he thought he did a decent job of pretending not to be very interested.

"I worked for the Chicago Library System," she said. "I was out in the suburbs, in one of their libraries there."

He grinned at her and cut a piece of French toast. "You have always liked the cold climate."

"It doesn't bother me," she said with a shrug.

"But Florida is *so* nice," Tex teased, drawing Bryce's attention. He stuck his food in his mouth, so he'd stop flirting so blatantly.

Abby actually smiled, and Tex could count on one hand

how many times she'd done that since he'd returned to town. "Humid there, though."

"It doesn't bother me," Tex said, and they smiled at one another. He sobered and cut another bite. "Lucky you got another job at the library here."

"I didn't go straight to running it," she said. "That's new too. I've only been at the helm for about eighteen months."

He nodded and took his bite of toast, glancing over to Bryce. His son had just flipped his bread, which meant Tex only had a couple of minutes before he'd join them at the table. "You didn't leave anyone or anything behind in Chicago?" he asked, this time failing to be casual.

Abby's eyebrows turned into hooks, and she gave him a glare. "I don't have to answer that."

"Nope," he said. "You sure don't." He glanced over to Bryce again, who openly stared at him. He gave his son a smile and dove into the deep end. "I met Bryce's mom in Boise, near the end of my last semester there." He looked back at Abby. "It was this whirlwind relationship, and we got married only six months later. Then I started working on Country Quad, and she had Bryce, and I was gone all the time." He left the explanation there and shrugged.

"How long were you married?" she asked, also failing at the casual tone.

"A couple of years," he said. "When we split, I moved to Nashville with Trace and Otis, who'd just graduated. We started writing songs and trying to get in front of record labels."

Bryce plated his French toast and started to pour syrup

on it. They had a full dining set, so Tex didn't have to give up his seat for his son to join them. When he did, Tex added, "Bryce would come join me in the summers, and any time I wasn't touring, I'd go to Boise and spend time with him. Had a house there too."

"Wow, two houses," Abby said.

"No," Tex said. "We gave up the apartment in Nashville once we got a contract and started touring. That's when I bought my place in Boise, but I mostly lived out of a suitcase and a trailer." He grinned at Bryce, because Tex did have happy memories of his band life. It might have cost him more than he'd known, but he hadn't been unhappy doing it. In fact, he thought he'd been downright lucky and blessed. "Right, bud? I think he liked the trailer until he was about twelve."

He chuckled, glad when Bryce smiled too. "The trailer isn't so bad," he said. "I just don't like sleeping with you." He stabbed a stacked bite of French toast. "He snores, Miss Abby. Loudly. You don't want any part of that."

Tex choked on his bite of bacon, and Abby's face turned bright red. "Bryce," he said. "My goodness."

"I wasn't sayin' you two shouldn't sleep together," Bryce said, and that got Abby coughing.

"Okay, stop talking," Tex said, thoroughly humiliated.

Bryce started to laugh, and that made Tex want to yell and laugh at the same time. He oscillated between mortified and giddy, and he got up to throw his plate in the trashcan. He started to chuckle too, because laughter lightened everything.

He returned to the table, still laughing lightly, to get Abby's plate. "Good?" he asked. "I can make more."

"Don't let him do that," Bryce warned again. "The other night, he nearly burnt the place to the ground heating up a can of soup."

"Hey," Tex said, his laughter drying up. "That was an accident."

"It still happened," Bryce said, grinning at him. "If you want more French toast, Miss Abby, I'll make it for you."

"I'm good, thank you," she said, handing her syrupy plate to Tex and turning back to Bryce. "But thank you so much. It was delicious. I haven't had banana bread French toast since the last time I ate over here."

"Sure," he said. "When was that?"

Tex walked away from the conversation while keeping one ear on it. "Easter Sunday," Abby said. "When your daddy was a senior in high school."

He bent his head over the dishes in the sink, because he only did them once per day. More than that was a crime, and he let the water run until it started to get warm. When he was a senior, Abby had been a junior. She had eaten over here a lot, especially once they'd started dating. His mama liked having her eye on Tex and Abby, and she told her mom everything. She'd told him once that she trusted Abby just fine. It was Tex she didn't trust, and he'd gotten mad at her. He was her son; she should trust him.

Of course, he was the one sneaking down into the basement to kiss his girlfriend, or convincing Abby to meet him in the barn before school so they could be alone. In a family as big as his, it was hard to find somewhere to be without a bunch of other people. That wasn't ideal when he had a girl he really wanted to hold hands with or kiss, so he'd had to resort to some…sneaky ways to be alone with Abby.

That wasn't a crime, but he supposed it did make his mother distrust him a little bit.

He lost track of the conversation, but he knew the moment Abby stood and walked toward him. She brought the smaller plate the bacon had been on, and she handed it to him. She stood at his side while he soaped, and when he handed her a washed bowl from earlier, she pulled the faucet over to her side and rinsed it.

He had to say something, because this was Abby, and he had all kinds of feelings for her. "You remembered Easter Sunday with perfect clarity," he said, immediately clearing his throat afterward.

She took the pan Bryce had cooked the French toast in and held it under the stream of water. "Yeah, I—" She sighed. "I remember everything with you, Tex." She looked at him, pure vulnerability in her eyes. "You're a hard man to forget."

He didn't know exactly what that meant, and he searched her face for more answers. She turned away from him to pull a towel from the stove handle. She started to dry the dishes she'd rinsed, all while Tex's heartbeat stampeded through his whole body.

He felt light-headed and weak in the knees, and he wondered if this was how Mav had felt when he'd first started dating Dani. Tex hadn't felt like this in years and years—probably since he'd signed his first contract for two albums with King Country. Then, he'd felt like he could float up to the clouds and shout for joy, just like he did right now.

And Abby hadn't even said anything all that good. She hadn't asked him to take her to dinner, and she hadn't accepted his invitation for a date.

"Good or bad?" he finally asked, hoping Abby would know he was simply continuing their conversation.

Bryce stood and brought over his glass, his eyes searching Tex's too. But he really needed Abby to answer first. "Abby?"

"Both," she said. "There's always good and bad with you, Tex."

"With everyone," he said, a stab of guilt going right through his heart. "Everyone has good and bad times."

"I'll give you that," she said with a weak smile. "I should go. You guys have band practice tonight."

"No," Tex said at the same time Bryce asked, "How'd you know that?"

She pointed to the wall calendar Bryce had hung next to the refrigerator and smiled. Tex had seen that grin before, and it made his pulse fly off the charts. "I saw it on your family activities calendar. I think that's great. I need to get one of those." Her face pinked up again, and she said, "I mean, if I had anyone to do any activities with. Which I don't."

"Well," Tex said, deciding to go full-send with the flirting, the presence of his son notwithstanding. He already had a million explanations to make. "You do have those two cats. Maybe the three of you could do some knitting or something."

Abby looked at him with such aghast that he burst out laughing. "That was a joke, Abs."

She held her head high as she re-hung the towel over the stove handle. "For your information, Mister Young, if my cats and I were to do something together, it wouldn't be knitting. I'm not seventy years old."

Bryce chortled at that, but Tex asked, "What would it be?"

"We'd watch a rom-com, of course," Abby said. "With plenty of caramel popcorn and hot chocolate."

"In the summer?" he asked.

"Tex, rom-coms, popcorn, and hot chocolate are year-round items." To prove her point, a rumble of thunder sounded overhead, causing all three of them to look skyward despite the ceiling in their way.

"The storm is here," Bryce said with glee. "I'm goin' out, Dad."

"All right," he said as his big kid ran for the back door. "Don't get struck by lightning." The door slammed before he'd really finished speaking, so Tex wasn't sure Bryce had heard him at all. "I did warn him."

"I should go," Abby said. "It's only a hundred yards or so, but I don't want to be running in the rain."

Tex reached for the towel and dried his hands. "All right," he said. "Thanks for coming over."

"Yeah," she said. "Thanks for feeding me."

They walked toward the door, and Tex hesitated at the

corner. He wanted to ask her out. He wanted to apologize for leaving her here in Coral Canyon without much communication. He wanted to learn everything about her and have her tell him about the past twenty years of her life.

Instead, he said, "Maybe I'll see you at church tomorrow."

She nodded, her jaw jumping. "Maybe."

"Or maybe you could come over and help me with the fields next week." His eyebrows went up. Maybe if he hid his desire to spend time with her behind the work this ranch needed, it wouldn't seem like a date.

"The fields?"

"They're wildly overgrown," he said. "I don't quite know how to get them into shape. I asked Wade, but…."

I want you sounded far too forward at this juncture in their relationship.

"Wade will know what to do," she said as another clap of thunder filled the air. She ducked toward the door, and Tex felt the world slipping through his fingers.

"Abby," he said as she opened the door to leave. She paused and turned back to him. He swallowed and once again committed to going all-in. He wasn't playing cards with his brothers, and this might have real losses and gains. "If you don't want to do the fields, maybe you could come on Wednesday evening, and I'll show you the blueprints for the basement."

Her eyes went wide, but Tex had pushed all of his chips into the center of the table. "Or I'll bring dinner over to your place one night when Wade is out with his girlfriend, and I'll show you then."

He was very clearly asking her out, and he'd tossed every ball he owned into her court. The first drops of rain hit the railing outside, making a clunky sound. Somewhere in the yard, Bryce whooped, and Tex smiled at the innocence of his son dancing in the rain.

"Think about it," Tex said. "And you better run, because it's coming down."

Abby didn't nod or confirm anything. She simply turned and left his house, racing down the steps and running across the fifty-two steps from his door to hers. Up onto her back porch she went, and right through the door without looking back at him once.

A sigh leaked from his body, and he went back inside, leaving the door open to hear the rain. He looked out the window above the sink to find Bryce soaking wet, his arms splayed out at his sides as he tipped his head back and smiled into the storm.

Tex's heart filled with love for the boy, and he hoped the rain would postpone the conversation his son would insist on having about Abby and Tex's obvious feelings for her.

"Thank you for my boy," he said to God. "And for the rain. And for Abigail Ingalls. Help me to do things right with her this time, and bless her to…know I won't hurt her again."

Tex realized with that prayer that he *had* hurt Abby all those years ago, and he added it to the things he regretted deeply. Maybe if he made it right, if he repented and apologized, their second chance could turn into happily-ever-after.

CHAPTER
EIGHT

Abby flipped her phone over and over and over against her leg, her nerves nowhere near settled though the sermon usually put her to sleep. Wade finally reached over and took her phone from her, giving her a nasty glare.

"Hey," she hissed, but he shoved her device under his leg and went back to holding Cheryl's hand. Abby looked from him—he stared straight ahead like he listened to Pastor Owens when she knew he didn't—to Cheryl.

She wore a look of sympathy on her face, but she didn't try to get Abby's phone back for her.

She needed that in case Tex texted. She smiled at those two words together. *Tex texting. Tex might text.*

He'd asked her to help him with the property they owned together. Her mind had been so mushy after he'd skated his skin along hers, fed her this amazing dinner—

even if his son had made it—and they'd talked about old times.

Then, he very obviously asked her to simply spend more time with him. Sure, he'd hidden it behind wanting to show her some blueprints, but not because he wanted her approval. He wanted…her.

She could see it plainly in his eyes. He hadn't tried to hide it, and Abby had no idea how to deal with that.

She'd tried last night, pacing from the front door, through the living room and into the kitchen to the back one. Atticus and Scout hadn't been pleased with her nervous energy or the storm, and they'd finally stalked down the hall to her bedroom, where she'd found them an hour later, curled up on her pillow together.

She hated that, because then her pillow was hot from cat-body heat, and she had to clean off all the hair and flip it over. They knew she disliked them on her pillow, but she supposed she had freaked them out a little, what with talking to herself and refusing to sit down.

Abby had deliberately gone to bed before Wade had returned home from his date with Cheryl, because then she wouldn't have to talk to him. She'd overslept that morning due to obsessing for hours alone in her bedroom last night, so they'd been rushed to get to church this morning.

She'd looked for Tex, of course. How could she not? Her eyes had a mind of their own as they'd swept the chapel for his big, broad shoulders and that characteristic white cowboy hat. So many men wore cowboy hats in Wyoming, and Abby hadn't spotted him.

"Wade," she whispered, her brother's name really a plea.

"You're drivin' me nuts," he said, pulling out her phone. "Hold still, for crying out loud." He handed her the phone, and Abby offered him a smile, though all she felt was anxiety and desperation to have a text from Tex.

She didn't. A sigh fell from her lips at the silent phone and empty text messages, and she tucked her phone under her own leg now. She didn't think he'd call or text her first. He'd already asked her to come see him several times, and he'd given her different ways to do it. Now, it was up to her to decide what she wanted to do, and when.

The sound of Pastor Owens' voice warbled on, and Abby closed her eyes. She could conjure up the most fantastic daydreams, and one started about her joining Tex and Bryce for lunch after this meeting. In her imagination, the sun was shining, which so wasn't reality. The storm which had blown in last night had decided to sit right over the valley and dump buckets of rain.

No one in Coral Canyon was complaining, because they needed the moisture. It would help everyone's crops and animals and lawns, Abby's included.

Her daydream broke with the sunshine that didn't belong, and she sighed again as she opened her eyes. Wade sent her another slicing glare, and she realized how loudly she'd been vocalizing her desire for Tex. Too loudly.

The sermon finally ended, and Abby got to her feet quickly. She could wait for Wade at the truck, because everyone wanted to talk to him after church. He and Cheryl were quite the couple, and Abby suddenly couldn't stand being at their side, the perpetual third wheel that everyone overlooked, while they chatted with their friends, the neighbors down the lane, and the elderly.

"Where you goin' so fast?" Wade called after her, but Abby didn't slow down or acknowledge his question. She wondered what Tex had told Bryce, because the teenager had his eyebrows up plenty last night. She'd seen him dancing in the rain as she stood at the back window in the kitchen and looked next door.

Tex had gone out eventually too, and the two of them had laughed and run relays from the house to the back fence, all while the rain soaked them to the skin. They'd gone in several minutes later, their hair plastered to their foreheads, Tex's a sexy gray and black that really had Abby's heart racing. Not only that, but he'd glanced over to her house more than once in the ten minutes he'd been outside with his son.

If she had to categorize the look on his face from a hundred and fifty yards away, she'd call it longing. She felt the same way inside right now. She longed to see him and talk to him. She longed to get a text or call from him. She longed to not have to spend the rest of the afternoon with Wade and Cheryl, while they held hands and laughed, watched movies and provided support and friendship for one another.

Abby wanted that so badly her stomach ached. She swallowed against her stubborness, and hurried to climb into Wade's truck so she wouldn't get soaking wet. She disliked the feel of rain against her skin, and she slicked it away once the door was closed.

She looked at her phone, still with no new messages. Before she could lose her nerve, she tapped to send Tex a message. In that moment, she realized she didn't even have his phone number.

"How is that possible?" she asked herself. The rain made plinking sounds against the roof and hood of the truck. She should've gotten his number when they signed the papers for the property. Wade had it—how had he gotten it?

She craned her neck to see if Wade and Cheryl were coming. She couldn't see them through the rain and the other people leaving the church building. Desperation clawed its way into her pulse, and Abby's frustration grew by leaps and bounds. Patience had never been her strong suit.

Someone knocked on her window, eliciting a yelp from her. She shrank away from the passenger window at the same time she turned in that direction.

The heavens had smiled upon her, because Tex stood there, a warm smile on his face and his cowboy hat protecting him from the rain. Abby quickly reached over and put the window down, not even caring that the rain joined her inside the truck. "Who goes around knocking on women's windows?" she asked. "You scared me."

Tex chuckled and actually waved at her. He waved, like he was fourteen years old. "Hey," he said. "I'm sure you have plans with Wade and Cheryl, but Mav's invited us for lunch, and I wondered if you wanted to come with me and Bryce."

"Today?"

"Yeah, today." His smile didn't waver, and Abby wondered where he got his confidence. "We're headed over there from here." He glanced over his shoulder at something, then looked back at her.

Indecision swam through her, and Abby blinked as she tried to find the right answer. She thought of the past sixteen hours and how much turmoil she'd been in, all because of Tex.

"It's—" he started to say, but Abby cut him off with, "Yes, I'd love to go to lunch at Mav's."

His grin kicked up a notch, because now it extended up into those eyes that pulled her in and drew her deep. "Fantastic," he said, opening her door and backing up. "Come on, Abs. We're parked on the other side of the lot." He looked at her shoes, which weren't the typical high heels most women wore. Abby couldn't stand jamming her wide feet into shoes like that.

"Do you want me to bring the truck closer?" he asked, sliding his gaze up her legs and back to her face. He reached up and pulled at the tie around his neck, his face turning a ruddy shade of red that made Abby feel sexy and desirable.

"I can walk," she said.

"Those shoes are going to disintegrate in the water," he said, eyeing them again.

She wore ballet flats, with a dress that almost reached the ground. She pulled it up to her knees as she turned toward him, the challenge accepted. "I'll be fine." She slipped out of the truck and closed the door behind her.

She shivered because of how near Tex stood, and she

hoped she could play it off as coming from the cool weather. "Hurry up, Tex. It's not exactly warm out here."

"Right." He turned and strode away from Wade's truck, and Abby hurried to catch him. She did have her brother's number, and she'd text him from the safety of Tex's truck. Part of her screamed that she was insane to be doing this, and another part reminded her of what waited for her at home.

Another meal she'd made, spent with two people who loved each other and would probably rather be alone. She was doing Wade and Cheryl a favor, and she pushed out her doubts and her fears.

This was Tex Young and his son. They weren't kidnapping her, and even if the food was the most disgusting thing she'd ever tasted, she'd be fine. She could get something to eat somewhere else later.

"I don't have my car," she said, slowing to a stop. "You'll have to take me home."

Tex turned and looked at her. "Abby, I live right next door to you. I'm goin' that way."

Foolishness filled her. "Oh, right."

He reached back for her, his hand hanging there in the air, obviously waiting for her to take it…or not. Acting out of that turmoil, she slipped her fingers along his, seating them between his, and got moving again.

Tex kept his hatted head down, but Abby saw his smile. It moved through her too, and she couldn't stop it even if she wanted to.

As they approached Tex's truck, Bryce got out of the

front seat and stepped to the back. "Hey, Miss Abby," he said in a perfectly pleasant tone.

"Hello, Bryce," she said formally, panic running through her all of a sudden. If she and Tex really dated and went all the way to marriage this time, she'd be that boy's step-mother. She couldn't do that. She absolutely couldn't, because she wasn't very maternal at all. She didn't nurture. She worked, and she organized, and things got done, sure. But she didn't baby Wade about his injuries; she simply took care of him.

When they were all seated in the truck, Tex took off his hat and tossed it in the back. "Dad," Bryce complained. "You just got me soaking wet."

Tex whipped around to the back seat. "I'm sorry, bud. I was tryin' not to."

"Well, you failed." His son sounded disgusted, and Abby didn't blame him. She slicked her hands through her wet hair, wondering what in the world her makeup looked like. She shivered, because now she wasn't moving, and her shoulders had caught a lot of water on the trek across the lot.

While Tex reached across her for some napkins to help his son get dry, his phone rang. He touched the fancy screen between them and said, "Hey, Mav."

"Hey, so, uh, we've had a bit of an issue here," he said, his voice higher than normal.

"He filled the house with smoke," a woman said through the speakers.

Tex started to laugh, and Mav said, "I did not. Just the kitchen."

"The alarms in the whole house were going off," his wife said. "We can't eat at our place, Tex. We're going to Garden Divine if you want to join us."

"Dad, that's a salad bar," Bryce said from the back seat, still not happy.

"I think we'll pass," Tex said. "Thanks, though. Good luck with the smoke."

"Yeah," Mav said. "Sorry, Tex."

"It's fine," Tex said. "I know how to cook." They said their good-byes, and Tex looked at Abby and then Bryce. "So our place? Or a restaurant?"

"I'm voting restaurant," Bryce said coolly. "Sorry, Dad, but you don't know how to cook."

"Hey," Tex said in a wounded voice. "We get by."

"Because I cook," Bryce said in a mock whisper, and Abby turned and grinned at him.

"I'm fine with whatever," she said.

"You know more about this town than we do," Tex said. "Where should we go, knowing that church just got out and it's Sunday right about noon?"

Abby cocked her head and thought for a moment. She and Wade didn't eat out a whole lot, but she did know every place in town. "If you can stand the drive, there's actually an amazing café out by the police dog academy. It won't be as busy, because it's not right in town and it's this really cute place."

"I want to see the police dog academy," Bryce said.

"It's pouring rain," Tex said.

"Maybe we'll get a miracle and there will be a break in the storm," Bryce said.

Tex shook his head but didn't argue. He put in the address to The K9 Café and pulled out of the parking stall. "So," he said, "What did you think of the sermon?"

"Oh." Abby swallowed, unable to tell him a single thing Pastor Owens had said. She'd spent the hour nervously flipping her phone and daydreaming about Tex. "Uh, it was great."

He started to laugh right in time with the swiping of his wiper blades. "You didn't listen either."

"I listened," she said defensively.

"I liked the part about slowing down to hear the Lord," Bryce said from the back seat.

"Yeah," Abby said quickly. "Me too."

"He didn't even say that today." Tex belted out a laugh then, and she'd been caught. She folded her arms and stared out her window. "Fine," she said. "I didn't really pay attention today."

Both Tex and Bryce laughed together, and then Bryce said, "Told you, Dad. I'm not the only one who struggles to listen."

"He's not the most dynamic pastor, is he?" Tex said, still chuckling. He looked over to Abby and reached over to take her hand in his. "Sorry, Abby. I didn't mean to embarrass you." He lifted her fingers to his lips and kissed them, sending lightning bolts through her whole body. Him kissing her in front of his son was definitely embarrassing, and she had no idea how to react.

"I'm glad to know you're not perfect," he said, not even realizing how stiff she'd gone. "Because neither Bryce nor I listened today at all."

"No?" she asked, letting their hands settle on the console. "What did you think about instead?" She didn't realize what a loaded question she'd asked until the silence filled the cab once and then twice over.

"Yeah, Dad," Bryce said with pure glee in his voice. "What *were* you thinking about during that sermon?"

CHAPTER
NINE

Tex groaned and adjusted his grip on the end of the huge beam. "Wait, wait, wait," he said, panic in his voice. On the other end of the beam, Bryce stalled.

"Got it?" his son asked.

Tex couldn't quite get the right hold, and he'd be going up the steps with the bulk of the weight of this thing on him. He found a good grip and said, "Yep. Let's go."

Bryce moved backward, calling, "I'm going up," when he reached the bottom step.

"Got it." Tex kept moving forward.

"I can't hold it," Bryce said. "All the weight's on you, Dad."

"I've got it," Tex said, bracing the beam with his shoulder. "Keep goin'." That had been his mantra this week. *Keep going. Don't stop. Keep going. Don't stop.*

After a pretty amazing lunch on Sunday, he hadn't seen

Abby for a couple of days. Nearly three before he went next door on Wednesday night with the blueprints for the basement remodel. He didn't have to show them to her and get her to sign off on them, and they both knew it.

Still, he'd spread them across the coffee table in the living room while Wade and Cheryl made dinner in the kitchen, and he'd gone through how he was going to make the bedrooms bigger, take out one of the bathrooms and make a Jack-and-Jill between the two bigger rooms and then expand the living room.

Abby had seemed impressed, and Tex could admit he liked that. They'd visited for a while after he'd rolled up his blueprints, and then Wade had insisted he stay for dinner. Tex had made a show of texting Bryce to make sure his son was okay finding something to eat without him, which was a total farce.

His son could drive, and he could go to town and buy anything he wanted for dinner. He hadn't, but Tex knew Bryce didn't care at all that he wasn't there. He'd talked to Jenny for a while, poured himself a bowl of cereal, and then started playing online video games with the friends he'd left back in Boise.

Tex had walked back into the farmhouse about the time darkness fell to cheering from Bryce's room. The boy hadn't missed his dad at all. In reality, it was probably a relief to Bryce not to have Tex hovering around him all the time.

"I'm throwing it right over the railing," Bryce said, and the beam started moving faster than Tex could keep up.

"Whoa, whoa," he said as if the pole was a horse and

he could stop it. Something twinged in his back as he stumbled to keep up, and pain ripped down to his heel. "You're going too fast."

"Sorry," Bryce said, panting. Tex reached the top of the steps and gave the beam one final heave and then joined Bryce on the small landing outside the back door to watch the beam tumble to the ground. They both breathed heavily, and Tex reached to press against his back.

"I gotta sit down. I ain't as young as I once was." He limped back into the house to get some painkillers, a bottle of water, and to find the couch.

Bryce followed him, saying, "Are you sure you're all right, Dad? I'm sorry. I didn't know you couldn't keep up."

Tex threw back the pills and collapsed onto the couch, stretching his legs out in front of him. "I'm fine," he said, knowing he probably wasn't. At the very least, his back would bother him the rest of the day. And in the morning? He'd have to put pills and a glass of water on the nightstand so he could take them before he got out of bed.

He leaned his head back and closed his eyes, the grumbling noise of a tractor outside hopefully belonging to someone down the street.

"They're here, Dad," Bryce said, checking through the blinds if the rattling told Tex anything. He didn't move or crack open his eyes.

"That's it for us today," he said, still trying to get a full breath.

"Really?" Bryce asked. "It's barely ten-thirty, and the mowers just arrived."

Tex didn't want Bryce to feel worse than he already did, so he groaned as he sat up. "Help your old man off the couch then. I guess we can mow a few fields down." He groaned again as Bryce pulled him to his feet, and Tex did a back bend to try to get the pinch there to go away.

It didn't, but he had faith that the pills would kick in quickly. He went to the front door and opened it, leading the way out onto the completely safe and refinished porch. He and Bryce had started with some of the most noticeable and most unsafe features of the farmhouse, so they could both feel comfortable living there.

He'd hired someone to come put on new roof shingles, as well as to clean the exterior and then paint it. They were booked until the end of July, so he and Bryce had to live with the dirty beige for another six weeks.

They'd torn out almost all of the flooring in the house, and new carpet and a fabricated tile that looked like hard wood had been laid last week. He hadn't done it, but he'd paid for it. The money flew out of Tex's bank account faster than he even knew, but when he saw the progress on the house and ranch, he could only smile.

"Jimmer," he called, smiling as he lifted his hand in a wave. His back didn't like that, and Tex quickly dropped his arm. The man couldn't hear him, and he started to power down the huge eighteen-wheeler he'd used to bring the mowers out.

He opened the door and got down from the cab, saying, "Tex."

"Good morning." Tex chuckled as he approached and then shook Jimmer's hand. "Thank you for getting these to us so fast." He surveyed the machines on the flatbed, wondering if he should be trusted behind the wheel of one of these.

"You got the fences out?"

"Most of 'em," Tex said. That had been Monday and Tuesday's job, and his back had already started to turn fragile from that work. "We won't mow over any fences, I promise."

"All right," Jimmer said, moving the toothpick in his mouth from one side to the other. "Sue-Ann here'll teach ya how to drive these."

Bryce looked like a kid in a candy store on Christmas Day, and Tex paid extra-close attention to Sue-Ann as she went over the type of gas the machines needed, how fast to drive them, and what to do to troubleshoot the most common things that made them stall.

"Got that?" she asked, her voice as weathered and rough as Jimmer's.

"Yes, ma'am," Tex said, taking the manual from her and flipping it open. "We got it."

"Call us if you need anything," she said, though she looked like one of those fluffy cats with the grumpy faces. She didn't smile. Her eyebrows were actually drawn on in the down position. She tipped her ballcap at Bryce and walked back to the truck.

Jimmer fired it up again, and the engine on that eighteen-wheeler could've deafened a man if he stood too close. The engine brakes hissed as Jimmer released them, and Tex looked up from the manual in time to see Bryce leaping onto the seat of the closest mower.

"Son," he said, plenty of warning in his voice. "These aren't toys."

"I know, Dad," he said. "Mom made me mow the lawn a ton in Boise. I can do this. You go lay down again."

Tex didn't think that was a bad idea, and he looked out toward the fields—which he couldn't see because the house stood in the way—and back to Bryce. "Nah. I'll come out with you."

Bryce frowned at him. "Dad, I'm not going to get in trouble."

"I know," he said. "Go. I'll walk out my back."

Bryce started up the mower, and it too sent an enormously loud growl into the air.

"You're supposed to wear auditory protection!" someone yelled, and Tex turned to find Abby striding toward them.

He waved his hands at Bryce, finally making sense of her words. The mower powered down, and Bryce asked, "What?"

"Get the headphones, son," he said. "Sue-Ann said to wear those."

"Right." Bryce jumped down and grabbed them from the bag sitting on the seat of the second mower. Tex couldn't think straight as Abby stepped to his side. She wore jeans, her cowgirl boots and hat, and a purple plaid shirt that had plenty of dirt on it. She smelled like straw and horses and freshly mown grass, and Tex wanted to sneak away with her and kiss her until he couldn't breathe again.

Bryce whooped as he got the mower moving, and he

dang near clipped the corner of the house as he went by. "That boy," Tex said, shaking his head as if his son had somehow hoodwinked him into getting these huge pasture mowers.

He touched Abby's hand, and she flinched away from him. The rejection sang through Tex, and he didn't know how to make it stop stinging. Abby looked at him as if she'd just realized he was there. "Sorry," she said.

"Haven't seen you in a few days," he said, putting a smile on his face to cover the sting. "You're not working today?"

"Not at the library," she said. "I have to drive the Bookmobile later tonight."

"Right," he said. "To Dog Valley."

She'd trained her eyes back on the corner of the house where Bryce had gone. "Yeah."

Without her hand to hold, Tex didn't know what to do with his. He folded the manual in half and walked over to the second mower. "Have you ever used one of these?"

"No," she said, plenty of disdain in her voice.

He turned back to her, surprised. He wanted her to do more talking, so he waited. "Go on," he prompted when she simply glared at the house and folded her arms. "Say what you want to say."

"I don't want to say anything." She switched her glare to him, and it definitely went down a few notches. The buzzing of Bryce's mower changed, and Tex tilted his head.

"Walk out there with me?" He started going toward the house without waiting for her to come with him.

She caught up to him quickly, saying, "Those things aren't good for the land, you know."

There it was. She'd always had opinons, and he didn't mind her voicing them. "Why not?"

"They cut too close," she said. "You'll end up killing everything."

"We *want* to kill everything," Tex said.

"You're joking." Her voice came out like a scoff, full of air and disbelief.

"No." He looked at her, frowning. "Abby, there's nothing to save out here. The fields are weeds. We want it all gone, so we can seed it with what we need for actual livestock."

"What are you getting?" she demanded, her long legs keeping up with him easily.

He went around the back corner of the house and found Bryce mowing along through the longer prairie grasses and weeds. He didn't seem to have a care in the world, and the chopped foliage went in the huge gray bag hanging off the back of the mower.

"Horses," he said, slowing his step. "A dairy cow or two. Chickens. It's too late to plant hay, so we're going to spend the summer getting things cleaned up and getting a few animals to take care of, and then we'll plant next year."

"You're going to be here next year?"

Tex rolled his eyes. "You don't have to sound so shocked about it."

"I...you said at least a year. Bryce is going to graduate.

Are you saying he won't leave you to run this ranch all by yourself?"

"I don't know what he'll do." Tex and Bryce had already talked about college, of course. Bryce wasn't that interested, the same way Tex hadn't been. It had been real important to his parents that he go to college, so Tex had gone through the application process to make them happy. He had decent grades, and he'd gotten in to the three places he'd applied. He'd chosen Boise State, because they'd given him the most scholarship money.

He and Bryce had also been talking about doing an album together. Tex hadn't heard from Otis, Luke, or Trace about the album they still owed King Country, and it suddenly needled his mind with the force of hail striking the earth.

They played their guitars together in the evenings, and Tex loved that. Bryce worked on music; Tex wrote lyrics. They worked on the house in the morning, in the cooler summer hours, took a break in the afternoon, and then did their music at night.

It was a slow, easy life, and Tex had really enjoyed his time in Coral Canyon so far. His phone rang just as Abby said something. He didn't hear her, and chose to look at his phone instead of her.

"Oh, it's Ames," he said, holding up his phone for her to see. "I asked him about a dog."

"Of course you did," she said, as if Tex getting a dog was a crime akin to driving drunk.

"What is with you?" he asked, his irritation with her

sparking. He swiped on the call and turned his back to her. "Ames, howdy."

"Howdy yourself," Ames said, plenty of growl in his voice. "Well, I have to say, Tex, that you must have someone in heaven lookin' out for you."

Tex chuckled and took a few steps away from the glare Abby cut through the back of his skull. "Why's that?"

"Francesca didn't pass her police exam," he said with a sigh. "I can't move her through the rest of the program. She won't get to be a police dog."

Tex heard the severe disappointment in Ames's voice, and his heart tore a little. "I'm sorry, Ames."

"You wanted a dog who failed my program, and well, now I've got one."

Tex's heart grew wings and flew right out of his chest. "You're kidding."

"Like I said, someone up there is watchin' out for you."

Tex laughed, suddenly feeling like dancing. "Well, that's great. When can I pick her up?"

"I'll bring her to you," Ames said. "How about tomorrow night? Doable?"

"Definitely," Tex said. "Bryce and I will just be home."

"Tell me where you're at, and I'll bring her by after dinner."

Tex rattled off his address, and Ames said he'd be there tomorrow. He hung up, joy mingling with shock as it coursed through him. He turned back to Abby, his smile permanently stuck to his face now. "Guess what?"

"You're getting a dog," she said dryly.

His euphoria faded quickly in the face of her salty attitude. "Why do you care?"

"I have to live next door to that dog," she said. "And they aren't quiet."

"Oh, like your cats are perfect," he said. "One of them was prowling around my garbage can the other night."

"Bite your tongue," Abby said, as if a cat eating out of the garbage can was the scandal of the century.

"I have a picture and everything," he said, already swiping on his phone. "It was Atticus, and." He paused as he tried to find the picture. Apparently he couldn't talk and see and swipe at the same time. He found it and showed it to her triumphantly.

She looked at it and glared at him. "And what?"

"And he was sleeping on my deck supplies yesterday afternoon."

"That is not true," she said.

"Oh, it's true," he said.

"Do you have a picture?"

"No."

"Then it didn't happen." She folded her arms and turned back to stare down Bryce. He didn't seem as attuned to Abby as Tex was, or else he was too far away for her glare to really hit him with the full force.

"You think they stay inside all day," he said. "But they don't. They're all over your farm and my ranch."

"They're not prisoners," she said.

"You're never home," he said. "You won't even be here if my dog barks. Besides." He held up his hand as she opened her mouth to argue. "She's a police dog, and they don't bark just because they feel like it. So if she's barking, you better put on your slippers and come see if I've had a heart attack."

She drew in a big breath, her eyes sparking with something dangerous. All at once, she exhaled, and the sparks turned into a glint. She smiled, and her eyes danced. "You're good, Tex," she said. "I'll give you that."

He grinned too, and this time when he touched her hand with his, she slid her fingers between his. They stood in the mid-morning sunshine and watched Bryce mow weeds to his heart's content.

Tex wanted to say something to Abby, but he wasn't sure what. "It's Saturday," he finally came up with. "After you get done with the Bookmobile, do you want to…I don't know. Do something?"

"Like what?" she asked.

He looked at her, so many hormones and synapses firing through his body. "Stay in? Go out? Come over? I could come over to your place? Watch a movie? Here? At the theater? Go to those concerts in the park? Get a sandwich and hike up to the waterfall?"

She started giggling and squeezed his hand. "All right, enough."

"There's literally a thousand things to do," he teased. "Or not do. I don't care. I just want to see you tonight."

The moment sobered, and Abby searched his face. "You do?"

"Uh, yeah," he said, grinning down at her. "Don't tell me I haven't been ultra-obvious, because I have been. Bryce tells me how embarrassing I am every single day."

"How would he know?"

"He checks my phone," Tex said simply. "Who do you think came up with the winning question to get you to let me in on Wednesday night?"

Abby smiled then too, and she looked back out to Bryce. "And he's okay with us…going out?"

"Yeah, I think so." He focused on Abby again and toed the ground. "What about you? Are you okay with us going out?" He watched her for her reaction, and Abby blinked a couple of times, clearly surprised by his question. "I'm really sorry I left you here twenty years ago."

"Tex," she said.

"No, I need to say it."

She gestured with her free hand. "Then say it."

"I left for college, and I didn't call or write or anything. You must've been so…mad. Hurt." Tex shook his head. "I was stupid, and young, and I didn't even think about it. I'm really sorry that I hurt you."

Abby leaned into his bicep and curled her fingers around his forearm. "Thank you, Tex."

Bryce turned the mower toward them, barreling across the land, bumping up and down like a maniac, all with a smile on his face.

"He's going to hit us," Tex said, and he started to pull Abby to the right. Bryce came to a stop several yards away and yelled something.

"He wants to know where he should empty the bag," Abby said, tipping up and yelling into Tex's ear too.

"How did you get that?"

She shrugged and smiled, and Tex had always known

that women could understand other humans better than men. Still, Abby seemed like a super-woman, and he hoped he could fix up this ranch to her liking, while fixing up himself to be worthy of her attention too.

He wanted someone to spend his life with, so no matter what Bryce decided to do, Tex's only option for companionship wasn't Mav and his wife.

Tex hadn't told anyone yet—he hadn't even admitted it to himself—but he wanted this house and this ranch to be utterly perfect so Abby would be happy here…with him.

CHAPTER
TEN

Abby plucked the Bookmobile keys from her boss's office and turned to get going. Mya stepped in front of her, a giddy smile on her face. "You live out on Mountain View Road, right?"

"Yeah," Abby said, sliding her eyes from Mya to Quincey, who'd joined them. She'd worked with the two part-time librarians for a few years now, and one of Tex's brother's—Mav—had a wife who'd started working there too. She considered herself friends with all three women.

Her very best friend in the world, besides her brother, was Georgia Beck, but if Abby had to name someone besides the two of them as friends, she'd say Mya, Quincey, and Dani.

Maybe not right now, what with the way Mya and Quincey exchanged a knowing glance that made her feel like she'd missed a very important memo. "What's going on?"

"Georgia said there's a hot new cowboy in town, and that he lives out on Mountain View Road."

Abby knew exactly where this was going. She cocked one hip and folded her arms. "Georgia said that?"

Georgia Beck owned a cute little bookshop sandwiched between the post office and the best barbecue place in Coral Canyon, and since so many women moved through the shop, she could start a gossip fire with only a few words.

Abby had been friends with her for a while now, as she loved to spend her time with books, both in libraries and bookshops.

"She's friends with Dani Young," Quincey gushed. "And Dani says her brother-in-law just moved to town and needs a girlfriend."

Abby squinted at Quincey. "Tex is almost forty, Quince. I think he might be too old for you."

"Not for me," Quincey said, waving her hand like Abby was being utterly ridiculous. "I'm married, silly."

Abby grinned widely "Oh, of course."

"For you," Mya said as if Abby hadn't already connected those dots. "He lives right on your road."

"Ladies," Abby said, leaning closer and smiling at them. "He lives right next door to me."

Quincey squealed and Mya started fanning herself. "Right next door? My goodness."

"Yeah," Abby said. Maybe she'd stood over the air conditioning vent a couple of times while she'd watched Tex carry debris out of the basement. She couldn't control that he wore tank tops that showed off his impressive muscles, nor how hot Wyoming was this summer.

"You should see what he did to his fields though." She clucked her tongue like he'd done a real number on them, which he had. She didn't agree with his philosophy of killing everything and starting over. The soil wasn't ready for that, and his parents would've never spent as much as he had to rent those mowers. They'd worked their ranch with love and respect, and it had taken a lot of Abby's willpower to keep her mouth shut about his tactics.

"You can still go out with him," Mya said.

"Can I?" Abby shook her head. "I don't know. I have to respect how a cowboy works." He had made some impressive improvements around the ranch and with the house, and she couldn't fault him for too much. "I have to go, girls. I don't want to be late getting to Dog Valley."

With that, she spun the keys around her finger as she walked away. "We'll figure out how to get him to ask you out," Mya called after her, and Abby turned around.

She walked backward as she said, "You really don't need to do that." She hadn't dated a whole lot here in Coral Canyon, and she appreciated her friends looking out for her. But she'd gotten a date with Tex Young all on her own, thank you very much, and she smiled to herself as she went down the back stairwell to the parking lot behind the library.

———

"Then," she said later that night, everything about her lit up from within. "The *cutest* little boy came to the Bookmobile tonight. You have to be five years old to check books out, you know, and his birthday was this week." She knew she was gushing, but Tex hadn't stopped smiling once, and Abby just felt so alive.

"His mama said he only wanted one thing for his birthday—to come to the Bookmobile and get his own books. He's been coming with his sister, you see, but he's never been allowed to take any books of his own." She reached for the saltshaker and shook it over her salmon and rice pilaf.

Tex had texted, which she loved, and he'd suggested they try Pearl's on Fifth tonight. He'd never been there, and she'd admitted she hadn't either. The food was farm to table and locally sourced from Wyoming, Idaho, or Montana, and she'd ordered the fish while Tex had gotten the meatloaf.

"Tonight, he got four books about trucks or insects, and he was so happy, Tex." She sighed, because she loved seeing children interacting with books. She'd loved reading for as long as she could remember, and her book friends had been some of the most real people in her life.

"That's amazing," Tex said. "I can't remember the last book I read."

"Yeah," she said. "It was that manual for the mower, remember?" She grinned at him, feeling like she'd shed her winter skin and had become a beautiful butterfly.

He chuckled and shook his head. "I really only needed

to rent one of those. Bryce didn't come in all day, even when I said he could."

"Trust me," she said dryly. "I know."

"Oh?" Tex's eyebrows went up and he swiped another bite of meatloaf through his mashed potatoes. "Did he disturb your beauty rest this afternoon?"

"As a matter of fact, he did," she said with a smile.

"I didn't think the mighty Abigail Ingalls slept."

She laughed, not caring that it was probably too loud and too flirty. Tex grinned with all he had, and that only made Abby feel even more beautiful than he'd already helped her to feel.

He'd picked her up properly, whistling as he dripped his gaze down the length of her body. Tonight, she'd stepped out of her jeans and plaid shirts and into a pair of slacks and a blouse her mother had given her for her birthday.

Other than church, Abby had no need to dress all that nicely, though she occasionally wore slacks or skirts to the library. She packed and unpacked a lot of boxes, had to get down on the floor often, and her boss didn't enforce a strict dress code.

Since jeans would do, and Abby felt the most comfortable in them, that was what she wore.

Tex had also leveled up his attire, and he wore a sports jacket with his polo and dark wash jeans. He always had that white cowboy hat on, and tonight, his boots had been black to match his pants.

"I was thinkin' about something," he said, moving his mashed potatoes through the pool of gravy on his plate.

"Oh yeah?" Abby flaked off a bite of her fish and popped it into her mouth. "What?"

Tex met her eyes, his throat working like he'd forgotten how to swallow. Her nerves fired at her like cannons, and she could barely get her fish down. "I have to make another album," he said. "Country Quad is under contract for one more."

"Oh." Abby didn't know what to say, but she knew people didn't make hugely popular country music albums in Coral Canyon, Wyoming. "You're leaving again."

"Not right now," he said hastily. "I don't know when, actually. Bryce and I have been fiddling around with some songs in the evenings." He looked at her with a slight edge of desperation in his eyes. "I want to be honest with you. At some point, yes. I'm going to have to go to Nashville to record."

Abby kept her head on straight. She didn't need to storm out right this second or anything. "How long does it take to record an album?"

"It depends on how well it's going," he said. "The fastest one we did took about four months. The one after that was a bit of a disaster, and it took us a year."

Abby pushed the rice around hre plate. "Where is Country Quad right now?"

"Mav was our manager," Tex said with a sigh. "He quit, and believe it or not, Morris has come on."

"Oh, good for him," Abby said, brightening again. "Gosh, how old are the twins? They were what? Ten years behind you?"

"Thirteen," he said, with a smile. "They'll be twenty-seven in a few months."

"Your momma is a saint," Abby said with a giggle. "Nine boys? She'll go straight to heaven, I'm sure."

Tex chuckled too, nodding. "What about you, Abs? Do you want kids?"

Her stomach cramped, and she hated that she'd only gotten one bite of her salmon before this serious conversation had started. "Uh, I don't know, Tex."

"I have a son. You know that, right?" He grinned at her, clearly teasing. When she didn't throw something back at him, he covered her hand with one of his. "Abby, just... what's goin' on in your head?"

He asked her that a lot back when they dated as teens. He'd asked her that in the past few weeks since returning to town too.

"I...." He'd been honest with her about his band, and she could tell him. "I'm not that maternal, you know? I don't...I don't think I'd be a very good mother."

Tex studied her, and she appreciated that he didn't immediately jump in and tell her how wrong she was. He'd always been a bit more observant, only speaking after he'd thought about something. "I think you might be wrong," he said. "I've seen you with Bryce, and that boy is seventeen years old. You talk to him like he's normal—he even mentioned that about you. You don't talk down to him."

"I talk to him the same way I'd talk to a baby," she said. "That's the problem. I'm not the...coo-y or baby-waby type, Tex." She shook her head, because she did know herself. "I'm not."

He withdrew his hand and went back to his meal. "All right," he said. "That doesn't mean you won't be a good mother."

She didn't think it would help, but she wasn't going to debate him on it tonight. "Do you want more kids?"

"Yeah," he said easily, as if everyone went around longing for more children.

"That would be a big gap for you," she said.

"I had Bryce when I was twenty-two," he said. "I'm not that old." He grinned again, then groaned. "Of course, my body aches all the time and tells me I am, so maybe I'm fine with a dog."

She pointed her fork at him. "That dog is going to be the death of you. Mark my words."

He laughed instead of marking anything. She basked in the sound of it, because Tex did have a beautiful laugh to match his gorgeous smile and winning charm. Honestly, how he wasn't married again was a mystery.

The band, Abby thought, another slice of fear moving through her. She did not want his band to break them up the way it had his first marriage. At least she assumed that was why he and his ex-wife had gotten divorced. He hadn't actually told her yet.

"Do you, I don't know." He cleared his throat. "See yourself getting married?"

Abby put another tiny bite of fish and rice in her mouth. She chewed excessively to give herself more time to think. "For a while there, no," she admitted. "But...."

She looked at him, willing to open this door to her heart if he wouldn't shove it closed again. "Can I tell you a secret?"

He leaned forward, over his plate. "I wish you would."

"I'm a little lonely," she said, the words raw and burning her throat. "When Wade got home, my life was consumed with taking care of him, taking over the farm, and dealing with stuff at the library. I didn't have time to be lonely." She set her fork down, not ready to eat more until the hard conversations ended. "But now." She sighed wistfully and looked out into the restaurant.

It was busy, because Saturday night brought out the families and couples. "Now, Wade has Cheryl," she said. "He doesn't need me as much, and he does most of the work on the farm. I'm...I think it might be nice to have someone the way he has Cheryl."

Tex gave her a few seconds of silence, and then he asked, "Are they going to get married?"

"It's highly likely," she said, sounding miserable about it. She picked up her fork again, only to cut off a piece of asparagus.

"I liked being married," he said. "I just chose the wrong person."

Abby's emotions wavered, and she said, "I know what you mean," with her focus down on her food. She'd had so much fun in Dog Valley that night, and she couldn't believe the word vomit about to spew from her mouth.

"You do?" Tex asked at the same time Abby looked up and right into his eyes.

"I was engaged in Chicago," she said, her throat closing around the last vowel.

Tex reached across the table and covered her hands again. "Tell me about him."

Abby didn't want to do that, but at the same time, she wanted to share her life with Tex. The good things, the bad things, the humiliating things. "You remind me a lot of him, actually."

"Uh oh," Tex said, grinning. "How's that?"

"He had a lot of money too, and he kind of threw it around sometimes."

Tex's hand slid away from hers, his face hardening. "I'm not throwing my money around," he said. "Do you have any idea—any idea *at all*—what I've invested into that ranch? Just the hours alone are insane."

"I didn't mean—" Abby clamped her mouth shut, because she didn't know what she'd meant to say.

Tex glared at her and leaned back in the booth. "Go on, then. Tell me what you meant."

CHAPTER
ELEVEN

Tex couldn't believe Abby thought he was "throwing around his money." She looked like she'd come upon an active mine field, and she'd barely taken two bites of food as it was. He sighed when she remained silent and said, "Forget it. It doesn't matter. I don't have to get your permission to fix up the house and ranch the way I want to."

"Tex," she said desperately. "I didn't mean you throw around your money. I just meant you pay for things I would never pay for. Like the mowers. That's all."

"How would you have cleared those fields?" he demanded.

"I'd have plowed them under," she said, some hardness entering her voice too. "I'd have put the nutrients back into the soil, not stripped them from it."

He shook his head. "I asked Wade, *and* I talked to three guys at the tack and feed. They said for land that hasn't been cultivated properly for years, the best thing to do is to burn it or mow it to the dirt." He couldn't even imagine the grief he'd be taking from her if he'd filled her clear sky with smoke for a week. "And for your information, we then *did* plow everything under. Thank you so much for loaning us your tractor and plow."

Her face went blank and she blinked.

"Oh, Wade didn't tell you?" Tex hated the poison in his tone. "Right. So you *don't* know everything then."

"I never said I knew everything."

He sliced off another corner of meatloaf. "Like I said, forget it."

"I'm sorry," she said, and that got him to lift his eyes. "You're right, and I'm sorry. I don't know everything going on next door, and I...don't need to." She nodded like that was that, her auburn waves swinging along the sides of her neck. When he'd picked her up tonight, all he'd been able to think about was touching that hair. Fisting his fingers in it as he brought her closer to kiss her. Sliding his hands through it as they kissed, and kissed, and kissed.

She slid to the end of the bench, and Tex thought she'd excuse herself to the restroom. All thoughts of kissing her on her front porch that evening vanished as he looked up at her. She put her napkin on the table and took two steps to his side. "Can I sit by you?" she asked at the same time she slid into the booth.

He moved over, shock coursing through him, to make room for her. "I—sure."

She linked her arm through his and threaded her fingers on her left hand through those touching him. "Tex,

I'm so sorry. I just ruined everything tonight, and I didn't mean to do that."

He looked down at her, but she kept her chin angled down, toward the table. "Abby," he said, his voice somehow throaty and filled with desire. He needed to clear that away quickly. "You've...changed."

"I should hope so," she said, finally looking up at him.

Five inches, and he could kiss her. He swallowed, the fantasy playing through his mind.

"I just meant to say that sometimes Jonas would pay too much for something, because he just wanted it done. The mowers reminded me a little bit of that. You don't throw your money around. That was a stupid thing to say."

He nodded, managed to swallow, and said, "Apology accepted."

"You two doin' okay here?" the waitress chirped, and Abby sat up straighter, her hands leaving his arm and falling to her lap.

"Yes," she said. "Thank you."

The waitress left, and Abby looked at him. "We're doing okay here, right? I didn't mess everything up too terribly?"

Tex leaned toward her, watching her eyes drift closed, a sense of satisfaction driving through him. He brushed his lips against her cheek and whispered in her ear, "We're doing great here, Abs."

She shivered, and Tex's blood turned to liquid lava. He put his arm around her and brought her back into his side. "Will you come over for lunch after church tomorrow? I'll send Bryce to his uncle's, and I'll show you all the progress on the inside of the house, and we can order pizza."

"I'm not eating from The Pipeline," she said, totally serious. "They're the only ones who deliver out as far as us, remember?"

"I'll order from Pie Squared," he said. "You said that was your favorite place in town."

Her eyebrows went up. "When did I tell you that?"

Tex chuckled, about to admit a few things himself. "Well, you didn't tell me, exactly. But I check Bryce's phone too, and he asked you which pizzeria was the best in town, so...." He shrugged one shoulder, which she promptly slugged.

"You have your son setting up our dates," she said, her voice full of accusation.

He laughed, and she got up and returned to her side of the booth, her mock irritation with him adorable and making him too hot all at the same time. "Hey, a man wants to be prepared," he said. "You can't fault me that. I just got your number last week. My son has had it for like, a month."

"You've been in town for a month," she said dryly. "And I can't help it if you're too big of a chicken to ask me for my number." She held her head high, forked up another micro-bite of fish, and ate it.

Tex tipped his head back and laughed, because he had been a little bit afraid to get her number, if only because then he might text her too much and annoy her. He sobered and looked her straight in the eyes. "I can't help it if you're stunning, and smart, and have me wishing I'd never left Coral Canyon." He swallowed, about to push all those chips into the middle of the table again. "Maybe I *was* nervous. Any man would be nervous to talk to a woman like you."

She scoffed, and he wasn't sure she'd heard him properly. "Don't be ridiculous, Tex."

"All right," he said easily. He'd spoken true, and Abby would analyze everything he'd said at some point. Just because she hadn't heard him right now didn't mean she wouldn't later. "But you can't tell me I'm the only one who's nervous."

She gave him that trademarked eyebrow. "How do you know I'm nervous?"

He stabbed no less than half a dozen green beans. "Because you haven't taken a real bite of food since we got here." He grinned as he shoved all the veggies into his mouth. He didn't have room for all of them, and one fell back to his plate.

Abby shook her head, the corners of her mouth twitching up ever so slightly. "Attractive," she said.

He finished the beans, which so weren't his favorite vegetable, and asked, "So is that a yes or a no to tomorrow?"

She studied him, those eyes doing a real number on his heart. "It's a yes," she said. "But I'm not telling your son any more of my favorite things."

"No problem," Tex said. "From now on, I'll ask you myself." He grinned at her, satisfied when she smiled back, and then finally—*finally*—took a bite of her food big enough to fill her mouth.

———

TEX EYED HIS PHONE LIKE IT WAS A POISONOUS SNAKE. Corrie's name sat there, and she'd called three times over the past three days. "I guess I have to talk to your mother," he said to Bryce, who currently held a cordless drill and used it to attach the cupboard door to the new bathroom cabinets. "I'll be right back."

Tex picked up his phone and went down the hall toward his bedroom. "Heya, Corrie."

"Finally," she griped at him.

"Sorry," he said. "I kept meaning to call you back." He entered the bedroom and went over to the new sliding glass doors. They'd eventually lead out onto the new back deck, which he and Bryce would build all along the back of the house. They could get to it from the side steps, or the sliding doors in the dining room. Then, from his bedroom too. One huge outdoor sitting area. "What do you need?"

She'd signed the custody paper his lawyer had sent her. Bryce was in his full custody until he graduated, and Tex didn't have to share him with Corrie. Bryce still spoke with her, of course, though Tex had told him he didn't have to.

"I just paid for Bryce on my health insurance. I thought you were changing him to yours."

"Yeah, I did," Tex said. He'd actually asked Mav to do that, as his brother had handled all of those kinds of tasks for Tex for years. All the band members, actually. He chose their insurance, and the band paid for it for the employees.

"I'm going to need you to send in proof of his other

insurance," she said with exhaustion raining through her voice. "Then I can get my money back."

"Okay," he said. "Tell me what to do." He pulled his phone from his ear and tapped to get to his recorder. Stuff like this bored him to death, but if he got it on tape, he could have Mav help him get it done.

Corrie finished quicker than he thought she would, and then she paused. "How's Bryce?" she asked.

"He's great," Tex said brightly. "We're doin' great here." He didn't need to go into details. When he'd asked about their son over the years, he didn't get detailed answers. He'd bought Bryce a phone when the boy was seven, just so he could talk to him more often and get real information right from Bryce.

"I do miss him," Corrie said, a wistful quality in her voice. Tex's fingers tightened around his phone, but he said nothing. He and Bryce were doing great, and if they could finish these cabinets, they could get to church.

Tex didn't want to think about after church with his ex-wife on the line. Thankfully, Bryce called for him, and Tex swung around. "I have to go, Corrie. We're putting cabinets together this morning."

"Okay," she said. "Will you ask him to call me?"

"Sure will," Tex said, and he let her end the call. He returned to the hall bathroom and held up his phone. "You're not talking to your mother?"

Bryce looked up from the half-hung cabinet door. "I am. Sort of."

Tex frowned and went to help with this last thing. Once

it was in place, he helped Bryce to his feet, and squared his shoulders at his son. "She's your mother."

"It's complicated," Bryce said. "Kind of like you 'sort of' dating Abby."

"Hey, I graduated into full dating," Tex said. Talking to his nearly grown son about girls and women hadn't been the easiest thing Tex had done. But he and Bryce didn't have secrets from one another, and everyone could see how much Tex liked Abby. "Son, you have to talk to me for this to work."

"Yeah." Bryce sighed and set the drill on the edge of the tub. "The cabinets look great, Dad." He smiled as he surveyed them. They were a bright white, painted in the factory and shipped to Tex to install himself.

Pride stole through him as he scanned down the hall to the kitchen too. With the new appliances—complete with the dishwasher—and the cabinets and the new flooring, the house looked like a million bucks. Tex smiled even though his shoulders hurt from hauling those cabinets up the steps. "They sure do," he said.

"It's just that Mom keeps asking me about college, and I don't know what to tell her."

Tex deliberately didn't look at Bryce. "You should tell her what you told me."

"She doesn't like that answer," Bryce said, moving over to the sink. He flipped on the water and started to wash his hands. "I really like this," he added.

"Define *this*," Tex said.

"Construction," Bryce said. "This renovation and remodeling. I like studying the blueprints and floorplans. I like doing installations and ripping out old stuff and putting in new."

Tex had never heard his son talk like that, and he let it all sink into his head. "There are vocational programs for construction," he said. "And college degrees."

"Yeah." Bryce turned off the water and reached for a towel. "I also really like making music." He faced Tex, his smile revealing the perfectly straight teeth Tex had paid for. Bryce really did look so much like him, with his square features and dark eyebrows and hair. He'd been shaving for about a year, but he hadn't bothered this summer, so he wore a pretty decent beard.

"I like the music too," Tex said. "Maybe we should go to Nashville next month. Take a break from all this work and go see Luke and Trace. I can introduce you around to the producers at King Country."

Bryce's face lit up. "Could we, Dad?"

"Sure," Tex said. "I mean, I don't have Mav to book flights for me anymore, but I think I can figure it out for myself."

Bryce chuckled, and Tex stepped over to him and curled his hand around the back of his son's head. He brought their foreheads together and said, "I love you, son. You're a good boy, and you're going to be an amazing man. Better than me, for sure." He pulled away slightly, so Bryce would know how serious he was. "But you have to call your mother. Once a week is what I'm asking you to do. Just check in with her and keep her updated. She raised you almost by herself, and she deserves that."

Bryce nodded, properly chastised. "Yes, sir."

"Good." Tex stepped back and sighed. "I know I haven't been perfect, Bryce. Far from it. Thank you for forgiving me and giving me another chance."

"Dad, of course."

Tex nodded, because he felt like he needed a lot of second chances right now. He realized that was why he was working so dang hard on this ranch—all it needed was a second chance, and he wanted to be the one to provide that to the house, the land, the fences, the outbuildings, all of it.

"You know what we should do?" he asked as he moved toward the back door to go to church. "We should find a rescue operation and get all of our animals from there. Give *them* a second chance."

"That's a great idea, Dad," Bryce said. "Maybe I'll just stay here and be a farmer-slash-rancher. We could start our own rescue operation. We have plenty of land here."

"A rescue operation," Tex mused, because the idea held plenty of merit for him.

"You'll save me some pizza, right?" Bryce asked as they buckled into the truck. "From your fancy at-home date?"

Tex laughed, because there wasn't much fancy about what he had planned for him and Abby. Pie Squared. He'd show her the progress on the house. Then…he had no idea what the afternoon held for them, and that got his pulse racing faster than it had in a good, long while.

He'd been praying for pleasant weather and divine guidance when it came to the ranch and house. He'd been asking the Lord to help him with Bryce for seventeen long years. His petitions to the Lord about Abby were still somewhat new, but he really didn't want to mess up this time, so as he and Bryce walked into the church a half-hour later, he once again asked the Lord to bless him and help him that afternoon.

He'd never really believed there was "one right person" for him, but as Abby rose from the wingback chair in the lobby at the church, Tex could only see her. He wanted so much more time with her, and he wondered if she was "his one," and he just hadn't been able to see it until now.

CHAPTER
TWELVE

Ames Hammond finished filling the dishwasher and bent to get a pod to start it. The tension in the house couldn't be washed away, and he'd have to face it sooner or later. He'd be fifty this year, and he felt every single day of his life descend upon him as he dropped in the pod, closed the dishwasher, and started it.

He turned to find his wife standing there, a cross look on her face. "Hey," he said. "Soph, I'm sorry." He crossed the expansive kitchen to her and took her in his arms. She put hers around him too, and Ames buried his face in her neck. "Those boys can't be at the academy if they can't behave."

"I agree," she said. She just didn't like how loud Ames could bark sometimes. In truth, his loud bark kept everyone safe. Without it, Lars might've been seriously hurt. She threaded her fingers through the long hair on the back of his head and pulled back slightly. "I've talked to the twins. They feel really bad."

"As they should," he said.

She sighed and looked past him. The back of the house held huge, magnificent windows that both he and Sophia loved. They held their family councils under all that light, as well as family game night, and in the winter, they closed all the shades and watched movies together.

He adored his family, he really did. He loved his two boys and two girls, but he absolutely needed them to obey him when they came to the police dog academy with him. He'd built it and ran it single-handedly for the past twelve years, and he didn't want to see his son's blood on one of his dog's mouths.

Ever.

"They just need to know you still love them," she said quietly.

"Of course I do," he said.

"They adore you." She looked at him again, an earnestness in her face he didn't see often. "They want to *be* you, Ames. All Chris talks about is how he's going to be a police officer when he grows up." A fond smile touched her lips. "And Lars, well, he just wants to train dogs as well as you do."

He didn't need the added pressure or guilt, and he stepped out of his wife's embrace. "I understand that," he said. "They're nine years old, still children, all of it." He paced over to the sliding door that led into the backyard. He kept dogs here at home twenty-four-seven. The ones in intense training went everywhere with him, and he had two of those right now.

He slid open the door and yipped, and both Lucky and Lois came toward him instantly. Their obedience had to be perfect or they couldn't work in the military or on the police force, and perhaps he'd expected his children to be a little too perfect.

"I'll go talk to them," he said, swinging around as he closed the door. "I have to take Francesca over to Tex Young tonight."

"Take the boys," she said. "I'll make cookies with June, and Jillian will pick a movie for us." She smiled at him, and Ames swept his arm around her and bent his head to kiss her.

"I'm sorry," he whispered again, and Sophia was his perfect match, because she always forgave him. When he worked too much and left her with their four children, she forgave him. When he forgot to pick up one of the kids, because his focus was on a malamute, she forgave him. When he barked too loudly at the twins, she forgave him.

"I am too," she said. "I didn't mean to indicate that they don't have to obey you at the academy."

The flash of teeth Ames had seen moving toward his son's face filled his mind, and he hardened again. "He could've been *seriously* injured, Soph."

She studied his face, and he hoped she understood. He'd done what he'd had to do to protect his son, and that extended to getting in the boy's face about being disobedient. "He shouldn't have been in that pen, and I'd told him maybe three minutes prior. He didn't listen, and Chris was the one who unlocked the gate. They're both to blame."

She nodded, her mouth turning down. "Maybe they shouldn't get to go for a while."

"How about a week?" he suggested. "I need them to know how serious the situation was." No one seemed to get it but him, and he supposed he shouldn't expect them to. He had come home bleeding before, and Sophia had been horrified. He probably understood better than anyone else.

"A week is fine," she said. "I've got to get the storage room cleaned out, and they can help me with that."

Ames grinned at his wife, feeling his mood lift and the tension in the house lighten. "They'll love that."

"They'll learn," she said. "All of them need to clean up that playroom too. It has a funky smell in it, and I can't find it."

Ames chuckled and kissed his wife again. "Okay." He exhaled heavily, and put on his stern-Dad-face. "I'll go talk to them."

He headed down the hall and then up the stairs to the second level. He thought of his own father, who still lived in Ivory Peaks on the farm where Ames and his brothers had grown up. His dad had run their huge family company in downtown Denver, and he'd been stretched thin for time and energy almost all of the time.

Ames had four brothers—one of which was his twin— and they'd gotten into so much mischief as children. That was what boys did, and he reminded himself of that as he approached his sons' bedroom door.

He pressed his eyes closed and murmured, "Dad, how would you handle this?"

His father's disappointment had been the one thing Ames had never wanted to shoulder. His dad had a way of simply looking at him, and Ames would hear the lecture without his dad having to open his mouth at all.

No matter what, after the conversation, his father had taken him into his arms and hugged him. He'd told him Ames was a good boy, and he loved him, and that stuck in his mind as he knocked and then twisted the doorknob.

Both Chris and Lars lay in their beds, and they both sat up as Ames entered the room. "Howdy, boys." He sighed as he turned slightly to close the door. He faced them and put his hands in his pockets.

Lars sniffled and launched himself from his bed. "I'm sorry, Daddy." He flew toward Ames and flung himself into his arms. Ames, almost fifty as he was, bent and caught the boy, lifting him easily off the ground and into his arms.

He held him tightly, his own emotions storming through him as Lars wrapped his legs around Ames's abdomen. Chris got out of bed too and came over, wrapping his arms around Ames's waist.

"I'm real sorry, Daddy."

Ames held Lars with one arm and put his other hand on Chris's back, pressing him into his thigh. "I love you boys," he said, his voice thick. "You cannot even imagine what I saw flashing before my eyes. I can't lose you at the academy, okay? They're working animals, boys. Okay?"

"Okay, Daddy." Lars sniffled and kept crying.

"They're not pets. We have a pet dog. You can wrestle with her. My dogs at the academy are trained to deal with bad guys, and they don't get the difference between you and them."

"We understand," Chris said.

Ames was strong, but he couldn't hold his nine-year-old with one arm anymore. He slid Lars to the floor and crouched in front of his sons. He put one hand on each of their shoulders, noting how alike they looked—and how much they mirrored him too.

"You have to obey me at the academy, and you didn't." He reached up and wiped the tears from Chris's face. "Momma and I think you can't come with me for a week. She's got chores here for you to do, and you *will* do them without complaining. If I hear even once that you're giving her attitude, I will not let you come with me for another week." He looked from Lars to Chris and back. "Am I clear?"

"Yes, sir," they said together.

"Daddy," Lars said. "What about Avalanche's run-through? You said I could launch 'im."

"Well," Ace said. "I don't know, Lars. It's on Thursday, and that's this week. I'll have to think about it."

His chin and lower lip wobbled, but he nodded. "All right."

Ames's knees ached, and he straightened. "All right. Momma's making cookies with June, and we're watching a movie in a little bit. You don't have to be confined to your room."

"I'm going to read," Chris said, turning back to his bed.

"My eyes are hot," Lars said. "Can I lay down up here?"

"Sure," Ames said. He tucked his son into his bed, then bent to kiss his forehead. "Love you, Lars."

"Love you too, Daddy."

He tousled Chris's hair and kissed him too. "Love you, Chris."

"Love you too, Daddy."

He went to the door and opened it. "Oh, I'm taking Francesca over to Tex's. Did either of you want to come?"

"I do," they said together, and Ames grinned at them.

"Okay," he said. "We'll go in about a half-hour, okay? Then we can take some cookies too."

"Okay," the twins said together, and Ames was reminded of how amazing it was to have a twin. He needed to call Cy, and maybe he and Patsy and their kids could come for the movie tonight. Ames didn't want to get rid of Francesca, and he'd be in a low mood. Cy would be able to cheer him up, and he texted his brother before he left his own twins' bedroom and went back downstairs.

Sure, Cy said. *I can go with you to drop her off too.*

That would be great, Ames said. He hated it when his dogs failed their final tests, because it felt like *he* was failing. Francesca had struggled through a lot of her training, but he'd believed in her so much. In the end, she'd be happier with a family, and while Ames didn't know Tex Young very well, the man had a good air about him.

Downstairs, he approached Sophia. "Hey, baby," he said, causing her to turn. "What do you think about inviting everyone for movie night tonight? I can ask Wes to bring his screen and we'll set it up in the backyard." He raised his eyebrows, hopeful. He needed this. He needed his nieces and nephews, loud laughter, his brothers rallying around him, and his wife at his side.

Sophia knew instantly without Ames having to say anything how he'd be once he got back from dropping off Francesca. She gave him a sympathetic smile and said, "Put it on your brothers' text, and tell them I'm making cookies, but I'm only one woman."

He grinned at her and swooped toward her for another hug. "Thank you," he whispered. "There will be so many cookies here, you won't even know what hit you."

She laughed as Ames stepped away and sent the text out to his brothers. Gray normally lived in Ivory Peaks too, but he came to Coral Canyon every summer with his family. If he and his kids weren't out on the lake, they'd be at movie night.

Messages started flying in, and within a few minutes, Ames had confirmation from all of his brothers that they'd be at his house in an hour.

He looked up, tilting his head back as if stretching his neck. "Thank you, Lord," he whispered. Giving up his dog would cost him part of his heart, but coming home to family would be the perfect balm.

"I'm gonna go get Franny," he said to Sophia. "I told the twins we'd leave in a half-hour. My guess is Lars will be asleep, but he wants to go."

"Okay," she said over her shoulder. She stepped over to June and pointed to something in the recipe book. Ames took a moment to enjoy the scene, because it was so normal and yet so perfect. He loved his wife and his family, and he loved that she taught their kids how to cook, clean, and be decent human beings. He was trying to do the same, and today, he'd show his sons how to do something really, really hard—like give a dog he'd worked countless hours with to a complete stranger.

———

A WHILE LATER, AMES PULLED UP TO THE APPOINTED ADDRESS. A couple of pick-up trucks sat in the driveway, and three men with guitars in their hands sat on the front porch. That made him smile, and his heart took courage.

"Look, fellas," he said to his boys. "They play the guitar."

"Daddy, can you ask him if he does lessons?" Chris asked, pulling on the back of Ames's seat as he sat up and leaned forward. "Please?"

"Who's gonna drive you to a lesson?" he asked his son.

"You could, Daddy," Chris said. "Or I'll ride my bike. Please?"

Chris had wanted to take guitar lessons for a while, and they'd just never worked out with his schedule. He already took an art class once a week, and played soccer in the spring and fall. Sophia had put Jane in piano lessons, and Chris, the more sensitive of his boys, wanted to learn music too.

"Come on, Franny," Ames said to the dog riding shotgun next to him. "Time to go meet your new owner."

"If he does lessons," Chris said. "I could check on Franny when I come. She'll like that, won't you, girl?"

The German shepherd, always with her tongue lolling out of her mouth, turned and looked at Chris when he said her name. Ames wondered if she knew she'd failed her test, if she was disappointed she wouldn't get to find bad guys, drugs, or bombs. He wasn't sure, but he sure did love her. Maybe Tex would let him come see the dog too.

The men had started to lean their instruments against the house, and Ames got out of the truck. "Howdy," he called.

"Howdy," they all called back, and Ames went around to the other side of the truck as his twins got out. He leashed Franny and said, "Let's go, girl."

She jumped down too, her keen eyes already scanning the area. She put her nose to the ground, probably trying to catch the scent Ames wanted her to. He patted her and said, "You're not workin' today, hon. You're meeting your new master." He sighed, his chest so, so tight. This was the absolute worst part of his job.

He'd rather turn a dog away before starting their training than go through the many months of work, hoping, praying, and then crashing when they didn't pass. The requirements were tough, and Ames had known that for years.

She's not the first dog you've given away, he told himself, and then he turned toward the farmhouse and Tex Young, yipping at the dog to stay right at his side. She did, of course, because Franny was an amazing dog.

Tex came toward him, his smile just as infectious now

as it had been the first time he'd met Ames. "How are you?" he asked, extending his hand.

Ames shook it and said, "Great," he said, looking down at Franny. "This is Francesca."

Tex crouched down right in front of the dog and held out his hand. "Howdy, Francesca." He let her sniff him, but she wouldn't lick. Ames trained his dogs religiously not to lick.

Tex scrubbed her face and up behind her ears, all while he chuckled, and Ames really liked the spirit oozing from him. He seemed larger than life but down to earth at the same time. He straightened and indicated the others. "You remember my son, Bryce. And he's my brother, Mav."

"Of course," Ames said, shaking Bryce's hand. Mav didn't look like Tex—where he was square, Mav was round. "Nice to meet you."

"I was talkin' about you to someone the other day," Mav said. "Lily Whittaker? I guess they live up at Whiskey Mountain Lodge, and she said all you Hammonds had been through there a time or two."

"That we have," Ames said. "My wife used to work up there."

"That's what she said." Mav smiled at him. "I think she said all of your wives used to work up there."

"Yeah, most of us," Ames said, thinking through his brother's wives. "Yep, all of us."

"So you and your brothers all live here?" Tex asked, sliding a look at Mav.

"In the summer," Ames said. "Gray lives part-time on

our family farm in Colorado. He brings his family here for the summer."

"See?" Tex asked Mav. "That's what we should do."

Mav simply nodded, and Ames wondered what the story was there. "This is our dad's ranch," Tex said. "I just bought it, and we're fixing it up. I keep tellin' Mav we gotta get all our brothers back here."

"There's more than a few of us," Mav said.

"How many?" Ames asked, thinking his family was big.

"Nine total," Mav said.

So his wasn't so big. "Oh." He looked from Tex to Mav. "Tex must be the oldest."

"Tex is," Tex said with a laugh. He took the leash from Ames without any problem at all, but Ames's heart tore a little as Franny went with him. She just went, without looking back at Ames at all.

Panic moved through him, and thankfully, his twins distracted him by galloping around the front yard. "Those are my boys," he said. "Twins. Lars and Chris. They're nine."

"Daddy," Chris said, plenty of pleading in his tone.

Ames sighed and looked at Tex, who'd gone to Mav's side. Franny sat at his feet, looking at Ames too. "They want to know if you do guitar lessons. They saw the three of you playing."

Mav looked at Tex, his eyebrows up. Bryce did too, so the answer was clearly up to him. He looked at his son. "I don't," he said. "But Bryce might."

"Dad," Bryce said. He rolled his eyes and looked at

Ames. "He taught me to play. He's amazing. He's the lead singer for Country Quad."

Ames's eyebrows rose. "That's how you know the Everett Sisters."

"They sang at my wedding," Mav said with a shrug.

Ames really needed to clue into the country music circuit. "Please?" Chris asked. "I will practice so much, I swear. My uncle even has a guitar I can use." He looked at Ames with pure pleading. "Uncle Colt does, Daddy. I've seen it."

"That doesn't mean you can use it, son," he said, gesturing for the twins to come back to him.

"Might be a good way for you to earn some money," Tex said to Bryce, who did perk up at that. "I'm sure between the two of us, we could do some decent lessons."

"Really?" Chris asked at the same time Ames did.

Tex chuckled again and looked down at his new dog. "Yeah, I think we could do it." He met Ames's eyes. "What do I owe you for Francesca?"

"Nothing," Ames said. "Just the best home for her."

Tex blinked, his eyes going wide. "That can't be true. These animals are worth thousands of dollars."

"He can pay," Mav said.

Ames shook his head. "I don't need the money. Just take real good care of her." He crouched down too and clapped his hands once. He told Franny to come in Dutch, and she trotted right over to him. He bent his head so it touched hers, his hands moving up and down along her throat. "I have to leave you here, girl," he whispered. "You're going to like it so much. Tex and Bryce are nice, and they'll take good care of you." He pulled back and stroked her ears flat, because she liked that. "Okay?"

She seemed to know what was happening, because she stuck her nose out and licked his face, just once. He grinned at her, his heart so full of love for her. "All right, then. Go on." He stood, and Franny sat in front of him, looking up at him with such high expectations in her eyes.

"You just tell her to *komen*," Ames said. "And she will. It means come in Dutch."

Tex looked at him, sympathy and compassion in his eyes. Bryce said, "*Komen*," and Franny turned toward him. She jogged over to him and sat, and Bryce looked like he'd won the lottery. In many ways, he had, and Ames didn't want to dwell here for much longer.

"We'll take real good care of her," Tex said, approaching Ames again. He shook his hand and then pulled him into a hug. "You come see her any time you want. Or I'll bring her to you." He stepped back, his hand still gripping Ames's tightly. "Okay?"

"Yeah," Ames said, his voice catching on itself.

"I've got your number, and I'll text you about guitar lessons." Tex released his hand and patted Chris on the shoulder. "You remind your Daddy, okay?"

"Okay," Chris said like he was Tex's personal soldier.

"Come on, guys," Ames said, turning back to the truck. "Let's get home to Momma. Everyone's coming for movie night, and she'll need our help."

CHAPTER
THIRTEEN

W esley Hammond caught sight of the "Welcome to Coral Canyon" sign up ahead, and if he didn't start talking to his son soon, they'd arrive at the park, and he wouldn't be able to. He'd gone down to Ivory Peaks to get Michael for the holiday weekend, something he'd never done before.

Not only that, but Hunter, Molly, and their new baby were coming up to Coral Canyon for the next couple of months too. How Hunter had managed to get away from his CEO duties at HMC, Wes would never know.

He's better than you were, he told himself, not for the first time. He loved Hunt as if he was his own son, and not just because he was so dang good at running their family company.

"Mikey," he said, and his son looked up from his phone. "You talkin' to Gerty?"

"Yes." Mike stuck his phone under his thigh and sighed.

"That doesn't sound good."

"No, it's good," he said.

Wes wasn't so sure about that. He didn't mind the boy having a girlfriend. The tricky part was that she lived several hours south of where Mike lived most of the time. He didn't seem to have a problem talking to girls, and he'd been to several school dances with a date. Maybe Bree was right, and Gerty wasn't a problem.

Wes didn't exactly think she was a problem. He just didn't want Mike limiting himself for a girl he saw three months out of the year and maybe on one holiday.

"You'll be sixteen soon," he said, not sure where he was going with this conversation.

"Yeah," Mike said, not offering anything.

Wes gripped the wheel and told himself to talk. He'd led a huge, multi-billion dollar company for a lot of years. He'd dealt with hard conversations before. "What do you think you'll do after high school?"

Mike rolled his neck, which probably hurt for how long he'd been staring at his device on the drive here. "I don't know, Dad."

"You've told me that before." Wes wasn't going to let this drop. He wasn't going to tell Mike he'd figure it out and he had lots of time. Both were still true, but Wes wanted more. "What are you really thinking?"

"I know what everyone wants me to do," Mike said. His voice sounded slightly sour. "Hunter's been running

HMC for five years or something, and if he just puts in ten more, then I'll be old enough to take over."

"Mm hm."

Mike sighed, the weight of the Teton range in the sound. "Dad, I don't know if I want to do that, but I don't know how to *not* do what's expected of me."

Wes reached over and slid his hand down the back of his son's head. "You're a good boy, Mikey."

"What if I don't want to run HMC?" He sounded like he'd swapped out his deeper voice for a mousy one.

"If you had no expectations," Wes said, his throat turning thick. "And you were twenty-one, with your inheritance money fresh in your bank account." He looked at Michael as the speed limit sign went by and he eased up on the accelerator. "What would you do? Where would you go? Who would you be with?"

Mike looked out the windshield, his brow furrowed as he thought. He was a smart kid—not as smart as Hunter, but Wes wasn't sure that was possible—and he could do anything he wanted. Absolutely anything.

"Mama wants me to go to college," he said.

"No expectations," Wes said.

"And I'm twenty-one and have all the money I could ever want."

"Yep." Wes focused on coming into town now. With the Independence Day weekend upon them, the whole town had been decked out in red, white, and blue. People descended on Coral Canyon from the smaller surrounding communities, and that meant more congestion, more pedestrians, and more traffic.

"It's not that far from now," Wes said. "Five years, Mike." Five years to a fifteen-year-old might as well be a lifetime. Wes knew that, but he wanted to hear what his son had to say.

"I wouldn't mind going to college," Mike said. "I've been thinking about that. I like working the farm too, dad. I especially like helping with the horses at Pony Power."

"Mm hm," Wes said. "So maybe you'll take over Granddad's farm."

"Hunt wants to do that."

Wes looked left, out his window. It didn't really matter what Hunter wanted to do. He ran HMC now, and he wouldn't give up the CEO office to just anyone. Wes knew what that office did to a man, even one as tender-hearted and intelligent as Hunter.

"Maybe you'll buy a farm of your own," Wes said. "Plenty of opportunity for that." He came to a stop at a light and looked at his son. Mike studied his hands, which meant he had more to say. Lots more.

Wes waited, because the boy usually needed time to get out his thoughts. Bree had taught Wes that, and once he'd known that about Mikey, he'd given him the time he needed instead of getting frustrated that his son wasn't saying anything.

They continued through town, the park where his brothers and their families had chosen to gather this year getting closer and closer. They spent the holiday with the Whittakers, which meant the Everett sisters always came. Their parents lived in town too, and Hunter had brought Wes's dad with him. There would be dozens of people with blankets spread out, and picnic baskets, baby wipes for their kids, and lawn chairs.

They'd rented a space with three grills, and Wes would be sorely disappointed if Celia Zuckerman didn't have a whole array of sides to go with the hamburgers and hot dogs Graham Whittaker had said he'd bring and make.

Not only that, but Ames had invited the man he'd given Franny to, as well as his parents and brothers. Wes hadn't met any of the Youngs yet, but Ames had spoken highly of the ones he'd met.

"I want to fly helicopters," Mike blurted out. "For the military."

Wes worked not to jerk the wheel or stomp on the brake. He managed it, but only just. "Okay," he said evenly. "Do you know how to get into that?"

Bree would not like that. *The military?* she'd ask. She'd worry herself to death over Mike being in danger even some of the time.

"No," Mike admitted. "I haven't looked, because I know Mama isn't going to let me do it."

"Son," Wes said, not wanting to speak against his wife. "You'll be an adult. Of course your mother and I will advise you on what to do. You'll want that, because it's hard to make huge life decisions without help."

Mike nodded, and Wes turned, the park now on his right. "But buddy, you'll be an adult. Your mama might not like it, but she can't stop you from doing it."

He looked at Wes, a glimmer of hope in his eyes. "What do you think?"

"About you flying helicopters in the military?" Wes

tilted his head, thinking and looking for a parking space at the same time. "I think you'll be phenomenal at anything you do, Mikey. That's what I think."

"Dad." Mikey sounded like he was rolling his eyes. Wes couldn't quite see, because he'd found a spot and was turning left into it.

He put the truck in park and looked at his son. "I mean it. Do the research. Figure out where you'd have to go and how long it takes. I can help if you want. As you learn more about it, you might not like what you see, or the Lord might lead you in a different direction."

Mike nodded, his eyes narrowing. "Dad, do you think the Lord led you to be the CEO?"

"I do," Wes said. "Yes, I was the oldest son. It was always mine if I wanted it, and you know what, Mike? I wanted it. I always wanted it, even while I went to college. There are some people who know what they want to do with their lives from a very young age. And then there's people who don't. There are people who change careers later in life, who go to college when they're in their sixties, all of that."

The only emotion Wes could feel and see coming from his son was fear. "You can't be afraid to make a wrong decision," he said. "There is no wrong decision for you. If you make a choice, then learn or decide it isn't for you, then you make a different choice."

Mike nodded, his eyes back on his hands. "All right."

"Mikey." He waited until his son looked at him. Wes gave him a smile, always able to get one in return. Even as a baby, Mikey had smiled for him first. "There is nothing you can do that will make me or Mama ever stop loving you. No matter what. There is no wrong decision for you to worry about."

"Yes, sir," Mikey said, his throat working like he'd swallowed a glassful of sand.

"All right," Wes said, reaching for his cowboy hat in the back seat. "Let's go see if Uncle Colt has eaten all the chocolate cake yet." He chuckled as he got out of the truck, his long legs glad to be back in Coral Canyon and straight for a change.

Across the street, his brothers weren't hard to find. They laughed and yell-talked with the Whittaker family, which included their mother and her husband—a race-horse breeder who lived up in Dog Valley. Wes sure did like Finn Barber a whole lot, as well as Celia's husband, Zach.

He had his daughter and son-in-law with them, and instead of trying to be heard above everyone gathered in their area, Zach signed to her.

Wes basked in the family spirit that came from the group, and Gray pointed first and said, "There they are!" as if Wes and his son were celebrities.

Colton turned, a chocolate cupcake in both hands, and came toward them. "This is for you," he said to Mike, handing him one cupcake. Everyone there knew he hadn't been saving it for Mike, but no one said anything. "You gotta come meet the Youngs," he said. "You're going to love them."

He took Mikey and Wes over to a group of tall, cowboy-hatted men standing in a semi-circle. Wes noticed several people out on the perimeter, talking and looking in their direction.

"Holy cow!" Mikey danced ahead of them. "Uncle Colton, that's Country Quad!"

"Who?" Wes asked.

"He's right," Colton said with a laugh. "Bro, they're famous country music stars. Look at those boys coming over to get autographs."

Wes and Colton and Mike had almost reached the Youngs, but Colt was right. A trio of teenage boys came over and he approached and heard, "What are you guys doin' here? Are you performing?"

"Not performing," one of the men said with a huge smile. "Our parents live here."

"Now some of us live here too," another said, and four of the seven of them signed some random piece of paper for all three boys.

"Fellas," Colton said, going right up to them. "This is the oldest of us Hammonds. Wes, and his son Michael." He presented Wes like he was a game show host, his smile just as wide and just as hitched as Vanna White's. "Wes, this is Tex Young—he's the oldest, and he's who owns Franny now. His son Bryce, who's seventeen and going into his senior year at the high school."

Wes glanced at Michael, who gazed at Bryce like he was a god. He shook his head, because celebrity meant nothing to him.

"Otis Young," Colton said. "He's the brains behind their lyrics, I'm told. Luke is the genius on the drums, and

Trace can play any stringed instrument from here to the Norwegian harp."

They all started laughing, and Trace said, "There's no such thing as a Norwegian harp."

"This is Morris," Luke said. "He's our youngest brother, and he's our new manager."

"Mav," Tex said, practically pushing another man forward. He turned back and gave Tex a glare, and Wes liked them all instantly. They seemed real, even if they had signed autographs a few minutes ago. "Used to manage us, but he found himself a pretty woman and they live here now."

"So two of you are here," Wes said.

"And our parents," Mav said, indicating an older couple already sitting in a pair of lawn chairs. "They've lived here their whole lives."

"They're younger than us," Colton said. "But Beau is a year or so older than Tex. Is that right?"

"We did go to high school together," Tex said. "He's a year younger than me. He's the same age as the woman I'm seeing."

"Oh, who are you dating?" Trace asked, his eyebrows sky-high.

"Dad," Bryce said, chuckling. "You stepped right in it."

"You're dating?" Luke roared, and Morris and Mav both rolled their eyes.

"People date," Mav said. "It's not a crime, remember?" He turned back to his parents and took a seat. "Sit down, you guys. Everyone is staring at us."

"No one is staring," Otis bickered back at him, but Wes

was pretty sure the whole park had been alerted of their presence, and if they wanted any peace tonight at all, they should move into the center of the group.

In fact, he suggested it, and that began the pilgrimage of the Youngs from the outer circle of the Hammond family barbecue to the middle of it. Before Wes knew it, Graham was serving hamburgers and hot dogs, and someone had found Tex, Otis, and Trace a few guitars.

They started to sing and play, and Lily, Rose, and Vi stood around them, harmonizing. Wes ate his fill of baked beans, potato salad, and chocolate chip cookies, and then he took Bree's hand in his and kissed the back of it.

"I love summer," he said with a sigh.

She smiled at him and leaned her head against his shoulder. "How was the drive?"

"Good," he said, deciding to keep his talk with Mikey to himself for now. "It was real good."

Just then, a pretty redhead approached the group with a brunette and a man in a wheelchair. Tex's guitar went silent and he jumped to his feet, handed it to his son, and jogged over to her.

She was obviously his girlfriend, if the way she grinned at him told Wes anything. Not only that, but Tex lifted her right off her feet and swung her around as if he hadn't seen her for a while.

"Aw," Bree said. "They're cute."

"Do you know them?"

"Sure," she said. "That's Abigail Ingalls, the librarian. She drives the Bookmobile too. Remember we took the kids when we were out in Rusk that one time?"

"Sure," Wes said, a vague memory coming forward from the back of his mind.

"And her brother," Bree said. "He got hurt in the military overseas. Lost both his legs, but he's been dating Cheryl Watts for a while now. She's the one I buy those tamales from for Cy."

"Ah."

Bree smiled at him again and then got to her feet. "Come on," she said. "Let's go say hello. I didn't know Abby was dating anyone, least of all a famous country music star."

Wes got to his feet too and took Bree's hand in his. "You know, to him and his son, and probably to Abby too, he's just a guy."

"You're right," Bree said. "He's just a guy."

"I bet he hasn't even been to all fifty states," Wes said, and that got Bree to giggle. He smiled too, and then he donned his personable skin so he could talk and not make a fool of himself.

CHAPTER
FOURTEEN

M averik Young looked toward the mountains, wishing he held a fishing pole or carried a backpack. Since meeting Gray Hammond a couple of weeks ago, he'd been fishing with the man and his son twice now, and Mav suddenly knew what he could do with all of his time in Coral Canyon.

Gray took all of his kids if they wanted to go, so he hadn't objected to Mav bringing Boston. Beth had deemed fish "yucky," and she'd stayed home with Dani.

"Is it ready?" Tex called, and Mav focused on his task instead of daydreaming about fishing in crystal clear mountain lakes.

"Yep," he yelled back to his brother. Having everyone in the band in town had been a blessing in his life, and Otis and Morris were currently staying with him in the house on the western highway. Trace and Luke had opted to stay here, with Tex and Bryce.

Tex had asked them all to help him around the ranch, and today, they were setting the last of the fences he'd taken out to get the fields and pastures and land cleaned up.

Mav could admit his brother knew how to work hard. He'd done amazing things with this ranch in only six or seven weeks, and he barely recognized it from the first time he'd come to see it. The grass had come back, and that alone had changed so much.

Tex had put on a new roof, installed new windows, and had the house painted a great shade of blue that didn't sting the eyes but didn't speak of robins either.

"Comin' down," Tex called, and the *cha-pop!* of the nail gun filled the air. As he secured the final top rung in place, the other brothers stepped out of the way and headed back to the house, comments of ice water and lemonade drifting to meet Mav's ears, who stood way down on the end.

Tex reached him last, and with the final nail in place, he smiled at Mav and started laughing. Mav loved his oldest brother's laugh, and how very happy he seemed here, and he chuckled with him. "You sure are a different man," he said.

Tex switched on the safety on the nail gun. "Am I?"

"I think so," Mav said, turning to face the house. "And look at Morris walkin' side-by-side with Luke and Otis." That really brought a smile to his face, and he couldn't look away to judge Tex's reaction.

"It's pretty incredible," he said.

"Heard from Blaze?"

"He'll be here this weekend," he said. "He and Jem are flyin' in together."

"Are they staying here or with Mama?"

"Mama," Tex said, lifting himself up onto the top rung. "Listen, I wanted to ask you about something."

Mav turned away from the other brothers and faced Tex. "Yeah? What?"

He looked left, toward the farm and house next door. Mav did too, but he couldn't see Abby. He did find well-tended-to barns and stables, a pretty substantial chicken coop, and plenty of hay almost in need of a harvest.

"Abby," Tex said.

Mav boosted himself up onto the rung too and took a moment to find his balance. "I haven't sat on a log fence in forever," he said, half afraid he was about to tumble off. "What about Abby?"

"Bryce said something the other day I can't stop thinking about." Tex took off his hat and wiped the sweat from his forehead. "Something about how I could marry her, and we could start a family, and it would be like me starting over." He frowned and brought his gaze back to Mav. "I didn't like that. I told him I didn't need to start over, and that he would be my son no matter what."

Mav nodded. "And?"

"And I think he feels like a burden, or like he doesn't belong." Tex sighed. "Corrie said some real cruel stuff before he moved in with me. He knows she didn't mean it, but...I don't know. I think it got inside his head, and he sees me with Abby, and he thinks he's in the way. That his mama doesn't want him, and for me to have the life I want, I'm gonna need to 'start over.'"

Mav exhaled, trying to put himself in Bryce's boots. "I don't know what to tell you, Tex."

"Yeah," Tex said with a sigh. "I just thought, you know, you dated with kids. You and Dani both had a child."

"They're far younger," Mav said. "Beth just finished kindergarten, and when I picked her up on the last day of school, she told her teacher she was going to live with 'her other mom' for the summer."

"Well, that's good," Tex said.

"Dani's great," Mav said, his heart still filled with insane love for his wife. "So is Abby. She won't let Bryce feel forgotten."

"Yeah," Tex said. "I just…I don't think he hears me when I tell him he is my son, and I will always love him, no matter where else my life takes me." He shook his head. "It's my fault," he said quietly. "I should've quit the band when he was younger, the way you did for Beth."

"Hey." Mav put his hand on Tex's back, but his brother didn't look up. "You can't change what you did, brother. It was the right thing for you at that time. There's no sense in beating yourself up about it."

"Yeah." Tex didn't sound convinced at all, and Mav suspected he hadn't heard him the same way Bryce didn't hear Tex when he told him he was loved and wanted right where he was.

Franny barked, and that startled both Mav and Tex. "Hey," Tex said, his voice suddenly hard. He jumped to the ground. "What are you barkin' at?" He scanned the land in front of him. "She never barks."

She took off running, really sprinting, and Tex yelped. Mav slid to the ground too, sudden urgency in his bloodstream too. "Let's go see what she's doing."

"She better not maul some newspaper boy or something," Tex said, his long legs striding after the dog.

Franny was mighty fast, and she disappeared around the side of the house where the steps came down. Mav had hated those steps as a child. He'd always thought he was going to trip and fall to the gravel below.

Tex had made them stronger and wider, and he'd extended the little landing, where Mav had once nearly gotten the wind knocked out of him as all nine brothers tried to get in the house first, into a huge deck off the back of the house.

It wasn't done yet, as Tex and Bryce weren't building it, but it had been framed, and the area below it, which would be the covered patio, had been poured with concrete and the pillars set.

"Franny!" Tex bellowed, and the only response that came was a man's laugh. Tex's stride immediately slowed, and he said, "Oh, Ames is here. Of course." The two of them came around the corner of the house, and Ames lifted his hand in a wave.

Tex picked up his pace again, and Mav went with him. "I don't know how you get her to stay," he said to Ames as the two of them embraced.

Ames shook Mav's hand, his grin as wide as the sea. "She failed her test for a reason," he said. "Good to see you, Mav." He looked back to Tex. "I just came to get Chris, but he wasn't on the porch. I didn't even speak."

"Did you shower today?" Tex asked, chuckling. "Maybe she could smell you."

"From two hundred yards?" Mav asked while Ames also laughed. "Come on."

"Daddy!" Chris yelled from the front of the house, and Ames turned that way.

"Backyard, bud. I'm comin'." They all walked toward the house, and Franny frolicked ahead to greet Chris too. "How was it, bud?"

"So great!" Chris jumped up and gave Ames a high high-five. "I know how to hold the guitar now, and Bryce gave me a book and an instrument the right size for a boy like me." He held up the black case, his whole face lit up like an entire Christmas tree farm.

"Wow," Ames said, chuckling. "How much do we owe you for that?" He looked at Tex.

"Nothing," Tex said. "It's a student guitar, but it's great for beginners. Has a real rich sound." He nodded toward it. "I learned on one of those."

"As did I," Mav said.

Another man came around the corner, and Mav nodded to Ames. "Daddy," he said. "What are you doin' here?"

"Mama and I came for dinner," he said.

"They actually *brought* dinner," Tex said, coming up beside Mav.

"Bryce and Trace are bringing it in," Daddy said as Mav embraced his father. "Hullo, Ames."

"Mister Young. We'll get out of your way." He bent down and patted Franny. "You stay here, girl." The dog stopped and sat, still watching Ames until Tex went to her side.

"Come on, Franny," he said. "Let's go see Mama. You like Mama, remember?" The dog looked up at him as if she could understand English. "You're welcome to stay, Mav," he added. "I think Abby texted Dani."

In that moment, Mav's phone rang, and he answered the call from his wife as Tex, Daddy, and Franny headed for the house. His wife's razzle-dazzle ringtone came out of his device, and he answered it with, "Hey, love."

"Will you tell Tex and Abby that I can't come," she said, clearly frustrated. "I had both kids in the car, and then Boston said he was sick. I didn't really believe him, but then he threw up."

"I'm on my way home." Mav jogged toward the driveway.

"You should stay," she said, and it was clear she was still in the car. If Boston had thrown up...he didn't even want to think about Dani cleaning that up alone.

"I'm not going to stay and enjoy dinner while you take care of our sick kids," he said. "Leave it for me. I'll be home as quick as I can."

———

A FEW DAYS LATER, MAV HAD JUST ABOUT HAD IT WITH cleaning up after sick people. First Boston had come down with the stomach bug, and then Beth. He'd been spared, and he believed it was only because of his obsession with washing his hands, washing blankets, sheets, bedding, stuffed animals, and towels.

"I must've done thirty loads of laundry this week," he'd said to Dani. She'd smiled and gone back to disinfecting the kitchen. Exhaustion pulled through him every hour, but the kids seemed to be better now.

Then, he woke in the morning to the sound of Dani throwing up in the bathroom. "No," he moaned as he got out of bed. "Hon?" He went to help her, fetching a glass of cool water for her and helping her back to bed.

"I'm fine," she said. "Really."

"No, you're not," he said. "Go back to bed. I'll get you the tub and make sure the kids are okay." He paused at the door and turned back to her. "It's a twenty-four hour bug, so it'll pass soon."

She curled into the fetal position, and her eyes drifted closed. Mav sent up a prayer for strength to get through the day with two barely-well children by himself. He'd check on Dani in an hour or so and hope for a miracle.

Out in the kitchen, all was silent and still. The kids hadn't gotten up yet, and Mav started making coffee. He checked the fridge for milk, and thankfully they had some. Then he could feed the kids cereal, call for pizza for lunch, and as he spotted a loaf of bread, grilled cheese sandwiches came into his head for dinner.

His phone rang, this time a classical piece indicating his ex-wife needed him. "Hey, Portia," he said after answering the call.

"Good morning, Mav," she said. "I'm surprised you're awake."

"Then why did you call?" He leaned against the island in the kitchen, his own stomach not feeling great.

"A couple of reasons," she said with extreme patience. "I wanted to check on Beth and see how she was feeling. Is anyone else there sick?"

"Yeah." Mav wrinkled his nose at the scent of the coffee as it started to drip into the pot. He normally loved his morning brew, especially with the hazelnut cream. But today, it made his stomach rumble and roll. "Dani's not doing great this morning, and honestly, neither am I."

"Do I need to come get Beth and Boston?"

The fact that she'd offered to take Boston told Mav how good of a person Portia was. "No," he said. "Literally all of my brothers are here."

"I thought Otis and Morris had gotten a hotel."

"They did," Mav said. "But they can take the kids. Or Tex will. He's got Luke and Trace and all the kids at his house. Blaze and Jem got in on Saturday too." The only brother who wasn't currently in Coral Canyon was Gabe, and Mav was still working on getting him there.

Not today, Mav told himself. He could barely stand upright.

"Okay," Portia said, and he yanked his eyes back open. "Mav, there's another reason I'm calling."

"Sure," he said, moving around the island to the barstools.

"Jackson proposed last night, and I said yes." She delivered the statement in an even, unemotional tone.

Mav smiled, because she'd been dating him for over a year. "Portia, that's amazing," he said. "Congratulations."

"Thank you." Her voice did carry a smile then, and she added, "Maybe not as fast as you and Dani, but we finally got there."

"There's no race," he said.

"No, there is not."

Mav's wave of nausea passed, and he got to his feet. "So when's the big day?"

"Christmas," she said. "We'll be married here in Jackson, and of course I want you and your family there."

"Sure," Mav said. "Tell me the date, and I'll get it on our calendar." Someone knocked on the garage entrance, and he turned that way as Dani's mother entered the house. She carried a couple of grocery sacks and a smile.

"I brought—oh." She closed her mouth when she saw him on the phone, and Mav waved her in.

"December twenty-first," Portia said, and Mav scrawled it on the whiteboard that hung on their fridge.

"Got it," he said. "Dani's mom just walked in."

"I'll let you go."

Mav put his phone down, the chime telling him Portia had hung up.

"I brought bagels and cream cheese," Dani's mom said, the food already on the counter. "You don't look well, Mav."

"Dani's down too." He looked at her with pure hope. "Could you take the kids to your house?"

"Of course," she said, glancing into the living room. "They must not be up yet."

"They aren't," he said. "I'll help you." The next twenty minutes blurred as Mav tried to hold onto the contents of his stomach while he packed a few things for Boston and Beth to spend the night at their grandparents' house.

"I'm sorry," he said to Susan. "Take them to a movie today. Whatever you have to do to get through the day."

"We'll have fun," she said brightly, beaming down at the kids. "Come on, guys. Let's go surprise Daddy Don."

Thankfully, neither Beth nor Boston caused any problems or raised a fuss about going with Susan, and Mav skipped the coffee and took a bottle of water into the bedroom he shared with his wife.

She looked over to him as he entered. "I'm feeling a lot better," she said, sitting up. "You don't look good."

"I sent the kids with your mother," he said. "Portia's engaged. I'm going to puke." He dashed into the bathroom to do that, and this time, Dani brought him a glass of water, stood by him while he brushed his teeth, and helped him back to bed.

"Portia's engaged?" she asked as she tucked him in. He breathed in and out, trying to feel normal when he knew he couldn't.

"Yeah," he said. "I put the wedding date on the fridge. She wants us there." He closed his eyes. "She said she'd take the kids."

Dani swiped her fingers across his forehead. "You're burning up."

"I'm just going to go back to sleep," he said. He wasn't sure if she said anything else or not. He wasn't sure how much time had passed until he woke the next time, but his stomach growled at him.

He tried to sit up, noting how dark the room was, and his body felt so weak he fell back to his pillow. "Dani," he croaked, but her side of the bed was empty. He reached for the bottle of water on his nightstand and guzzled, thinking that probably wasn't a great idea.

His stomach bubbled, but he didn't need to run to the bathroom. He looked for his phone, and Dani had plugged it in for him. He wasn't sure he could get out of bed, as weak as he felt, so he texted his wife, noting that it was a full twelve hours after he'd sent the kids with Dani's mom.

She came into the room, flooding it with light as she opened the door. "You're awake," she said.

"Yeah," he said. "Sorry. I didn't mean to sleep all day."

She handed him a single graham cracker. "Try eating this and see if you can keep it down." She offered him a kind, loving smile, and Mav took a bite. He chewed slowly, the taste of honey and cracker one of his favorites.

"You're not sick," he said.

"Not really." She turned and opened the curtains, and because it was summertime, there was still plenty of light left in the day. She faced him again and said, "Mav, I was sick this morning because I'm pregnant."

Mav swallowed, but his hand had frozen with the graham in his hand. "You're pregnant?"

A beautiful smile filled her whole soul, and Dani nodded slowly. Joy burst through him, and as weak as his body felt, his mind and soul couldn't contain his excitement and happiness. "Come here," he said, and she flew into his arms. He held her tightly, stroking her hair. "Oh, I love you. I love you so much." He pulled back and searched her face. "Are you happy?"

"Yes," she whispered, her hands cradling his face. "I'm so excited."

"I want to kiss you, but then you'll have the stomach flu on top of your morning sickness."

"I'm willing to take the risk," she said, touching her mouth to his and kissing him. Mav touched everything he loved and wanted as he held Dani's face lightly in his hands and kissed his wife.

CHAPTER
FIFTEEN

O tis Young stood on Isabella's front porch, the *ding-ding-dong* of her doorbell chiming through her house. He was leaving town today, as he didn't see the point of staying in Florida now that Morris had left. Everyone in his family seemed to be up in Coral Canyon for the summer, and he'd been there too for the past few weeks.

He'd realized how much he liked it there, and since he hadn't been able to pen anything for the last album Country Quad had under contract, he'd decided to return to his hometown for now too.

Luke, Trace, and Morris had, and getting one of the twins back into the family felt like a miracle Otis shouldn't overlook.

He did look back to Isabella's door and reached to knock this time. She should be home. They'd made lunch plans before his flight back to Wyoming. While he'd been in Coral Canyon, he'd spoken to her every day. They'd talked about their relationship and her perhaps leaving her educational counseling job here and going up to Wyoming with him.

Mav had done it, and while Otis was fifteen months older than Mav, he didn't mind following in his brother's footsteps.

She still didn't come to the door, and Otis pulled out his phone and called her. The line rang and rang, making his heartbeat do strange flips in his chest. "Isa," he said to her voicemail. "I'm on your front porch. I thought we were goin' to lunch today before I head back to Coral Canyon."

He didn't know what else to say, so he hung up. Frustration built beneath his breastbone, making his lungs work harder to expand. "Where is she?"

Otis had a temper that flared from time to time, and he had to force himself back to a reasonable place mentally. Only then could he think straight. He'd barked at Mav about dating Dani, and then sixty seconds later asked him about the app. That was about how Otis lived—in sixty second chunks where he reacted, took a minute to think, and then acted like a rational human being.

He was trying to get better about skipping that first step and lashing out, but it was hard for him to undo what felt natural to him. Right now, he wanted to bang against Isabella's door with both fists and demand to know where she was.

She'd never left him high and dry like this, and Otis turned away from the door so he wouldn't act on his impulse to pound it to the ground.

The Florida sunshine blinded him, and he settled his sunglasses in place beneath the brim of his cowboy hat. He looked and felt foolish standing on the woman's porch, and he returned to the rental car. His tall frame barely fit inside, but he managed to fold himself into the driver's seat, where he immediately texted Isa.

I'm going to Benito's, he said. *That was our first date, and I thought you'd like that before I left town.*

He waited ten seconds, watching his phone without blinking. Surely she'd answer. Tell him she'd run into some traffic and she'd meet him there. Explain that her boss had called an emergency meeting she couldn't miss.

Otis wasn't a genius with arranging flights—Mav had been doing that for him and the rest of the band members for over a decade—but he could figure it out. If Isa couldn't see him for a few more hours, he'd wait.

His pulse flipped oddly again, telling him something. He looked up from his phone and to Isabella's front door. She wasn't there. She hadn't put up a note.

He also had the very distinct feeling she wasn't going to call him back or respond to his texts.

She'd ghosted him.

Panic clawed at his ribs now, trying to separate them so it could get to his heart. He pressed one palm to his erratic heartbeat, feeling it jump against his fingers as it tried to get away from the inevitable.

When he and Lauren had finally called their marriage over, Otis hadn't really felt anything. He'd been numb from the months of counseling, of trying to be the man Lauren wanted him to be—a man he wasn't.

She'd taken their daughter home, as they'd been touring with him at the time. She lived in Dog Valley with Joey now, and Otis saw his daughter as often as he could. She was seven and going into third grade. She loved to read and do crafts, and she made Otis smile every time he thought of her.

He'd been steadily falling in love with Isabella Marquez, but he hadn't introduced her to Joey yet. Not live and in person, at least. He'd shown her plenty of pictures, especially over the past few weeks as he and Joey had been together in Coral Canyon.

Otis leaned his head back as his heart gave one loud, booming beat in his chest, and then cracked. He gasped for breath, confusion riddling his mind and making him frown.

"This isn't what's happening," he said, though he knew it was. Deep down, he *knew*. He told himself that things with Isabella had been going so well. He'd been dating her for eight or nine months now. No, she hadn't come to Mav's wedding, but that had been in April, during a very busy semester change for her.

No, she hadn't introduced him to her parents, but they'd been traveling all the times Otis had been in town.

No, she hadn't let him kiss her until they'd been talking for about three months and they'd been out about a dozen times. That was normal.

"It is," he told himself. Lots of women didn't want to move very fast. Heck, he was fine going slow too, because he still had an album to make with his brothers, and his future wasn't set in stone.

He could admit that he'd been paving a path in his mind. One where he helped Isabella pack her belongings and move them north. One where she adored his daughter, and they started a family in Coral Canyon, where Tex and Mav lived now.

His mind spun, because his next thought told him that Tex would have to go to Nashville to make the album, same as Otis.

Otis shook his head. "Call her again." He took a deep breath to try to calm himself. His phone had connected to his car, and he tapped the screen to call Isabella again.

She didn't answer.

He didn't bother leaving a message.

"Can't sit here," he said to himself. His flight didn't leave for another four hours, but he backed out of her driveway and headed for the airport.

He didn't cry, because the anger kept the tears at bay. He kept his phone plugged in on the way, and no one called or texted. By the time he returned the rental and went through security, the numbness had set in.

Once in the member's lounge, he tried texting Isabella one more time. *I'm at the airport. I don't know what happened or when I'll be back in Florida. Call me tonight.*

He sent the message, knowing she wouldn't call that night. For one, Isabella never called him. He always called her.

As he sat there, waiting waiting waiting for his flight, his irrational mind churned up all the things about his relationship with Isabella that should've told him he was far more into her than she was him.

Pure humiliation filled him, and he leaned his head back and closed his eyes. He let his mind drift, and his thoughts went wherever they wanted. Here, there, up, down, and around.

All at once, the lyrics to a song came forward, and Otis's eyes snapped open. He scrambled for his phone, humming a tune to go with the words. He started thumb-typing, and he couldn't get his fingers to move fast enough to keep up with the song streaming from him.

Title: When She Won't Call Back

He practically punched the top of the app and put that in, then went back to the lyrics he'd hastily typed out.

Twenty minutes later, the inspiration dried up, and Otis sagged into his seat again. He'd been struggling with the songwriting for six solid months. Nothing would come. No music. No words. Nothing.

He should've known that country music can only be penned from a place of desperation and agony. Country Quad did play some upbeat songs, but those usually came into Otis's mind from things he did with his family. He and Tex had started a song just after the Fourth of July that Bryce and Tex had been working to finish.

All of their ballads came from Otis and Luke, and they always spoke about loss and how to recover from them.

Otis had no idea how he'd tell everyone waiting for him in Coral Canyon that his girlfriend had ghosted him. "It reflects more on her than you," he said to himself as his phone notified him that his plane had started boarding.

He stood up, checked to make sure he hadn't left anything behind, and headed for the gate. Every step closer to Wyoming told him that it didn't matter why he went home. His parents wouldn't mind that he'd lost Isabella. They wouldn't blame him. They wouldn't demand to know why he was such a monster.

They'd envelop him in their arms and tell him how sorry they were. His brothers would surround him with love and sympathy—sometimes to the point that Otis would start to get irritated with them.

Embarrassment squirreled through him, mostly because he'd been so blind to Isabella's dislike of him. She sure had acted like she liked him, and a warning from the band's agent from years ago entered his mind.

You guys have to be careful, he'd told then. *You're celebrities now, and sometimes there are people who just want to separate you from your money. They sometimes just want to see if you can help them, not if they can fall in love with you.*

He wasn't sure if that was what Isabella had done or not. He hadn't given her any money. He hadn't helped her get into the music industry or get a promotion at work or anything like that.

On the plane, he texted Mav that he thought Isabella had broken up with him by completely ghosting him, and then put his phone on airplane mode. He needed a few hours before he could handle the condolences.

He thought of his disastrous relationship with Lauren.

He thought of his daughter.

He thought of Tex fixing up their boyhood home and ranch.

He thought of Mav and Dani's wedding and how perfect it had been.

He thought of Ames Hammond giving Tex that beautiful German shepherd and how he must've felt doing that.

Another song crowded into his mind, this one about grieving the loss of something that never really belonged to you. A woman, a dog, a ranch.

Otis wrote two songs on the way home from Florida, and when he landed in Jackson Hole, he found Mav, Dani, Beth, Boston, and Joey there to greet him.

"Daddy!" His daughter ran toward him, and Otis dropped to his knees, overcome with relief and joy to see her. He caught her and hugged her tightly until she said, "Daddy, you're squeezing me to death."

"Sorry, Kangaroo," he said, pulling back and smiling at her. Tears did burn in his eyes then, the gratitude he felt for his daughter overwhelming him. He was also so grateful he hadn't introduced Isabella into Joey's life, so she didn't have to feel as shredded and tattered as he currently did.

He got to his feet and took Joey's hand in his. Mav wore compassion and worry in his eyes, and he hugged Otis for a good, long minute without saying anything. When he pulled back, he said, "It's going to be okay, Otis. We've got pizza in the truck, and you can stay with us as long as you want."

"Thank you," Otis said through a raw throat. Eight months. He wasn't sure why the past eight months were going to scar him so badly, only that the wound was open, and he didn't see it closing any time soon.

CHAPTER
SIXTEEN

A bby let Wade get the door, because it would be Cheryl and his parents. She slid the tray of pizza pockets back into the oven, wishing Wade's favorite meal could be made in the slow cooker. The oven heated the kitchen, and she'd deliberately made his cake the previous day.

Knocking sounded on the kitchen entrance, and she turned that way as Bryce entered. "Hey, Abby," he said, his smile genuine. His father came right behind him, and Tex also wore a grin with his jeans, his dark blue polo, and cowboy boots. That hat never went anywhere, but as he swept his arm around her waist and pressed a kiss to her forehead, he'd clearly showered after his work around the ranch next door.

"Smells good in here," he said, smiling down at her. She looked at his mouth, wondering why he hadn't kissed her yet. They'd gone out several times, held hands, and he used those lips to kiss her cheek or temple. Never her lips, and her heartbeat skipped around her chest before going back to where it belonged.

"Abby," her mom said, and she turned toward her. "Cheryl has something for you." She smiled at Tex and added, "Howdy, Tex."

"Hello, Mrs. Ingalls." He moved in front of her and gave her mom a cheek kiss, then let Abby squeeze by and into the living room. The doorways in this house could use some widening, but Abby would never do it. She didn't have the vision or muscles Tex possessed.

In the living room, she'd set up two long tables and covered them with bright blue cloths. Wade's favorite color, of course. He'd sprinkled confetti in white and navy down the center of the table, and Abby had put paper plates and plastic utensils at the end of both tables.

"Cheryl, hi," she said, giving her brother's girlfriend a hug. "You have something for me?" Abby genuinely liked Cheryl, and they'd gone to lunch a few times in recent weeks. Abby had invited her friend who owned the bookshop, Georgia, as well, and the three of them had had fun. More fun than Abby could ever remember having with her girlfriends.

Cheryl smiled at her and held out a small box. "Yep. I saw this at the farmer's market this morning, and I thought of you."

"Oh." Abby took the small box and lifted the lid. A glass hummingbird sat there, and she pulled in a breath. "Wow, thank you." She looked up at Cheryl and hugged her again. "I can add it to the wind chime on the porch."

"Wade says you love hummingbirds." She looked at him with love in her eyes, and he put his arm around her and brought her into his side. He wore his prosthetics today, and he'd already practiced getting down on one knee and then both knees. He needed help getting up, but Abby had assured him multiple times that there would be plenty of people willing to help him stand after he proposed to Cheryl.

Not only that, but she'd reassured him at least that many times that Cheryl would say yes to his question. Abby found it interesting how differently Wade could see things than she could.

"Dinner is almost ready," she said, handing her new hummingbird to Tex. "Look at my new wind chime gem."

"It's real pretty," he said, gazing at it and then her. "What do you need help with?"

"I've got the salad," her mom said, coming out of the kitchen.

"Have you met Cheryl's parents?" Abby asked, bringing Tex to her side too. She introduced him and then his son, and they shook hands with Cheryl's mom and dad. With her parents there, and Cheryl and hers, and Tex, everyone who'd been invited to Wade's birthday dinner had arrived.

The timer on the oven went off, and Abby turned that way. "Those are the pizza pockets." She hurried into the other room to get them out, then used a pair of tongs to put them on a cool platter.

She carried it out to the living room, where she'd also pushed all of the furniture against the walls while Wade had been out doing their morning farm chores. "Okay," she said with a sigh, looking around. Emotion jumped into the back of her throat, and she couldn't say anything else.

Seeing everyone there in their small living room—all the people she loved the most—snuck up on her and made her realize how very blessed she was.

She'd said she'd welcome everyone and lead them in Happy Birthday. "The cake," she blurted out, her voice too high. "My goodness, I forgot the cake."

"Abby," Wade said, but she'd already spun and dashed for the door. She pulled the sheet cake from the fridge, pocketed the candles and lighter she'd already gotten out, and returned to the living room.

"Wade wanted to do cake first," she said. "He's forty-three today, and that means he gets to have dessert first if he wants it." She beamed at him, the very solid rock in her life. "He's put up with me mothering him for the past five years, and that also deserves plenty of cake as well as his favorite dinner." She met Tex's eye, which was a mistake. Her emotions spiraled out of control again, and she managed to control them by clearing her throat.

"Let's sing," she said. "And then Tex, will you pray for us?"

He nodded, and she wished they were to the level where she could brush her lips against his and tell him thank you. She needed to find out why he hadn't kissed her yet. Maybe he was waiting for her to kiss him. Or for her to give him some sort of message that it would be okay to make a move.

Maybe she needed to ask him.

"Honey," her mom said, and Abby blinked, realizing she'd been giving directions and had blanked out.

"You don't have to have cake first," she said. "But anyone can who wants to. I made pizza pockets, which are Wade's favorite food. There are pepperoni and cheese ones, as well as spinach, chicken, and Alfredo. Those are marked with a little leaf of spinach on the top."

She nodded at the pizza pockets and then Tex. He swept that sexy cowboy hat off his head and waited for the other men to do the same. He looked at her as his eyes fell closed and he seemed to concentrate so hard before he started to speak.

Abby found him utterly adorable, and her chest and face heated as he said, "Lord, we're so grateful to be gathered her for Wade's birthday as family and friends. We acknowledge Thy hand in our lives, from the littlest things to the largest. Bless this house and those who live here that they'll have the blessings they need."

He paused, and Abby didn't dare look at him either. Her hands trembled, and she pressed them tighter against her arms. "Please bless this food. Amen."

"Amen," everyone said, and Abby stepped out of the way to make room for Wade. She'd done everything they'd rehearsed, and he took a couple of steps into the middle of the room and all the people, then turned toward Cheryl.

"Before we eat," he said, his voice gruff and low. Abby sent up a fast, silent prayer that he could do this to his liking. He dug in his pocket and took out the diamond ring he'd bought weeks ago.

Abby's lungs stormed as he dropped to one knee, his

bone making a thunk against the wood floor. She cringed, but no one else seemed to notice. Tex's warm hand slid along her hip and back as Wade made it down to his second knee.

"Wade," Cheryl said, her voice pitching up.

"I love you, sweetheart. I know our lives won't be easy, but I'd rather have a harder life with you in it than an easier one without you." He held up the ring. "Will you marry me?"

"Yes," she said instantly, and she fell to her knees in front of him too. Abby's eyes burned with tears, because Cheryl always knew exactly what to do to make Wade feel normal. She flung her arms around him and hugged him, then pulled back and kissed him quickly before he slid the ring on her finger.

"I love you," she said, looking at her hand and then cradling his face in her hands. He kissed her again, and then he stayed still while she put her hands on his shoulders to steady herself as she got to her feet. Then she stood very still and offered him both of her hands so he could get up too.

He managed it, though Abby saw her father twitch toward them, ready to help. The congratulations started then, and Abby's feelings assaulted her. She couldn't stay in this room.

She turned to leave, Tex's hand catching on her waistband. "Abby," he said, but she couldn't stay. She just couldn't.

She burst out of the front door and went down the steps, sucking at the August heat. It didn't matter. It held more oxygen than the engaged air inside. She went left across the lawn instead of right toward the driveway.

"Abby," Tex said after her, and she broke into a jog. She wouldn't be able to outrun him, and she'd have to explain. What, she didn't know. She didn't understand her feelings, which meant she couldn't tell someone else why she suddenly felt like sobbing her eyes out.

In the shade on the side of the house, she stopped and pulled in breath after breath. Tex came around the corner, anxiety emanating from him. "Abby." He strode toward her and took her by the shoulders. "Are you okay?"

She shook her head, a wildness inside her she couldn't name. "I'm happy for him."

"Of course you are." Tex drew her into his chest. "It's just a big change."

She wrapped her arms around him and held on tight. "A really big change." And Abby didn't like change that much. She needed gradual steps over time, and then she was okay. Or she could figure out how to be okay.

She sniffled and stepped back, wiping her eyes. She'd worked hard on her makeup that afternoon, and she couldn't go back into the house with messy mascara and red eyes.

Tex tucked her hair gently, the movement so tender and soft. "Talk to me, Abs. What else is going on?"

She took a steeling breath. "He and Cheryl want to live here. At the farmhouse. And they should. Of course they should. He's lived here and worked the farm for the majority of the past thirty years." He'd gone into the military for about five years before he'd gotten injured and returned.

She'd gone to college and then Chicago, and of course she couldn't live here and make Cheryl and Wade live somewhere else.

"When are they getting married?"

"Christmas, I think," she said, shaking her head. "I don't know. They'll have to set a date, but I know they've talked about Christmas."

"That's lots of time," he said, stroking his hand down the side of her face again. He ran one behind her head and curled his fingers along her neck.

She looked up at him, deciding she might as well expose herself completely. "I like you so much, Tex. Is there…? I mean, why haven't you kissed me yet?"

He searched her face, as sober as she'd ever seen him. He wasn't irritated with her, and he wasn't joking. Emotions ran rampant across his face, and then a half-smile kicked up the corner of his mouth.

"You want to kiss me?"

Abby ducked her head, but Tex brought it right back up. "Sorry, that was so arrogant. I'm dying to kiss you." He leaned down as she slid her hands up his chest. He hesitated for a moment, swallowing hard, and then she closed her eyes, telling him she was ready. Beyond ready.

His lips grazed hers, and fire licked down her throat and out to her arms. She wrapped her hands around the back of his neck, and when Tex touched his mouth to hers again, he really kissed her. Not a touch. Not a brush.

This was a *kiss*, and it was the most magnificent one

Abby had experienced since he'd kissed her the first time all those years ago.

She imagined herself to be living on that ranch and in the farmhouse next door that had been left dormant for so long. He'd put a new roof on it. He'd ripped out the old things and put in new ones. He'd made a lot of improvements, and he'd painted and stained worn wood to make it shine again.

While he'd been doing all of that, he'd been fixing all of the broken things inside of her too. He'd made her feel seen. He'd called her beautiful many times, and as he kissed her, she actually felt beautiful. He listened to her, and that had healed so much she hadn't even known needed to be healed.

He was a fixer, and she didn't mind him working on her, that was for sure. She hoped she fixed something inside him too, and because he kept kissing her, maybe she did.

CHAPTER
SEVENTEEN

Tex had never kissed a mouth that tasted like Abby's. Not even the first time he'd kissed her. His memory wasn't that good anyway, and this felt like a brand new first kiss he wanted to prolong and prolong so it never had to end.

He paid attention to where he put his hands, because Abby had clearly spent some time doing her hair and makeup for her brother's birthday. He didn't want to mess any of that up, because they'd have to go back inside and eat. People were probably already wondering where they were. Abby hadn't invited that many people to the party, and Tex felt blessed to have been invited at all.

A shiver ran across his shoulders, and he enjoyed the way Abby's fingers moved through his hair. He hadn't put his cowboy hat on again after the prayer, so he wouldn't have to pick it up afterward. That also meant he wouldn't have anything to hide behind.

He told himself he didn't need to hide from Abby. She'd trusted him with her emotions, and she'd told him how she felt in words and actions. He stroked his lips against hers, a growl moving through his whole body at the sweetness she introduced into his life.

He finally broke the kiss, the tightness in his chest telling him he needed to breathe deeper than kissing allowed. He kept his eyes closed and his face real close to hers, getting the floral hints of her perfume as well as the fruity taste of her mouth.

"Frosting," he whispered. That was what she tasted like. Not fruit. Frosting. He opened his eyes and put a bit more distance between them. Enough that he wouldn't have to go cross-eyed to look at her. "Abs, I like you a whole lot."

She smiled, and he wanted to drink it right up. He grinned too, matching his curved lips to hers. That didn't really work for a kiss, and he chuckled. "So much," he said, sobering. "Some days, I think I might be falling in love with you."

She pulled in a breath. "Tex."

"I'm serious," he said. "I've been afraid to kiss you, because then I would have to face that."

She leaned into him, her hands still up around his neck. "I can't believe a big, tall cowboy like you is afraid of anything."

"Just losing you," he whispered, letting his eyes drift closed as he pressed his cheek to hers.

"Why would you lose me?"

Tex's own fears and doubts roared through him. "There's so much in my life that isn't stable," he said. "When I have to go make the album, I might need help with Bryce."

"What else are good neighbors for?" Abby teased, and Tex pulled back and smiled at her again. He wanted to kiss her again, and he leaned in to get the job done.

"Dad?" his son called as if summoned by Tex saying his name a few moments ago.

He stepped out of Abby's arms with a sigh, and said, "Busted." He liked the way Abby giggled as he walked away from her, and he arrived at the corner of her house a moment later. "Right here, bud."

"Is Abby with you?" he asked, coming down the steps. "Her daddy is worried about her."

"Yeah, she's over here." Tex looked back toward her and found her fixing her hair. "She just...needed a minute. Couldn't breathe in there after that amazing proposal." He turned back to Bryce, hoping he didn't wear too much of Abby's lip gloss. He wasn't entirely sure she'd been wearing any, but he still had to force himself to keep his hand at his side.

Bryce slowed a few steps away, his phone ringing in his pocket. A startled look crossed his face, and Tex catalogued that. His son silenced his phone without answering it and said, "I'll tell her dad."

"I'm coming," Abby said, and Tex let her come up beside him. "Sorry, Bryce." She smiled at him as she went past Tex, not a look for him at all. She reached up and touched his son's face as she went by, something unspoken moving between them.

They both stood in the front yard and watched her go in, and then Tex asked, "What was that?"

"I was going to ask you the same thing," Bryce said, facing Tex once the front door closed. "You kissed her, didn't you?"

"Yes," Tex said, seeing no reason to deny it.

His son settled his weight on one foot. "Are you going to marry her?"

"I don't know," Tex said. "It was our first kiss, Bryce. You don't know stuff like that with a first kiss." At least he didn't want Bryce to think he should. He smiled at his son and slung his arm around him, turning him back toward the front door too. "Did you save me a pepperoni pocket?"

"Yes," Bryce said, and he didn't sound happy. Tex didn't know how to have this conversation with his nearly grown son, and he questioned whether now was a great time to be so involved with Abby. He had an album to make, a son to support through his senior year, and they still had plenty to do around the ranch and inside the house.

Otis had returned several days ago, and he wasn't doing great after his break-up with Isabella. He'd come home, and Tex wanted to make sure he could provide the support his brothers and parents needed too. He and Bryce had helped Dani and Mav with their kids while they got over the stomach flu, and he'd been grateful he was available and present to be able to do that.

Adding a serious relationship felt unwise to Tex, but

he'd also said the truth. He didn't want to lose Abby. Not again.

He followed his son back inside, where the party had continued without him. He found his hat hanging on the rack just inside the door, and he grabbed it and put it back on his head. Abby had an empty seat beside her, and Tex spotted his pizza pocket. Bryce said, "I didn't get you any salad."

"I'll get it," he said, giving his son a smile he hoped would convey to Bryce how appreciative he was. The boy had spent all summer with him. He'd made no attempt to find kids his own age and make friends, but he had been teaching guitar lessons to two of the Hammond kids. Chris and then Cy's boy, Thomas.

He served himself some green salad and took his seat between his son and Abby. He usually loved participating in conversations and getting to know people, but today, he just listened. He watched Wade and Cheryl, who obviously loved each other powerfully. He wondered what other people saw when they looked at him and Abby.

He wished he didn't worry so much about the unknown, but the truth was, without the safety and security of being in the band, where someone managed his life and schedule for him, Tex worried. He feared. He doubted. He hated not knowing when he'd be called back to Nashville, and what he'd do about Bryce at that time.

"How are you, Tex?" Abby's mother asked, and he pushed away the questions and put a smile on his face.

"Just fine, ma'am. You?" He prayed he could be present tonight and worry later, because he didn't need to come off as a sulky cowboy to his girlfriend's parents. The future would work itself out, because it usually did. Tex just needed to have faith that he could live his life without Mav managing it for him.

LATER THAT NIGHT, TEX KNEW THERE WAS A PROBLEM THE moment he opened the back door. The banging of pots and pans met his ears, and he tapped the door closed with his cowboy boot and went around the corner. "Bryce?"

His son threw him a death glare, and Tex couldn't stop himself from reaching up to wipe his mouth. He'd stayed over at Abby's to help her clean up after the birthday dinner, and yeah, he'd kissed her again before coming home. It wasn't a crime, as Mav had told Luke and Trace several times over the course of his dating relationship with Dani.

"Whoa," Tex said, bending down to scratch Franny behind the ears. "What did I do?" The canine sat right on his left foot, half protecting him and half comforting him.

Bryce cracked an egg with one hand, his head bent. Tex would be lucky if he saw his face during this conversation at all.

"Is Otis here?"

"Yeah," Bryce said. "I mean, no. He ran to town to get more salami and crackers so he doesn't have to leave the house tomorrow."

Otis stayed in the basement, on the couch in the living room, as the bedrooms downstairs weren't done yet. Tex had paid a landscaper to dig out part of the lawn to make a walk-out basement with steps leading up to the patio he'd poured when the deck had been framed. In the beginning, there'd been so much progress around the house and ranch, and now Tex felt like it had slowed.

"Did he say something to you?"

"No," Bryce clipped out. "I mean, not something he shouldn't have." He kept cracking eggs, finally tossing the broken shells into the sink and facing Tex. "You still have an album to make."

"I know," Tex said.

"Otis has been writing songs like mad since he got here, and he's got a call on Monday with King Country."

Tex swallowed, because this was exactly what he'd been worried about for weeks now. "All right."

"No, it's not *all right*, Dad," Bryce said, picking up the milk and splashing some into his bowl. "They're gonna call you back to Nashville. They'll call you back, and you'll have to go. You have a contract."

"Bryce."

"And school starts in three weeks. Here, Dad. What am I supposed to do? Transfer to freaking Nashville?" His chest heaved, and he whipped those eggs as if punishing them for Tex's country music contract.

"Son," Tex said, risking his life as he moved over to the countertop where Bryce worked and took the fork from him. "Stop for a second."

Bryce wore the angriest look Tex had ever seen, beating the one he'd given him in April when Tex had shown up to get him for Mav's wedding. Then, he'd begged Tex to ask

Corrie if he could have him for the summer and for senior year. He hadn't wanted to live with her anymore, and Tex felt like he'd done everything wrong in the boy's life right now.

Bryce's fury cracked and a sob lurched from him. Tex tossed the fork, not caring where it landed, and wrapped his son up tightly in his arms. "Hey," he said, his voice as soothing as he could make it. "I'm right here, and I'm not going anywhere."

Bryce gripped him tightly too. "How, Dad? *How* are you not going anywhere?"

"I...I'm working on it," he said, but his mind was still blank. He'd been praying for an answer to this exact problem, and nothing had come. Absolutely nothing. Standing in his kitchen, holding his emotional, worried son, Tex still couldn't come up with a solution to the album he was contractually obligated to make.

He couldn't let his label down. He couldn't let down Otis, Luke, and Trace. They all counted on him to be there to sing the lyrics that Otis wrote so beautifully. Yes, since Otis had been back in Coral Canyon, he'd written an entire album's worth of songs at lightning speed. He'd told Tex that country music came easier when he wasn't happy, but Tex hated that he wasn't happy.

Otis claimed he'd find his way back to living joyfully again, but if Tex didn't specifically ask him to help with a project around the house or ranch, Otis spent most of the day at the dining room table, writing music or lyrics.

With Trace and Luke in town too, the usual talk

surrounding a new album had been at an all-time high. Tex's anxiety was too, and so was Bryce's, obviously.

"Listen," Tex said, stepping back. He held Bryce with his fingers around the back of the boy's neck, his thumbs going up in front of his ears. "You're my son, and I will always choose you first. I know I've been awful about that in the past, but that changed this spring."

"How are you going to make an album in Nashville while I go to senior year here?"

"I'm not going to Nashville," Tex said, a ray of heavenly light appearing in his mind. "I'm going to build a recording studio right here on the ranch."

Bryce looked at him with pure hope in his eyes. He searched Tex's face, and Tex started to laugh. "Yeah," he said. "That's right. There's two hundred acres here. We'll put up a barn, and we'll fill it with a recording studio."

"Dad," Bryce said, his voice mostly made of air.

"What?" Tex said, releasing his son. "It makes sense." He paced away from the stove, his mind whirring now. "All the boys are here. We live here. We shouldn't have to all fly to Nashville and find apartments while we record. How long can it take to build a studio? I get the equipment and install it, and we're good to go."

He turned back to Bryce, his own hope starting to lift. He'd been stewing over this for weeks, and he couldn't believe it had taken him this long to come to this solution. Just like it had taken him a while to get up the gumption to kiss Abby.

"This could work, right?"

Bryce went back to his eggs, pouring them into the hot

pan, where they hissed as it had been heating for too long. "You're the charmer, Dad." He looked over to Tex. "Work your magic on your producer."

Tex didn't believe he possessed any magic, but he knew he couldn't go to Nashville for months on end to make the last album on his contract. The other boys might be able to, but Tex had Bryce full-time now, and he wasn't going to send him back to Corrie in Boise. He wasn't going to ask Abby and Wade to watch him for months.

He'd thought about asking his parents, but Tex was tired of having someone else take care of his responsibilities. No. It was time for him to be the father he should've been this whole time, and he wasn't leaving Bryce here and recording in Nashville.

Bryce had just plated his scrambled eggs when the doorbell rang. They looked at one another, and Tex asked, "Are you expecting someone?"

"No," Bryce said, putting his plate on the table and sitting down. He could see the front door from his spot, but he nodded toward it while he forked up a bite of his second dinner.

Tex rolled his eyes and went to answer the door. He pulled it open, and a pretty blonde woman stood there. Tex cocked his head and said, "Good evening."

She carried a plate of cookies in her hands and a look of apprehension on her face. "Good evening," she said politely. "Is Bryce here?"

"Bailey?" Bryce jogged to the door now, his dinner forgotten. He tried to muscle Tex out of the way, but Tex wasn't having any of that. "Hey, Bailey." He exhaled like he'd run a mile not ten steps.

"I texted," she said. "But you must not have seen it." She flicked her gaze toward Tex, who pressed into the back of the couch and stared at the side of his son's face. Bryce ignored him with supreme perfection and took the cookies.

"Let's talk outside." He went out onto the front porch with the very pretty Bailey No-Last-Name, and pulled the door closed behind him.

Tex moved over to the window and peered through it, but Bryce wasn't stupid. He didn't sit with Bailey on the front porch. He took her back down the sidewalk, and they moved out of Tex's line of sight.

Tex held his ground in the living room and started researching what he needed to build a recording studio in a barn that didn't exist yet. Ten minutes later, the front door opened again, and Bryce walked in, a soft, happy smile on his face.

Oh, Tex had seen a smile like that on a man's face before. "Who's Bailey?" he asked.

Bryce yelped and dropped the plate of cookies. "Jeez, Dad, have you been standing there the whole time?"

"Yes, sir," Tex said, moving to stand in front of his son. "Who's Bailey?"

"You've met her, so calm down." Bryce went past him and into the kitchen. "It's Bailey McAllister. She's Graham Whittaker's step-daughter." He took his cold eggs to the garbage and started scraping them into it. "We met her at the Fourth of July thing at the park they invited us to."

"Ah." Tex kept his eye on Bryce, who smartly opened

the fridge and leaned into it, using the door to block himself. "And you're...seeing her?"

"No, Dad," Bryce said, like Tex's question was the dumbest one ever asked.

"Have you broken up with Jenny?"

Bryce sighed the sigh of the century as he closed the fridge. "Yes, okay? Yes, I broke up with her. I didn't see the point. She lives in Boise, which is hundreds of miles from here. I'm not going back there, and she's not coming here."

Tex's eyebrows went up. "When did this happen?"

"I don't know. Last week?"

Tex ignored the swooping in his stomach that testified of how left out he felt. He thought Bryce told him everything. "And we've been texting Bailey since...?"

"It's friendly," Bryce said. "She's going to college in Montana in a month, Dad."

"But you like her."

"So what?"

"She likes you." He had eyes, after all.

"Again, so what?" Bryce folded his arms and glared at Tex.

"Son." Tex marched toward his boy. "You can't be dating her now and have her leave. I did that to Abby twenty years ago, and it hurts. She'll hurt you."

"I'm not dating her." Bryce looked right into his eyes, and Tex couldn't tell if he was lying or not.

"I hurt her," Tex said, his voice breaking. "And I've hurt you, and I've been working *so* hard to fix it all this summer." He realized in that moment the reason why he'd been laboring so hard around this ranch. He was trying to fix *everything* he'd neglected for the past two decades.

"Dad," Bryce said quietly, his bluster falling. "You haven't hurt me. You've got to stop beating yourself up about that."

"I wasn't there for you when you needed me."

"Actually," Bryce said. "You were. You *were*, Dad. Every single time. You didn't miss a birthday, and remember how you fixed things when she scared me with all the drinking? And when I needed to get away from Mom, you were there, no questions asked. You got full custody of me when I needed you to, and you really have to stop trying to make up for something that doesn't need to be made up for."

Tex didn't know how to sort through the jumble of emotions in his gut. He grabbed onto Bryce and hugged him again. "I love you," he said.

"I love you too, Dad." Bryce pounded him on the back and stepped away. "Aaaand…I might have a date with Bailey tomorrow night."

"What?" The word exploded from his mouth. "You just said you weren't dating her."

"I'm not," Bryce said. "One date is not dat*ing*."

"I don't understand," Tex said, frowning.

Bryce chuckled and shook his head. "Otis is back. You can ask him about it."

"Right," Tex said, turning as Bryce went past him. "I'm going to ask my heartbroken brother about how young people date. That's *such* a great idea."

"Okay," Bryce said over his shoulder. "I'm going to play with Jordan and Woody."

"I want to see your phone before you go to bed," Tex called after him, and not three seconds later, the front door opened, and Otis said, "Some help here, Tex?"

Before Tex could get to his brother, he dropped the twelve-pack of soda he'd been trying to bring in with four other grocery sacks hanging from his arm.

CHAPTER
EIGHTEEN

A bby tried to dodge the evening wind as she ran toward The Magic Noodle. One couldn't actually avoid wind, and it pulled at her hair and tugged against her blouse. She'd left the library a while ago, but the groceries in the back of her SUV hadn't shopped themselves.

Tex had then called about going to dinner, and she hadn't wanted to. It had been a very busy week, what with Wade's birthday, all the cooking and prep for that, the near mental breakdown over his engagement, and then that kiss with Tex last night.

More than one kiss, actually, but Abby wasn't counting. She smiled every time she thought about Tex, and when she'd suggested she grab something and then eat in that night, he'd agreed.

"Hey," she said to the girl at the cash register. "I have

an order for Tex Young." He'd called it in, and she could see it on the counter behind the woman.

"Just a sec," she said, bending her head toward a woman standing with her. The Magic Noodle was busy already, but it was a Friday night. The waiting area held quite a few people, but this restaurant had those buzzers, so there could be more in the nearby shops.

Abby just wanted her food, and then she'd run by Georgia's shop to confirm lunch next week.

Someone approached the counter too, and Abby glanced over, edging out of the way. Tex had said he'd pay, and all she had to do was grab and go. The food was right there. She could see his name on the receipt.

She did a double-take as her brain caught up with her eyes. "Bryce?"

He looked at her fully, surprise coloring his expression. "Abby," he said, and he leaned in for a quick hug. That meant he had to release the hand of the woman at his side, and Abby's pulse picked up speed. Did Tex know about this date?

Abby couldn't keep a secret from him. Bryce shifted his feet and indicated the pretty blonde woman. Abby pulled in a breath. "Bailey," she said. "How are you?"

Bailey McAllister hugged her too. "I'm good, Miss Abby. How's the library?"

"We close early on Friday nights," she said. "Thankfully."

Bailey laughed lightly, her hand slipping right back into Bryce's. Abby certainly didn't blame her, but…. "Are you still at Montana State?" she asked.

"Yes," Bailey said, shooting a look at Bryce. "Heading back in a few weeks."

"Back?" he asked, and Abby's stomach fell to her shoes.

"Yes," Bailey said lightly. "I'm a sophomore there this year."

"You are?" He searched her face. "I thought you'd just graduated from high school."

She shook her head and pressed her lips together. The woman looked at Abby again, and of course Abby knew Sierra Selzer. "I'm sorry. You said Tex Young?"

"Yes." Abby cleared her throat. "I can see it right there."

Sierra turned and picked up the single plastic bag of food. "It's all paid. There you go."

"Thank you," Abby said, turning toward Bryce. He still held Bailey's hand, so her being *two* years older than him must not be that big of a deal. The discontent in his eyes suggested otherwise, and she stepped in closer to him. "You're still going to come help me with those barrels in the morning, right?"

"Yes, ma'am," he said, something unspoken moving between them. She liked Bryce a lot, because he worked hard and respected his father.

"Great," she said. "See you then." She walked away, willing to keep her thoughts to herself until morning.

The following day, she found Bryce by her stables when she backed up in Wade's truck. "Morning," she said to him as she dropped from the truck and pulled on her gloves.

He turned and tipped his cowboy hat at her. "Morning, Miss Abby."

She indicated the row of barrels. "We need to get these into the back of Wade's truck. He's taking them to town for the flea market."

"Okay." Bryce wore gloves too, because she'd texted him to bring some. She couldn't lift a barrel by herself, and together, she and Bryce loaded all six of them into the back of her brother's truck. The job had taken maybe ten minutes, and Abby hadn't said anything to him about Bailey.

"You know," she said, peeling her gloves off. "I dated your dad in high school. He was a year ahead of me, and he graduated and went off to college while I stayed here."

Bryce looked at her with some interest, but mostly wariness in his eyes. "I've heard that."

That surprised her, but she just nodded. "It sure seemed like you didn't know Bailey was a sophomore."

"I didn't." He hung his head, and he looked so much like Tex doing it. She hoped to the heavens above she wasn't overstepping.

"I didn't tell your dad I ran into you two last night."

"No?" Bryce looked up. "He must have some sixth sense or something, because he questioned me relentlessly about Bailey last night."

Abby smiled at him. "Did he?"

"He was wearin' the same look you are right now."

She looked away, because she could never hide her true feelings. "And what's that?"

"Worry," Bryce said. "Concern."

"I can live with that," Abby said, moving her gaze back to his. "I do worry about you, Bryce. You're a good boy. You don't deserve to be left behind the way I was."

Bryce's Adam's apple bobbed as he swallowed. "My dad feels so bad about that," he said. "He beats himself up about it daily."

Abby frowned, as Tex had apologized almost the very week he'd returned to Coral Canyon. "Really?"

"Really."

Abby shelved that away to deal with later. "I'm sure she won't mean to hurt you. Bailey is a good girl too. She used to come into the library all the time. Studied more than anyone else I saw that year. She was the valedictorian, and she earned big scholarships to any school she applied to."

Bryce took his gloves off too. "She did tell me that. I guess maybe I misunderstood when she'd graduated. She said she told me, but I don't remember."

Abby gave him a partial smile. "Maybe you were blinded by her beauty."

Bryce chuckled and didn't deny it. "Maybe." He took a big breath and looked at her. "You think I should break up with her."

"Are you dating?"

"No," Bryce said. "I mean, maybe."

Abby stepped over to him and patted his chest. "Bryce, I think I'd figure out if I was dating before I decided if I needed to break up with someone."

"Fair point."

She moved to get behind the wheel so she could drive

Wade's truck back to the house. "And of course, it really doesn't matter what I think. I'm not your mom. But I do like you, Bryce, and I don't want to see you get hurt the way I was. It was not pleasant, and no one wants to feel left out or left behind."

She paused and looked at him, watching what she'd said sink into his ears. "Okay?"

"Yes, ma'am," he said quietly.

She got behind the wheel and reached to close the door just as he said, "Abby?"

The door slammed, and she quickly rolled down the window. "Yeah?"

"I know you're not my mom, but you're great." He came up beside her window. "I like you too."

"Thank you," she said, a genuine smile lifting her lips.

"Do you think...I mean, if my dad...uh...if you guys got married, you'd be my step-mom, right?"

"Yes," she said, trying to keep all emotion out of her voice. He'd be an adult before that happened. Tex had said his birthday was in December, and he'd be eighteen then.

"Would you...would you like that?"

"I—" She didn't know how to answer, and she didn't know the situation with his mother. "I'm not what anyone would call maternal or nurturing. But if Tex and I got married, I would work very hard to be a good stepmother, I think."

Bryce smiled at her and said, "I think you would too." He backed up and waved, then turned and jogged toward the ranch next door.

Abby watched him go, the questions he'd asked

revolving through her mind. A feeling of peace moved through her when everything finally aligned. Bryce liked her. He thought she was great, and that she'd be a good mother figure for him.

She had serious reservations about that, but she would try hard. She'd had a sensitive conversation with him, and neither of them had gotten upset. That had to count for something, right?

She hoped so, because she was starting to feel big things for Tex Young, and she hoped she would be part of his life for a long time to come. Bryce was an integral part of Tex's life, and that meant he'd be part of hers too.

––––––––

"THERE SHE IS," SHE SAID AS DANI CAME AROUND THE corner. She lifted her hand, and Dani came toward her, reaching up to pull her ponytail tighter.

"Sorry I'm late," she said, giving Abby a quick hug. She looked at the other two women at the table, pure nerves in her eyes.

"This is Georgia Beck," she said, indicating the curly-haired woman against the wall on her side of the booth. Abby slid back into the booth while Georgia said hello to Dani. "She owns the bookshop just down the street."

"My kids love that shop," Dani said. "I haven't seen you in there though."

"I have an assistant in the summer," Georgia said. "We're so busy, I spend a lot of time in the back or in my office." She smiled at Dani, then Cheryl, and then Abby.

"And Cheryl Watts," she said, indicating the woman Dani had just sat beside. "She's engaged to my brother, Wade." She grinned at Cheryl as she said hello to Dani.

"Guys, this is Danielle Young. She works at the library with me, and she's Mav's wife. Mav is Tex's brother."

Abby wasn't usually the one to bring friends together, but these women represented the three sides of her life. A friend she'd known for years. A future sister-in-law. And a co-worker and possible future sister-in-law.

None of Tex's other brothers were dating right now, and Abby thought it would be nice to get to know Dani better.

"How long have you been in Coral Canyon?" Georgia asked, reaching for her soda.

"I moved here just before Christmas last year," Dani said. "Mav and I got married in April."

Congratulations went around, and Abby felt like a brand new person. It took a long time and a lot of conversations for her to trust people and truly let them in. She and Georgia had been lunching together for years, but that relationship had literally taken that long to cultivate. They both loved books, and they both worked with them on different aisles.

Bringing Cheryl into the group had felt natural, as Abby only had the one brother and she wanted to enjoy family events where they all celebrated together. Cheryl was literally the nicest person alive, so it hadn't been hard to let her into her heart.

She knew Dani decently well through their work at the library, but she'd been at Tex's over the weekend, and

Abby had been texting with Georgia about lunch. She'd felt the prompting whisper telling her to invite Dani, so she had.

"Tex is doing amazing things with that ranch," Cheryl said, and all eyes turned to Abby.

She sipped her cola and nodded. "He's a miracle worker."

"Yeah," Georgia said with a grin as wide as the moon. "He got you to go out with him."

Dani looked at her with open curiosity on her face. Cheryl giggled, and Abby couldn't deny it. "Sometimes you just need the right person to come in and start cleaning out the cobwebs, you know?" She nudged Georgia. "I don't see you dating anyone."

"CJ keeps calling," Georgia said with a sigh. Her whole countenance fell, and Abby's internal alarms went off.

"You're ignoring him, right?" She looked from her best friend to the two women across the table. "CJ is her *ex*-boyfriend, and he's really bad at understanding what 'break up' means."

"Oh," Dani said.

"I'm ignoring him," Georgia said. "He comes into the shop sometimes. That's awkward."

"Does he do anything?" Cheryl asked.

"No, not really." Another sigh told Abby that CJ's presence in the shop bothered Georgia more than she'd admit. She knew Cheryl a little bit, as the three of them had gone to lunch a few times now. But Dani was brand new to the group, and Georgia wouldn't say much in front of her. Especially not much negative.

She had a glass half full mentality, and she gave everyone the benefit of the doubt. She gave them second and third and fourth chances, which was why CJ was still sniffing around.

"Maybe you need a new boyfriend," Abby said. "He'd get it then."

"Yeah," Georgia said, her blue-green eyes lighting up. "That's not a bad idea." She took another drink of her soda. "I don't suppose you ladies know where I can just pick me up one of those?" She trilled out a laugh, and the others joined in.

"I met Mav on a dating app," Dani said, and everyone's eyebrows went up. She laughed and nodded. "It was really great, actually." She looked at Cheryl. "How did you meet Wade?"

"We met at a cider tasting," she said, the happiest look crossing her face. "He was there with his parents, and I don't know. There was something about him that made me look twice."

"That would be the prosthetic legs," Abby said, smiling for all she was worth at Cheryl. Cheryl didn't say anything but simply shook her head and looked down at the table.

"He's handsome," she said. "He has the kindest spirit. I noticed his prosthetics, but they aren't why I looked twice."

Abby loved her in that moment, because she'd seen the really important things about Wade the very first time they'd met. "I live next door to Tex," she said. "Now, *and* when we dated as teens. So Georgia, what are your neighbors like?"

Georgia's expression grew horrified, and she shook her head. "Nope. I'm not dating a neighbor." She shuddered, and everyone at the table laughed.

"Might be a dating app then," Dani said, her blue eyes twinkling with friendship and fun.

"Or you better start getting out more," Cheryl said. "The apple cider tasting is coming up. They do it out at the Foxhill orchards. The ones on the way up to Dog Valley?"

"I've been," Abby said, "Not for a long time though." She looked at Georgia.

"I try to avoid the outdoors," Georgia said with an uppity hint in her voice.

"Oh, honey," Dani said. "No wonder you can't meet anyone. You know you live in Wyoming, right? Literally *everyone* I've met here adores the outdoors."

Georgia blinked at her, but Dani's smile held only playful notes that Abby started to giggle. Cheryl did too, and she said, "She's right, Georgia." She picked up her phone. "So let's see what there is that's outdoor adjacent."

"What's outdoor adjacent?" Georgia asked.

"You know, like things where you're outside for only a few minutes," Cheryl said.

"On flat ground," Abby added.

"In the summer," Dani said.

Cheryl looked up from her phone. "There's an ATV ride-along up into the hills."

Abby burst out laughing while Georgia's look turned into something sharp enough to cause death. "She's not a personal vehicle person," Abby said, still giggling. "No snowmobiles, ATVs, boats, canoes, dirt bikes, any of that."

Cheryl went back to her phone, and Abby grinned at the other two at the table. She reached across it and covered Dani's hand. "Thank you for coming. It's fun to get to know you better."

"You too," Dani said, and Abby looked at Georgia again.

She put her arm around Abby and said, "I'm glad you're happy, my friend."

"Me too," Abby said, leaning her head against Georgia's. She'd been unhappy for so long, she hadn't even remembered what happy felt like. Now that she did, she wanted to hold onto it and let it erase all the disappointments and setbacks in her life. "I feel rebuilt, and it's nice," she admitted.

"It's amazing what a handsome cowboy boyfriend can do," Georgia said with a grin. Abby didn't argue with her. Yes, Tex had stitched together a lot of the things that had been quietly weeping in Abby's life. She felt like she'd been working on herself for such a long time, trying to be a better version of herself each day, and no one had seen it. No one had acknowledged it.

But Tex did. Tex had healed her, and he'd seen how she'd changed and the work she'd done on herself. She hoped she would be enough to keep his attention this time, that she would be important enough to him to keep him in town when he had the opportunity to leave.

Familiar anxiety rose up her throat, but then Cheryl said, "I've got it, Georgia." Her face glowed as she glanced up. "There's a five-K in two weeks, and they need volunteers to help check people in." She put her phone down as if she was dropping a mic. "That's it. That's what you need to do."

Georgia looked at Abby with questions in her eyes. Abby shrugged one shoulder. "It's not like you'd be *running* the five-K, and maybe you'll meet a man with running muscles." They all laughed again, and Abby thanked the Lord for this new level of happiness and friendship in her life.

CHAPTER
NINETEEN

Tex stood at the back window in his bedroom, the one that faced west and looked out over the ranch. The deck had been finished yesterday—sealed and ready for use—and the foundation for the new barn-slash-recording-studio had been dug the day before that.

The huge cement trucks had come yesterday, all while he looked for horses online. He and Bryce had done a metric ton of work around the ranch and farmhouse in the past couple of months, and his son would start senior year in just two more weeks.

He'd decided he didn't have to do so much anymore. He'd hired someone to finish the floor in the basement so it was level, and then he'd order carpet for the family room down there, as well as the bedrooms, and tile for the bathroom.

The progress on the walk-out part of the basement was

still happening, and then Tex would be done with the house. It looked completely different than it had when he and Bryce had stopped by, almost three months ago.

It was a different color, with a new roof that shone like motor oil in the sunshine. The barn would be the same, and Tex could only pray that when King Country called, he'd be able to convince them to let him and his brothers record right here on the property.

It would be ideal for everyone. The arguments he'd been amassing in his head started again, and Tex turned away from the three men outside, all of them working to organize the lumber they'd use to frame. The concrete foundation had to cure for at least seven days, and that was seven more days Tex was behind.

Anxiety built beneath his tongue no matter how hard he tried to swallow. He picked up his phone from the nightstand where it was plugged in and yanked out the power cord. He looked at the screen as it brightened, a picture of him and Bryce grinning at the camera meeting his eyes.

Bryce had gone fishing with a couple of the Hammonds —Hunter and Gray and Wes, if Tex remembered right. He'd enjoyed teaching the guitar lessons that summer, and he was really good with kids. His son would excel in music, Tex knew that.

He sank onto the bed. "I just don't want him to make the same mistakes I did." He tilted his head back and looked up at the ceiling. "Please, Lord. Don't let him make the same mistakes I did."

When Tex looked at his phone again, the time had

come to make the call he'd been dreading for a week now. Otis has been in Louisville for the past four days, and every message from him told Tex they were getting closer and closer to recording.

He tapped and found Taylor's name. He practically punched the phone to get it to dial, and then he lightly tapped the speakerphone, feeling wild and nervous beyond anything he'd felt in the past several years.

Maybe. not as nervous as he'd been to talk to Corrie about Bryce moving in with him, and oh, then the two of them leaving Boise. Both of those had darn near put Tex in the hospital. But he'd done them, because Bryce needed him to be his champion, and Tex wanted to be that protective father for his son.

This was no different.

"Tex Young," Taylor said with a laugh. "How's my favorite country music Rockstar?"

Tex grinned too, because his agent always made him feel like the most important person in the word. "Just fine, Taylor," he said. "You?"

"Oh, I'm gettin' by," Taylor said. "I heard from Otis yesterday. He says things are going well with Larry at King Country."

"Yeah, I heard the same thing," Tex said, getting up from the bed and pacing back over to the door. He wished the barn he'd imagined and had sketched by a contractor stood there, ready for cowboys who could sing, instruments, and music producers.

"So why are you calling me?" Taylor asked, never one to drag things out.

Tex sighed, and somehow all of his nerves dried up. "I can't record in Nashville this time, Taylor. I need you to do something about the contract that will allow us to record here in Coral Canyon."

Taylor didn't say anything, and Tex didn't like that. He felt like he needed to fill the silence with more explanation, but he held his tongue.

"I'm pulling up your contract now," he said. "Let's see what it says. They don't often say *where* something needs to be recorded, only that it does...."

"I'm building a recording studio on the land I bought at the beginning of the summer," Tex said. "I'll do it to their specifications. I'll meet with them to get those, go over what they need, all of it. But it won't be done right away."

"How long?" Taylor asked.

"Uh, I don't know," Tex said. "We'll need to talk to them about equipment and whatnot."

"They'll have to fly their sound engineers out there."

"It's a trade-off," Tex said, his argument for that ready to fly from the tip of his tongue. "They'd fly us all to Nashville to record. So they'll fly a few people here instead."

"Mm." Taylor was probably reading, so Tex let him do that, pressing his eyes closed into the silence and praying that the contract didn't specify that the album had to be recorded in Nashville. "All right, Tex." Taylor let out a long breath. "There's no stipulation in the Country Quad contract that says you have to record at the King Country studios."

A smile burst onto Tex's face. "Perfect." Heaven had

smiled on him, and Tex tilted his head back and thanked the Lord silently.

"You have clauses about producers and sound engineers, and as you know, they don't usually work on one album at a time. A few hours each day, right?"

"Yeah," Tex said, moving his gaze outside again. "I'll talk to them. If I know the contract, I can talk to Meryl." His producer had been a Godsend for Country Quad, and Tex didn't want to burn any bridges. He simply couldn't afford to light the ones he'd built here in Coral Canyon on fire either. The casualties would be far too high. Bryce's and Abby's faces both flashed through his mind, and he couldn't lose either one of them. Not again.

"It'll be expensive for them to send their big wigs up to Wyoming and spend their time *only* with you."

"I hear you," Tex said. "What else won't they like?"

"Where are they going to stay in Coral Canyon?"

"I can work out accommodations," he said. Or Mav could. Morris could. They'd all found places to stay that summer, and there seemed to be plenty of rentals in Coral Canyon.

"How long will the album take?"

"I don't know. Otis is working on that."

"The two of you should go in there with a plan," Taylor said. "Heck, all four of you. Are your brothers on-board with this idea?"

Tex didn't answer, because he couldn't. "I'll talk to them," he finally said.

"Mm hm," Taylor said. "I'm going to email you the contract for these last three albums. That's what we're operating from right now. Then you'll have it if you need it."

"Yes, sir," Tex said, though he relied on his agent to negotiate the contracts and understand what was in them.

"And Tex," Taylor said. "Lisa at King Country called me last week, wanting to know what the band's plans were. They're interested in more albums."

Tex turned around and walked away from the windows. "That's great," he said.

"It sounds like you're not going to be traveling much anymore," Taylor said. "So is it great?"

"There might be a different version of the band," Tex admitted. "What that is, I don't know."

"You're their star."

"Right now," Tex said with a frown. He opened his bedroom door and left the room. "There are others who could be stars."

"All right," Taylor said with some level of doubt. "Just so you know where they'll be coming from."

"Thank you, Taylor." Tex hung up and paced the length of the kitchen a couple of times. He'd just had one hard conversation, and he had at least one more to get through. Probably two or three or four.

"Start with one," he said, and he got back on his phone to the band group text. His fingers flew, and surprisingly, it only took two minutes and four paragraphs to spell out what he wanted to do with the barn he was building out back.

He read over the message and fixed a couple of typos, took a deep breath, and sent it.

He immediately navigated away from that string, which would blow up in a matter of seconds, he was sure, and called Abby.

"Howdy," she drawled at him, clearly smiling and flirting with him.

A smile came to his face again. "Howdy yourself," he said back. "Wondering if you're free for dinner tonight."

"As a matter of fact," she said, and Tex tensed for a rejection. "I am."

He sighed, his smile still stuck in place. "Great," he said. "Out or in?"

"Let's go out," she said.

"Perfect," he said. "I'll swing by your place about six, okay?"

"Okay."

That wasn't Tex's hard conversation with Abby—that would come that evening when he took her to dinner. He said, "Bye, Abs," and ended the call. Ignoring the swarming bees in his stomach and the band group text, he instead called Bryce.

"Hey, Dad," his son said after three or four rings. "Sorry, I nearly dropped my phone in the lake." He chuckled, and Tex did too. He wanted to be everything for his son, and he couldn't believe he'd ever chosen something different.

"Okay, don't freak out," he said. "But we need to go to Nashville before school starts. I want to take them the things we've been working on this summer. We can play for them, show them the music, even make a few demos before we go if you want. I want to introduce you around, and—" His throat tightened, and Tex cleared it. "And I have to figure out how to get them to let us record here, in Coral Canyon."

Bryce took a moment, and then he said, "Okay. When are we going?"

"I'm going to call them right after this and set something up for next week. Could be as early as Monday."

"All right."

"Bryce." Tex had so much to say, and no words to put his feelings into.

"I know, Dad," his son said quietly. A few seconds went by, and then he said, "You'll find a way to make it work," in a bright voice. "You always do."

"I'm going to try," Tex said with only misery flowing through him. "I really am."

"You'll get what you want," Bryce said. "It's your superpower." He laughed, and that helped lighten the mood.

"Love you, son," he said.

"Love you too, Dad."

With that done, Tex dialed Meryl in Nashville, knowing he'd get the man's secretary. Sure enough, Jason answered with, "Meryl Osbourne's office. How can I help you?"

"Jason," Tex boomed, hoping to come across as upbeat and positive. "It's Tex Young."

"Tex!" Jason burst out laughing and said, "We were literally just talking about you ten minutes ago."

"I need to get down there and talk to Meryl," he said. "When can we make that happen?" He faced the fridge, where a small calendar sat, the picture of the real estate agent who'd dropped it off in the corner. Tex had no plans, and as long as he could get Bryce back here before the first day of school, he'd do whatever Jason said.

"How about Tuesday?" Jason said. "We just talked to Otis today too, but I think he's headed home for the weekend."

"Is he?" Tex asked. "I'll have to check my messages. Those boys in the band send so many, I have that string on silent." He forced a chuckle out of his mouth as another call came in.

He pulled the phone away from his ear to see who it was as Jason confirmed a meeting with the music producer on Tuesday at ten-thirty only to see Otis's name.

Tex swallowed and went back to his call. "Tuesday at ten-thirty," he said. "Jason, I'll have my son with me. We want to talk about Country Quad and our next album, of course. But Bryce and I have some stuff to show Meryl."

"I've got you down," Jason confirmed without giving Tex any grief at all about bringing Bryce and new music. That call ended, and Tex was almost done with the things he had to do before talking to Abby that evening.

Gathering his courage, he held it close and tapped to open the group text again. As he'd predicted, everyone in the band—including Morris—had responded multiple times. He scanned quickly, seeing several positive responses, including one from Morris that said, *I'd love to be closer to Mama and Daddy. Make it happen Tex!*

"Yeah," Tex whispered to himself. If he could just wave a magic wand and make things happen, his anxiety wouldn't have eaten a hole in his stomach.

His phone rang again, and this time, Tex answered the call from Otis with, "Sorry, I was on the phone with Jason, scheduling a meeting for next week."

"Oh, boy," Otis said with a chuckle. "Catch me up with what's goin' on inside your head, brother."

Tex took a big breath, because there was so much to tell. "All right," he said with a smile, exhaling out that breath. "But you asked for it."

———

WHEN ABBY OPENED THE DOOR AT HER PLACE LATER THAT evening, Tex's spirits already soared somewhere above Coral Canyon. She stepped back and finished putting in her right earring, and Tex couldn't move though he wanted to.

She wore a forest green dress with short sleeves and a wide leather belt around her waist. The hem of the dress fell to her knees, and she wore a pair of cowgirl boots with it, no colored stitching in sight.

"Evening, Tex," she drawled, and that seemed to thaw him.

"You are gorgeous," he said, the words scraping his dry throat. He stepped into her house then, knowing Wade wasn't home. He'd seen the man leave, freshly showered and dressed for his own Friday-night date, a half-hour ago.

Tex closed the door with the heel of his cowboy boot and took his girlfriend into his arms. He barely had time to inhale properly before he kissed her. She melted into his touch, and he sure did like that. He liked the way she pressed into him, and the shivers her fingernails sent scattering across his shoulders.

He liked the way she tasted like milk and honey—she'd probably eaten her favorite treat, graham crackers soaked in milk—and he liked the heady scent of her perfume in his nose every time he inhaled.

"Tex," she whispered as she gently pushed him back. She searched his face, and he let her. "Good day?"

"Yes," he said, grinning and swooping down for another kiss. "You? Or did you have to have your graham crackers after work to soothe something?"

She giggled as he moved his mouth along the column of her neck. "It was an okay day. Nothing too bad."

"You just like graham crackers."

"Guilty," she said, pulling in a breath when his lips tasted her earlobe. "You're handsy tonight."

"I missed you." He did slide his palms along her waist as he stepped back, a hint of humiliation pulling his head down. "Are you ready?"

"Yes," she said. "How could you miss me? You came over this morning and helped with the chickens."

Tex turned away from her, too many dangerous things in the back of his throat. He was good at hiding how he felt, but he needed a moment to cage it all away. "Maybe I want to be with you all the time." He opened the door and went out onto the porch, where more oxygen cleared his head.

Abby joined him, her hand slipping into his. "What's got you so happy?"

"Talked to Otis today," he said, leading her down the

steps. "He wasn't surprised when I told him Bryce and I have been working on some music I want to try out on the new album." He didn't dare look at her, not yet.

"That's good," she said after a beat of silence, her voice pitched up. He opened her door and met her eyes then. She drew strength into herself and climbed up, her jaw clenching and unclenching in time with her pulse.

Tex rounded the truck and got behind the wheel, some of his euphoria fading. "I talked to our producer in Nashville," he said as he started the ignition.

"So you're going to Nashville," she said, some resignation in her voice.

"I mean, yeah," Tex said. She knew that. She'd always known that.

"When?"

"Monday," he said.

"We can help with Bryce," she said.

"I don't need you to help with Bryce," Tex said, confused. "He's coming too." He looked at her as he backed out of her driveway, but she'd trained her eyes out her window, her arms clenched across her middle.

"When are you coming back?" she asked once he pointed them toward town and started driving.

"Uh…I don't know."

She sighed, and Tex didn't like the sound of that. "What?"

"If you have no plan to come back, that means you're not coming back."

"Yes, I am," he said, suddenly realizing what she was upset about. He hadn't imagined this conversation going down this track at all. "Bryce is starting school in a couple of weeks. We'll be back before then."

"So you're not recording?"

"Not on this trip," he said. "Hopefully not in Nashville at all."

She swung her attention toward him. "What does that mean?"

"It means, sweetheart." He grinned at her, hoping she'd lighten up. "That I'm going to try to get our producer to agree to let us record the album here in Coral Canyon."

Abby's eyes went wide, her surprise radiating off of her the same way Tex had heard it in his brother's voice earlier. "Here?" Then she went right for his jugular when she asked, "Where are you going to record *here*?"

CHAPTER
TWENTY

Abby's cells stormed inside her body while she waited for Tex to answer her question. He suddenly seemed so intent on driving, and she didn't like that. "Tex," she barked.

"On the ranch," he said. "I'm going to build a recording studio on the ranch."

"No, you're not," she said with a dry laugh. "Don't be ridiculous."

"Why is that ridiculous?" He looked at her with genuine confusion.

"You *can't* be serious, Tex. Mountain View Road gets maybe four people driving on it per day. *Four.*" She studied his face, and he sure wasn't smiling or looking at her like he'd gotten her good.

"It's going to be a barn," he said. "No one will even know what it is."

The new foundation he'd poured a couple of days ago

suddenly made sense. She hadn't asked him about it, and he hadn't volunteered any information. Now she knew why. "And are all of your fancy music producers going to walk out there in their shiny shoes?"

"There will be a path."

"We don't even have paved driveways, Tex. Are you going to pave the road so all your city-folk can get back to that *barn*?"

He glared at her, and she gave it right back to him, her arms clenched around her stomach. "Why do you care? Music studios are sound-proof. I'm not going to ruin your perfect country silence with my music."

"I care, because you're changing everything. I own that ranch too, you know."

"No," he bit out. "No, you don't, Abby."

"Well, the seventy-five grand I paid says otherwise."

"If you'll pick up my phone there, sweetheart, you can find a spreadsheet with all of the things I've done around the ranch this summer. It's over a hundred thousand dollars. So your seventy-five isn't even a third of what that ranch is worth now."

Abby's chest felt like she'd swallowed bleach and she was slowly getting burned from the inside out. "What?"

"That's right," he said, plenty of acid in his tone. "You don't get to decide what I do with the ranch, remember?" He looked at her and the road, back and forth, several times. He sighed, some of the fight leaving him, when she didn't answer.

She also didn't pick up his phone. She didn't need to see the evidence in black and white numbers. She could see it in the front porch that didn't sag anymore. She saw it in the huge back deck he'd added to the house. In the fences that stood tall and straight and proud around mowed fields. In the garden plot he and Bryce had worked to put in last weekend, though they wouldn't plant anything until next spring. In the beautiful, freshly painted house and the stunning, newly painted red barn not far from his back door.

She could see money everywhere she looked when she looked south to his farm—and she'd just thought of it as his.

"Do you want to buy me out?" she asked, her voice sounding small and tinny.

"Yes," he said quietly. "We should probably talk about that too." He continued on to town and to Beef and Leaves, a steakhouse that had a salad bar and hot bar to go with any cut of beef. Abby did like coming here, because she could get a delicious steak and her salad too. They had a delicious corn chowder too, and Fridays meant surf and turf would be on the menu.

She thought about the life she had on Mountain View Road, knowing it was all about to change. Not only with a recording studio, but Wade and Cheryl would get married, and Abby wouldn't even live on that road anymore.

When he opened her door to help her down, she met his eyes. "Tell me the truth. How many people does it take to make a record?"

He gazed back at her evenly, though his dark eyes burned with something hot. "Our producer will come. Maybe his assistant. We have people who check the mics and run the equipment. People who check the quality of the music. Mix it. That kind of stuff."

"So how many?" She got down, only touching his shoulder for a moment.

"Six or seven," he said.

"Where will they all stay?"

"A hotel."

Morris would deal with that, Abby knew. Tex didn't deal with details. He never had. She hated feeling like she was a detail to him and not the main event, but the feelings came anyway. Her chest squeezed against her lungs, removing the air and not allowing her to get anymore.

He might not be building a high-rise condominium, but he was going to pollute their small-town ranching community on the outskirts of Coral Canyon all the same.

"How long will it take to make the album?" she asked as he opened the door to the restaurant for her. The line nearly reached the entrance, but they joined it anyway. They just had to get through this, and their orders would be in and they'd be escorted to a table.

"It depends," he said. "But Bryce is here, and I can't go to Nashville for months. None of the other boys have to be in Nashville, and I talked to our agent today too. Our contract doesn't say we *have* to be in Nashville to record."

Abby nodded, wishing the spaces between her fingers didn't long for his. His devotion to his son was admirable, but she wished she'd been part of who was here in Coral Canyon preventing Tex from leaving. She was a bad person for wanting to be as important to him as his son, and yet, she couldn't change how she felt.

He'd told her last week that he might be falling in love with her, but the problem with *might* was that he *might not* be falling in love with her. When things between them were good, they were really good. He was a funny guy, with loads of personality and every ounce of a hard working spirit Abby liked.

He asked her about her job, her friends, her family, and he listened. He brought her food and stopped by in the morning to help her get her chores done faster so she wouldn't be late for work at the library.

And no one could challenge how handsome he was. Any woman in any of the western states would gladly shove her aside so they could be standing next to Tex Young in this line for a dinner date.

Tears filled her eyes, and Abby just wanted to go home. She couldn't feel Tex looking at her, but his hand slipped into hers and he said, "Let's go."

She didn't argue with him. He took her back outside, where she managed to look away from him and wipe her eyes with her free hand. He put her back in the truck and leaned into the doorway. "I'm sorry, Abs. I didn't think it would be this big of a deal."

"You liar," she said, half laughing and half crying. "You were nervous about telling me, and you know it."

He sighed and shook his head. Without saying anything, he closed her door and went to get behind the wheel. She composed herself, sniffling and wiping all she wanted until he opened his door and vaulted into the truck.

"I was nervous," he said, starting the truck and backing

out of the parking spot. "Because I knew you'd react the way you did. I thought you'd come to realize though, that I haven't done anything to that house or land that isn't respectful and amazing. The recording studio in the barn will be no different."

She didn't say anything, because there wasn't anything to say. Perhaps she had overreacted. Some of the anxiety and worry drained from her.

"I was thinking you'd get outside your head and trust me," he said, driving his point home. "There won't be more people than when Bryce and I have my family over. Most of the people coming will be Youngs."

Abby watched the town roll by, her stomach mad at her for ruining the date when it wanted steak and blue cheese dressing. "I know, Tex," she said. He didn't answer, and maybe she hadn't spoken loud enough.

She turned to look at him, and he nodded. "I'm sorry I can't be the man you want, Abby."

"It's not that," she said. "At all."

"Isn't it? Your natural default with me is straight to an argument. You don't stop for even a *second* and think, 'hey, I know this guy. He's not going to do anything I won't like.'" He shook his head. "It's fine. I'm just glad we figured it out now before we did something stupid."

He stopped there, thankfully. Abby could fill in his unspoken words—*like get married*. Or *like try to raise a family together*. Or any number of other things.

The drive back to her house happened in less time than she knew possible, and Tex didn't walk her across the narrow strip of grass to her driveway and then to her front stoop. He waved to her on his way to the steps that went up to his back door and said, "I'm sorry, Abby. I really am."

Numbness spread through her, and while he hadn't said, "I don't want to see you anymore," the message had been driven home with his apologies.

"Tex," she said, but the wind snatched her voice and whipped it away from his ears. "I'm sorry. Don't go."

He went anyway, and Abby had no choice but to go home alone. Again. Always alone, because her attitude couldn't be contained and hidden for longer than two seconds.

She'd been trying to change. She'd been trying to listen to Tex the way he listened to her. He'd said something wrong—it wasn't that he couldn't be the man she wanted. It was that she wasn't the woman he deserved.

———

ON SUNDAY EVENING, ABBY STOOD AT HER BACK DOOR, looking through the open screen. She and Wade had eaten lunch hours ago, and her brother had laid down for a nap. He'd woken an hour ago, and Cheryl had arrived, and they currently worked out on the farm. He'd wanted to start teaching her some of the chores they'd be responsible for doing once they got married and Abby didn't live here anymore.

A huge truck had just growled its way into the driveway next door, and four cowboys spilled from it. The band had arrived—Otis, Luke, Trace, and Morris. They laughed and joked as they went up the back steps and into the house, no knocking necessary.

Only a moment later, the gravel crunched again, this time with Mav and his family. A third truck, this one rounded and older so it clearly would be Tex's parents, pulled in behind Mav. Abby shrunk away from the doorway as Dani dropped to the ground, her eyes immediately coming to the door where she'd been standing.

She helped her son down from the back, then called to Mav. He turned and waited for Boston, looked next door too, something on his face Abby couldn't read without looking fully at him, and continued toward the house.

Dani came Abby's way, and she suddenly needed to find something to do. Too bad she'd been cleaning the house for two straight days, except for the few hours she'd spent in the Bookmobile last night.

Tex always had dinner for her at his house after her Dog Valley Bookmobile run, and she'd spent most of the evening weeping as she cleaned out the fridge, folded laundry, and then went to visit the horses who preferred Wade over her.

It seemed everyone preferred someone or something else over her. "You don't make it easy for them," she muttered. She also couldn't think faster than it took for Dani to arrive at the back door.

"Knock, knock," she called cheerfully. "Are you home, Abby?"

"Yes," she said, stepping around the corner where she'd faded into the background.

"Oh." Dani pressed her palm to her heartbeat, obviously startled. "I wasn't expecting you to be right there."

"I'm right here," Abby said, reaching for the door handle on the screen door. "Come in, Dani."

She did, easily embracing Abby. "How are you? Georgia says you haven't texted her back all day, and I said I'd be out your way tonight and I'd check on you."

Blast Georgia, Abby thought, though the bookshop owner was her best friend. Had she confided in her, Georgia would've closed her shop and shown up in less than twenty minutes.

Dani pulled away, and Abby hung her head. "I'll text her back," she said. "I've been...busy today." She'd skipped church that morning, for fear she might not be able to keep her composure if she saw Tex. That, and the pastor had a way of saying things that pushed her over the edge when she already felt like her life was crashing down around her, the pieces huge and life-threatening.

The only place she wanted to be when she felt like that was here at home. Her home. She had no idea how she could possibly leave this farm and this house and try to make another place hers. Only hers.

Always alone, she thought.

"Yes, this place smells like lemons and Clorox," Dani said knowingly. She looked around the kitchen. "Are you coming next door for dinner?"

"No," Abby said, moving over to the refrigerator. "We ate already." Lunch, but Dani didn't need to know Abby hadn't even thought about dinner yet. Surely they had milk to go with her Cocoa Krispies. When she felt down, she always soothed herself with chocolate and cream.

When Dani didn't say anything, Abby forced herself to turn and face her friend. "What's wrong?" she asked, and when faced with such a point-blank question, Abby couldn't lie.

"Tex and I...aren't really together anymore," she said.

"Ah." Dani once again nodded knowingly. "And you're miserable."

"I've been miserable before," Abby said. "I'll survive."

"Abby, honey."

"Please," Abby said, her voice breaking. "I'm better miserable when I'm alone." She tried for a smile, and Dani wrapped her in another hug.

"I'll set up a lunch for this week," she said. "I'm assuming you know the boys will be in Nashville."

"Yes." Abby stepped away and wiped her eyes. She wasn't going to sob all night tonight. "Is Mav going?"

"Yes," Dani said. "Just to help Morris through a few things."

"I think it's probably more for Tex than Morris," Abby said with a small smile.

Dani grinned too. "You really do know him well. Both of them."

"They toured together for a long time," Abby said, shrugging one shoulder. "Tex said Mav managed his whole life, and he was figuring out how to do it himself."

"Well, maybe he's not that good at it yet," Dani said, smoothing back Abby's hair. "Once he figures out he can't live without you, he'll be back."

Abby wanted to tell her that the problem didn't lie with Tex. It was her. It had always been her. Instead, she simply smiled and said good night to Dani. She stood at the door and watched her cross the distance over to the farmhouse next door and go up the steps. She too went inside without knocking, and Abby leaned against the doorjamb, wishing she could do the same.

At the same time, perhaps Tex was right. Perhaps they'd always butted heads a little too much and they always would. He did fire up something inside her, and she always felt so inadequate at his side. She supposed she *had* to challenge him to make herself feel...not so insignificant.

And she didn't really want a bunch of people rolling up to the house next door to make an album. "But would you like him to leave town again?" she asked herself.

Of course she wouldn't. He'd found a solution—a really intelligent solution—to his problem, and she should've supported him not come at him with question after question.

She sighed and closed the back door, cutting off the sight of Tex's house next door. "Perhaps we were never meant to be," she said to herself, feeling the lie pull through her entire being.

"But if we are," she said as she went into the living room and turned on the TV to distract herself. "Lord, it would be nice to have an inkling of how to get him back."

CHAPTER
TWENTY-ONE

T ex couldn't help looking to the white house next door as he reached the bottom of the steps. His carryon bumped down beside him, and the only thing he experienced was pure exhaustion. The past couple of days had been a whirlwind of activity, from laundry to packing to band meetings.

Everyone seemed as excited as him to build the recording studio on the ranch and make their album right here in Coral Canyon. Everyone except the one person Tex wanted to be happy for him.

He tore his eyes from Abby's house. She wasn't there, as it was mid-morning on Monday, and she'd gone to the library hours ago.

"Move, Dad," Bryce said with some urgency in this voice as he came down the steps behind Tex. Tex hauled his bag out of the way to make room for his son, and together, they managed to get their luggage over to the truck and in the back.

"Ready?" Tex asked.

"Did you get the music I left on the piano?"

"Yep."

"What about the demo CDs?"

"Got all three of 'em," he said, grinning at his son. He put one hand behind Bryce's head and touched his forehead to his son's. "This is going to be great. Don't be nervous. They already think I'm a Rockstar."

Bryce chuckled, and Tex dropped his hand. "Because you are, Dad. But I'm not." He moved toward the passenger side of the truck. "You're better than me, and they'll know it with two chords."

"I am not better than you," Tex argued. They got in the truck and he looked at his son. "You're far better than I am, Bryce. They'll see it." He started the truck and backed out. "They won't say it, but they'll see it."

Bryce's excitement filled the cab of the truck, and Tex basked in it. He didn't like being with his own thoughts, and he told his son to cue up the music that would get them to the airport in Jackson Hole.

"Aren't we getting Uncle Mav?" Bryce asked.

"No," Tex said. "He took Beth back to Portia last night, so he's already there. He'll meet us at the airport."

"Oh, I thought he said he needed a ride."

"Changed his plans," Tex said, his eyebrows folding down into a frown. "He called last night after you went to play video games with your friends. I guess Dani isn't feeling well, and school's starting soon, so he took Beth back to her mama."

"Dani looked real tired last night," Bryce said.

"Yeah." Tex suspected his brother's wife was pregnant, but Mav hadn't made any sort of announcement yet, and Tex wasn't going to ask. When Mav wanted to share, he'd share. With the country music playing, the drive happened quickly, with Bryce singing along while Tex let his thoughts go into the corkscrew they'd been on for several days.

He told himself time and time again that he'd prepared for the meeting tomorrow. He'd gone over his arguments with Otis, then Luke, then Trace. Separately, and they'd pretended to be Meryl, asking hard questions and refusing to give in to Tex's ask to record in Wyoming.

He'd then refined his arguments and points and presented to all of them, Morris and Mav included. He'd gotten some good feedback. Morris had a good idea to mention how he would arrange everything for the people who needed to come to Coral Canyon for the recording. Mav had reminded Tex of how Meryl liked to think he'd come up with the ideas. There was so much going on inside Tex's head, and he needed it all out.

Still, Abby managed to crowd herself into the midst of everything else going on inside his mind, and that made him calm for a moment. Then he remembered he'd broken up with her, and he glanced over to Bryce.

His son typed away on his phone, probably texting with his friends he gamed with or Bailey. Maybe one of

Tex's brothers. No matter who, Bryce seemed happy. *That's the most important thing*, Tex thought.

He needed to create a stable life for Bryce. His son needed him right now to be his father, help him know what to do with his future, and Tex couldn't do that unless he could get King Country to agree to his idea to record in Coral Canyon.

He had to focus on that and worry about Abby later. He thought about texting her just before the plane took off, but he wasn't sure if that would make things better or worse between them.

In the end, he stayed silent. He dozed on the way to Nashville, courtesy of his sound-cancelling headphones. With the majority of his brothers on the plane with him, the headphones actually saved his sanity.

They had an evening before the meeting at the record label, and they all piled into a huge van Morris had rented for them. "Just like the tour bus," Otis joked from the way-back.

"Come on," Luke said. "If this were the tour bus, your knee wouldn't be in my back."

"You like it," Otis said, chuckling.

Tex buckled himself behind the wheel and looked at Bryce, his navigator. "You ready?" he asked as Morris and Trace started arguing with Otis about minding his manners. Mav sat in the row right behind Bryce, shaking his head.

"Come sit up here," he finally barked at Luke. "Move this luggage there if Otis's knees are that big of a problem."

"Let me up there," Luke said, trying to climb over Trace, who hadn't had time to move a muscle.

Tex rolled his eyes but waited patiently while suitcases and men got rearranged. When everything quieted down, he looked in the rear-view mirror. "Are we ready, boys?"

"Yes," Luke practically yelled. "Let's go."

Tex had actually booked all of their rooms at a hotel near to King Country, and he'd been to Nashville so many times, he didn't really need a navigator. He'd brought Bryce through the city a few times too, but a few years had passed. His son exclaimed over the differences he saw, as well as the old things they'd tried and loved.

"Dad," he said, swinging his attention wildly toward Tex. "Can we go to that hot dog place where they put the sweet-and-sour sauce on the bun?"

Tex chuckled and said, "Sure."

"Are we playin' cards tonight?" Trace called from the second row where he now rode alone. Otis and Morris sat in the back, and they'd been quiet since Luke's movement.

"Are we?" Mav asked.

"We have time," Luke said in a bored voice, his eyes out the window.

"Did anyone bring cards?" Tex asked.

"Did anyone bring cards," Mav muttered. "Twenty bucks says they *all* brought cards."

Tex pulled up to a red light and looked once more in the rearview mirror. Luke met his eye and nodded, a slow smile pulling across his face.

"I did," Otis said at the same time Morris said, "I

thought we always played cards when we got to a new city."

"This ain't a new city," Trace drawled, looking over his shoulder. When he faced forward again, he added, "But I brought cards too."

Tex grinned at everyone in the van and said, "Sounds like we're playin' cards tonight then." He glanced over to Bryce, whose smile mirrored that of a mad man.

"This is so great," he said, and Tex enjoyed his boyish enthusiasm. He didn't want to spoil the fun for anyone, so he said nothing. He'd play cards and try to enjoy himself. He'd go over his notes one more time. He'd talk to Trace privately and get the reassurance he needed.

Then, he'd get down on his knees and pray. He'd pray for the band, for the meeting to go well, for Meryl to see his point of view, and for his own clarity of mind.

After that, he'd pray for Abby, and then he'd beg God to help him find the road back to her, that prayer already starting to stitch itself together inside his mind.

He wasn't sure why he'd let one of their arguments go all the way to a break-up. He didn't want to break up with her. In fact, if Tex would just allow himself to admit it, he'd say he was in love with Abigail Ingalls.

"Dad, that's the turn," Bryce said, and Tex pushed his personal problems out of his mind. Right now, he needed to focus on driving and tomorrow, business.

He could figure out how to get back to Abby after that.

———

THE FOLLOWING MORNING, TEX FELT LIKE HE HAD AFTER THAT first and only night in the rental in Coral Canyon—like he'd swallowed a dozen spiders. His stomach lurched to the left and right with every step he took. Coffee only made his blood buzz louder.

Trace, Morris, and Mal showed up at his and Bryce's hotel room with their favorite pastries from Ringgold's, but Tex could barely get the gooey cinnamon roll down his narrow throat.

"Come on," Trace said. "Let's just go, and maybe you'll calm down."

"Bryce," Tex said, and his son came out of the bedroom and into the suite. He carried the small pack with their demo CDs and the folder of music. "Got it all?"

"Got it all," he confirmed. "I'm bringing this box of sweets with us." He picked that up while Mav grinned at him, and Tex simply allowed himself to be led down to the van.

"What about the others?" Tex asked as Bryce got in the front passenger seat.

"This isn't their meeting," Trace said, not moving to get in the van.

"I said they could come."

"Yeah, well, I told them not to come."

"Trace."

His brother wouldn't look at him. "You're already a basket-case, Tex. You don't need Luke's temper in the room, or Morris's nerves." He slid a look at Tex, who didn't like what he heard but he could admit it was probably true.

Mav said, "I know you haven't said anything about Abby, but I know something's wrong there."

"Yeah." Tex looked back toward the hotel, not wanting to talk about his girlfriend in front of anyone. Mav raised his eyebrows, and Morris stood back, watching. "Like Dani's been sick for weeks now."

"No," Mav said way too fast.

"Then we don't need to talk about this right now," Tex murmured.

"Fine," Mav agreed.

"Come on, Tex," Morris said. "Mav and I are going with you."

"Just for the beginning," Mav said. "I'll introduce Morris around, and then we'll wait in the lobby."

Tex looked around at everyone, wishing they'd all come in with him. "Fine," he said. "Let's go."

He got behind the wheel of the van, and the drive to the studio happened in silence. Tex exhaled as he looked up at the tall building, the windows reflecting the late summer sunshine. He said nothing as he got out of the van, and he put on the brightest smile he could when Bryce stepped out of the vehicle.

"Ready, Dad?"

"Yes."

"I've heard all of your arguments. They're going to agree with you." His encouraging smile gave Tex more courage than he normally possessed, and he led the way inside. The woman sitting at the welcome desk several feet inside the lobby had the same curly hair and winning smile, and Tex's step lightened.

"Ramona," he said with a laugh. "I can't believe you're still here."

She stood, also laughing, and came around the desk. "Tex Young, my boy." She stood barely over five feet, but Tex wouldn't try to sneak anything against the rules past her. He bent down and hugged her, lifting her right up off her feet.

"I thought you were going to retire," he said.

"I am," she said as he set her back on her feet. "At the end of the year." She beamed at Mav and squealed. "Maverik, how's your new wife? Did you get the basket we sent?"

"Sure did," he said, grinning for all he was worth. "Didn't you get the thank you card?"

Ramona stepped back and indicated the wall behind her desk. "It's right there."

Mav just smiled at her, though Tex would've been asking why she'd asked.

"And who is this fine-looking young man?" she asked, eyeing Bryce.

"My son," Tex said. "Bryce. Bryce, this is Ramona Wiggs. She runs King Country."

"Ho, no," Ramona said. "I do not run King Country." She shook Bryce's hand and trained her eyes on Morris. "And you must be Morris. I've heard all about you."

"Oh, boy," Morris said with a chuckle.

He shook Ramona's hand too, while Mav said, "Good things, Morris. I promise."

She rounded her desk once everyone had been greeted sufficiently. "I saw you on the schedule. Go on up, fellas."

"Thank you," Tex said, the tension in his stomach easing up a little bit. He tried not to think of Otis, Luke, and Trace, all waiting to see how he'd performed. He couldn't look at Morris or Mav or Bryce. The one person he wanted to comfort him and soothe him wasn't speaking to him right now.

He looked up at the ceiling on the elevator and once again called upon the Lord to help him. *Just a little strength,* he prayed silently. *For a little longer.*

He opened his eyes when the elevator slowed and came to a stop, and he found everyone looking at him. "Ready?" Mav asked.

Tex didn't feel wildly different than he had a few seconds ago. But he knew the Lord had always been on his side, and that allowed him to step out of the elevator with confidence.

Jason greeted them moments later, with offers of water or coffee, soda or juice. Tex said, "I'll take a water, Jason. Thanks."

He introduced Bryce to everyone who rose from their desks to say hello, and Mav did the same for Morris. Tex's heart filled with love for the pair of his brothers, especially as he watched Morris smile and exude confidence and charisma like he was born to be the band's manager.

As he glanced around, he realized how King Country had prepared for his arrival that day. No less than three album covers for Country Quad papered the cabinets, the walls, and a floor-to-ceiling poster of their last tour covered Meryl's closed office door.

"Wow," he said as he looked around. "You guys go all out."

"We're just thrilled to have you back in Nashville," a woman gushed at the lot of them.

"Thank you, Lucy," Mav said, because it had always been his job to know everyone's names and handle all of the details. "This is Country Quad's new manager, Morris."

Tex and the others shook hands until Jason returned, and while Meryl's assistant moved swiftly to his desk, Tex uncapped the bottle and took a sip. He told himself not to guzzle it, because that would show his nerves.

He'd never been nervous at King Country before. Everyone here treated him and his brothers like royalty—like they were right now. Morris turned down offer after offer for muffins, and finally Bryce said, "Hey, I brought some pastries too."

Someone led him into a conference room, and Tex caught something about much he looked like Tex. He looked back at Jason, who held his desk phone at his ear. "Yes, they're here. We'll be in conference room four, sir."

He hung up and gestured for Tex to go into the room where Bryce had already been taken.

"We'll stay out here," Mav said, giving Tex a meaningful look. Morris chatted with Larry, who worked primarily with Otis and had to okay all of their songs before they even started learning them.

Tex went into the conference room alone, with Jason bringing up the rear and closing the glass door behind him.

Glass. Tex couldn't believe he'd forgotten he'd have to give his pitch to the whole dang office. His nerves bubbled and brewed, and he could only smile as Jason said, "We've been getting a lot of fan mail recently. Did you guys know one of your songs is trending on social media right now?"

Tex took the oversized bag of mail while Bryce instantly pulled out his phone. "Really?" he asked. "I'll find it."

Tex swallowed, wishing he'd made cards for his notes, but everything had been held in his head. That wasn't a great place to be right now, and he stared at the various doughnuts, muffins, and bear claws that sat on the table.

"Oh my heck," Bryce said a few seconds later. "Look, Dad. It's *Wish You'd Gone First.*" He held up his phone, the Country Quad song blaring from the speakers while teenagers in cowboy hats did something. Tex blinked, confused as to what he was looking at.

"Yep, that one," Jason said. "Ah, here's Meryl now. He never makes our biggest stars wait for long."

Tex got to his feet as he twisted to see the famous record producer—the top dog at King Country—pass by the windows toward the door. He slicked his hands down his jeans, glad he'd dressed as if he'd be performing on stage any moment now. Jeans. Cowboy boots. Bright plaid shirt in blue, black, and thin yellow stripes. The white cowboy hat that sat on the front of all eight Country Quad albums.

He added a smile as Jason moved to open the door for the music mogul, and then Meryl entered the room with a laugh—as well as Mav and Morris. "Tex and the Young brothers," he boomed. "My favorite cowboys." He engulfed Tex and Mav in a hug, one of them in each arm, the scent of his old-school cologne thick and making Tex choke.

He managed to turn that into a laugh and he looked at Meryl as he stepped back. "Howdy, Meryl." The man had gray hair from root to tip, but the brightest pair of blue eyes Tex had ever seen on a man. Those eyes knew, and they saw, and Tex could only send up one more prayer that they'd agree with him.

"Sit, sit," he said. "You didn't get a doughnut?" He reached for a maple-frosted one, and Bryce followed him and took a twisted tiger's tail. "My word on Fridays," Meryl said, his eyes landing on Bryce. "Is this your twin, Tex?"

"My son," Tex said with a forced chuckle. "Bryce, this is Mister Bigler. Meryl Bigler. Sir, my son."

"The pleasure is all mine," Bryce said with precise diplomacy, and Tex couldn't be prouder of him in that moment. Meryl undid his suit coat button and pulled out his chair. He sat, and that meant everyone else could too.

Tex did, Mav did, Morris did, Bryce did, Jason did. Meryl looked at Tex, and said, "It's your meeting, son. What's on your mind?"

Tex's mind went blank, and he clutched his own hands, trying to find a thread of thought. A whisper would be great. So when Bryce said, "It's really my issue, sir. See, my dad has full custody of me now, and I'm a senior this year in Coral Canyon, Wyoming."

The sound of his son's rich, handsome voice spurred

Tex to get his act together. He met Bryce's eyes, and his son nodded at him. With the two of them perfectly in sync, Tex faced Meryl.

"Yes," he said. "Which means I can't be here to record the album in Nashville."

Meryl said nothing, but he did take an astronomically huge bite of his doughnut.

"I know Otis has the songs almost ready to go," Tex said. "We did a dirty run-through of our favorite one in my kitchen on Sunday night. Bryce has it in there, and we can listen to it if you'd like."

Meryl nodded, those eyes as bright as sapphires, and that helped Tex to keep breathing and keep speaking too.

"So," he said. "Once we pass the initial stage of song selection and approval—which Otis can do here in Nashville. All the boys can except for me, and I can be looped in via video or phone call. But after that." He drew a deep breath, all of his arguments saved in his mind should he need them.

"I'd like to propose that the band and I do all of the recording in a custom-built studio on the ranch I own in Wyoming."

There. He'd said it, and Meryl could respond. Tex took another breath as Meryl finished his bite of doughnut and swallowed, the silence in conference room four about to swallow him whole.

CHAPTER
TWENTY-TWO

Morris paced in the lobby of the hotel, getting more and more antsy by the moment. "Where are they?" he asked for the tenth time. His impatience had gotten the best of him many times in the past, and he shoved against it again. "We were finished when Mav and I came downstairs."

He and Mav had brought the van back to the hotel, and Tex and Bryce had stayed to play for Meryl, Larry, and a couple of other executives whose names Morris couldn't remember. His brother and nephew would get a cab back to the hotel, and they should've been here by now.

"They're talking," Otis said without looking up from his device. "It takes forever over there."

"I should've stayed," Morris said. Luke, Trace, and Otis all lounged on the couches in the lobby, none of them all that concerned.

"No," Trace said, looking up from his novel. "Trust me,

you don't want to be at King Country. Everything there takes an age and a half. Let Tex deal with it."

"You'll have to stay for the full meetings soon enough," Mav added.

"Plus, Tex and Bryce were playing. That takes a million years." Luke tossed his phone a moment later in disgust. "I can*not* beat that level. It's impossible."

His phone buzzed and chimed at the same time, and so flipping loud, Morris felt sure the entire hotel had heard it. He frowned at the phone and then his brother, who clearly had a hearing problem.

"What?" Luke asked.

"Your phone just went off," Morris said as it did again. He peered closer at it, his heart sinking to the floor when he saw Blaze's name there. "It's Blaze."

Luke dove for the phone then, so violently that his cowboy hat—which Morris believed to be permanently glued to his head—got dislodged. He narrowed his eyes at Luke, but his older brother didn't even look at him. He got to his feet as he tapped and swiped, and he practically bellowed, "Hey, Blaze," before he went around the corner.

Morris glanced at Otis, who'd craned his neck to look at Luke too. He met Morris's eyes, his wide. "Blaze?"

"I was going to ask you that," Morris said. "Since when are Luke and Blaze chummy?" Blaze was almost a decade older than Luke—he *was* ten years older than Morris—and he'd been riding the rodeo circuit since before Luke had graduated high school.

Without looking up from his novel, Trace said, "Blaze is

thinkin' about quittin' the rodeo. Hurt his back or hip or something a couple of weeks ago."

Otis sat up from the couch and picked up his cowboy hat from where he'd left it on the table. "Really?"

"Yep."

"Why didn't he tell all of us?"

Morris nodded to that. He'd been so isolated for so long, and he'd hated it. When Mav had started texting and calling about managing the band, Morris's whole heart had started to beat with real blood again. He'd known he needed to take the offer, even if it didn't pan out, because it was time for him to return to the family.

Gabe didn't feel the same way yet, but Morris prayed for his twin every single day. He texted and called him that often too. He knew Gabe struggled to feel wanted and appreciated in the huge, loud, stuffed-with-talent Young family. He knew, because he and Gabe had talked about their brothers for years.

Morris had been so thankful for Gabe over the years. He'd told him more than once that the only way he'd stayed sane for the past decade was because he had a twin. God had known they'd need each other, and they'd promised to never leave one another out.

He was trying real hard not to do that, but now that he was the official band manager, Gabe had to feel *some*thing. Morris suspected not something good.

"Trace," Otis said, and he looked up from his book.

"What?" he barked back.

"Why didn't Blaze tell us all about his injury?" He shot a look at Morris, who leaned forward too. He'd learned from Mav that he had to act as the mediator between band members sometimes. Turned out that Youngs didn't always get along, even if they were in the elite band together.

"I don't know," Trace said. "He felt embarrassed or something? Luke's tryin' to recruit him for the band."

"What?" Morris and Otis asked together. "Why?" Morris added solo.

Mav finally looked up from his phone, some curiosity in his face too. He said nothing, and he probably knew about Blaze's injury, because he kept tabs on all the brothers.

Trace rolled his neck along the back of his shoulders. "Oh, Luke is so pessimistic. He's sure the band is going to break up after this next album, because Tex isn't going to stay. Mav's gone, and well." Trace shrugged. "I agree with Luke. Tex is doing this album, and then he's done."

"You think so?" Otis asked, plenty of interest in his voice. "He hasn't said that to us."

"He hasn't even said that to me," Mav said. "And you two are close, Trace. Has he said that?"

"He's dating Abby hard-core," Trace said, hitching up one shoulder.

"Yeah, but he's building the recording studio in Coral Canyon," Morris said, concern spiking through him. He'd just gotten this job. He didn't want the band to break up.

"Truth be told," Trace said, his eyes locked on Otis's. "I think Otis is considering hanging up his hat too, and well, Luke and I want to continue the band for a while longer."

Otis didn't confirm or deny his departure from Country

Quad, though Morris practically stared a hole through the side of his face. "What about Bryce?"

"Yeah, he's on the list," Trace said. "But we still need one more. Luke's talkin' to Blaze. As Mav would say, it isn't a crime."

"He's right," Mav said. "It's not a crime to talk to your brothers."

Otis looked at Morris then, some worry and doubt prevalent in his eyes. "Interesting," he said. "I'm being replaced, and I didn't even know it."

"You haven't even quit," Morris said.

"I wasn't planning to quit," Otis said, leaning back into the couch and bringing his hat over his face. "I'm pretty sure I just wrote the best album of my life in less than a month. Must not be good enough. You're out, Otis."

"Come on," Trace said, plenty of disgust in his voice. "I didn't say you were out, Otis."

"Luke is talkin' to my replacement," Otis said, and Morris didn't like how the voice came from his very still body, his face covered.

He looked at Trace, who hooked his thumb at Otis like it was Morris's job to fix this. He had no idea what to do, and his heart palpitated like it did when his team had less than a yard to go to score the game-winning touchdown and only two seconds to do it.

"There's no way Blaze is quitting the rodeo," Morris said. "Your place is in the band as long as you want it, Otis." He nodded like he'd just decreed it as such, and no one answered him.

He cut a look at Mav, who'd gone back to his phone.

He allowed a small smile onto his face, and he gave a single nod, his way of saying that Morris had said the right thing.

This time, Trace's phone rang, and he said, "Sorry, boys, I have to take this. It's Lady Bea." A smile popped onto his face, and he stood too, saying, "Hey, princess. How are you?"

"Lady Bea?" Morris asked as Trace wandered at a much slower pace toward the revolving door leading into the hotel. "Who is that?"

"She's a legit princess," Otis said as he pushed his hat back just enough to reveal his eyes. "Trace met her at some high-society function in New York city a few months ago. Right after Mav's wedding."

"So he really does only date celebrities," Morris said, awed. He'd seen the jokes about Trace's dating habits on the brothers' text string; he just hadn't known Trace well enough to know if Tex and the others were ribbing him or speaking true.

"Totally," Otis said. "Just don't let him hear you say that." They chuckled together, and Morris went back to obsessively staring at the entrance to the hotel.

Luke returned, and he brought a certain tension and awkwardness with him that he couldn't seem to feel. He sat on the opposite end of the couch where Otis sat, and Morris watched the two of them. Luke probably couldn't hear the weird vibe he'd brought with him, and Morris said, "So, Luke, have you thought about getting hearing aids?"

"What?" Luke looked up from his game, annoyance on

his face. Yes, Morris and Gabe had often annoyed Luke growing up. He was only three years older than the twins, and Jem was two older than him, so for a couple of years there, everyone had gone but the three of them. Luke claimed that Gabe and Morris ganged up on him. The twins always said Luke left them out of everything. Literally everything.

It had been a particularly sour poison when Luke had joined Country Quad, that was for sure. He was the only younger brother in the band, and Gabe had particularly struggled with how he felt Luke didn't represent the younger Young brothers very well.

"You can't hear very well," Morris said gently, leaning forward but not speaking any louder. "You've been playing very loud drums for a very long time. I wondered if you'd thought of getting some hearing aids."

Luke blinked at him, surprise replacing his irritation. He looked at Otis, who mouthed something. Luke leaned closer while Morris held onto his composure. He was going to break any second.

"What?" Luke asked, and Otis moved his mouth again, no sound coming out.

Morris burst into laughter, relieved and overjoyed when Otis and even Mav did too.

"I hate you," Luke said, getting to his feet and shaking his head. He moved over to the other couch opposite the coffee table and Otis and sat back down.

"Come on," Otis said. "That was funny. Plus, Morris is right. You yell everything, and your phone deafens people because you can't hear it."

"I can hear it fine."

"Because it's *so loud*," Morris said.

"I'm not getting hearing aids," Luke said.

"They make 'em really small now," Morris said. "No one would even know—"

"That's Tex," Otis said, and Morris's thought about hearing aids vanished. He jumped to his feet as Otis did, with Luke not far behind.

"Trace," he called, and his brother turned from the fountain in the back of the lobby. Morris pointed toward Tex and Bryce, both of whom had now entered the hotel.

Trace stopped talking, lowered his phone from his ear, and marched toward them. He arrived at Morris's side about the same time Tex and his son arrived in the seating area. No one said anything.

"Well?" Morris prompted, trying to search multiple faces simultaneously. Tex and Bryce wore masks of iron, without a single emotion he could identify. "What did Meryl say?"

CHAPTER
TWENTY-THREE

Otis's pulse pounced through his body, and he growled, "If someone doesn't say somethin', I'm going to start punching things." He zeroed in on Tex, who would do the talking. "You're closest, brother."

Tex's face split into a grin, and he threw both hands into the air. "They're going to let us record in Wyoming!"

The lobby erupted with cowboy cheering, Otis's voice right there with his brothers'. He grabbed onto Tex without fists and hugged him as he said, "Yes! Good job, Tex!"

Luke was definitely the loudest of them all, and he always went on just a bit too long. He'd thrown his cowboy hat up into the air as he whistled through his teeth, then grabbed onto Morris—his nearest victim. Morris laughed, and it did Otis's heart and soul good to see his youngest brother there with them. He communicated with Gabe, but the other twin still wouldn't talk to anyone but Morris and Mav.

Otis tried; he knew Tex tried. Even Trace had reached out. A lot of hurt existed there, and only Gabe could wade through it all.

He stepped away from Tex and said, "I'm gonna call Lauren and let her know." He strode away from the cowboy crowd just as a sharp-dressed man came out from behind the podium. Oh, his brothers were in troub-ble, but Otis couldn't stop smiling.

He hadn't realized just how badly he wanted to be in Wyoming for the recording until he'd come to Nashville last week to start playing through the songs for the production team at the label.

He hated being here by himself, and at first, he'd reasoned that he wouldn't be. His brothers would be here, and they'd stay in adjoining rooms like they'd always done, and they'd record. He loved making the music he'd written with the band, and he couldn't imagine his life without it.

At the same time, Lauren wasn't well. A whole new kind of worry dove through Otis as he waited for his ex-wife to pick up her phone. She didn't, and Otis hung up without bothering to leave a message. She'd see he called and give him a ring back when she could.

He quickly checked the clock, and it wasn't too early in Dog Valley, where she lived with their daughter Joey. Otis called his daughter, because school hadn't started yet, and she should be able to answer.

Lauren hated that Joey had a phone, but Otis had

insisted. He paid for it to text and call and nothing else, because his girl was only seven years old. He wanted to be able to communicate with her while he was on the road, and he and Joey had agreed to keep the phone out of Lauren's sight as much as possible.

"Daddy, hello," Joey said, her voice so cute and so full of chirpy happiness.

"Heya, baby," he said, his smile as genuine as it ever had been. "Where's Mama?"

"She's sleepin'," Joey said, and alarm rang through Otis. He needed to be near Dog Valley, and he'd already been looking at houses there.

"Has she been up today yet?" he asked, trying to keep his voice light and airy.

"Yeah," Joey said. "She made scrambled eggs and we ate 'em with lots of syrup." She giggled, and that made Otis's whole world brighter. "Then she said she had a headache and had to go lay down."

"Okay," Otis said. "Listen, Kanagroo, I called her, and I'm sure she'll call me back, but I wanted you to know that we got approval to record our next album in Coral Canyon!"

"That's great, Daddy-Bear," she said, and it sounded like she meant it. He'd enjoyed seeing her more this summer—he usually had her all summer long—and a voice whispered in his head that he better get ready to be a full-time dad in the very near future.

He swallowed and pushed the thoughts of Lauren's as-yet-undiagnosed condition from his mind. He couldn't deal with what-ifs. He dealt with facts and data, and until she had those to present to him, he wasn't going to wallow in worry.

"If Mama's asleep," he said. "What are you doin'?"

"Grammy Echo came to get me," she said. "I'm at her house, and we're makin' sourdough bread."

"Wow," Otis said, a flash of love for Lauren's mother filling him. "You be sure to tell her thank you like, a hundred times."

Joey giggled, and Otis leaned against the wall in the hall, wishing he was already home. "Daddy has a few more meetings this week, and then I'll be back, okay? You'll come stay with me for a bit while Mama gets better."

"Can I, Daddy?"

"Yep," he said, glad his little girl didn't think he was a horrible father. He beat himself up for that day in and day out, and perhaps Trace and Luke had picked up on some unspoken cues about how Otis felt about continuing with the band. "All right, Roo. I have to go, but you give Grammy a kiss from me, and tell Mama I'll be home soon."

"Bye, Daddy."

He said, "I love you, Joelle."

"Love you too."

He ended the call and sighed as he heard Luke's voice heading his way. He pushed away from the wall as his brothers rounded the corner, both Morris and Mav on their phones too. Tex spoke with pure joy and animation in his face, and Bryce responded in kind.

"Hey," Otis said, moving into step with them. "How did your demos go?" He watched Bryce, because the boy wanted a career in music. Otis couldn't fault him for that. Bryce had serious talent, in multiple areas of the industry. He could write music and songs. He could play the guitar. He sang better than Tex, though Otis would never tell his brother that.

Bryce got brighter, if that was possible. "So great, Uncle Otis. Meryl *loved When a Girl Kisses You.*"

Otis grinned at his nephew. "I told you that was the one."

"Meryl liked our duets too," Bryce said. "He said I need an agent." He shone like the sun, and Otis slung his arm around his nephew.

"You're so talented, Bryce."

"Don't get his hopes up," Tex said as the elevator dinged.

"Why not?" Otis said. "He can help us record some of our songs and be on this album."

"The boy will have school," Tex said, marching onto the elevator. "He won't be hanging out with us in the recording studio." Otis exchanged a look with Bryce, who hadn't dimmed at all.

He rolled his eyes and said, "Don't worry, Uncle Otis. I know how to handle my dad." Then he got on the elevator too, his joy still at a mega-wattage level. Otis wished he still had that innocence of youth, and he stole some of it from his nephew as he joined the crew on the elevator.

"When we meet with them tomorrow, I need Luke to handle the equipment list." Tex looked at Luke, who nodded.

"You got it, Tex," he said.

"Morris, you're going to get all the details about who they're sending and what accommodations they'll need."

"Yep," Morris said, glancing at Mav, who gave him a single nod of reassurance.

"Trace, I'm going to need you to keep Meryl's daughter happy."

"Excuse me?" Trace looked like he'd swallowed a whole bushel of lemons.

"She's apparently in the office," Mav said. "And driving Meryl mad."

"So I have to miss the meeting to entertain her?"

"You hate the meetings," Tex said. "She has a couple of albums out too, and I'd call her a...B-list celebrity."

"C-list," Mav coughed, and Trace's frown deepened. He didn't confirm or deny that he'd accept and carry out his assignment, but Otis suspected he would.

"Otis," Tex said.

"I know," Otis said. "Get the songs approved as quickly as possible. I've been working on it."

The elevator dinged, but Tex said, "Hit the panic button, Mav."

Mav did without question, and everyone faced Tex. He swallowed once and said, "I really appreciate all of the support on this recording-studio-in-a-barn idea. I mean it." He opened his arms wide and settled them around Bryce and then Morris.

That continued until the seven of them were a connected circle, and Otis finally felt a true sense of calmness enter his life. Family. *Family* was what mattered most, and he needed to make sure he focused his attention in that direction from now on.

———

A WEEK LATER, OTIS PULLED UP TO THE SMALL-TOWN bookshop in Coral Canyon, Beck's Books. It hadn't existed when he was a child, and his parents didn't have money to buy extraneous entertainment like books. Mama had taken the boys to the library to instill in them a love of reading.

Otis wasn't that son, not the way Trace was, but he'd checked out plenty of guitar manuals, and he'd learned to play from the music books he'd gotten at the library. His family didn't have money for lessons either, and Otis had paid for his own once he'd turned twelve and could work to earn the money.

He'd mowed lawns all over town to get the money he needed for guitar lessons, and he'd completed plenty of chores around the family ranch too.

"Are we goin' in, Daddy?"

He swung his attention to Joey, who'd unbuckled her seatbelt and had her door open. She peered at him with her pretty brown eyes, framed by her long lashes and her cute, pink pair of glasses.

"Yes," he said. "Come on, Roo. Let's go see if they've got the new Blueberry Girls book."

She giggled as she dropped to the ground from his truck, and he smiled to himself as he got out too. "It's Strawberry Shortcake, Daddy."

"Is it?" He opened the door for his daughter, and she

went into the shop first. The place smelled like lemons and flowers, and Otis could admit it held a certain charm that women and girls obviously liked.

He could appreciate a well-run shop, cleanliness, and good management, and a woman nodded at him while she continued to help another customer. Joey went straight to the kids area, and Otis wandered toward the part of the bookshop which didn't boast books at all. Bookmarks, book-related baubles, and brightly colored T-shirts took up the wall next to a hallway that went toward an office.

He browsed there, not really looking at anything, until his attention got alerted to another voice coming from down the hall.

"…no," the woman said. "We're *not* together, CJ. Don't you dare come in here and disrupt my shop again."

Otis could tell a damsel in distress when he heard one, and he peered further down the hall. More shadows existed down there, so he took a step in the direction of the natural light spilling out of an open doorway, which was probably an office.

"Too late?" the woman screeched, and she burst out of the office a moment later. Her eyes met Otis's, and he froze. She did not. "I'm hanging up, and I better not see you in here." The phone lowered, and she moved toward him. "You, get in here."

"Me?" he asked, but she'd already turned around and started back to her office, her curls bouncing with her angry movement.

"Come on," she said, and Otis obeyed.

He filled the office doorway and took in the disarray

here that stood in direct contradiction to the organization in the front of the shop. The brunette with the pretty curls turned and faced him, a sigh falling from her mouth.

"My ex-boyfriend doesn't get the message," she said. "I've broken up with him."

"All right," Otis said, more confused than ever about what he was doing there.

"Georgia," a man said, and Otis flinched away from it, moving further into the office as another man came down the hall.

"Kiss me," Georgia hissed, panic in her face and prevalent in her voice now.

"What?" Otis asked, his adrenaline spiking for the second time in as many seconds.

"You're my boyfriend, and I need you to kiss me," she said. "Now." She stepped into him, grabbed onto the collar of his shirt, and kissed him.

Otis stood as still as a statue while his brain caught up to the situation. Then he tasted raspberries and chocolate, and his body remembered how to hold a woman and kiss her. His hands slid around her waist, and his lips stroked hers as if they really had been dating for a couple of months and he simply couldn't wait for her to get off work before he kissed her again.

"Georgia," a man said, and Otis started to pull away. Georgia's fingers in his collar tightened, and Otis went back to kissing her, wondering how long she was going to make her ex stand there and watch.

CHAPTER
TWENTY-FOUR

Georgia Beck couldn't believe how well she fit into this Young brother's arms. She'd recognize a Young any time she saw one walking the streets, even if they came and went from Coral Canyon as quickly as the weather around here changed.

He wasn't Tex, but he did have a hint of gray along his temples, so she thought he might be Trace or Otis.

It doesn't matter, she thought, sinking further into his kiss. Boy, this cowboy could *kiss* a woman, and Georgia's legs trembled as he brought her closer to him and broke their connection. "How long do you want me to keep goin'?" he whispered.

CJ hadn't spoken again, and Georgia didn't dare look past the kissing cowboy to see if her ex still stood there. She took a deep breath of the cotton in the cowboy's shirt, wondering why her heart had started bumping so strangely about the time she'd seen this guy standing in the hallway outside her office.

He shouldn't have been there, and yet it sure seemed like the Lord had dropped him into her life right when she'd needed him most.

CJ cleared his blasted throat, and that sent another dose of sourness down her throat and through her veins.

"I've got it," Cowboy said, and he turned while keeping her sheltered in the shadow of his body.

"No one's supposed to come down here," he said, his hand slipping into hers. Everything that had been cold in Georgia's life warmed up, and she had no idea what that meant. She couldn't be attracted to this man. She'd just needed help in the form of a kiss for a few seconds.

She'd kissed him for longer than that, she knew, but she wasn't going to apologize for it. It had been the single best kiss of her life, even if it had been done in a moment of extreme desperation.

CJ stuttered something Georgia didn't even pretend to listen to, and Cowboy said, "She's not interested in getting back together with you, brother. Sorry." He didn't sound sorry, and for some reason, that made Georgia like this Young brother even more.

Footsteps sounded down the hall, fading as CJ left. Cowboy turned back to her and blew out his breath. "All right, he's gone." He reached up with his free hand and wiped his face like the activities of the past five minutes had made him sweat.

That couldn't be the case, because she hadn't attracted anyone's attention in a while. Well, anyone worth attracting, that was. Looking up into Cowboy's deep, rich, dark brown eyes, she could've sworn she, one—swooned. Two —saw desire flickering in the depths of his eyes. Three— felt the earth move for a second time that day.

"Daddy?" a girl called, and Cowboy spun toward the doorway.

"I'll be right back," he said, jogging out of the office and down the hall. She heard his deep voice talking to his daughter, and Georgia steadied herself against her desk with both palms pressed flat against the wood.

"What have you done to yourself?" she murmured. She reached for her phone to text Abby, because she'd know what to do. She'd know which Young brother had a daughter, and if Georgia could get the name of the girl, Abby could pinpoint who he was.

She didn't even get a text off before Cowboy returned, this time his eyes roaming her office instead of locking onto hers. "My hat," he said. "There it is." He swooped to the ground to pick it up, and she hadn't even noticed he'd lost it. The kiss was that good.

He did look at her then, and sparks filled the entire room, making popping, crackling sounds fire in her eardrums. "You, uh…can I get your name?"

She tried to speak, but her mouth had turned to sand-paper at some point. She cleared the roughness away and said, "Georgia Beck."

"Ah, Beck's Books." His smile could fill entire towns of children with wonder, and she found herself returning it.

"Yes," she said.

"I'm Otis Young," he said, reaching to shake her hand.

He chuckled with a nervous undertone as he did. "Seems like we're doin' things in quite the opposite order." He looked at his daughter. "This is my girl, Joey." He released her hand and put that arm around the girl's slight shoulders.

"Hello," Joey said, clutching three books to her chest.

"She owns the shop, Roo," he said.

Joey's face brightened then, and Georgia's soul lit up as she met another book lover. "Looks like you've got some books there."

Joey nodded, suddenly shy as she dipped her head toward the floor. With her pink tee, she wore a pair of short shorts and flip flops, her legs spindly and long, just the way Georgia's had been growing up. Hers still were, but she concealed them well behind cute skirts and masterful pedicures. If people looked at her toes, they weren't judging her legs and making comments about how they couldn't possibly hold up her body.

"I'll be right out, baby," he said. "Go look at that dog book you were excited about."

Joey did what he said, and he watched her go back down the hall, his smile only faltering as he turned back to Georgia. "Did that work?"

"Did what work?" She reached up to tuck her hair back, but it just sprang right back out. Her curls betrayed her all the time, so she wasn't sure why she'd hoped they'd cooperate with her now. At least they hadn't gone into frizz mode yet.

"The kissin'," he said with a grin. He leaned into the doorjamb, and his arrogance floated on the air like a scent.

She busied herself with moving papers around on her desk, heat filling her face. She blushed fairly easily, especially around handsome cowboys, and she hated that about herself. "I think so," she said. "He left, didn't he?"

"He sure did."

Georgia looked up and into Otis's eyes again. "Thank you," she said sincerely. "I mean it. I've been trying to get him to accept the break-up for over a month. Maybe longer."

Otis let his gaze drip down her body to those immaculate toes, and his eyes zipped back to hers. "You're not wearing shoes."

"I work indoors," she said.

"I suppose you don't step on books," he said.

She tilted her head at him, wondering what that meant. His face began to turn red too, and my, wasn't that adorable? She smiled at him. "Not very often."

"I just meant—if you did, you might get a paper cut." He pressed his eyes closed, and Georgia once again found him charming in a soft yet incredibly arrogant sort of way.

"No paper cuts on my feet yet," she said, looking back at the nonsensical papers. She'd messed them all up when CJ had called, and again just now. She wasn't even sure what she was looking at right now.

"Well, I have to go," he said. "It was real nice meetin' you, Georgia. If you need any more help with CJ, you let me know." He reached up and tipped his hat at her, then walked smoothly out of her office.

She forced herself to stay beside her desk until she couldn't hear the clomp-clomp-clomp of his cowboy boots against her hardwood floor. She hadn't told him that she sometimes did get splinters in her feet from that floor and her personal no-shoes-in-the-office policy. That was something she could maybe work into a conversation later.

A scoff came out of her mouth. "There isn't going to be a *later*, Georgia," she chastised herself. Then she picked up her phone again and called Abby.

She had no idea what time it was and if her best friend could answer a call right now. On the third ring, Georgia started to lower the phone. Then Abby said, "Georgia, you'll never believe who just called me."

She sounded breathless and not in a good way. So it wasn't Tex.

"Who?" Georgia asked, falling into the chair behind her desk. Her feet rejoiced to get some relief, but every cell in her body perked back up when Abby said, "CJ."

"What?" she demanded. "Why would he call you?"

"He wanted to know who you were dating now."

Georgia's blood turned to ice in her veins. "What did you tell him?"

"I said I didn't know what he was talking about, and even if I did, I didn't have to tell him."

Georgia nodded. "Yeah, that's good. Good job, Abby." Abby did have a sharp tongue, and she certainly didn't hold back from using it. Georgia liked that about her, because it meant when Abby was sweet, she really meant it. She was *real*, and Georgia didn't need any more fake in her life.

"He said you were kissing a cowboy in your office, and he *demanded* to know who it was."

"Oh, uh...." Georgia couldn't find the right words, though *Otis Young* streamed through her mind at the loudest volume she'd endured.

Abby gasped. "So it's true? You were kissing someone in your office? Who? Who was it?"

Georgia let out a long, hissing sigh. "Abby, don't get all excited."

"I'm not excited. I'm *irritated* you didn't tell me you've started seeing someone new."

"Because I haven't." Georgia put her head in her hands —well, the one not holding the phone. "CJ called and said he was bringing lunch. I told him under no circumstances would he do that. He couldn't come here. He said he was already there, and I went out into the hall to see. There was this...guy standing there."

So she omitted how good-looking Otis was. Abby didn't need to know that. She was in a crisis with Tex right now, and Georgia would not—she *would not*—tell her who he was.

"Oh, juicy," Abby said, clearly not irritated at all. She'd probably said that just to get Georgia to talk.

"Anyway, I said I needed him. Or something. I asked him to come into my office? Either way, he came into the office, and CJ showed up, and I begged the guy to pretend to be my boyfriend and kiss me." She lifted her head, the adrenaline of that kiss returning to her body. "This is all *your* fault anyway. You told me I just needed a new boyfriend and CJ would leave me alone."

"My fault?" Abby repeated, clearly not amused. "I

didn't tell you to pull in the first random stranger and start going at it."

"That is *not* what happened at all," Georgia said. The kiss had been sweet, unrushed, and absolutely perfect. The kind a caring, real boyfriend would give to his girlfriend in her office at her quaint bookshop when he'd stopped by with his daughter to get a few tomes.

Oh, she was in trouble. The kind with a capital T, because she couldn't start dating Otis Young for real.

Could she?

"So you don't know his name?" Abby asked.

"I...uh, sort of knew who he was."

"You didn't ask afterward?"

"He introduced himself."

Abby made an impatient noise. "Well? Are you going to tell me who it is or what?"

Georgia opened her mouth to spill the news, but she couldn't force herself to do it. "I'm going to plead the fifth," she said. "And insanity."

"Insanity? Then I should definitely get to know."

"Can I just...I don't know. Keep it to myself for a little bit? I...feel like a fool already." She did, and she just wanted to keep that kiss between her and Otis forever. Maybe if she did, that first fake kiss could become a first real kiss between the two of them.

"All right," Abby said, but Georgia knew she'd try to get it out of her any way she could. She'd sweeten her up, throw a question into a conversation out of nowhere, or needle her to death until Georgia finally told her. "How about we go to lunch this Saturday? Rosco's. I'll pay."

And there was the sweetening. Georgia decided she might as well take the offer, because Abby wouldn't make it twice. "Sure," she said. "I'll get us a table."

The call ended, and she sat at her desk, staring at the spot where Otis had leaned in the doorway. She could see him there, as well as in her life. She didn't know what that meant, but she knew she had some investigative work to do to figure out if Otis was seeing anyone right now and how open he was to a girlfriend if he wasn't.

She couldn't ask Abby, and she didn't have the man's phone number, so that meant she'd have to resort to... more underground ways. She picked up her phone again and called her mother.

CHAPTER
TWENTY-FIVE

Abby spent ten days standing at the back door, watching various people show up at the ranch next door and go about the jobs they'd been hired to do. Someone came and finished weather-proofing the deck. Men came and worked on the landscaping around the new barn. She actually had to stand on the back porch to see at that angle.

The younger of Wes Hammond's sons came to mow the lawn. Every morning, Abby walked into the kitchen to find Wade and Francesca there, and she didn't dislike the presence of that dog in her life. In fact, she reached down to pat the animal right now, and Franny started to pant.

"It's too hot to stand with the door open," Wade said as he wheeled himself into the kitchen.

Without replying, Abby fell back far enough to close the door. It did feel instantly cooler in the house, and she couldn't wait for the predicted storm to arrive. When she arrived at the library each morning, she looked west. She did the same thing every evening when she left. The sky had started to darken last night as the storm rolled over the Teton Mountains in the distance, but it hadn't reached Coral Canyon during the night.

"I'll help with the chores this morning," she said, stooping to pick up her boots. "It's supposed to start raining by lunchtime."

"Yeah, I saw," Wade said. He didn't move to pour himself a cup of coffee the way he normally did. He liked routine as much as Abby, and he always started the coffee first thing in the morning. Then he'd go shower and get ready for his day on the farm, come back, pour his coffee, and make something for breakfast.

Sometimes she cooked, if she was feeling particularly like eggs or pancakes or oatmeal. Most of the time—especially since Tex had walked away from her with an apology hanging in the air between them—she ate a banana and a piece of toast while Wade poured himself a big bowl of cereal.

"He's supposed to be back today," Wade said.

"Who?" Abby asked, though she knew darn well who.

"Come on," Wade said, giving her a frowning glare. "Tex. Your boyfriend. The man next door who you're in love with." He didn't phrase any of them as questions.

"We broke up." She shook her head, wishing she could glare back. She couldn't. Everything inside her felt so... broken. "He's not my boyfriend." She couldn't truly refute the last thing he'd said, so she simply closed her mouth.

"Abigail," Wade said, and he rarely used her whole name. "I don't understand why you punish yourself."

Franny moved over to him, and he scratched the dog behind the ears. Smiling at her, he said, "I'm gonna get a dog like you, Franny." He looked up at Abby. "Once Abby moves out, there will be room."

She scoffed, though Wade had just driven a spike into her heart. "That dog is too big for this house." They'd perfected the dance of maneuvering around his wheelchair in the small kitchen. "I just want a banana, and I'll go get started with the horses." She paused as he handed her the yellow fruit. "And you know, another woman is going to be moving in here. It's not like you'll be by yourself."

"I'm aware," he said dryly. "Have you looked at any apartments in town? I heard there's a new townhome development going in only a couple of blocks from the library."

Abby wrinkled her nose, the monster insider her cracking open its eyes. "I would never live in a development like that," she said.

"You lived in something like that in Chicago," he said.

"It's different there," she said, when she really meant *she'd* been different there. She didn't have the room to spread out and let her spirit fly in the city or the suburbs. She'd lived on the second floor, in a condo-ish townhome. The bottom level had been mostly garages, for three houses that existed on three different levels. Hers had been on the second level, and she could access it from inside the garage or from a front door that someone had to walk around the building and be a super-spy to find.

She didn't want that life. She wanted wide open skies and plenty of space between her and her neighbor. She wanted tall, mature trees, with land and buildings that exceeded her age. She wanted the scent of horses in the air, and fresh sunshine on her face no matter where she stood in her own house.

She peeled her banana and tossed the peel in the garbage can. "I can't look for an apartment yet, Wade. It's far too early. When they list rentals, they're ready now."

"You could move any time," he said with heavy nonchalance in his voice. "I'd be okay here alone."

"I know," she said, and then she walked out of the house. She couldn't stand that conversation. Of course her brother didn't need her anymore. Tex didn't need her. The land next door didn't need her. No one needed her.

"Abby," Wade called after her, and instead of stomping away like a child, she turned back to face him. He came down the ramp their father had built off the back of the porch, his eyes on hers. "I'm sorry. I know you don't want to leave the farm, and...."

"It's fine, Wade." She looked up into the sky, mostly to keep her tears where they belonged. "I'll start looking for something, okay? You don't need to worry about me."

"I worry about you constantly," he said quietly, that big sky she wanted above her house nearly drowning out his words. "I'll talk to Tex if you'd like."

"I would never like you to do that." She gave him a hard look. "I can handle him."

"Abby." He sighed and looked down at his lap. "He's

not a horse. He's not a dog. He's in love with you too, and he just wants you to…."

"Say it," Abby said, plenty of challenge in her voice. "Or don't. I know what you're going to say anyway." She turned away from her brother and walked toward the stables. Franny trotted alongside her, and Wade's wheels creaked and made noise on the dirt path behind her. "He doesn't need to be handled," she said. "He doesn't need to be told what to do like he's a naughty little boy."

She sighed, as she'd already realized all of the things she'd done to Tex. She'd held him down and clipped his wings when all he'd wanted to do was soar too. "He doesn't want me to criticize his ideas. He wants me to listen to them and then help him make them better."

"Yes," Wade said quietly.

"He doesn't want me to point out all the things he's not good at, because he already knows those." Heaven knew she did. "He wants me to love him despite those things." Her voice broke, and she couldn't win against the tide of tears this time, no matter how far up into the sky she looked. "He wants me to point out what he does excel at, and he wants me to support him in his trials and challenges."

She sobbed, and Wade pushed himself harder to get in front of her. "Hey," he said. "Come on and sit down."

"I can't," she said, tears pouring like a waterfall down her face. "I'll help you with the horses and then I have to get to work."

"Abby." Her brother looked up at her, pure compassion

and concern on his face. "Sit with me for one minute. Just one."

She didn't want to be so alone anymore. She didn't want to even think about moving out of the farmhouse. She didn't want to cry so much either.

She sat on his lap, and Wade put his arms around her. Franny came to their feet and leaned against them, and Abby cried into her brother's shoulder for a few seconds. "I'm sorry," she said. "I know I'm critical, and I have a short fuse, and I swear I've been trying to do better at both."

Wade said nothing as he ran his hand up and down her arm from shoulder to elbow. After a few moments, he said, "When I got released from the hospital and came home, you were the only person I wanted in the house. Remember?" He tilted his head, but she kept hers down, unable to look at him.

"I wouldn't even let Mama or Daddy come in. I didn't want them to see me how I was. But you...you were and are and have always been such a safe place for me."

"Stop it," she whispered.

"You took care of me completely," he said. "I needed all new clothes, and who did it? You, and you hate shopping. I had a thousand pills to take every day, and you made sure I took them at the right time. You checked all of my bandages, and you cleaned up horrible things."

"Wade, you're my brother. The only sibling I have."

"Tex could be your husband," he whispered. "The only one you have. The only man you need. If you can apologize to me and tell me you've been trying, then you can say the same things to him."

She lifted her head then. "It's not that easy."

"Yes," Wade said, his dark eyes earnest and kind. "It is. You call him right now, and you say, 'I'm so sorry. I miss you so much. I love you, and I'm trying so hard to be your biggest champion. I just need more time to practice. Can't we have more time so I can get better at it?'" He gave her a smile and wiped her face. "Okay? So don't worry about the horses. Go call him right now."

He made it sound so easy, and Abby searched his face, hoping for more amazing words that fit into the right sentences.

"You care about him in a different way than you cared about me," he said. "A more powerful way. A way that's stronger than the bonds between siblings." He nudged her. "Go on and get up. My legs are starting to tingle." He chuckled as she hurried to get to her feet.

They continued toward the stable, this time in the country silence that allowed her mind to think through tough things. She thought about what Wade had said. She thought about Tex and the tether that had always been between them. Even when he'd left, she'd been left holding one-half of that connection.

It had returned easily and quickly when he had, and Abby wondered if she'd severed it too completely to be fixed this time.

After she finished with the horses and left her brother to do the rest of the farm chores that day, she changed out of her work boots and into a pair of sandals. At the library, she weeded through useless emails, attended a boring meeting, and confirmed she'd be in Dog Valley in the Bookmobile for their Harvest Weekend—both Saturday night and Sunday afternoon. She thought about getting a hotel up there—Dog Valley had a couple of places for visitors to stay—only so she wouldn't have to torture herself by either skipping church or going and having an awkward interaction with Tex.

"Maybe you'll be back together by then," she murmured to herself inside her quiet office. The clock read just after noon, and while she didn't have Tex's itinerary, she didn't think he'd be back from Nashville yet. Not with a flight and then the drive from Jackson Hole.

She didn't have to drive the Bookmobile tonight, and Abby suddenly didn't want to return to the farm that had always been the safest place on the planet for her. She picked up her phone when it rang and quickly answered the call from Georgia.

"Hey, girl," Georgia said, plenty of upbeat vibes in her voice. They were set to go to lunch this Saturday, but she still wouldn't reveal the identity of the mystery cowboy who'd kissed her in her office a couple of days ago.

"Hey," Abby said, getting up and turning to look out her window. "What's up?"

"I'm wondering if you have—now hear me out."

"Oh, brother," Abby said, rolling her eyes. "I'm not taking another stray cat. My barns are mice-free, and we've still got the German shepherd."

"This is not about a stray cat."

"Praise the Lord."

Georgia giggled, and that alone alerted Abby to the direness of the situation. "I have a date." She hit the T on the last word pretty hard. "I'm wondering if you'd help me tame my curls after our lunch on Saturday. And can we maybe move that to breakfast? I'm going out for dinner, and I don't want to be too full."

Abby sputtered, not quite sure where to start. Helping Georgia with her hair was an all-day event, as her curls could really get out of hand sometimes. Abby believed them to be the most beautiful things in the world, but they did require some tender loving care—and a lot of relaxation hair products that sometimes had to sit for twenty minutes or more.

"Who are you going out with?" she asked, deciding to get that out of the way first.

"It's not the cowboy who kissed me a couple of days ago," she said.

"Okay," Abby said, a stab of disappointment hitting her between the ribs. "Then who is it?"

"You know him," Georgia said. "James Rylon?"

Abby did know the Rylons. Their family had lived in Coral Canyon for a long time, and they owned a ranch on the south side of town. "Wow," she said. "How old is James?" Older than her and Georgia, she knew that.

"His age is irrelevant right now," Georgia said, her soft, whimsical voice gone. "He asked me out, and I said yes. *That's* what matters."

"All right," Abby said, sighing. "I'll bring my kit and do my best."

Georgia laughed and thanked her. "Now," she said. "Why did you pick up my call so fast?"

"Oh, I...." Abby turned away from the window and straightened her shoulders. She had been about to call Georgia. "Tex is coming home today, and I'm not ready to face him. I was hoping I could stay in your guest room for a couple of nights. Just until Saturday."

Feeling like a coward, she sank into her desk chair. She'd get a hotel in Dog Valley on Saturday night, and maybe by Sunday evening she'd be ready to see Tex's truck in the driveway next door.

"Hmm," Georgia said. "Only if you'll let me brainstorm ways to get the two of you back together."

Abby sighed the biggest sigh of her life. "Fine."

"I'll talk to the cats," Georgia said. "You'll be taking their bedroom, you know."

"Georgia."

She must've included the right amount of pleading, because Georgia laughed and said, "Yes, come over tonight. I'll be home by six."

"Perfect," Abby said. "I'll bring our favorites from The Magic Noodle." The call ended, and she spun in her chair to look out the window again. She knew she was running and hiding, but right now, she didn't have a better solution.

She needed more time to come up with the right thing to do and say to repair the damage she'd done to Tex, and to their relationship.

After her talk with Wade that morning, she'd tapped

the words he'd said into her notes app, and she opened that on her phone and re-read them.

I'm sorry.

I love you.

I'm trying.

I just need more time to practice.

Can't we have more time?

Below that, she started typing out the reasons she wanted Tex in her life.

Makes me smile.

Listens to me.

Challenges me to be a better person.

Holds my hand just right.

Could be my family.

"Family," she whispered, thinking of how Wade had described her as his caregiver. She'd morphed from that as he'd healed, and he had eventually let their parents into the house, of course.

Abby felt so much like him. She didn't want anyone to see her yet. Only Wade knew how bad her wounds were, and she simply needed more time before she could allow Tex to see her.

"Soon," she said to herself, her eyes moving right back to that last word she'd spelled out. *Family.*

She wanted to belong to one of those so very badly, and she couldn't think of a better one than the big, loud Young family.

CHAPTER
TWENTY-SIX

Tex noticed that Abby's SUV wasn't in the driveway as he and Bryce pulled in. She didn't come home that night either. Her car wasn't there the next morning, and Bryce went to help Wade with the morning chores on the farm next door while Tex stayed secluded inside the farmhouse he'd been putting back together one textile at a time.

Things had gone swimmingly well in Nashville, and the celebrations he'd had with his brothers made him smile. A glance out the back window to the curing foundation of what would become the single most important thing he'd built on this ranch brought joy to his heart.

That recording studio would allow him to be the father he needed to be. Why couldn't Abby see that instead of all the traffic it would bring?

Why did he want to celebrate his good news with her—and only her?

He didn't care about the dinners in Nashville, the junk food binges, the card games with his brothers. They were fine. He enjoyed them. But all he'd been able to think about in Nashville with every victory he and the band had achieved was how he couldn't call Abby and tell her.

"Bryce first," he told himself as the boy came into view. He laughed with Wade, and Franny trotted ahead of the pair of them. "This has been so good for him." His son was a different person than he'd been when Tex had picked him up in April for Mav's wedding, and a completely different person than he'd been at the start of the summer.

"You have an album to make," he reminded himself next. "Perhaps after that...." He left the words there, looking next door though he couldn't see through timber and drywall. He sipped his coffee and heard Bryce outside before the door opened.

Franny bounded inside, her face bright and full of happiness and hope. Tex laughed and crouched down to scrub her face and throat. "Hey, girl. Did you help on the farm? Did you?"

"Dad," Bryce said, closing the door behind him. "Guess what Wade just told me?"

"What?"

"He knows of a horse auction in a couple of weeks that sells abused horses from around the west." He too wore joy and hope on his face. "Can we go? We can get some horses and start our rescue ranch."

Tex straightened, his mind buzzing at him not to kill this dream too quickly. "I thought we weren't going to get any animals until next spring," he said. "Then we don't have to go out in the dead of winter and take care of them." He picked up his coffee cup and took another sip. "It'll get mighty cold out there in the winter, son."

"I know," Bryce said. "Wade said he'd help me get the stables ready for winter."

Tex could see this wasn't going to die. "Do we have everything we need to take care of abused horses?"

"I'll do some research," Bryce said. "School doesn't start until Monday, and the auction's not until after Labor Day."

"Mm."

Bryce pulled out a box of cereal and then a bowl. He clanged around the kitchen, putting breakfast together for himself, and then he sat in his usual spot at the end of the dining room table. The seat that faced the front door and had a bird's eye view of the kitchen too. Behind him, he could've gone out the new sliding glass doors to the deck.

"I thought you wanted to be a country music star," Tex said, maintaining his ground in the kitchen.

Bryce had just stuffed his mouth full of sugary puffs, and he shrugged. "Maybe," he said around the cereal. He swallowed and added, "Let's see how this album goes first."

Tex nodded, the wisdom in his son inflating a balloon of pride in Tex's chest.

"What are you gonna do about Abby?" Bryce asked, immediately filling his mouth with more cereal.

"Uh, nothing?" Tex guessed. "There's nothing to do."

"Dad," Bryce said. "You like her so much."

"Yeah, I know I do." Tex lowered his head, wishing

he'd put his cowboy hat on that morning. He hadn't left the house yet, and it hung by the back door. "But you know what? Mav said once that that doesn't matter. If she doesn't like me, then there's nothing to do. I can't make her fall in love with me. I can't force that on someone. I'm not going to beg her to be with me."

She'd always had strong reactions to Tex, and he knew that was what they were—reactions. She usually calmed down and got into her rational thoughts and came around. But sometimes she barely seemed like she liked him at all. Other times, Tex was sure they were meant for one another.

"Wade says she's been really unhappy since you guys broke up."

"Well, join the club," Tex said darkly. Movement caught his eye outside, and he saw a couple of men wearing tool-belts heading toward the foundation. "I'm going to go talk to the construction manager." He turned away from his son, grabbed his hat, and left the house.

He looked at Abby's for as long as it took him to get down the steps, little stabs of regret and disappointment over their broken relationship hitting him in different spots in his lungs. The punctures didn't make breathing any easier, especially now that he'd returned to this higher elevation.

"Morning," he called as he got closer to the barn. "Are we framing soon?"

"We're checking," the manager said, and he smiled at Tex. "You're back."

Tex reached him, smiling too. "Yep," he said. "Got in

last night." He surveyed the concrete foundation. "And I got approved to record here by my label, so I need this done as soon as possible." He looked at Joel and his partner Cameron, who'd bent over the corner of the concrete. "How fast can you guys do it?"

"Depending on what we find today, I'd say it shouldn't take that long," Joel said. "There's no plumbing. You want two rooms, the whole thing soundproofed, and finished."

"Electrical is extremely important," Tex said. "And I am thinking of putting in a bathroom." Otherwise, everyone would have to use the house. Which he could handle.

"Well, plumbing is a different story. We didn't plumb it or prepare it for plumbing."

"But electrical is fine."

"Definitely," he said, turning in a circle back to the house. "It's what? Two hundred yards? I bet your septic tank is somewhere close to the house. And it's downhill from here. We could plumb it." He looked at Tex, his eyebrows up.

"Let me talk to the boys," he said. "How much time does that add?"

"Oh, not much," Joel said. "Another couple of days, and we have to dig up your yard."

Tex didn't need to talk to anyone. He didn't have a life manager anymore. This was his ranch, and his recording studio, and he said, "I want a simple bathroom in it then. Nothing fancy. A sink and a toilet."

"Let's look at the plans," Joel said, setting down his bag of tools and plucking a clipboard from the top of it.

Tex focused on the task, the Wyoming wind trying to

steal away the floorplans as he and Joel looked at them. When the rain started to fall, Tex said, "Let's get inside."

Cameron pulled the tarp back over the cement, and the three of them ran for the house. Tex was still soaking wet by the time he found shelter, and he offered the two men coffee. Joel said yes and sat at the table, got out his tablet, and started to sketch in the bathroom he and Tex had just talked about.

Five minutes later, after Tex had changed his shirt and returned to the kitchen, Joel had the new floorplan done. He slid the tablet toward Tex, and asked, "What do you think? Does that still give you the space you need for your equipment?"

Tex picked up the tablet and looked at it. Joel had not only added in a bathroom in the front corner of the studio, he'd also added a foyer. "Wow," he said.

"It's an entryway," he said. "Sounds like you boys might be recording in the winter, and this'll give you a place for your boots, hats, coats." He pointed to the entryway, which spanned the front of the barn, where the entrance sat.

"Then," he said. "The bathroom is off that. Takes up the same width as the entryway, and everything else is the same."

"It pushes everything back four feet," Tex said, catching the number on the screen. "That's perfect."

"More privacy for the recording too," Cameron said, standing next to Tex and peering at the plan. "Anyone coming in and out isn't really in the studio until they go through the door."

"Right," Joel said.

"It's amazing." Tex handed the tablet to Bryce, who'd just come in from the porch. "What were you doin' out there?"

"Bailey left for Montana today," he said. "She stopped by to say good-bye." He held the tablet and looked at it. "What's this?"

"New floorplan for the studio," he said. "These boys think it'll be done by...Halloween?" He looked at Joel, who nodded.

"Way before Halloween," he said.

"I can get Tom out here to dig the plumbing tomorrow," Cameron said, looking up from his phone. "Should I?"

"Yes," Joel and Tex said together. He walked away from the conversation and looked out the big glass doors to the tarp-covered foundation.

"Thank you, Lord," he whispered, a thread off peace and comfort moving through him. Building this studio was the absolute right thing to do, because Tex wanted to stay right here in Coral Canyon with his son.

And Abby, he thought, and the discontentment that had been his constant companion these past several days perked up again. He had to do something about her.

But what?

CHAPTER
TWENTY-SEVEN

Bryce Young left the farmhouse through the front door just as a rowdy round of laughter filled the whole world. His uncles could be *so* loud, and he hurried to pull the door closed behind him.

The silence enclosing around him actually made his ears buzz with the absence of noise, and he reached for the guitar he'd left propped in the corner from that morning's lessons. He'd loved giving those this summer, but he'd decided to take a break for the next couple of weeks until everyone got settled into school.

Three more days, he thought as he settled onto the top step and laid the guitar across his lap. School started on a Tuesday, and why it wasn't Monday, Bryce didn't know. He didn't much care. He had a new backpack, and his father had bought him plenty of new clothes Bryce didn't even need.

He wouldn't know a single other senior, as the few

teens he knew were younger than him. He often felt trapped between two worlds. He wasn't quite an adult, but he didn't really belong in the child column either. Right now, his younger cousins had gathered downstairs in the basement to watch a cartoon while their dads worked through the songs which had been approved by their music moguls.

Joey was seven, Corrine four, Boston seven, and Harry eleven. Bryce felt decades older than them, though he was technically only six years above Harry.

He also didn't quite fit in with the band inside. Mav had come, and he wasn't technically part of the band either, but he was in the same generation as the other Young men in the house. Bryce wasn't. He once again existed on the cusp of a group, and he wasn't sure where he belonged.

Other than here with his dad, that was.

He looked down at the guitar, his fingers sliding along the familiar strings. His dad had given him guitar lessons every time he was home, and he'd funded them over the years. This instrument had saved Bryce on more than one occasion. His father had too.

When his mom drank too much and started sobbing and screaming, Bryce could escape to his room, lock the door, and play over the noise she made. Bryce had told his dad, and his mom didn't drink anymore. At least at home.

Then, if she brought home her boyfriend of the week, Bryce could once again retreat to his room, lock the door, and play to drown out whatever he didn't want to hear. He'd told his father about that too, and his mother stopped bringing men home. She still dated a lot, but Bryce didn't have to know about it.

In truth, his father had been there for him every single time Bryce had needed him. He loved his dad with a power he couldn't fathom, because his father had always come to his rescue and protected him, no matter where he was physically.

Sometimes, Bryce wondered what his life would've been like had his parents stayed together, or if he'd lived with his dad full-time instead of his mom. He dismissed the first scenario, because he didn't want to waste his imagination on what-ifs. What would be the point? To make himself feel bad about what he hadn't had?

The second he currently enjoyed, so he didn't spend any time trying to figure out if he should've asked to be with his father at an earlier age. He traveled so much, and it wouldn't have been possible.

Bryce thought he heard a voice floating on the air, and he looked up from the strings. He glanced south, where his ears thought the sound had come from, the but the road in front of the house remained as empty as ever. Their ranch extended that way for about three-quarters of a mile, and Bryce saw no one.

He plucked a few chords, his throat starting to hum with a song. He'd played and practiced with the boys inside on the two songs he'd be performing with them. Their plans for a tour weren't solid. They weren't even a gel. At this point, anything could happen, and the record wasn't even done yet. They hadn't even started recording, but apparently everyone had to memorize everything before they got into the studio, and now Dad worried that it would be done before they'd be ready to use it.

He shook his head, smiling at the way his father worried over so many things.

His head jerked up and left this time, looking north toward the Ingalls' place as he heard the voice again. He couldn't make out what it said, nor if it was a man or a woman, but something whispered inside his brain that he better go see who needed help.

He stood and leaned his guitar back into the corner of the house and jumped from the porch. He went toward Wade's house, but the man's truck wasn't in the driveway. Bryce had already been next door this morning to help with the chores, just like he usually did. Sometimes Wade drove further onto their farm and parked back by the barns.

The Ingalls owned about half as much land as his dad had bought on their ranch. Wade had told him once that it was a hundred and ten acres, and Bryce knew they owned two hundred. Wade and Abby took care of a half-dozen horses, three or four dairy cows, a whole mess of chickens, and a couple of pigs.

Wade had laughed as he'd told Bryce about the other animals they'd raised over the years. "Every few years or so, I get a hankering to raise a side of beef. So I'll do that. One year I got three turkeys and raised up right, just to eat 'em for Thanksgiving and Christmas."

The pigs they had now, in fact, would become dinner at some point. Wade kept a good farm, and past the huge garden that he and Abby worked all summer long sat the enormous chicken coop. The stable stood on the other side of the road, and down past that waited a pair of barns.

Wade kept one full of hay and the other housed supplies, tools, and tack. Out past the stables, the fields took over, most of them filled with hay. An equipment shed stood out there too, and all of the tractors and equipment that Wade used had been specially fitted so he could drive it without his legs.

Bryce walked past the garden, which still held plenty of green and producing things, another yell filling the air. Alarms rang in his head, one voice yelling at him to, *Run!*

Breaking into a sprint, he called, "Wade!"

"Bryce!"

"Where are you?" He rounded the corner, the stable right in front of him. Wade's truck sat parked there, but Bryce couldn't see him. "Wade?"

"Behind the stable," the man yelled, and Bryce took off past the truck and then to his left when he reached the corner of the stable. Wade's wheelchair came into view, and seeing it toppled onto its side made Bryce's blood run cold.

"Wade," he said, his heart pounding, because he still didn't see the man. "Wade!"

"Right here."

Bryce burst past the edge of the stable, the whole of the farm coming into view. Wade lay on the ground at least fifteen or twenty feet from his fallen chair. Bryce rushed toward him, taking in the blood on the man's face, hands, and arms.

"What happened?" he asked, falling to his knees and

skidding a little. Pain fired at him for only a moment, and then it faded under the adrenaline coursing through him. He didn't know where to put his hands, and his first thought was to call his dad.

"I called Abby already," Wade said, putting his hand on Bryce's shoulder. "She's on her way out."

"What can I do?" Bryce asked. *Get the chair. Get him in it.* He jumped to his feet and said, "I'll help you back into your chair." He jogged over to it, grabbed it, and sat it upright. It went across the gravel and slightly rutted ground to where Wade now sat up.

"My ribs hurt," he said, the only time Bryce had ever heard him complain. "There was a wild dog, and it came out of the stable right as Aristotle and I got back. The horse spooked, reared up, and threw me."

He nodded toward the corner of the paddock. "He's over there now, actin' like a cat and keepin' his head down, as if he can't see me then I won't be able to see him." Wade shook his head, and Bryce hoped he hadn't hit that too hard.

"You've got a lot of blood on you," he said. "Let me check your head."

"It's from my hands." Wade held up his right one. "This one caught most of my fall, along with my ribs and back, and it got cut up on the gravel." His right hand still wept blood, and Bryce wasn't convinced that was the man's only injury.

He held the chair still by putting on the brakes and bracing the front wheel with his foot. Wade put his left hand on Bryce's shoulder, and Bryce said, "One, two, three."

Wade did most of the work, pressing hard on Bryce to get himself up. He twisted and turned in midair, landing in his chair the right way. He groaned, and Bryce quickly released the brake on the chair.

He moved behind it and started pushing.

"I can do it."

"Nope," Bryce said. "I've got you. House or stable?"

"House," Wade said, tucking his bleeding hand inside his shirt and holding it tightly with the other one.

Bryce couldn't push and text, so he paused for a moment to take out his phone to dial.

"I tried your dad," Wade said. "You too. You guys didn't answer."

Bryce frowned. "My dad's got all his brothers over. They're practicing their set. But I was just on the front porch." He hadn't heard his phone ring or chime. As he looked at it, he did have a missed call.

From ten minutes ago.

Fear and regret made his blood run cold. "I'm sorry," he said sincerely. "I was inside when you called, and it's so loud in there."

"It's fine," Wade said, his voice tough and resigned. "Abby's almost here."

"Where's she been?" Bryce asked, his voice pitching up. He could admit he liked Abby a whole lot. She spoke to him like a regular person, and he'd enjoyed getting to know her as they did chores together on the farm. "Haven't seen her the past couple of mornings."

"Hiding," Wade said darkly. He looked up at Bryce.

"Hey, we should work on her together. See if she'll go talk to your dad. She's a right mess. Been stayin' at her friend Georgia's house, because she didn't want to run into him."

Bryce frowned and looked down the driveway once he turned the corner. "Is she still mad at him?"

"She never was mad," Wade said. "She just has a mouth that she can't control sometimes. Happens to the best of us."

"My dad wouldn't really say what happened," he said. "Just that they'd broken up." He looked to the farmhouse he and his father had spent so much time, effort, and money on that summer. "He's not super happy with himself with what happened."

"Wait'll you see Abs," Wade said. Her SUV came into view, and she dang near took the corner on two wheels she pulled into the driveway so fast. Bryce met her eyes, and he found pure panic in hers.

As they registered him, she relaxed. She still jammed the car in park before it had come to complete stop and jumped from it in the next moment. "Wade!" She ran toward them, arriving several seconds later. "My word, you're *covered* in blood. Where are you hurt the most?" She pulled a wad of brown paper napkins from her pocket. "This is all I had in the car, but it'll be okay. We'll get you inside and get you cleaned up, and—"

"Abby," he said, cutting her off. Bryce was glad about that, because he wasn't sure how much higher her voice could get. "I'm fine."

Her hands fluttered with the napkins, and Wade took

them from her. "Bryce here helped me back into the chair. I
think the biggest problem is gonna be the ribs."

"Did you break one?" She fell into stride on Wade's
right side, and Bryce noted that she didn't look toward his
house, not once.

He pushed Wade up the ramp while he continued to
tell Abby he was fine. No, he hadn't broken his legs, either
of them. No, his head didn't hurt. No, he wasn't bleeding
anywhere that he knew of besides his hands and lower
arms. No, he wasn't going to the hospital. No, he hadn't
called Cheryl yet.

Inside the house, Abby flew into motion, getting
several clean cloths warm and mopping the mess from her
brother's face and ears. Sure enough, he hadn't been cut on
his face. The only scrape Bryce could see sat along the back
of his neck, and Abby handed him a first aid kit and told
him to bandage it.

Bryce did that, all while he kept his mouth shut. Abby
had plenty to say about Aristotle, and once Bryce was
convinced Wade wasn't going to bleed out, he met the
man's eyes.

Wade nodded, clearly not enthused about the lecture he
was enduring.

"I'll go put Aristotle back in the stable," he said in a
brief pause while Abby took a breath.

"Thank you, Bryce," she and Wade said together, and
he ducked out of the house. He went back down the ramp
and back out to the stable. He coaxed the horse away from
the fence and into the building, taking several long

minutes to brush him down, give him a treat, and make sure he was safe and secure in his stall.

He could just go home now, but one look at his shirt, and everyone next door would freak the heck out if he walked in like that. Covered in blood. So he went back up the ramp and into the Ingalls house.

Wade wasn't in the kitchen anymore, but Abby was. She stood at the sink, rinsing cloths, and she looked over her shoulder when Bryce entered. "You dear boy," she said, wringing the life out of one rag. "Come get cleaned up. You have blood all over you too."

"I didn't hear him call," Bryce said, his adrenaline gone and some numbness starting to set in. He sniffled, and he wasn't sure why he was suddenly so emotional. "He called my dad, and then me, and we didn't answer."

Abby turned fully, pure sympathy on her face. "It's not your fault, Bryce." He rushed at her, and she opened her arms to him. "Come on, now," she said, her voice soothing and quiet. "You heard him calling, and you came. That's all that matters."

Bryce closed his eyes, and he saw Wade down on the ground, all that blood everywhere…. He sobbed into Abby's shoulder, and while he probably stood a foot taller than her, she offered him maternal comfort and support in a way he'd never gotten from his own mother.

"Sorry," he said only a few seconds later. He stepped back and took the warm washcloth she offered him. He covered his face with it, breathing in the moist heat and taking a moment to further compose himself. He wiped up through his hair and down to his collar. "I don't know what that was."

"You were scared," she said, taking the cloth and handing him another. "Because you love Wade."

"Yeah," he said. He used this rag to wipe his hands clean, going all the way up to his elbows. "Just like you love my dad."

She sucked in a breath, and Bryce kept his head down but lifted his eyes. "Right?"

"Bryce," she said. "I don't—I don't know what to tell you."

An idea popped into his head. He could see the whole scene in front of him in less time than it took for him to take a breath. "Come next door with me," he said. "He's home right now, and he wants to see you."

She started to shake her head before he finished talking, but Bryce leaned forward, his enthusiasm and excitement back. "Please, Abby."

"I saw the mess of trucks," she whispered. "All your uncles are there."

"Yeah," Bryce said. "Abs, that's the perfect time to walk in. Remember when Dani showed up at the hotel for Mav? And we were all there? I mean, you weren't there, but I was there. Dad was there. Dad helped her make sure the band was there, so everyone would know how crazy she was for him." He grinned at her. "They're all there, Abby."

She looked like she might throw up. "First, I'm not Dani. Secondly, I don't even know what to say."

"You won't have to say anything," Bryce said, his imagination taking the scene and morphing it. "Trust me. I

know my dad, and I know my uncles. You walk in, and...
my dad will take over. He'll say everything, and then all
you'll have to do is kiss him." He grinned at her. "Please?
Come on, we can go right now."

"I can't go," she said. "Wade is here, and he—"

"Wants you to go next door," Wade said from the doorway. He wore his prosthetic legs now, and he leaned
against the doorframe, all evidence of his tumble gone.
He'd changed his clothes, and the bottom part of his legs
extended out of his shorts. "If you don't go next door, I
will, because I need help with the chores this afternoon.
I'm gonna ask Tex. So he'll come over here, because then
I'll have to invite him to dinner. And you're here, and you
won't leave, because my rib might be broken."

He lifted his shoulder, a grimace marring his normally
handsome face. "Maybe two or three of 'em."

Abby's eyes were as wide as Bryce had ever seen them,
and she looked from Wade to him. He took her hand in his.
"I'll go with you, and anything that's too hard for you to
do alone, I'll do for you."

"Go," Wade said, and Bryce sent up a prayer that the
Lord would soften her stubbornness enough to get her to
take the first step.

Abby turned toward the door, and Bryce took the first
step.

She took the second.

CHAPTER
TWENTY-EIGHT

T ex put his hands around the back of his neck and squeezed. "That chord isn't right," he said, but his voice got lost among the other brothers as they continued to argue.

"I don't like how we're smashin' a three-syllable word into two beats," Luke said.

"It works," Otis said, who had been tired of defending his songs for at least the past hour. "Because it rhymes with the lyric down here." He practically punched the music stand which held the innocent pages.

Having everyone in his living room had started to wear on Tex about thirty minutes ago, when Bryce had snuck out through the front door.

He turned away from Trace and Morris, who both leaned over the music stand, both of them still arguing. He looked out the front window, but Bryce wasn't on the front step where he expected him to be.

His stomach growled, and Tex pulled out his phone to find something for dinner that night. On a Friday, he wouldn't want to sit down and eat, because it seemed like everyone in Coral Canyon went out to eat at the end of the week. He could call and order something, make the drive, and Bryce could run in and pick up the food.

If he could just get rid of everyone first. "All right, fellas," he said, turning back to the lot of them. Mav sat casually on the couch, flicking through his social media on his phone, and a powerful jolt of jealousy hit Tex. He was so relaxed, and he didn't have to deal with any of…this.

"It's time to wrap it up for today," he said. "It's almost dinnertime, and Bryce and I are going to head to town to pick up food."

"What?" Luke asked. "We can't stop now."

"This song isn't even close to done," Morris added.

The look on Otis's face at that comment could've killed Morris, and Tex quickly stepped between the two of them. "Otis," he said through clenched teeth. "Get the music off the stand."

"Right." Otis lunged for it and rolled it up in his fingers. "Tex is right," he yelled over the protests. "This isn't how our best songs are made."

Trace stepped back and folded his arms, but at least he wasn't as vocal as Luke. He did glare in Tex's direction, but Tex simply raised his eyebrows and indicated how Luke was still arguing with Otis about something that had already been put away.

Mav got to his feet and said, "I'll get the kids."

"I've got to find my son," Tex said, turning back to the

window and leaning further toward it. "He's not on the front porch." He rested his forehead against the glass and twisted his head to the right, trying to see all the way in front of the door.

Behind him, everyone finally turned silent, and Tex said, "I wonder where he went."

"I know where he is," Mav said, his voice perfectly even.

Tex straightened and turned. "Where?" fell from his mouth at the same time his eyes landed on his tall son. His eyes traveled to where Bryce held hands with Abigail Ingalls, and the world went white for a moment.

When he opened his eyes, he focused on Abby. He opened his mouth to say something, but his brain was still catching up to the silence—and the fact that Abby was here.

She was *here*.

"Dad," Bryce said, smiling at him. He nodded to Abby. "I was just next door, and look who I found."

"Evenin', Abby," Otis said, and he gave her a side-squeeze. "It's good to see you."

"You too, Otis."

"I'm just gonna, uh, go grab my daughter."

"Me too," Mav said. "Except I don't have my daughter. I have my son, so I'm gonna grab him."

"Get mine too," Trace said. "I just need to use the bathroom."

"Luke," Otis barked from the kitchen. "Come get Corrinne."

"Oh, right." Luke high-tailed it out of the living room, and Morris took a couple of steps after him.

"Mav's my ride," he said. "Good to see you, Abby."

She nodded at him, and Tex catalogued that they'd all started to leave. He blinked and took a breath and stepped toward Abby. "You're here." He drew her away from his son and into his arms, his eyes drifting closed at the scent of her hair. She smelled like books and the air freshener in her car...and something else his brain couldn't quite identify.

"I missed you," she said. "I'm so sorry, Tex."

"Shh, no," he said. "You don't have to apologize to me."

Her arms went around him, and Tex smiled into the embrace. "I just need more time to show you that I'll support you in anything you do."

"You got it," he said.

"Tex, you're—I need you to understand." She stepped back and wiped her eyes.

He watched her, slightly confused. "Understand?"

"Yeah," she said. She pressed her palms together and then ran them up his chest. "I don't mean to come at you with all of my attitude. I've been working on listening first and reacting second. Of course I want you to build a recording studio here, so you can be here with your son and with me. I don't care how many people come to the ranch, as long as *I* get to come over here and kiss you."

Tex smiled down at her. "You're welcome any time, sweetheart."

"Tex, I'm in love with you." Her eyes crinkled as she

smiled and then a slightly manic giggle escaped her lips. "Wade said all I'd have to do is apologize and say I was trying and tell you I love you, so I guess I've said it all now."

Tex took a moment to absorb all she'd said. *Tex, I'm in love with you.*

"Abby," he said, aware of all the feet scuttling along his kitchen floor, just around the other side of the wall. People started crowding into the wide, arched doorway that went into the dining room and kitchen.

"Shh," Luke said, holding his daughter in his arms. Otis had a hand on Joey's shoulder, and Harry stood at Trace's side. They all watched him.

Tex looked at his son, his eyes seeing details he hadn't before. Something wasn't right with his boy, but he stood there breathing and grinning like Tex had brought home a pair of ponies carrying guitars.

He cleared his throat, suddenly everything he wanted to say right in front of him. "Abby, I don't have much more to say. I think I fell in love with you the moment I saw you marching across the crunchy grass toward me on the very first day I got back to Coral Canyon."

"Tex, I'm really going to try harder to be the support you need."

"I heard you the first time," he said, taking her face in his hands. "I appreciate that, and I want that. The truth is, I have a lot of good news, and the only person I wanted to call when I was in Nashville was you. I've been dying since I walked away from you two weeks ago. I'm sorry I did that. I'm sorry I didn't call you from Nashville. I love you, and—I yeah. I love you."

"He loves you," Bryce said, chuckling.

"He *looooves* you," Otis said in a mocking tone, laughing afterward.

"He so loves you," Mav said, grinning.

Tex pressed his cheek to Abby's and whispered, "This is the madness you'll have to endure." He turned her gently to look at their audience, and he grinned at them.

"He's been in love with you forever," Trace said, smiling back at them.

"I don't know how we all survived in Nashville with his brooding and longing sighs," Luke said, rolling his eyes. He grinned at Tex in the next moment, and Tex ran his hands down Abby's arms to her hands.

"Even I know Tex is in love with you," Morris said, smiling at the pair of them.

"So how many of you knew I was in love with him too?" she asked.

"I knew," Bryce said, raising his hand.

Everyone slid their eyes over to Bryce, and Otis sucked in a breath. "Boy, what happened to you?"

Tex hadn't even kissed Abby yet, but he too took a closer look at his son. He sucked in a breath when he realized the stains he'd seen earlier were actually from blood. "Why are you covered in blood?" he asked, and Bryce looked at Abby and they both burst out laughing.

CHAPTER
TWENTY-NINE

"He's fine," Abby insisted. "Really, Tex. You don't need to go check on Wade." She looked from Tex to Otis, silently begging him to do something.

"I'll go," Otis said, his face turning a shade of red that didn't fit the situation. "Come on, everyone. Let's go check on Wade."

Before she could stop the tide that was the Young brothers, they flooded out of the house. "Oh, uh," she said. "Maybe I should text my brother so he knows what's coming."

"I'm going to go change my clothes," Bryce said, and he went in the opposite direction of his uncles.

"I don't think you have time to text Wade," Tex said, turning her in his arms so they faced one another again. "Because by my count, we're by ourselves, and it's not going to stay that way for long." He wore his country music star mega-watt smile, and Abby couldn't help sinking into that.

"I suppose you want to kiss me," she said.

He shrugged slightly. "A little."

"I guess I could stand that," she said. She looped her hands up behind his neck and drew him down to her. She waited, her eyes closed, and when Tex finally kissed her, Abby's pulse rocketed up to light speed.

She breathed in, every cell in her body tingling as the love mingled between them. Now that Tex had said how he felt about her, she could feel it in every stroke of his lips against hers. She hoped he could feel it in her touch too.

He pulled away after only a few seconds, when Abby wanted to kiss him for a lot longer. "Abby," he said as he breathed in. She liked the airy quality of her name in his voice. "Do you want to try dinner tonight?"

"No," she said, smiling up at him. "I want whatever you have here and to just spend the night talking. The two of us."

"I do have a son," he whispered, his lips skating along the edge of her jaw. Her brain buzzed at her, and she wasn't sure how Tex had known to wear her favorite cologne while he simply worked on songs with his band in his own home.

"Yeah," Abby said. "I really like him too, Tex."

"It seemed that way," he said, pulling back. "I saw him holdin' your hand."

Abby beamed up at him, so much happiness flowing through her, she could finally see how perfectly miserable she'd been without him. "He helped get me over here," she said, a measure of nervousness returning. "I've been wanting to come talk to you since you walked away."

"I'm sorry I did that."

"It's not your fault," she said. "I'm the one who acted like someone building a barn on their property was against the law." She couldn't believe herself sometimes. "I really am trying, Tex."

He searched her face, then dipped his head and kissed her. "I love you just the way you are, Abs," he whispered, and then he kissed her again. He couldn't have said more perfect words, and Abby fell in love with him a little more because of them.

Her phone rang, Wade's ringtone, and her heartbeat catapulted up into her throat. She pulled away, a pulse throbbing in her neck. "That's Wade."

"Yeah," Tex said with a chuckle. "He probably wants you to come save him from my crazy brothers."

She silenced the call and looked up at Tex. "The last time he called, he'd been thrown from a horse."

"Let's go see 'im," Tex said. Leaning closer, he added, "The night is young. We can kiss later."

She giggled and tucked herself into his arms. "All right, cowboy."

"Bryce," Tex called. "We're goin' next door."

"Kay," his son called back. "I'll be over in a little bit."

Abby looked down the hall. "What's he doing?"

"He might be talking to his friends in Boise," Tex said, glancing toward the bedrooms too. "Or Bailey. Or maybe he just needs a break. He left the house to get away from crazy, and then came home covered in another man's blood." Tex grinned at Abby, and she'd always been able to get lost in his eyes. Now, everything felt different. Now, she loved him—with a real, grown-up love—and he loved her.

She didn't want to kiss him later. Well, she did, but she wanted to kiss him right now too. She pulled his face toward hers while he chuckled and said, "You're going to make every one of my brothers talk."

"Let 'em talk," she whispered just before his lips touched hers.

———

"HAVE A NICE DAY," ABBY SAID TO THE MOTHER AND CHILD who'd just finished checking out their books at the self-serve kiosk. The library here in Coral Canyon only had one, and she'd just finished reshelving the non-fiction titles and had returned to the desk.

Margot Gatwood nodded at her and herded her boy toward the exit with some measure of relief on her face. Abby couldn't stop smiling, though in the past, the thought of dealing with a whiny, crying child would've irritated her.

Today, the next person she saw brightened her whole world, and she practically vaulted over the waist-high doorway that led out of the desk area to get to Tex.

"Hey," he said as he caught her in his arms. He laughed and pressed a sloppy kiss to her neck. "How are you?"

"Good," she said. "Now that you're here."

"Yeah, because I brought lunch." He held up the brown

paper bag giving off the delectable scent of garlic and butter.

"Did you bring the floorplan?"

"Freshly printed," he said with a smile as he stepped back.

She led the way into her office and closed the door. She had a few printouts to show him too, but she'd been asking him for a week to show her the floorplan for the recording studio, and he'd claimed not to have it.

"Really," Bryce had finally told her. "They mocked it up on a tablet. I don't think he has it."

So Tex had asked his contractor for it, and well, contractors didn't seem to understand the need to get back to people very quickly. With all of the rain in the past week, they hadn't done anything to the foundation in Tex's backyard, and she knew his frustration had started to grow roots and branches.

Hers had too, because the rental market in Coral Canyon was intense. She hadn't told anyone—not Tex and not Wade—that she'd started looking at potential places to rent. The first had been during lunch two days ago, and she'd left in a coughing fit from all the dust.

That's a no, she'd told her real estate agent. He'd said that dust could be cleaned, but Abby didn't think anyone could vacuum up all of the dirt and grime in that carpet. Oh, no. It would have to be ripped out and replaced, the way Tex and Bryce had done at their farmhouse. Abby wasn't going to do that, not for a rental.

She'd gone to another place after work yesterday, because she didn't have to drive the Bookmobile, but all she'd learned was that "quaint" meant "microscopic" and "you can't even fit a twin bed in this place so don't bother."

Another no.

She wasn't discouraged yet. She had patience and loads of time to find somewhere. She simply didn't like the process. It reminded her of all she was leaving behind, and she'd rather just get it done quickly.

She sighed as she sat behind her desk, and that drew Tex's eyebrows up as his attention centered on her. "That didn't sound good." He pulled out the first carton of food and read the writing on the top. "This is your ravioli."

"Thanks." Abby looked down at the printouts of the houses she'd looked at that morning. Fisting them, she picked up several. "Will you help me look through these? Maybe come with me to look at some of them, if your schedule allows?"

Tex took the papers, curiosity written in the lines of his face. "What are these?" He studied the top one. "Rentals?" He looked at her, his curiosity morphing into concern and compassion. "You're already looking to rent?"

She pulled her food toward her and said, "Yes. Wade is getting married in less than four months. I don't have to live there now. He's a grown man." Her worry carved a way through her belly, but she thought she did a pretty good job containing it.

Tex said nothing but went back to the papers. He tucked the first one behind the others and got his food out of the bag too. Abby liked that he didn't jump right into the conversation, offering his opinion and bossing her around. She'd endeavored to be more like that in the past couple of weeks—more silent, more thoughtful, less vocal about things, even if she didn't agree.

She'd never be as good at it as him, and she'd come to terms with that. She didn't need to *be* Tex. She could still be herself, and his words to her in his living room—*I love you just the way you are*—had assured her and reassured her over the passing days.

She ate a few bites of ravioli while he assessed the pile of rentals. He finally sighed, straightened them all together, and put them on the edge of her messy desk. He unwrapped his plastic silverware and took off the lid on his steak and spinach pesto.

"Here's what I think," he said, finally looking at her. His eyebrows went up again, nearly touching the underside of that cowboy hat, as he asked her silently if she wanted to hear his opinion.

She nodded for him to go on, because she so desperately did.

"You don't need one of those," he said, waving at them dismissively. "Wade and Cheryl are getting married just before Christmas, right?"

"Yes," she said, surprise not allowing her brain to function very well. "December twenty-second."

Tex mixed his pasta together, his eyes down, that cowboy hat obscuring her view of his face. "I'll talk to Wade."

"What?" Abby asked. "Tex, you're not making any sense."

He forked up a piece of steak and a piece of penne.

"Actually, it's probably Cheryl I need to talk to. Wade won't care."

"Care about what?" Abby leaned toward him, wishing she could read minds. His eyes met hers, and oh, that mischief shone through. Excitement bubbled in her stomach. "Tex," she said with plenty of warning in her voice.

"It's kind of a crazy idea," he said.

She couldn't eat another bite until she heard it all. She told herself to hold her sharp tongue too. So she folded her arms and blinked at him, clearly telling him to go on and spit it all out.

"That's it?" he asked, grinning at her. "You're not going to throw some witty comment about how building a recording studio in a barn was crazy too?" He chuckled and put his food in his mouth. He shook his head, charm and charisma flowing from him as he ate. After he swallowed, he said, "Abby, you don't have to change for me."

"I'm not changing for you," she said, plenty of bite in her tone. "I'm changing for me. So I'm not so unhappy all the time. So I don't lose you and have to go through that again."

His dark eyes burned in her direction. "It feels like you're doing it to please me," he said. "I don't like it. I never asked you to be anyone different than you are. Or act any differently."

"I know," she said. "I'm waiting to hear the crazy idea, because yes, it might be just as amazing—insane, sure. But amazing—as building a recording studio in a barn so that you can stay right here with your son. And me."

"And you," he said, pointing his fork at her. "You got that part right."

"I know Bryce is your focus," she said. "As he should be. That boy...he's something, Tex. You're not going to be able to contain him in a box, that's for sure."

"I'll have to ask my mama and daddy how they let me do what I did," Tex said, chuckling, and they were so far off-topic now that Abby wanted to scream. He seemed to understand her slow internal combustion, because he sobered.

"All right," he said. "Hear me out."

"I'm all ears." She swallowed, the few bites of ravioli she'd taken not enough.

"I don't think you need to find somewhere to rent," he said. "Because if I talk to Cheryl and she says it's okay, we could get married on the twenty-second with her and Wade." He nodded as if he hadn't just dropped a bomb.

Two bombs. Two nuclear bombs, one right after the other.

Abby kept breathing, but only because her body did that by itself. Everything in her tightened, clenching to the point of pain. She exhaled and released all the tension in her muscles. "Tex Monroe Young," she said calmly, reaching to pick up her fork. "That better not have been your proposal."

He burst out laughing and shook his head. "No, ma'am."

She stabbed a ravioli and looked at him again. "It's insane."

"I know," he said, grinning.

"It's less than four months."

"Yep."

"You barely know Cheryl." That wasn't a good argument at all, not that Abby was trying to argue with Tex. He usually got his way, because he was so darn likeable and he didn't even know it.

"Oh, I know her fine," Tex said, waving that one away as Abby expected him to. "The real question, sweetheart, is if *you* think you can be ready to marry me in less than four months." He took another bite, his eyes never leaving hers.

She couldn't hold his gaze, and she dropped her eyes to her food. She took a bite too, not ready to tell him she'd have married him when they were eighteen-year-old kids. In that moment, she realized he wasn't asking her if she *could* marry him. He was asking if she could *be ready* to marry him.

"Because if not," he said. "There's no point in me embarrassing myself with Cheryl. Seein' as how we'll soon be family and all."

"Again," she said sarcastically. "That better not have been a proposal."

He chuckled and shook his head. "That's gonna blow your mind," he said. "Don't worry. You'll know it when it comes." He'd been saying that for a few days now, ever since they'd talked about getting married.

"Here's what I think," she said slowly, separating out a chunk of tomato from her ravioli. She didn't like the big chunks in the sauce. Her heart thumped wildly in her chest. "I'm ready to marry you, Tex. Right now. Today. Now, as for being able to get ready with flowers, and cake, and a dress...." She gave him a wide grin, unable to keep it hidden for another moment. "I can do it, Tex. By December twenty-second."

His smile grew too. "I know you can."

"You can help," she said. "You're not even working right now."

"I'm not even working?" he demanded, his eyes flashing with dark fire. "Are you serious? I can't believe—" He cut off when she burst into giggles, and he tossed his fork on the desk as he got to his feet.

"You think you're so funny," he said, coming around the desk.

She squealed as she realized he wasn't slowing or stopping. He bent and started to tickle her, despite her efforts to spin her chair away from him. They laughed together, and Tex ended up on his knees in front of her as the moment sobered.

Abby reached out and swept his graying hair off his forehead. "You're looking old, Mister Young." She really liked the mature silver in his hair and beard, and this wasn't the first time she'd told him.

"Yeah," he said softly.

She met his gaze, the love there stealing her breath. "I know you work hard," she said.

"You'd marry me right now? Today?"

"Yes," she said.

He took her face in his hands, so gentle and so tender. "I'd marry you right now too. Today." He kissed her, and Abby loved his touch, his taste, him. She loved him.

"I know I'm crazy," he said, leaning his forehead

against hers. "But I cannot stand the thought of you living anywhere but right next door to me. I don't want you to move, and when you do, I want it to be in with me and Bryce." He put some space between them, and Abby heard and saw how genuine he was.

She smiled at him and traced her fingers down the sides of his beard. "I like your brand of crazy."

"So I'll talk to Cheryl?"

She nodded, biting her lip. "I can if you want."

"No, I will," he said. He pulled back and went back to his spot in front of her desk. When he faced her again, he wore a soft smile. "You can eat now." He nodded to her food, but Abby shook her head.

"No?" he asked.

"One more thing." She pulled the paper out from under her plastic container, wondering how she'd gotten even a few ravioli down. She handed him the single sheet, something so lightweight yet carrying something so heavy.

Tex didn't ask what it was this time, and his eyes read quickly. "Abigail."

"If I'm going to be living on that ranch anyway, what's the point of having two different owners?" She got to her feet and went toward him. She sat on his lap, the paper flapping out to the side as he made room for her within the circle of his arms. "I want you to buy it from me. It's yours, and it's stupid that I bought half of it anyway."

She smiled down at him, but he simply gazed up at her. "Say something."

"I'm trying to figure out what," he said softly. "Does *I love you so much* work for you?"

Abby's grin felt like it would never fully straighten. "I think I could handle hearing you say that, yes."

He finally cracked a small smile. "So I sign this and give you the money, and the ranch is all mine?"

"Mm hm," she said. "I had Cyrus look it over, and he says it would be binding."

"I'll stop by the bank after lunch," he said. "Figure it out."

She looked up to his cowboy hat and delicately removed it, twisting slightly to set it on her desk. Facing him again, she ran her hands through his hair, liking the way he tilted his head back and let his eyes drift closed.

With her hands cupped around the back of his head, said, "Soon enough, it'll be *ours*," and then she kissed him.

CHAPTER
THIRTY

"N o, leave it," Tex said to Franny at the end of September, his mood already foul. "Leave it." The dog finally left the wadded up hamburger wrapper she'd stolen from the garbage can, and Tex dared to reach down and pick it up. Last time, she'd very nearly bitten his arm off. The scratch from her teeth still stung on the back of his hand.

Bryce should be home from school soon, and Tex wanted to ask him how his invite to the homecoming dance had gone. The boy was instantly popular at the high school here in Coral Canyon, if the parade of teenagers Tex had endured since school had started was any indication.

He wasn't that surprised, because Bryce was a charismatic and talented boy. "He'll be a full-fledged adult soon," Tex reminded himself as he went to put the wrapper back in the trashcan. He'd fashioned a lid out of a cardboard box for now, and he'd ordered a new garbage can that came with a lid.

He glared at his dog, who put her head over her paws and looked up at him sorrowfully. As she should. He couldn't stay mad at Franny for long, because he hated being cooped up inside while it rained and rained too.

Refusing to look out the window to the recording studio—if a pile of cement and lumber could be called such a thing—he washed his hands so he could truly assess the wound on his hand. It turned out to be nothing, and he went to Franny and bent down to pat her.

"Are you hungry?" he asked. She wasn't, because she was a grazer and her food sat out all day long. "I wish we could go outside too." She leaned into his touch, and Tex gave her a hearty scrub.

His brothers had been at his house almost daily for the past month, and he didn't mind so much. They worked on memorization, music tweaks, and getting things perfect. They'd had some good times—a lot of laughs—some down times, like when Otis told them all that he thought his ex-wife was seriously ill, and some times when Tex would seriously be happy if he never saw any of them again.

In the end, however, his family meant a great deal to him, and he wasn't surprised in the least to hear the grumble of a truck engine pulling into his driveway. He'd bought Bryce a truck to drive to the high school, something that had happened as an after-thought, because Tex sure didn't want to drive him to school every morning, and neither of them had really thought about it that summer.

He straightened and looked out the window to find Trace's truck there, and a smile touched his face. Trace was his oldest and best friend, even if they didn't spend every waking moment together. Tex trusted Trace with anything and everything, and he wasn't surprised to see his brother get out of the truck, frown into the rain, and then open the back door.

A bright yellow umbrella emerged from the truck, and that meant Trace had brought Mama with him. She and Daddy came up the walk with Trace, and Tex had the front door open for them before they got to the porch.

"Howdy," he said, grinning. "What brings you guys out here?"

"Goin' crazy at our place," Daddy said, grinning at Tex. He embraced him on the stoop and then went inside.

"Mama." Tex hugged her too, giving her an extra tight squeeze as Trace shook out the umbrella and put it down.

"Do you have plans this afternoon?" she asked.

"Just questioning my son until he regrets coming to live with me," Tex said with a chuckle. Mama smiled like that was normal behavior and went in the house.

Trace quirked one eyebrow. "Why are you questioning Bryce?"

"He's supposed to be asking this girl he likes to the homecoming dance today. I want to find out how it went." He hugged Trace too and asked, "Why are you guys really here?"

"Daddy is going crazy," Trace said in a low voice. "But

mostly because of Mama. So I suggested we come out here, then she'd have someone else to talk to, and maybe he could get a nap." He looked past Tex and into the house, apparently finding the coast clear, because he continued with, "I've never seen the man put his shoes on so fast."

Trace laughed, and Tex grinned with him. Trace's laughter didn't stick for long, and that meant something to Tex. "And what about you?" he asked, reaching to pull the door almost all the way closed. The porch had a roof, and it wasn't terribly cold that afternoon. Just drizzly and miserable.

September had brought brown with it, and the grasses and gardens had started to prepare for their winter slumber. Tex still thought it was beautiful, and he sat on the new bench he'd bought for the front porch, clearly indicating that Trace should join him.

Trace did, a massive sigh pulling through his chest. It sounded like it came from way down deep in his gut.

"Sounds like you have something on your mind," Tex said, keeping his eyes out on the front yard. Inside, his dog whined, and the door opened as Franny used her snout to get it to swing wider. "Come on," he said to her. "Come sit over here."

She did, the German shepherd slinking toward Trace. She put her face on his knee, because she always seemed to know who needed the most comfort.

Tex didn't prompt Trace again, because he'd already driven all the way out here. He'd talk when he got the words right. Right now, he stroked Franny, his smile only halfway formed, and when he looked up and out toward the road, Tex tensed.

"I don't know how to ask this."

"Mav says to just get it out, and then it's there, and we can talk about it," Tex said.

"Yeah, he's told me that too." Trace looked at Tex, and Tex met his eye with plenty of strength in his gaze.

"Whatever it is, I'm here."

"Val's moving to Europe," he said, referencing his ex-wife. She was a supermodel in every sense of the word. Tall, great body, wore the fashion sunglasses everywhere she went. She worked all over the world, and she returned to Wyoming less than Trace did.

Harry, their son, lived with her parents, and Trace took him as often as he could. For a couple of years, he'd even homeschooled his son while they worked on their albums in Nashville. With the tour, he'd gone back to his grand-parents, but Trace had bought a place here in town and had his boy all the time now.

"She's gone to Europe before," Tex said.

"She's not *going* to Europe," Trace said without a hint of bitterness. "She's *moving* there, Tex. She said she's not coming back. Ever."

"Ever?" Tex searched Trace's face, finding the misery there.

"I don't know what to tell Harry. He loves his mother."

Tex nodded, because of course he did. "You just tell 'im, Trace." His mind flew back to the hard conversations he'd had with Corrie about Bryce. "Once, I found out that Corrie was drinking too much at home. She'd go into these sobbing fits and end up screaming. She scared Bryce." He spoke barely above a whisper. "I had to call her and tell her she better knock that off right now. I mean, I said it nicer than that. I offered to get her into a rehab program. I told her I'd be there in the morning to get our son if she did it again. It was not a pleasant situation."

"I didn't know any of this."

Tex kept his face turned away from his brother. "Then I had to call my son and tell him that people weren't perfect. You know? I'm not. He's not. His mother isn't." He nodded, because he still believed that. "I did my best, for what I could do and what I knew at the time." He shook his head. "But I wish I'd realized what his situation was and gotten him out of there sooner."

He swallowed, his chest storming, and faced Trace. "So maybe this isn't a bad thing, Trace. She's barely here as it is. She makes promises to the boy she breaks constantly. Maybe this way, the two of you can just have the stability you need. You and him. You're not going anywhere for a while, and even if we get another contract, our lives will be different with the studio here."

"Yeah." Trace nodded, though his mind clearly kept working. He probably beat himself up in his quiet moments the way Tex did. In fact, Tex knew he did, because he knew Trace.

"You've got a house here now," he said. "Harry's happy there. He's got a paper route and everything." Tex put a smile on his face, but Trace didn't mirror it. "You'll bring him over here in the afternoons if you need help with him or even just need a break. He loves Franny, and

I'll have work for him to do. We'll make sure the two of you are okay." He slung his arm around Trace's shoulders, and his brother hung his head, the slightest tremor shaking his strong frame.

"Thanks, Tex," he whispered.

"Of course," Tex said. "Now." He drew in a deep breath. "You're not still dating that princess, are you?"

"No," Trace said. "I broke up with her last week. I don't even think she cared." He looked up but not at Tex, and Tex saw the pain on his brother's face.

"Maybe someone more...normal," Tex said. "Maybe someone right here in Coral Canyon."

"Not all of us have high school girlfriends waiting in the wings," Trace said dryly, and Tex chuckled with him. At least he'd gotten a small laugh.

"You're still helping me with the proposal, right?" Tex asked. "Dog Valley, at the church on Fixture Street. She's there right at five."

"We'll be there at four," he said. "Don't worry."

Tex was worried, despite all the preparations he'd made. He couldn't help it. He worried; that's what he did, and he didn't see a reason why he should stop now.

He could worry and still pray that the proposal he'd planned down to the second would go off without a hitch.

Three more days, he told himself as Bryce's truck drove in front of the house and turned into the driveway. "All right," he said, getting to his feet. "Here we go."

"Tex," Trace said from the bench.

"Hmm?" He looked from his son to his brother.

"Sit back down and let the boy get out of the truck." Trace nodded to the spot Tex had just occupied. "Now."

Tex fell back to his seat, his voice mute.

"Give him two seconds to breathe," Trace said. "Isn't that what you're always tellin' me about Luke?"

"Luke needs a year to breathe," Tex quipped, and the two of them laughed.

Bryce came down the walk and saw them. "What are you two chuckling about?"

Tex looked at Trace, and Trace looked at Tex. "Nothing. How was school?" Tex asked his son.

"Great," Bryce said, just like he always did. He wore his backpack on one shoulder, and he tucked his hand through the other strap and hefted it up onto both. Right there in the pouring rain, he grinned at Tex and Trace. "I asked Melinda to the homecoming dance in front of our whole ASL class."

Tex's face split into a grin. "Oh, was that today? How'd it go?"

Bryce shrugged and came up onto the porch and out of the rain. "I got an A on the assignment." He bent and patted Franny and stepped into the house. "And she said yes."

Tex's anxiety settled back into a quiet hiss in his stomach. "Great about the A," he called after his son.

Bryce poked his head back outside. "And I know you've been stewing about this for at least an hour. 'Oh, was that today?'" He scoffed and shook his head. "Nice try, Dad."

Trace burst out laughing, but Tex held onto his straight

face. "Nana and Pops are in there. Go talk to Gramma so my dad can take a nap."

"Yes, sir," Bryce said with a grin, disappearing back into the house.

"You're not helping," Tex said.

"Are you kidding?" Trace stared at him incredulously. "If he'd seen you standing at the top of the steps like an over-eager mother hen, he wouldn't have even told you that he'd asked."

"I still didn't get any details."

"So come with me to get pizza and some of that chocolate chip cookie dough you bake at home, and then we'll bribe the whole story out of him with food." Trace lifted his eyebrows, his hopes high. "I've got to pick up Harry in forty-five minutes, and Mama and Daddy are fine here."

"There's at least more room for them to exist in separate rooms," Tex said.

"Yep." Trace stood, groaning as he did, and said, "I'll meet you in the truck."

Tex let his brother go down the sidewalk, and then he got up to go tell everyone they were going to get dinner. Before he went inside, he sent a quick text to Abby.

Having pizza and cookies at my house tonight. Bring everyone who wants to come.

Then he sent up a prayer for Trace and Harry, as well as anyone else in the Young family who needed one.

———

Saturday arrived, and Tex's nerves skyrocketed. He'd only been this nervous on the flight to Nashville earlier this year, and that had gone fine. "It went fine," he told himself as he leaned forward to see out the window better.

The rain had stopped. "Thank you, Lord," he breathed. His proposal wouldn't work in the rain, and he'd been obsessively checking the weather for days now. The sun wasn't exactly shining, but a few patches of gold lit the sky, and Tex held onto his high hopes for the day.

He wasn't sure what he did that day other than survive, and before he knew it, he and Bryce had everything loaded in the back of the truck, the tarp tied down, and their seatbelts on.

He had told the story of how he'd signed his invitation to the homecoming dance for Melinda, only spelling her name at the end. He'd laughed when he said only about six kids in the class even knew what he'd done, because the others couldn't follow along with the sign language.

Melinda could though, and her whole face had turned red. They couldn't speak in the ASL class, so the teacher had signed to her that she better answer the "poor boy" up front, and that was when the whole class started cluing in that something besides another boring memorized paragraph had been signed.

She'd made the sign for S, which was just a closed fist, and nodded it—the sign for yes. Bryce, ever Tex's son, said he'd whooped and gathered her into his arms, saying right out loud, "Great, Mel. We'll have so much fun."

He'd gotten in trouble for talking out loud, and the

teacher had made him sign that part too. They'd all laughed over the pizza and cookies, even Trace.

His brother hadn't left Tex's thoughts for long, and he ran through ways he could help with Harry so Trace wasn't too overwhelmed. Otis needed help with Joey too, and Tex told himself he better check with Otis about his situation.

The church in Dog Valley arrived far sooner than Tex imagined it would, and everything sat in benign silence. No one had parked in the lot. The leafless tree branches drifted in the breeze.

"Not too windy," Bryce said, peering through the windshield.

"No." Tex looked at his son as he pulled into a spot way down on the end so Abby could park the Bookmobile where she usually did. "You'd tell me if you didn't want me to marry her, right?"

"Dad," Bryce said, plenty of disbelief in his voice. "Of course I would. But I wouldn't ever tell you that. She's perfect for you, and I'm glad you two found each other again." He grinned that winning Young smile, and Tex reached for him.

"I love you, bud," he said, curling his fingers along the back of Bryce's neck in a strange side-hug.

"I love you too, Dad."

"She loves you too, you know."

"I know," Bryce said.

"Did she tell you?" Tex dropped his hand and watched his son.

"No," Bryce said slowly, looking out the windshield.

"It's just...I can feel it in how she treats me." He gave Tex another smile and unbuckled his seatbelt. "Come on, Dad. Uncle Luke just got here, and if we don't put him to work, we're gonna hear about it."

"You don't have to tell me twice," Tex muttered as he got out of the truck too. Getting Luke to come help erect a huge banner that spelled out Tex's proposal was a miracle in and of itself. He didn't believe in love, marriage, or any of it. He had a heart, but it had been badly beaten and scarred from his first marriage, and he'd told everyone he could get to listen how he was never doing that again.

"Hey," Tex said as Luke and Mav approached his truck. "The banner is fifty-two steps long."

"Steps?" Mav asked.

"Who measures a banner in steps?" Luke asked, already disgruntled.

"I do," Tex said. "It's about a hundred and fifty feet. Happy?" He handed Luke a post and a hammer. "Let's get started."

CHAPTER
THIRTY-ONE

A bby saw the crowd waiting at the church for her Saturday evening Bookmobile appearance, and she couldn't believe how many people had come. "This is odd," she muttered to herself.

Thankfully, they'd left the spot open where she parked, but a whole slew of cars and trucks had filled the church parking lot. Maybe the local congregation had something going on in their building that night.

No lights shone from the church, and everyone stood outside but not in their usual places. Sure, a few kids and teens with books in their hands stood on the sidewalk where it dipped for wheelchairs and other handicapped accessibility. But most of the people stood back on the grass, and they didn't have books with them.

"Something's going on," she said, scanning the crowd as she bumped-bumped over the high entry into the lot.

She got her ancient Bookmobile in place, set the brake, and enjoyed the hiss as the vehicle settled.

She went into the back, proud of herself for not dislodging a single book on her drive up today. She flipped on the lights, because October sat right around the corner, and that meant it got darker earlier in the evening.

After unlocking the door, she went down the steep steps and outside. "Hello, everyone," she said, the same way she always did. The people back on the grass hadn't pressed closer, and Abby turned away from the sea of faces she couldn't focus on to hook the door open. If it got too cold, she'd close it and run the floor heaters until she had to leave.

Her fingers fumbled on the hook, and the door swung closed again. The slam hurt her ears and echoed up into the Wyoming sky. That was why she didn't let anyone get on the Bookmobile—or even approach it—until she'd hooked open the door. It could be lethal if it got away from her.

With a second try, she got the door in place, and she took a big breath and blew it out as she turned to face everyone again.

Tex stood right on the sidewalk now, and he definitely hadn't been there before. Any breath left in her lungs dried right up at the sexy sight of him in his dark jeans, those cowboy boots and that hat, as well as a black polo with a dark brown leather jacket over that. He was the pattern for what other country music gods were made from, as he also held a guitar in his hands, the strap over his shoulder just like he wore it during his concerts.

He grinned at her, his neck working as he swallowed. Then he started to play, and he visibly relaxed. They hadn't talked about what he'd do after this last album was made. It might not be his last, and watching him play and how it soothed him, she didn't want it to be.

Tex looked up and met her eyes, his rich tenor voice filling the air only a moment later.

"Sometimes," he said. "You meet a woman at work."

Other guitars joined the fray, and Abby pressed her hands to her chest as Bryce stepped out of the crowd and moved forward slowly.

"Sometimes," he and Tex sang together, which was a lovely, gorgeous sound. "You meet a woman on the street."

Otis and Trace emerged from the sea of people, and then Mav, Morris, and Luke. Every single one of them held and played a guitar, and with all that talent sending such beauty into the world, surely the heavens would rejoice.

"Sometimes," several voices sang together, and Abby didn't know where to look. "You meet a woman next door."

Her eyes filled with tears. Tex had said his proposal would be perfect, and Abby believed he'd nailed it so far.

"Sometimes," they sang. "You meet her at school, the library, the store."

She had no idea if *library* was the right lyric, but she didn't care. A sob-laugh came from her throat, and she grinned at Tex.

"But when you meet the woman who makes you whole," the Young family sang. "You know you better not let her go. Ohhh-ohh. You better not let her go."

Tex walked forward then, his smile so real and so full that it reached his eyes, his hands, his very soul. He came all the way toward her while his family kept singing the song. She couldn't see anyone but him. She could only hear his guitar.

He stopped playing, and the other instruments quieted.

"I love you, Abigail Ingalls." He practically yelled the words, and surely the whole crowd could hear him. "I don't want to let you go, ever. *You're* the woman who makes me whole, and—"

The guitars started up in earnest again, and Tex lifted the neck of his, clearly a cue. Then he stepped to her side, both of them facing the band, the church, the crowd.

Except there was no crowd anymore. Only a huge, monster-long banner that said, "Will you marry me, Abby?" in huge, hand-painted blue letters.

The music quieted again, and every living creature seemed to be holding its breath. Abby turned to Tex, who had just finished handing his guitar to his brother. Bryce stood at his side now, and how the two of them could move like ninjas, she didn't know.

Tex slung his arm around his son and looked at Abby. "What do you think? Do you want to make a family with us?"

"Yes," she said, her voice not nearly loud enough to hear in all this openness.

Tex leaned toward her, his grin so contagious "I don't think they heard you."

She turned toward the crowd, now able to pick out her parents, Wade and Cheryl, her friends from the library,

Georgia and her new boyfriend, and lots and lots of people she knew from Dog Valley, from Rusk, and from Coyote Creek. Everyone who came to the library and the Bookmobile.

Her heart swelled with love for each of them, for the Young family who was present, for Tex and Bryce, and for...herself.

She felt so loved in that moment, and she lifted her chin and held her head high as she called, "Yes!"

The crowd applauded instantly, a roar rising up with cowboy whoops and country hollers, and she turned toward Tex and threw herself into his arms.

They laughed together, and then he lowered his head and kissed her. "I love you," he whispered.

"I love you too," she whispered back.

The crowd surged toward them, and Georgia intercepted her first. "Oh, girl, I'm so happy for you." They hugged, and Abby closed her eyes in happiness.

"Thank you," she said.

Her mom arrived, and then Wade and Cheryl, and Abby lost Tex in all the excitement. Soon enough, she encountered the men who'd helped Tex set up this elaborate display, and he stood with them. She went down the line and hugged each one of them.

"I can't believe I have to attend two weddings back-to-back," Mav said as he hugged her. "But I suppose you're worth it, Abs."

Tex took her hand, his tight in hers, and shook his head, otherwise ignoring the comment. Mav's ex-wife was getting married the day before Wade and Cheryl.

"You don't have to go to your ex-wife's wedding," Luke spat beside Mav, and Abby grabbed onto him and hugged him too.

"Thank you, Luke," she said, because she knew this had cost him something. She didn't know what, but something.

He held her tightly too, his voice surprisingly quiet. When everyone had congratulated her, and the crowd had started to disperse, she stood at Tex's side and gazed at the banner. "It's incredible," she said. "Did you paint it?"

"No," Tex said, his arm snug around her waist as he held her against his warm body. "All the kids did. Bryce supervised, but we had Harry, Boston, Beth, Joey, and Corrine over one afternoon and got it done. It's been in my basement for a few weeks."

"Wow, a few weeks," she teased. "What were you waitin' for?"

"The rain to stop," he said dryly, and Abby looked up at him. He grinned at her and leaned closer to her. "The banner is fifty-two of my steps long. That's how far it is from the bottom of my side stairs to the steps that go up to your back porch."

"Fifty-two steps, huh?" An idea percolated in her head, and she didn't immediately dismiss it though it was kind of crazy. He'd taught her that crazy ideas could be some of the best ones.

"Yep."

"Are we getting married with Wade and Cheryl?"

"Yep," he said again. "Eighty-three days." He squeezed her tight. "Is that enough time, my love?"

"I'll make it work," she told him, turning into his body. He brought up his other hand and held her, their eyes meeting. "I can't wait to marry you."

"*I* can't wait to marry *you*," he said, touching the tip of his nose to hers. "Then you won't be fifty-two steps away, and we'll be on *our* ranch together."

She smiled at him, and he smiled at her, and when he kissed her this time, only love existed between them.

———

Read on for a sneak peek at **OTIS**, featuring Otis Young, the next member of the Young Family who's got a lot happening in his life...and maybe Georgia Beck will be the one to finally show him what true love looks like.

(It's a secret, but... You'll get Mav and Dani's complete love story, more insight and background into the brothers in the Young Family, and more Country Quad band fun, once **MAV** comes out this April! Newsletter subscribers will find out about it first, so **join today!**)

SNEAK PEEK! OTIS CHAPTER ONE:

O tis Young pulled up to the address his truck had navigated him to, already admiring the house. It looked as good in real life as it had on a computer screen, and he knew in that moment that he'd be purchasing this home.

"Look, baby," he said to his daughter who rode in the back seat. "It has a tire swing in the tree."

"Can I swing on it, Daddy?"

"Sure," he said without thinking too hard about it. He'd done all of his heavy thinking in the recording studio that day. The executives from the label would be here next week, and Otis wished he'd made this move already.

"We have to wait for Dave," he said, putting his truck in park. "Plus, there's still a lot of snow in the yard, and you're not wearin' your boots." Moving in the winter would be terrible, and Otis once again blamed Mother

Nature and the whole state of Wyoming for why he still lived in the rental close to the center of Coral Canyon.

This house sat on the northern boundary of the town, in a cute neighborhood—the last one before the highway became faster and only apple orchards separated Dog Valley from Coral Canyon. If he bought this home, he'd only be fifteen minutes from his brother's ranch, fifteen minutes from his ex-wife's house, and fifteen minutes from Joey's school.

It was perfect, and he almost didn't care what the inside looked like. He'd seen the inside of Tex's farmhouse —the house where he and all the Young boys had grown up, Otis included—when he'd first bought it. He and his son had ripped everything out and remodeled and renovated.

Otis could do the same thing to this house should it need it. The location was what he needed, because Lauren, his ex-wife, wasn't well and wasn't getting any better. He didn't have the greatest relationship with her—they weren't Mav and Portia—but they'd sat down over the New Year break and decided that Joey should come live with Otis full-time.

He wasn't touring with his country music band. He lived in town already, tweaking and perfecting the music he and his brothers would start recording next week, when the producers from their record label showed up.

He'd been driving Joey to school since last fall, picking her up, and taking care of her anyway. At this point, she barely slept at her momma's anymore, and Otis didn't like dropping her off there. He had a much bigger support network, and his parents or his brothers had no problem stepping in and helping with his seven-year-old.

"What do you want to do for your birthday, Roo?" he asked her as they waited for the realtor to show up. "Let me guess: A cake shaped like a book. No, a rainbow." He grinned at her in the rearview mirror, her fair face lit from within.

His precious daughter would be eight in a couple of weeks, and Otis hadn't heard Lauren say one thing about it. He wasn't going to bother her with it. He'd get all the presents, the cake, the balloons, everything, and make sure Joey had an amazing birthday.

"Can we still go roller skating?"

He'd forgotten about that, but he said, "Yeah, of course."

"Can I invite Mya and Timmy and Eleki?"

"Yes," Otis said, starting to feel like he'd jumped into the lake up the canyon a bit, and the water was freezing and dragging him under by his sopping wet clothes.

"That's what I want to do," she said. "All the cousins can come, of course. And the uncles."

He grinned as he looked out the window. "Of course," he murmured. He'd already gotten over a dozen texts that morning, all from Joey's uncles. They each wanted to know the moment he bought a house, which one it was, and when he could move in. They weren't being nosy. Otis liked to call it supportive, and when he got tired of answering their texts and questions, he withdrew from them a little.

Everyone did it; he just happened to be the quietest

about it. It helped that he didn't have all the eyes on him the way Tex did. As he thought of his oldest brother, he remembered Tex's wife had also texted him, and Otis hadn't responded.

He picked up his phone and quickly sent a message back to Abby, telling her he was currently waiting at the first house, and yes, it looked nice. She worked at the library in town, and she didn't always have access to her phone, especially if she was in a meeting.

He sighed and rested his head against the cold window, his thoughts going somewhere they shouldn't.

Beck's Books.

The quaint bookshop on Main Street, stuck between the post office and one of Otis's favorite barbecue joints, Bam Bam's. So *of course* he had to go by there often. Joey liked to read, and Otis wanted his daughter to be happy. Not only that, but he had things to mail all the time, and his hankering for brisket could keep him up at night until he satisfied his cravings.

The real craving was another taste of Georgia's lips. She'd called him into her office once, late last summer, and she'd demanded he pretend to be her boyfriend and kiss her. Then she'd kissed him, and wow, Otis had not minded that one bit.

It was pretend, he told himself for probably the eight hundredth time in the past six months. It obviously hadn't meant anything to Georgia, who'd never called him again for help with her ex, and who'd started for-real dating someone else very soon after that.

Movement in his rearview mirror caught his eye, and

Otis said, "Here we go, Roo. He's here." He unbuckled and got out of his truck, opening the back door to help his daughter down.

Dave apologized for being a few minutes late, they shook hands, and Dave led Otis up the cleared driveway to the house. The sun shone today, glinting off the snow in the yard. "The driveway is heated," he said. "As is the front sidewalk. It's nice for small storms, and it helps with the bigger ones too."

Otis looked at the decorative stone in the driveway and leading up to the front door. It wasn't regular cement, and it felt too uppity to him. Was he the type of man who owned a house with a heated driveway?

Dave went on about the double-wide oak doors, the reclaimed barn wood shutters, and how the pillars were original to a historic home that had unfortunately burned beyond saving about five years ago.

Otis didn't care about any of that, so he said nothing. He wanted somewhere that felt safe to him. Somewhere Joey could have her friends over, she could keep practicing the piano, she could have a little book nook with a bean bag so she could curl up and read while he worked on his song-writing. Or whatever.

Dave unlocked the house with a code, and he opened the door. He didn't lead the way in. He smiled at Otis and said, "You two go on in. Look around. Gather your questions. We'll talk in a few minutes."

Otis hadn't been expecting that. When he'd searched for rentals last summer, the landlords always hovered only twelve inches away, anxious to assure him that everything worked properly and what didn't would be fixed or wasn't their fault.

He peered into the house, took Joey's hand in his, and went up the single step into the foyer. Yes, this house had a legit foyer. It wasn't one of those huge sprawling mansions on the southeast side of Coral Canyon, but this house dripped with wealth.

Not in square feet. Not even in land, as the lot was only a half-acre. That was enough for Joey to set up a tent in the backyard during the summer and to roller skate around the front driveway—well, year-round, what with that heating system beneath it.

The house boasted four bedrooms and four baths, and Otis knew instantly that it had been designed by someone with an eye to use every space as wisely as possible. An office led left off the foyer, and he could see his collection of guitars there. His piano. All his sheet music. To the right from the foyer waited a small mudroom, with shelves and lockers for boots, hats, gloves, and backpacks. No one did that off a front entrance, but Otis loved it. He didn't want messy, muddy boots just left on the tile to rot, and he'd hated picking up all of Joey's things from where she happened to drop them after school.

From where he stood, he could see into a family room large enough to hold a couch and love seat, television, and a rocking chair. The kitchen sat behind that, with a long, long island where he could probably feed all of his nieces and nephews. A dining room table stood right in front of him, and he could see out the back door, which slid open into the backyard.

A sense Otis could only describe as *home* washed over him, making him warm from head to toe in less than a breath. It felt like God had taken a blanket straight from the dryer and wrapped it around his shoulders, whispering, *You're home, Otis. You're home, and I'm right here with you.*

He turned around and opened the front door again. "I'll take it," he said to a very surprised Dave.

"Really?" the real estate agent asked.

"If I pay cash, will they skip the appraisal?" he asked, meeting the man's shocked blue eyes. "And if they do, and I pay cash, when can I move in?"

———

Otis circled the block again, wondering why so many dang people needed to use the post office in the middle of the afternoon on a Thursday. He just wanted to dip into the bookstore and get Joey a gift.

For real.

He wasn't even going to see Georgia Beck. He hadn't the last five or six times he'd casually stopped by for some light reading for his daughter, and he couldn't expect this time to be different.

Georgia knew and was real friendly with Abby, but Otis hadn't seen her out at the ranch at all. Abby hardly talked about her friends with him or any of the other brothers, but Otis's heart pounded hard as he saw a car backing out of a spot only a few yards in front of him.

He flipped on his blinker and waited for the woman to

vacate her space. Then he quickly pulled into it, thrilled with how close to Beck's Books he'd gotten. He wasn't right in front of it, but a quick glance to the right showed a new window display since the last time he'd been here. He wondered if Georgia or her assistant did those as he picked up his phone, then his wallet, and then pressed the button to turn off his truck.

He still didn't get out, something strange keeping him in his seat. A woman came out of the shop, a brown paper bag in her hand with the embossed double B on it Otis had seen lots of times, usually on his own bag of books he'd bought.

Most people on the street right now seemed to be frequenting the post office, and after another couple of breaths, Otis felt like his legs would support him enough to walk. And walk he did, right up onto the curb, down the street a bit, and through the door of the bookshop.

The bell dinged, a high-pitched sound that echoed through the shop. No one came to greet him, as they had in the past. The shop waited in silence, and Otis froze, his footsteps suddenly too loud.

"Be right there," someone called, and his heart jack-hammered through his ribs as it tried to flee his body.

That was Georgia's voice.

He suddenly couldn't get his to work, and Otis reminded himself that he'd been out with women before. This wasn't even a date, and he scoffed at himself as he stepped over to the bestsellers shelf as if he cared about any of the titles there.

He had, in fact, forgotten why he'd come in here at all.

His mind fuzzed, and then he remembered Joey. Of course. Joey. He wanted to get her the new limited-edition collection of the Animal Hunters books she loved so much.

Rounding the bookshelf, the kids' section came into view. In that moment, a terrific crash filled the air at the shop, startling Otis enough to kick his pulse back into high gear. "Hello?" he called, now striding with purpose toward the back of the shop where he knew a hallway waited.

It came into view, but no one responded to him. "Georgia?" he called this time, and again, got no answer.

He hurried down the hall and looked in her office. She wasn't there. Another foot or two down, another doorway on his right showed him a huge storage room, with bookshelves around the outside of it, and standing down the middle.

The scent of paper and cardboard hung heavily in the air, and Joey would love that. She'd stand here and say, "Can you smell it, Daddy? It smells like adventure." She wasn't one who loved to go hiking, skiing, or fishing. She preferred her outdoor experiences to come from the books she read, and Otis had long ago given up trying to get her to go play outside. Instead, he hung a hammock in the yard and let her read outside.

"Georgia," he called, knowing he'd heard her voice.

A moan sounded somewhere, and Otis spun back toward the hall, the sound clearly coming from behind him. "O—tiiis."

"Where are you?" he called. "Georgia? Where are you?" He dodged back over to her office, but she wasn't there. His panic picked up speed, like a runaway train, and that was when he noticed the spilled books and toppled cart beside her desk.

Yes, this place was a mess, but Georgia would never leave books on the floor. He ran toward her deck, her legs coming into view. "Georgia!" He knelt beside her, the sight of her passed out, her eyes closed and her head bent at an odd angle against the wall haunting and terrible.

"Georgia," he said, pressing his palm to her stomach. "Wake up, honey. It's Otis Young, and I'm right here."

Her eyelids fluttered, and Otis's hope took flight. "That's right. Wake up."

Georgia opened her eyes, but they didn't focus on him right away. She blinked, her eyebrows drawing down into a V. Then those gorgeous blue eyes that had been teasing and taunting him for weeks locked onto his.

"Otis?" she asked.

SNEAK PEEK! OTIS CHAPTER TWO:

Georgia Beck had no idea how she'd gotten on the floor. Her head sent a throb of pain through her skull to the spot right between her eyes, and she groaned.

"You fainted," Otis Young said, and she had no idea how the man kept getting himself into her office. Her lips tingled, betraying her, at his presence. Sure, she'd seen him around town. At church. Once from a few aisles over at the grocery store. Driving around with his brothers.

"I fainted?"

"Yeah," he said. "Best that I can reckon, at least. I heard this terrible crash, and I called but no one answered."

Georgia sat up—or she tried. Her body didn't feel like it currently had any operating muscles, and Otis thankfully put his hand on her back and helped her sit all the way up. "There you go," he said. "You okay?"

The care and compassion in his voice rang loudly in her

ears. James had never spoken to her like that. His stern tone and set-in-his-ways routines were just two of the reasons Georgia had broken up with him before Christmas.

She did miss him.

No, she told herself as she reached up to touch the back of her head. *You miss being with someone. Not him.*

Yes, she went to lunch with her friends. She worked hard here at the bookshop, and she currently had her assistant living with her. Harper had fallen on some hard times with her own significant other, and she'd lost her apartment in the break-up. Georgia could admit she really liked going home when she didn't have to walk into a silent house, darkness, and her scowling cat staring at her from atop the refrigerator.

"Georgia?" Otis asked, and her brain sharpened. She looked at him, and the world stopped. It didn't matter that she'd fainted for some unknown reason. Or that her back ached in a whole new way that didn't come from hauling cases of books from the storage room to the showroom. Or that her stomach grumbled at her for something to eat.

Only Otis existed, with those black-as-coal eyes, that jaw that almost took on an angle, and the scent of his strength and power. He smelled like wood smoke and safety, and Georgia wanted to curl into his warmth.

She remembered kissing this man in vivid detail, right down to what he tasted like. How could she not? Their fake kiss was still the very best one of her life, and she shivered as her eyes broke the connection with his only to land on that mouth.

"Hey," he said tenderly, gathering her into those arms

so easily, like he'd done it every single day of his life. She wished, and oh, she wished mightily. "It's okay. You're shaking."

She did tremble for another moment, and then she stilled. "I don't know what happened," she murmured. "I was standing here, going through the books on the cart. I'm redoing one of the display shelves out front."

"Mm hm." Otis didn't release her, and Georgia had no idea how her arm had gotten up and around his, her hand resting lightly on his shoulder. All she knew was that she liked touching him.

"I thought—I'm hungry. I should get lunch. And then...I don't know. My stomach sort of swooped a little. I yelled to someone, I think? Someone came in the shop?" She pulled away from him slightly, her eyes now searching his.

"You called to me," he whispered, his throat working hard as he swallowed, almost like he had a rubber ball he was trying to get down. "Then I heard the crash a few seconds later."

She nodded, because that sounded right. "I got sweaty in like, an instant. I thought—I should sit down. Then I remembered I had a customer, and...well, that's all I remember."

"You fainted," he said again. "I came running, but I couldn't find you for a few seconds."

"How long do you think I was out?"

"A minute?" he guessed. "I looked in here, but you were behind the desk. So I ducked over to the storage room, but you weren't there either. Then you...." He cleared his throat and looked away.

Georgia needed to stand up. Her hip couldn't keep getting twisted this way. She groaned, and Otis put both arms around her and, with the help of him and the desk, Georgia got to her feet. She kept both palms pressed into it, and Otis did not remove his hand from her back.

"Okay?"

"Yeah," she said, the kink in her hip working itself out. "Thanks." She sighed, her head still a little light.

"You haven't had lunch?"

"No," she said, looking at him again. "What time is it?"

"Honey, it's almost time for me to go pick up my daughter from school. It's after two-thirty." Only concern existed in his eyes, and a love-hate battle started within Georgia. She loved that he was concerned for her, but at the same time, she hated people fussing over her.

"You okay?" he asked, stepping back and dropping his hand.

"Yes," she said with a nod.

"Is lunch here?" he asked.

She shook her head. "I was just going to go down the street and get whatever sounded good."

"What sounds good?" He pulled out his phone as if he could make all of her favorite dishes appear with a few texts. Knowing him, he probably could.

You don't know him, she told herself. One kiss did not make them friends. Or dating. Or anything. In truth, she knew very little about Otis Young, other than he was Otis

Young, a talented singer-songwriter who'd grown up here in Coral Canyon, the same way she had.

He was three or four years younger than her, and she pressed her eyes closed in an attempt to get her brain to stop regurgitating the information she knew about this man.

"Yeah," Otis said. "I'll call the school. Thanks, Luke." The sound of his voice brought Georgia back to the present.

She opened her eyes and looked at him. "I think I need to go home." If he suggested he take her to the hospital, she'd claw his eyes out. She wasn't going to go there. Never, ever again was she going to go to the hospital.

"Yes, you do," he said with the flicker of a smile. "But first, you're going to sit right down here on the floor." He eased her back to the ground without waiting for her consent. "I'm going to go get some food for you, and you're going to call me if anything goes awry. Anything at all."

He crouched in front of her, his eyes set on Very Serious. "Where's your phone?"

"Uh, the desk?" Georgia reached up and brushed her errant curls off her forehead.

"Got it," he said. "I'm going to put my number in it, and you're going to hold it with my contact info on the screen. You're going to call me if you feel faint or sick or anything at all." He tapped and swiped as he did it, and a moment later, Georgia held a great prize in her hand.

Her phone with his number in it.

He put his fingers under her chin and lifted her face up toward his. "Tell me I'm okay to go."

"You're okay to go," she said, her brain fog clearing even further. "Really, Otis, I'm okay."

"I'm going to get you some food," he said. "There's a bottle of water right here. You sip on that."

She started to get up as she said, "I can get—" but Otis put his heavy hand on her shoulder.

"Georgia," he said, those eyes not playing games with her now. The fire in them did lick through her, bringing excitement and danger. Oh, how she needed some of both of those things. "If you get up, I'm taking you to the hospital, not going to get something to eat. You choose."

She glared at him. "I'm not going to the hospital."

"Then will you please sit right there and wait for me to get back? I'll be incredibly fast, and I'm already on the screen. All you have to do is tap." He nodded to the phone, and sure enough, it was on, with his name sitting there, his number underneath it. All she had to do was touch the green phone icon, and she'd call him.

"Okay," she said.

"Thank you." He leaned down and pressed a kiss to her forehead, sending a shockwave of sparks and heat down to her toes. "I'll be right back." He straightened, nodded once, and strode out of her office.

Georgia watched him go, marveling at how quickly her afternoon had changed from a mundane one where she redid the display shelves for the fiftieth time that year and contemplated closing the shop early, to sitting in her office waiting for Otis Young to bring back lunch.

She sighed and leaned her head back against the wall. A twinge of pain scampered down her neck, and Georgia reached up with her free hand and began to probe her skull. She'd fainted and fallen. She had to have a goose-egg somewhere.

After searching every centimeter of her scalp, she still hadn't found anything. No blood. No bumps. "A miracle," she whispered. It was also a miracle that she hadn't been in the shop alone when she'd fainted. If she had, who knew how long she'd have laid there, cold and alone and injured?

She didn't want to think about that.

Her phone rang, startling her, and she glanced at it. Abby's name sat there, and tears jumped to Georgia's eyes. She swiped on the call and said, "Hey, Abs."

"Where are you?" she demanded. "Are you okay? I can be there in ten minutes." She sounded like she was running, and Georgia suspected she was on her way to her office to get her car keys.

"I'm in my office, Abs," she said. "I'm okay." She closed her eyes, the warm touch of air from the furnace brushing her skin. "How did you know I was hurt?"

"Otis called me," she said, her voice slowing with each word. "Are you sure you're okay?"

"Otis went to get food," she said. "I just need to eat. I haven't...."

"You didn't eat again," Abby stated, not asking. "Georgia."

"I know," Georgia said, annoyed with herself and not needing a lecture. "Listen, Abby." She lifted her head and opened her eyes as she looked toward the open office doorway. "Do you believe in...I don't know. Fate? Kismet?"

"What do you mean?" Abby was no longer rushing, which meant she wouldn't come to the shop. She would most definitely be at Georgia's house tonight, probably with a lot of food. She'd even section it off into individual lunch-sized portions, each in their own container, so Georgia had no excuse not to eat on time.

"I mean...I have to tell you something."

"Okay."

"So Otis was in the shop today, right?"

"Yeah, Tex said he stopped to get a book for Joey's birthday."

Georgia nodded, though Abby couldn't see her. "Remember that mystery cowboy I kissed last fall? The one who helped me get CJ out of my life for good?"

"Yes," Abby said, and then she sucked in a horribly loud breath. "Georgia, tell me that wasn't Otis Young."

Georgia shrugged one shoulder, her voice weak and mouse-like as she said, "It was Otis Young."

"By the Dewey Decimal System," Abby said, her voice shocked and full of air. "Georgia. Why didn't you tell me?"

"Because," Georgia said. "Then you'd start swearing in Librarian language instead of helping me figure out what to do."

Abby remained silent for a moment, and Georgia didn't like that. A silent Abby meant a thinking Abby, and Georgia didn't need her thinking too hard about this. "Why do you need to figure out what to do?"

"Because," Georgia whispered. "I liked kissing him, okay? I *liked* it. I like *him*. But then I started dating this other guy—who was a total idiot and so not right for me—and then months later. Months, Abs, I pass out and who's there? Who's the only person in my shop?"

"I'm back," Otis said, and Georgia looked up at him, her eyes wide and every organ in her body storming at her to hang up and hang up now.

"Otis," she said at the same time she lowered the phone.

"Georgia!" Abby cried. "Don't you dare hang up on—" Her voice cut off as Georgia ended the call.

Otis looked at it and then her as he came closer. "Everything all right?" He got down on the floor and parked himself right next to her, his shoulder touching hers and everything.

"Yes," she whispered.

He nodded to the phone, which still showed who she'd been talking to for the past four minutes and thirteen seconds. "Talkin' to Abby, I see." He handed her a warm plastic container that smelled like heaven in mashed potato form.

She didn't have to say yes. The evidence stared them both in the face.

"I called her," Otis said. "To make sure you didn't have any food allergies." He popped the top on his barbecue container, the spicy scent of Bam Bam's signature sauce joining the party on the floor in her office.

"Ah." Georgia nodded. "Makes sense."

"You didn't tell her about us...you know. Kissing last

year. Did you?" He looked at her, something scared in his expression.

"No," she said, her stomach heavy though she hadn't eaten since last night. He nodded and went back to his food, but she had to tell him. Abby could be relentless, and now that she knew the mystery cowboy was Otis.... Georgia didn't want him walking into a war zone out at that ranch where he recorded music with his brother, Abby's husband.

"I didn't tell her about that until just now."

Otis made a slight squeaking noise and yanked his attention back to her. "Why would you do that now?"

"Because," Georgia said, emotions streaming through her like kite tails caught in a strong wind. She stirred her pulled pork into her potatoes and lifted a bite. She wouldn't take it until the words inside her mouth made room for the food. She offered Otis a tiny smile that fled as soon as it touched her lips.

He searched her face, alarm and resignation mingling there. Georgia drew from his strength and reminded herself that just because she'd fainted didn't mean she was weak. "I told her now, because once we start dating, she'll find out anyway."

Otis blinked at her rapidly. "We're gonna start dating?" She wasn't sure if he was intrigued or horrified.

Georgia shrugged that same single shoulder she had while on the phone with Abby. "Maybe," she said. "If you play your cards right." With all the words—flirty words too, which made Georgia smile internally—out of her mouth, she could finally take a bite of her lunch.

Otis remained quiet for several long seconds while they both ate. Then he said, "I'm pretty good at cards. The best out of anyone in the band." He looked at her, and she looked at him, and this time, there was no doubt in her mind that his eyes fired desire and attraction at her.

"Great," she said. "Well, let's see what happens then."

———

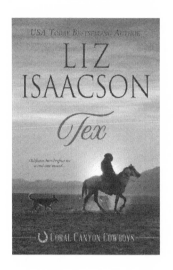

Tex (Book 1): He's back in town after a successful country music career. She owns a bordering farm to the family land he wants to buy...and she outbids him at the auction. Can Tex and Abigail rekindle their old flame, or will the issue of land ownership come between them?

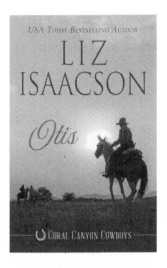

Otis (Book 2): He's finished with his last album and looking for a soft place to fall after a devastating break-up. She runs the small town bookshop in Coral Canyon and needs a new boyfriend to get her old one out of her life for good. Can Georgia convince Otis to take another shot at real love when their first kiss was fake?

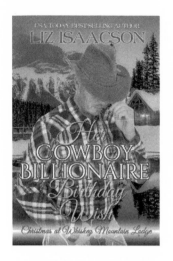

Her Cowboy Billionaire Birthday Wish (Book 1): All the maid at Whiskey Mountain Lodge wants for her birthday is a handsome cowboy billionaire. And Colton can make that wish come true—if only he hadn't escaped to Coral Canyon after being left at the altar...

Her Cowboy Billionaire Butler (Book 2): She broke up with him to date another man...who broke her heart. He's a former CEO with nothing to do who can't get her out of his head. Can Wes and Bree find a way toward happily-ever-after at Whiskey Mountain Lodge?

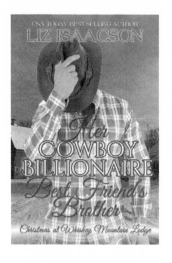

Her Cowboy Billionaire Best Friend's Brother (Book 3): She's best friends with the single dad cowboy's brother and has watched two friends find love with the sexy new cowboys in town. When Gray Hammond comes to Whiskey Mountain Lodge with his son, will Elise finally get her own happily-ever-after with one of the Hammond brothers?

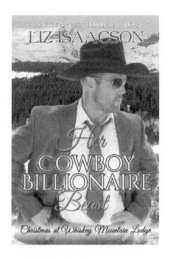

Her Cowboy Billionaire Beast (Book 4): A cowboy billionaire beast, his new manager, and the Christmas traditions that soften his heart and bring them together.

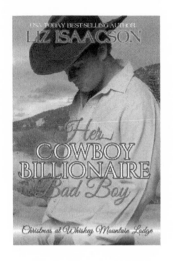

Her Cowboy Billionaire Bad Boy (Book 5): A cowboy billionaire cop who's a stickler for rules, the woman he pulls over when he's not even on duty, and the personal mandates he has to break to keep her in his life...

BOOKS IN THE CHRISTMAS IN CORAL CANYON ROMANCE SERIES

Her Cowboy Billionaire Best Friend (Book 1): Graham Whittaker returns to Coral Canyon a few days after Christmas—after the death of his father. He takes over the energy company his dad built from the ground up and buys a high-end lodge to live in—only a mile from the home of his once-best friend, Laney McAllister. They were best friends once, but Laney's always entertained feelings for him, and spending so much time with him while they make Christmas memories puts her heart in danger of getting broken again...

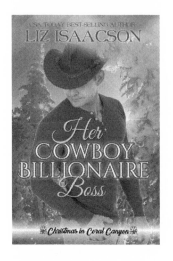

Her Cowboy Billionaire Boss (Book 2): Since the death of his wife a few years ago, Eli Whittaker has been running from one job to another, unable to find somewhere for him and his son to settle. Meg Palmer is Stockton's nanny, and she comes with her boss, Eli, to the lodge, her long-time crush on the man no different in Wyoming than it was on the beach. When she confesses her feelings for him and gets nothing in return, she's crushed, embarrassed, and unsure if she can stay in Coral Canyon for Christmas. Then Eli starts to show some feelings for her too…

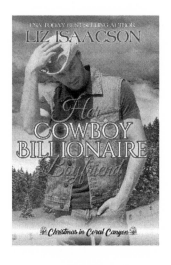

Her Cowboy Billionaire Boyfriend (Book 3): Andrew Whittaker is the public face for the Whittaker Brothers' family energy company, and with his older brother's robot about to be announced, he needs a press secretary to help him get everything ready and tour the state to make the announcements. When he's hit by a protest sign being carried by the company's biggest opponent, Rebecca Collings, he learns with a few clicks that she has the background they need. He offers her the job of press secretary when she thought she was going to be arrested, and not only because the spark between them in so hot Andrew can't see straight.

Can Becca and Andrew work together and keep their relationship a secret? Or will hearts break in this classic romance retelling reminiscent of *Two Weeks Notice*?

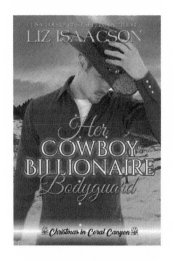

Her Cowboy Billionaire Bodyguard (Book 4): Beau Whittaker has watched his brothers find love one by one, but every attempt he's made has ended in disaster. Lily Everett has been in the spotlight since childhood and has half a dozen platinum records with her two sisters. She's taking a break from the brutal music industry and hiding out in Wyoming while her ex-husband continues to cause trouble for her. When she hears of Beau Whittaker and what he offers his clients, she wants to meet him. Beau is instantly attracted to Lily, but he tried a relationship with his last client that left a scar that still hasn't healed…

Can Lily use the spirit of Christmas to discover what matters most? Will Beau open his heart to the possibility of love with someone so different from him?

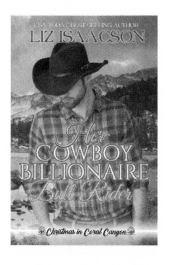

Her Cowboy Billionaire Bull Rider (Book 5): Todd Christopherson has just retired from the professional rodeo circuit and returned to his hometown of Coral Canyon. Problem is, he's got no family there anymore, no land, and no job. Not that he needs a job--he's got plenty of money from his illustrious career riding bulls.

Then Todd gets thrown during a routine horseback ride up the canyon, and his only support as he recovers physically is the beautiful Violet Everett. She's no nurse, but she does the best she can for the handsome cowboy. **Will she lose her heart to the billionaire bull rider? Can Todd trust that God led him to Coral Canyon...and Vi?**

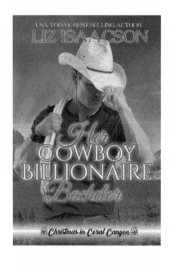

Her Cowboy Billionaire Bachelor (Book 6): Rose Everett isn't sure what to do with her life now that her country music career is on hold. After all, with both of her sisters in Coral Canyon, and one about to have a baby, they're not making albums anymore.

Liam Murphy has been working for Doctors Without Borders, but he's back in the US now, and looking to start a new clinic in Coral Canyon, where he spent his summers.

When Rose wins a date with Liam in a bachelor auction, their relationship blooms and grows quickly. **Can Liam and Rose find a solution to their problems that doesn't involve one of them leaving Coral Canyon with a broken heart?**

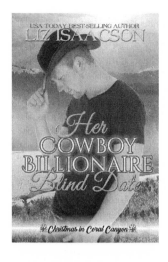

Her Cowboy Billionaire Blind Date (Book 7): Her sons want her to be happy, but she's too old to be set up on a blind date...isn't she?

Amanda Whittaker has been looking for a second chance at love since the death of her husband several years ago. Finley Barber is a cowboy in every sense of the word. Born and raised on a racehorse farm in Kentucky, he's since moved to Dog Valley and started his own breeding stable for champion horses. He hasn't dated in years, and everything about Amanda makes him nervous.

Will Amanda take the leap of faith required to be with Finn? Or will he become just another boyfriend who doesn't make the cut?

Her Cowboy Billionaire Best Man (Book 8): When Celia Abbott-Armstrong runs into a gorgeous cowboy at her best friend's wedding, she decides she's ready to start dating again.

But the cowboy is Zach Zuckerman, and the Zuckermans and Abbotts have been at war for generations.

Can Zach and Celia find a way to reconcile their family's differences so they can have a future together?

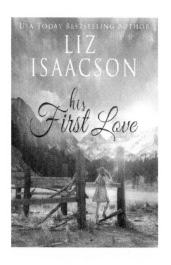

His First Love (Book 1): She broke up with him a decade ago. He's back in town after finishing a degree at MIT, ready to start his job at the family company. Can Hunter and Molly find their way through their pasts to build a future together?

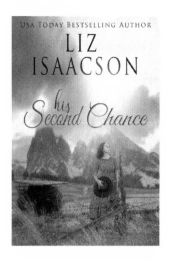

His Second Chance (Book 2): They broke up over twenty years ago. She's lost everything when she shows up at the farm in Ivory Peaks where he works. Can Matt and Gloria heal from their pasts to find a future happily-ever-after with each other?

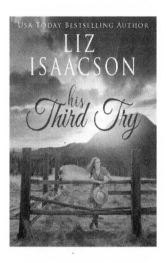

His Third Try (Book 3): He moved to Ivory Peaks with his daughter to start over after a devastating break-up. She's never had a meaningful relationship with a man, especially a cowboy. Can Boone and Cosette help each other heal enough to build a happily-ever-after...and a family?

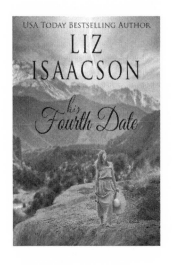

His Fourth Date (Book 4): Their relationship has been nothing but loose goats, a leaking roof, and her complete humiliation after he pays her mortgage so she won't lose her farm. Travis wants to go back in time and start over with Poppy, but he doesn't know how. Can a small town speed-dating event get their second chance off on the right foot?

The Mechanics of Mistletoe (Book 1): Bear Glover can be a grizzly or a teddy, and he's always thought he'd be just fine working his generational family ranch and going back to the ancient homestead alone. But his crush on Samantha Benton won't go away. She's a genius with a wrench on Bear's tractors...and his heart. Can he tame his wild side and get the girl, or will he be left broken-hearted this Christmas season?

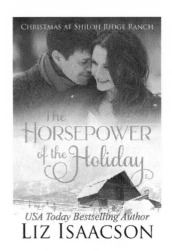

The Horsepower of the Holiday (Book 2): Ranger Glover has worked at Shiloh Ridge Ranch his entire life. The cowboys do everything from horseback there, but when he goes to town to trade in some trucks, somehow Oakley Hatch persuades him to take some ATVs back to the ranch. (Bear is NOT happy.)

She's a former race car driver who's got Ranger all revved up... Can he remember who he is and get Oakley to slow down enough to fall in love, or will there simply be too much horsepower in the holiday this year for a real relationship?

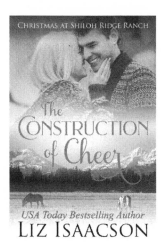

USA Today Bestselling Author
LIZ ISAACSON

The Construction of Cheer (Book 3): Bishop Glover is the youngest brother, and he usually keeps his head down and gets the job done. When Montana Martin shows up at Shiloh Ridge Ranch looking for work, he finds himself inventing construction projects that need doing just to keep her coming around. (Again, Bear is NOT happy.) She wants to build her own construction firm, but she ends up carving a place for herself inside Bishop's heart. Can he convince her *he's* all she needs this Christmas season, or will her cheer rest solely on the success of her business?

The Secret of Santa (Book 4): He's a fun-loving cowboy with a heart of gold. She's the woman who keeps putting him on hold. Can Ace and Holly Ann make a relationship work this Christmas?

The Harmony of Holly (Book 5): He's as prickly as his name, but the new woman in town has caught his eye. Can Cactus shelve his temper and shed his cowboy hermit skin fast enough to make a relationship with Willa work?

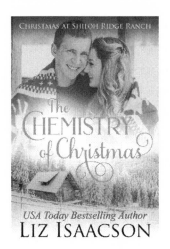

The Chemistry of Christmas (Book 6): He's the black sheep of the family, and she's a chemist who understands formulas, not emotions. Can Preacher and Charlie take their quirks and turn them into a strong relationship this Christmas?

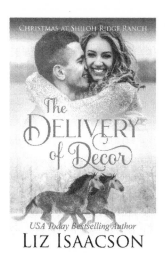

The Delivery of Decor (Book 7): When he falls, he falls hard and deep. She literally drives away from every relationship she's ever had. Can Ward somehow get Dot to stay this Christmas?

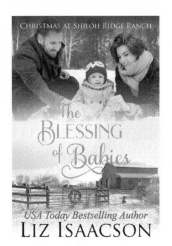

The Blessing of Babies (Book 8): Don't miss out on a single moment of the Glover family saga in this bridge story linking Ward and Judge's love stories!

The Glovers love God, country, dogs, horses, and family. Not necessarily in that order. ;)

Many of them are married now, with babies on the way, and there are lessons to be learned, forgiveness to be had and given, and new names coming to the family tree in southern Three Rivers!

The Networking of the Nativity (Book 9): He's had a crush on her for years. She doesn't want to date until her daughter is out of the house. Will June take a change on Judge when the success of his Christmas light display depends on her networking abilities?

The Wrangling of the Wreath (Book 10): He's been so busy trying to find Miss Right. She's been right in front of him the whole time. This Christmas, can Mister and Libby take their relationship out of the best friend zone?

The Hope of Her Heart (Book 11): She's the only Glover without a significant other. He's been searching for someone who can love him *and* his daughter. Can Etta and August make a meaningful connection this Christmas?

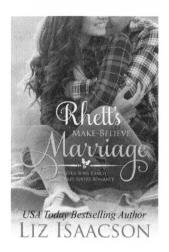

USA Today Bestselling Author
LIZ ISAACSON

Rhett's Make-Believe Marriage (Book 1): She needs a husband to be credible as a matchmaker. He wants to help a neighbor. Will their fake marriage take them out of the friend zone?

USA Today Bestselling Author
LIZ ISAACSON

Tripp's Trivial Tie (Book 2): She needs a husband to keep her son. He's wanted to take their relationship to the next level, but she's always pushing him away. Will their trivial tie take them all the way to happily-ever-after?

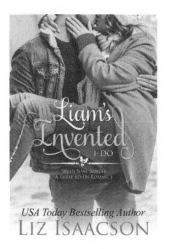

Liam's Invented I-Do (Book 3): She's desperate to save her ranch. He wants to help her any way he can. Will their invented I-Do open doors that have previously been closed and lead to a happily-ever-after for both of them?

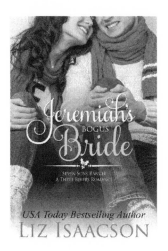

Jeremiah's Bogus Bride (Book 4): He wants to prove to his brothers that he's not broken. She just wants him. Will a fake marriage heal him or push her further away?

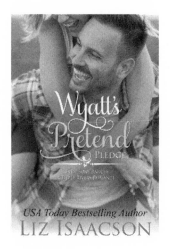

Wyatt's Pretend Pledge (Book 5): To get her inheritance, she needs a husband. He's wanted to fly with her for ages. Can their pretend pledge turn into something real?

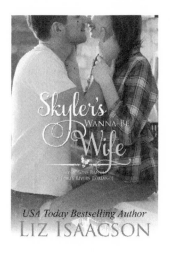

Skyler's Wanna-Be Wife (Book 6): She needs a new last name to stay in school. He's willing to help a fellow student. Can this wanna-be wife show the playboy that some things should be taken seriously?

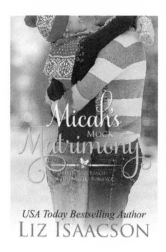

USA Today Bestselling Author
LIZ ISAACSON

Micah's Mock Matrimony (Book 7): They were just actors auditioning for a play. The marriage was just for the audition – until a clerical error results in a legal marriage. Can these two ex-lovers negotiate this new ground between them and achieve new roles in each other's lives?

ABOUT LIZ

Liz Isaacson writes inspirational romance, usually set in Texas, or Wyoming, or anywhere else horses and cowboys exist. She lives in Utah, where she writes full-time, takes her two dogs to the park everyday, and eats a lot of veggies while writing. Find her on her website at lizisaacson.com.

Made in the USA
Monee, IL
03 June 2022

97369565R00245